TWO FRIENDS

TWO FRIENDS

Alberto Moravia

EDITED BY SIMONE CASINI
TRANSLATED FROM THE ITALIAN BY MARINA HARSS

WITH AN INTRODUCTION BY
THOMAS ERLING PETERSON

OTHER PRESS
NEW YORK

Copyright © 2007 RCS Libri SpA

Originally published in Italian as *I due amici* by RCS Libri SpA, Milan, Italy, 2007

Translation copyright © 2011 by Marina Harss
Introduction copyright © 2011 by Thomas Erling Peterson

Production Editor: *Yvonne E. Cárdenas*
Text Designer: *Simon M. Sullivan*
This book was set in 12.5 pt Scala by
Alpha Design & Composition of Pittsfield, NH

10 9 8 7 6 5 4 3 2 1

LIBRARY OF CONGRESS CATALOGING-IN-PUBLICATION

Moravia, Alberto, 1907–1990.
  [Due amici. English]
  Two friends = I due amici / by Alberto Moravia ; translated by Marina Harss ; edited by Simone Casini ; introduction by Thomas Erling Peterson.
      p. cm.
  ISBN 978-1-59051-336-1 (trade pbk.) — ISBN 978-1-59051-421-4 (ebk.) 1. Young men—Italy—Fiction. 2. Communists—Italy—Fiction. 3. Male friendship—Fiction. I. Harss, Marina. II. Casini, Simone. III. Title.
  PQ4829.O62D8413 2011
  853'.912—dc22

                                      2011013258

CONTENTS

INTRODUCTION

Alberto Moravia (1907–1980) was Italy's most successful novelist of the twentieth century. A prolific author
of fiction, theatre, essays, film criticism, and travel correspondence, Moravia remained until his death a cultural icon and presence in Italian public life. A master
of the novel and short story, he created characters who
typically were embroiled in problems of money and sex
interrelated in ingenious plots that reveal the moral
weakness of ordinary people caught in predicaments of
their own making. At the same time, there are protagonists in Moravia's tales who evoke empathy and admiration; these are humble and heroic characters who resist
the alienating forces of modern society.

Moravia's first novel, *Gli indifferenti* (*The Time of Indifference*, 1929) was a tragicomic portrait of a Roman family that many saw as an indictment of the Fascist elite,
but which the author maintained was an honest picture
"from within" of his own world. The precocious work
depicts that world in spare, acrid prose, unforgiving in
its existential rendering of a dysfunctional family that is
"indifferent" to the higher values of humanistic culture.
Moravia achieved great success after World War II with

the short novel *Agostino* (1945). Based on the contemporaneous discovery of sexuality and social awareness by a pre-adolescent boy on a summer beach vacation with his mother, this was the first of a series of highly successful works that would firmly establish Moravia's literary reputation. Equally successful was the monumental *La romana* (*The Woman of Rome*, 1947), a lengthy novel written over four months between 1946 and 1947 and based on a brief experience from ten years earlier when Moravia encountered a beautiful young prostitute who was assisted in her profession by her mother. From this point forward, Moravia was a public figure whose steady stream of novels, essays, and journalistic reportage earned him a place of prestige among the Italian people.

La romana initiated a period in the postwar years when Moravia explored the "national popular myth" in his fiction. The other great novel in this populist phase is *La ciociara* (*Two Women*, 1957). Spied on by the Fascists, Moravia and his wife, Elsa Morante, had spent from 1943 to 1945 living in a sheepherder's cabin above Fondi, in the mountains southeast of Rome. *La ciociara* was conceived at this time. Moravia quickly drafted eighty pages in 1947, then put the manuscript aside in order to gain more historical distance from his subject. In the meantime he wrote four novels more purely creative in character: *La disubbidienza* (*Luca*, 1948), *L'amore coniugale* (*Conjugal Love*, 1949), *Il conformista* (*The Conformist*, 1951), and *Il disprezzo* (*A Ghost at Noon*, 1954).

After this inventive interlude, Moravia returned to *La ciociara*, a lengthy novel centered on a Roman shopkeeper named Cesira and her daughter Rosetta. The novel is largely faithful to external events and is an heroic chronicle of the Resistance. Also belonging to the national popular period in which the author investigates virtuous working-class characters are the short-story collections *Racconti romani* (*Roman Tales*, 1954) and *Nuovi racconti romani* (*More Roman Tales*, 1959). These stories capture the foibles and insecurities of ordinary working people in Rome; they are gems of textual economy and authentic cultural snapshots of daily life that turn around the primal emotions of love, jealousy, suspicion, fear, and joy. Here one sees the artisan Moravia, with his great attention to language and form, merge with the Roman Moravia, wryly aware of the mischief and wonder that exist in all of the city's populace irrespective of class. While Moravia lived his entire life in Rome, he was also an avid traveler and renowned travel writer (with a special love for Africa). He symbolized the cosmopolitan and worldly side of Rome and was a wry critic of its more baroque and provincial sides. Moravia's prose possessed an unmistakably direct and communicative quality, a fact that no doubt contributed to his broad appeal.

An astute essayist and commentator on a broad range of subject matter—from politics and literature to film and the arts to world cultures—Moravia upheld a humanistic viewpoint during a period in which humanism was under attack by ideologies on the right and left. He was a personalist and a humanist who believed in the ultimate dignity and complexity of the individual. It was precisely the personhood of the individual that was under threat and stood at the center of a modern existential crisis. In the essays of *Man as an End*—composed between 1941 and 1963—Moravia states that contemporary civilization has lost its moral compass, that humanity has become a means but not an end. One of the most obvious means by which this has occurred is through authoritarian ideologies that have eroded human dignity.

After World War II, the so-called communist aesthetic, as in socialist realism, was seriously considered by Western intellectuals. Moravia upbraided the communists for their notion of art as superstructure, which inevitably leads to its reduction to a form of propaganda: "Communist critics usually contrast art for art's sake with party art. But this contrast does not really exist, for neither the one nor the other could be said to be healthy and direct expressions of a given society. Healthy and direct art is born of an encounter between society and the artist on equal terms."[1] There was also a virtuous element in the enthusiasm over communism. As Moravia states in the essay "Hope, or Christianity and Communism," the communist movement is not driven by a rationalistic support of Marx's ideas but is instead a kind of religious faith: "What is more important in Communism, the idea of the advent of the kingdom of freedom or the lengthy and very complicated explanations offered by Marx on the internal laws of Capitalism? Without hesitation we answer that what counts above all in Communism is the idea of the advent of freedom."[2]

Harking back to the Renaissance, Moravia defended the autonomy of art: language is only a means, but art is an end. By the same token, neocapitalism's dominance in the West had created abstract and decadent art, which was ironically similar to socialist art: "They both withdraw from reality whose real needs are study, patience, humility, sincerity, sense of truth, and disinterestedness."[3]

[1] A. Moravia, *Man as an End: A Defense of Humanism*, trans. Bernard Wall (New York: Farrar, Straus & Giroux, 1965), 133.

[2] A. Moravia, *La speranza, ossia Cristianesimo e Comunismo* (Rome: Documento, 1944), 38.

[3] A. Moravia, *Man as an End*, 127.

These ideas invariably find their way into *Two Friends*, a projected novel about a confused young man gripped by an inferiority complex who latches onto communism as a panacea for his personal problems. The Italian publication of *I due amici*—the title assigned by the publisher to a novel planned then abandoned by Moravia in the early 1950s—coincided with the 2007 centenary of the author's birth.[4] The typescript of three drafts of this work were found in a worn suitcase in the basement of the author's Lungotevere della Vittoria residence in Rome; since he typically destroyed all working drafts, this discovery is of great value, especially given the finished nature of these texts, the lack of *lacunae*, and the sense of progression from one draft to the next.

Two Friends was written at a critical time in Moravia's life when he was quite active but also troubled: about his marriage with novelist Elsa Morante and the reception of his recent fiction. When *The Conformist* (1951) received negative reviews, Moravia grew depressed, and his productivity suffered. Loosely based on the 1937 assassination in Normandy of Moravia's cousins, Carlo and Nello Rosselli, *The Conformist* is the story of Maurizio Clerici, the Fascist bureaucrat empowered by the regime to carry out the assassination of his former philosophy professor, a socialist living in Paris. Critics found it difficult to relate to the tormented character of Clerici, whose repressed homosexuality, dissociation, and sadism is traced back to his childhood and his troubled family. There is some continuity here with the psycho-sexual-political plot of *Two Friends*.

Driven by moralistic impulses, Sergio Maltese is led astray by the notion that the promised liberation of his

4 Alberto Moravia, *I due amici. Frammenti di una storia fra guerra e dopoguerra*, introd. and ed. Simone Casini (Milan: Bompiani, 2007).

newfound ideology can somehow satisfy his personal need for love and friendship. As is true throughout Moravia's fiction, the prose possesses an emphatic clarity about matters of indecision and doubt. The motivations of the subjects are translated through the minimal events of daily life, the gestures and pentimentos, the provisional agreements and sudden separations. Thus Sergio's obsessive attempts to bargain with his sentiments—with his lover and his friend—for the sake of political ideology are translated into the language of material needs, desires, and lacks. In Moravia's view, Sergio is converting his affection and esteem into a means rather than an end. Thus in his day-to-day living with his lover, the intrinsic morality of true affection is undermined by the attempts to convert it into a value, such as a new set of clothes or ultimately the desire that his bourgeois friend Maurizio capitulate by adopting Sergio's chosen ideology of communism.

Version A begins "around 1938," the year of the Italian Race Laws and the formation of the Rome-Berlin Axis, when Sergio Maltese, a sexual innocent, and his occasional friend Maurizio, an experienced but bored Don Juan figure, are twenty years old.[5] It concludes after the fall of the Fascist regime on July 25, 1943. Sergio, the son of a government bureaucrat, is unemployed and finds himself in the grips of a "mortal lack of will." Inert, Hamletic, apathetic, Sergio is an ardent anti-Fascist who is, nevertheless, ambivalent about what a Fascist defeat would mean for his country. His brother is fighting for Italy on the Russian front while the sons of the privileged classes, like Maurizio, have found ways to

---

[5] The *Leggi razziali* denied Italian citizenship to Jews and prohibited them from positions in the government or in the professions of education and banking. Marriages between Italian citizens and Jews were banned.

avoid combat service. The war years pass, arriving at the fall of Fascism and the Allied struggle to liberate Rome. Encountering his old friend Sergio, the dissipative, self-indulgent Maurizio invites him south to the island of Capri to wait out the end of the war (echoing an invitation made to Moravia by friend Curzio Malaparte, the author of *La pelle*). Sergio elects to stay in Rome, and as he drops off a copy of his first article for a new Resistance newspaper—a kind of *j'accuse* against those responsible for the Fascist debacle—at Maurizio's house, an Allied bombing raid ensues, forcing Sergio, Maurizio, and Maurizio's family into the air-raid shelter in the basement of the Villa Borghese (the Roman museum housing Bernini's sculptures). Here one has a kind of bourgeois drama acted out in the darkness at the archetypal heart of Baroque Rome. Through the darkness, Sergio glimpses the feminine profile of Nella, a working-class woman whose name calls to mind the peasant heroine of Giovanni Verga's early short story *Nedda*. In the concluding scenes of Version A (it is easy to speak of Moravia's fiction in theatrical terms) Sergio accompanies Nella to her rented room (a seeming echo of Sonia's apartment in *Crime and Punishment*), as one has a glimpse of the sexual theme that will be prominent in the other drafts. Version A succeeds in establishing a foundation, but does not yet cohere in the sort of unifying "idea" that Moravia demands of his novels.

In Version B Sergio has joined the Italian Communist Party (PCI) to free himself from the label of intellectual; it is 1945, after the war, and he is working for a pittance as a film reviewer. Nella is here named Lalla, and the relationship with Sergio has been going on for some time. The couple lives together in a dingy Roman flat on a subsistence budget, their only luxury their sexual compatibility. Moravia's descriptions of the female anatomy are always particular, dwelling on peculiarities such as a small head or a long neck. The sexual relationship stands like an island apart from Sergio's political obsession, which is articulated through the friendship-rivalry with Maurizio. Sergio has become a communist for selfish reasons, seeking in the Party what he lacks in his personal life. Though Maurizio had been a convinced fascist, Sergio believes he is a communist unawares, a ripe fruit ready to fall from the tree of the bourgeoisie. What is in fact ripening is the relation between Maurizio and Lalla, who admits that Maurizio has asked her to marry him and can provide her the material advantages she desires. The rivalry intensifies to the point where Maurizio proposes a deal: he will join the PCI if Sergio will let him sleep with Lalla. As Sergio dissects the offer, he wavers, sensing that a political commitment must be voluntary to be authentic. But by accepting Maurizio's money, which he uses to buy Lalla a new wardrobe, he shows he is taking the offer seriously.

In the meantime, Lalla has befriended Moroni, a wealthy widower who takes English classes from her. Lalla, Sergio, and Maurizio set out for a weekend visit to Moroni's country house. It is here that Version B reaches its perfunctory ending, as Lalla is drawn to the protector Moroni after his poignant confession of unending regret and undying love for his deceased wife, Laura, and after Sergio's attempt to follow through with the "trade." In contrast to Maurizio's vanity and Sergio's "love" for the Party, Moroni can offer true love to Lalla. Summarizing the outcome, Maurizio states: "We are the predestined cuckolds of history . . . we argue over humanity but instead it betrays us . . . and it betrays us because in truth we don't love it for what it is without second ends." Here then is the unifying idea that Moravia requires in order to proceed to the following draft. The author seems to know at this point how the eventual work will end; faithful to a heuristic method, he now recommences and focuses more keenly on developing the characters and rendering the plot less schematic.

In Version C we are again at war's end. Sergio, now a first-person narrator, explains how he joined the Party because Maurizio called him an intellectual and a bourgeois, labels he could not deny and found odious. By joining the Party, he reasons, he could erase those labels and turn the tables on Maurizio, whose sense of superiority and condescension derive from his wealth. The extent to which Maurizio exercises control over Sergio's psyche (though the two rarely see one another) suggests a pathological attraction whereby Sergio projects his deepest desires and fears onto the figure of the Other.

Nella, who is twenty-three to Sergio's twenty-seven, loves him with great passion and unquestioning allegiance. Sergio meets her at her workplace, an Allied military office in newly liberated Rome. Their immediate attraction to each other results in her being dismissed from her job for inappropriate behavior. A passionate embrace ensues as the couple repairs to the closest lavatory; almost as quickly, Nella agrees to move in with Sergio. Sergio senses he is loved but that Nella cannot truly comprehend him and his political commitment; this results in growing feelings of scorn and contempt (*dispetto, disprezzo*). The attempt to convert Maurizio to communism is not presented in terms of a "trade" of Nella, though the thought does occur to Sergio and might easily have been included had the draft been completed. As Simone Casini writes in his introduction to *I due amici*, here one sees both the selfish and the disinterested sides of communism in Sergio's thought, the latter being a faith in the regeneration of society.

Version C has a subtler and richer narrative with more characters and mise en scène. Moroni is a small-time movie producer working with Maurizio who, when he meets Nella at a party at Maurizio's house, offers her a screen test. But here the text abruptly ends. The cinematic theme will carry over into *Il disprezzo* (*A Ghost at Noon*), the novel Moravia will then go on to write. So too will the theme of contempt carry over, but with the tables turned, as the wife, Emilia, is overtaken by contempt for her screenwriter husband, Riccardo. In addition, one sees the first-person narration employed in Version C, which Moravia would now retain for all his future novels.

It is difficult to second-guess an author as methodical and circumspect as Moravia as to why one project is curtailed and another begun, but in the case of *Two Friends* one might suppose that the core idea of communism (or ideology itself) grew stale and could not support the emotional complexity that formed the basis of the author's inspiration. This complexity was always a moral one in Moravia's fiction, as we suggested above with reference to his essays.

Two Friends is a kind of time capsule that seemingly survived only because of an oversight; its brilliant trajectories provide the material for a classic Moravian tale, founded on human foibles and psychological material that emerges unexpectedly from the unconscious. Here one sees the author's method of eliminating and adding, combining and substituting episodes in complete redrafts of the same project. The prose possesses an economy and vividness that make the characters seem visibly present and gripped by a tense network of common emotions. By trusting in the intrinsic life of his characters, Moravia allows them to steer the plot in the pursuit of what he once called "the absolute and moral justification of action."[6] Herein lies the debt to Dostoevsky as well who, in Moravia's view, had revolutionized the novel by displacing its focus from the world at large onto the interiority of the individual. In Italy this change had seen its first great exemplar in Italo Svevo.

Walter Benjamin has written of "the most European of all accomplishments, that more or less discernible irony with which the life of the individual asserts the right to run its course independently of the community into which he is cast."[7] Moravia's opus exemplifies this phenomenon, and *Two Friends* is no exception. It is ironic first of all—in Moravia's view—that so many Italians were tolerant of authoritarian ideologies, such that the nation seemed poised after the fall of Fascism to forgive the regime and repeat its errors (there having been no systematic attempt to remove former Fascists from positions of power in the postwar era). There is irony in the commonplace assumptions about the social classes, in the physical descriptions of interiors and settings, and in the precise, often unflattering descriptions of the human figure. There is a parody as well of normal sexual behavior. Scenes of lovemaking are bold but not prurient; the reader is not titillated, but exposed to a kind of ritual carried out by the lovers—in a garret or a public building, or even while fully clothed on a streetcar ride—to satisfy their animal needs. There is irony too in the fresh and sullen beauty of the Moravian heroine; the

[6] A. Moravia and A. Elkann, *Vita di Moravia* (Milan: Bompiani, 1990), 271.

[7] W. Benjamin, *Reflections: Essays, Aphorisms, Autobiographical Writings*, introd. and ed. P. Demetz, trans. E. Jephcott (New York: Harcourt Brace Jovanovich, 1978), 73.

descriptions of the woman at her humble *toilette* suggest the paintings of Courbet or Vuillard. Lastly there is the self-irony by which Moravia instills in his protagonists the gist of his own personal crises. The author experienced an existential malaise throughout his adult life, whether it is called indifference, boredom, or contempt. Distrustful of the autobiographical direction in modern fiction, he succeeded in retaining the personalist core of his deepest presentiments and forged them into an exquisitely disinterested fiction.

Two Friends comes at a pivotal point in the author's career when the subject matter of his fiction and the mode of narration itself are shifting. It also coincides with a time of great debate concerning the social function of literature, in particular the novel form used to reflect the struggle between the social classes. If Moravia had respected the work of Zola and Verga in this regard, his inclination was not naturalistic but was founded on the interior reality and contradictions of the individual. *Two Friends* represents a heuristic key to understanding this phase of Moravia's fiction; it is a phase when the Roman author is still committed to the working-class myth seen in *La romana* and *I racconti romani* (which will conclude with the publication of *La ciociara*) and yet has adopted a first-person narrator and inserted ample discussions of political ideas into the text, anticipating the Moravian essay-novel of the 1960s.

THOMAS E. PETERSON

EDITOR'S NOTE

The numbers that appear in the margins indicate the numeration of the original typewritten pages in the so-called Dossier Number 6 ["Incartamento 6"] at the Fondo Alberto Moravia. The few that come from Dossier Number 4 are indicated with an asterisk.

The marking "[. . .]" indicates a break in the text; "<. . .>" indicates an addition.

The marking < in the right margin indicates the existence of an alternate version of the text, to be found in the appendix.

TWO FRIENDS

*Fragments of a Story Set During the War
and the Postwar Years*

Version A

[. . .] The woman, a widow, lived alone in her tiny apart- 231
ment. Maurizio usually went to s<ee> her in the evenings. During the day he kept his old habits and often
s<aw> Sergio. The woman, who was jealous and did
not completely trust Maurizio, often subtly reproached
him about his friendship with Sergio. She was a conventional woman; in her eyes, poverty was the worst
possible defect a person could have. In her opinion,
Maurizio, who was so much wealthier than Sergio,
should associate only with his equals. Moreover, she
believed that Sergio was not a true friend and attached
himself to Maurizio only because of his wealth. How
could Maurizio not see this? And on, and on. The
woman, who was German by birth, concealed her hostility toward Sergio; in fact, she always affected a sick-
eningly sweet manner in his presence. But she often
said to Maurizio: "I'm sure that if I made eyes at your
dear friend, he would not think twice about betraying
you." Though Maurizio was convinced that this was
not true, and was sure of Sergio's loyalty, he did not
vigorously protest, because, deep down, these insinu-
ations were convenient to him. It was almost as if he
thought that through this [. . .].

The woman felt that she had heard enough, and 162
she sent Sergio away, with the pretext that Maurizio
was so late already that he would probably not come
at all.

That same evening, when Sergio was having dinner with his family, Maurizio called. Sergio came to

the phone, thinking that his friend wanted to make an appointment for the next day. But instead, Maurizio said: "What did you say to Emilia? What ideas have you gotten into your head?" He sounded irritated, but there was something else as well. Sergio thought he heard contempt in his voice. He answered vehemently: "Nothing that wasn't true." At the other end of the line, Maurizio's voice pressed on, more violently: "Indiscreet and voluble as usual . . . There are things one just shouldn't do . . . You don't visit your friend's lover in order to speak ill of him . . . You have no manners . . . It's completely crazy." Hearing these words, Sergio felt flames of anger and shame sweeping over him. He responded brusquely, "I only said the truth . . . Leave me alone, why don't you? Goodbye!" and quickly slammed down the receiver.

Later, reflecting on this phone conversation, Sergio realized that he hated Maurizio, though he also felt a trace of regret. Despite their rivalry, Maurizio was still the only friend who mattered to him. He realized that the woman had drawn him into a kind of trap, and, as he reconstructed their conversations, he also realized that she had constantly tried to undermine his friendship with Maurizio. Still, Maurizio had been too quick to offend him and even, it seemed, to bring about a break between them. After lengthy and painful consideration, Sergio decided that he would not call Maurizio back. It was up to Maurizio, who had been so quick to insult him on the slightest pretext, to take the first step toward a reconciliation.

Maurizio, on the other hand, regretted his phone call almost immediately. But partly out of pride, and mainly out of fatuousness and selfishness, he did not want to take the first step. He was convinced that Sergio was somehow inferior to him, and that Sergio knew this; and he was convinced that his friend's sense of inferiority would drive him to take the first step. Vaguely, and not in so many words, he sensed that he was not so sorry to lose Sergio. In recent times, Sergio had been overly critical and had made it quite clear to Maurizio that he disapproved of certain aspects of his personality. Maurizio was troubled by these criticisms, and it did not help that he had to admit that many of them were true. There was an additional factor that persuaded him not to seek a rapprochement with his overly candid friend.

Even though he was still very young, Maurizio had already developed a Don Juan–like attitude—he could not tolerate a serious bond with a woman, and preferred to pursue many light, inconsequential affairs rather than devote himself to a singular, deep relationship. For some time now, this woman's attachment had been an inconvenience to him, especially because his lucid intuition told him that this attachment was not unselfish on her part. On the day of his conversation with Sergio, Maurizio had gone to see Emilia and told her what had happened. He explained that his friendship had probably come to an end. The woman did not hide her satisfaction, and Maurizio suddenly realized—though he had not reflected on this possibility before—that the quarrel with his friend might also be an opportunity to free himself of this woman. He told her that she should not be so happy, since after all Sergio had always been and was still his best friend; that she had done her best to come between them; that she had probably encouraged Sergio to speak ill of him in order to create discord between them. This was the truth of the matter, and Maurizio had been able to see it by remembering her attitude as well as Sergio's. She confirmed his intuition by exclaiming: "There you go; you trust Sergio more than me . . . Who knows what that hateful man has said?" Maurizio answered that Sergio had said nothing at all, and that he was not the least bit hateful. He would probably never see Sergio again, but he regretted the loss of a friend who, all in all, had always shown himself to be affectionate 164 and loyal. At this point the woman became irritated and responded that evidently, if he spoke to her in this manner, he was more attached to Sergio than he was to her. This was the reaction that Maurizio had been hoping for with childish shrewdness. Quickly, and with a certain coldness, he told her that she was right; he was more attached to Sergio than to her. The woman, who until then had flattered herself with the idea that she held Maurizio through the power of sensuality, responded brutally that he should go back to his dear Sergio and leave her alone. Maurizio immediately got up and left.

Once he was in the street, he breathed a great sigh of relief. Without much difficulty, he had managed to free himself of a relationship, one which might have been difficult to extricate himself from under different circumstances. Regarding his friend, he once again reflected: if Sergio called, all the better, and if not, tant pis. Maurizio's cynical nonchalance had another cause as well: he was interested in another, much younger woman, who was receptive to his advances. He climbed into his car and went directly to her place.

The days passed and the two separations became definitive. Sergio did not call, and Emilia was unable to reach Maurizio; he had ordered that whenever she called she should be told he was out. She wrote him a letter, called again, wrote another letter, and then resigned herself to the situation and found another lover. Sergio didn't call. Maurizio continued down the path he had laid for himself. The girl who replaced Emilia was herself replaced, and on it went. Maurizio was twenty years old and thought only of love.

[II]

Sergio was also twenty years old, but he had other 165 things on his mind. Whereas Maurizio rushed headlong down the path suggested by his senses and his youth—a path unencumbered by ambition, material struggles, scruples, or emotional aspirations—Sergio found himself, because of the ambitions, emotional aspirations, oppressive material struggles, and scruples that constantly tormented him, in the difficult situation of a traveler seeking a path through a desert or a forest never before visited by man. He had no precise vocation, only a certain intellectual attitude toward life and a facility for writing; he was poor, and his dreams for the future were vast but vague. Youth did not inspire in him the same joyful, fulfilling vigor felt by Maurizio; if anything, his youth inspired a continual discomfort and struggle between contradictory emotions and purposes. He was extremely serious and felt seriously about everything he did, read, loved, discussed, or experienced. And yet he was not able to free himself—despite all his seriousness—from a constant feeling of insecurity and impotence, in other words from what is usually referred to as an inferiority complex. This complex had many elements, all of which seemed to converge toward something that he was unable to identify but was obscurely aware of. He felt socially inferior to Maurizio and Maurizio's circle; he felt inferior to the women he pursued; and he felt inferior to so-called men of action. To Sergio, action required innumerable profound, subtle reflections which usually resulted in inaction, out of fear or shyness. Instinctively, he sought an explanation for his frame of mind, but he might never have pinpointed it if Maurizio had not revealed it to him by chance, with cruel carelessness. It was a few years after their break. Because they lived in the same city, they often crossed paths. Whenever this happened, Sergio was

166 stone-faced, embarrassed, filled with unspoken reproaches and a feeling of irritated impotence mixed with a secret attraction. Maurizio—to whom Sergio was simply one acquaintance among many—treated him with the jovial, indulgent condescension one affects with old schoolmates with whom one has lost touch. During these casual encounters, he would greet Sergio with jokes and quick repartee, aggravating his friend's sense of inferiority and ill-concealed rivalry. These meetings, which usually took place on the street or in cafés or other public places, were always very brief. After inquiring about work and life, Maurizio would depart with a joke and a smile, leaving Sergio to feel unhappy and wonder in vain

why, given that there was no longer real friendship between them, he even bothered to stop and talk to Maurizio.

On one of these occasions, Maurizio was sitting in his car, parked on an elegant street. As Sergio— gloomy and sloppily dressed—walked toward him along the sidewalk, Maurizio called out casually: "Well, how is the intellectual doing today? What have you been up to?"

The word "intellectual" had an unpleasant ring to it, but in some strange way Sergio knew it to be tinged with truth. He heard himself say, almost resentfully: "Who are you calling an intellectual?"

"Why, you of course," Maurizio said, smiling.

"Me?" Sergio repeated, as if the word sounded strange applied to him. "So you consider me an intellectual?"

"Of course," Maurizio said, smiling, "otherwise, what are you?" He laughed, adding, "See you later, Sergio . . . Got to run . . . Good luck." He turned on the ignition and drove off.

Sergio ruminated on Maurizio's words for a long time. On the one hand, he realized that the word "intellectual"—like the word "bourgeois" and many others—had been degraded over time to the point that it now had a decidedly negative connotation. On the other hand, he could not help but recognize that despite Maurizio's coarseness and ignorance, he had done something that Sergio, with all his education and subtlety, had never been capable of: he had defined him in a single word. Wasn't he in fact an intellectual? And how had he managed not to realize this before? After that meeting, he reflected often on his appearance and his state of mind, and each time was forced to recognize that Maurizio's jocular, off-the-cuff epithet fit him perfectly. To begin with, he had the physical attributes of the intellectual: he wore glasses and was on the small side, and often wore a serious expression on his unshaven face; his clothes were frayed and worn, his pockets full of slips of paper, his shoes covered in mud. Not to speak of his personality and his attitude: he was educated, intelligent, and versatile enough to quickly scribble an article on almost any subject, or write film reviews—as he did, for a second-rate newspaper—but not dedicated enough to be a professional writer, dependable and serious. As he saw it, the word "intellectual" was a kind of cliché, and in fact Maurizio was someone who often expressed himself in clichés. And yet, it was true that Sergio's appearance and personality fit the cliché; here was the proof that clichés are often based on realities and behaviors that are actually quite common. In the end, he realized that he was an intellectual precisely because it displeased him that he should be seen as one by others. But no matter how he tried, he could not free himself of this displeasure, or accept Maurizio's epithet with indifference or, better yet, with pride. He did not know why it displeased him so much; in part it was of course because he saw being an intellectual as something completely negative. But more important, it displeased him because it was Maurizio who had defined him in this way and, by so doing, had placed Sergio in a clear category, defined him as a type, with no possibility of change or surprise. Worse yet, it proved that Maurizio had a negative, unfavorable opinion of him.

It was just before the start of the war, sometime around 1938, and, like everyone around him, Sergio was suffering from the suffocating weight of the tempest, heavy with war and destruction, which was gathering over Europe's skies. In his case, the suffering was redoubled by his feelings of impotence and lack of confidence. Though he was opposed to all dictatorial regimes, he feared that his opposition was not strong enough, or decisive enough, or based on reasons that were sufficiently well founded or convincing. He envied the Fascists, for whom the choice was so clear, and he also envied Maurizio, to whom these events were clearly and uncomplicatedly indifferent. One day when they bumped into each other in the street, Maurizio had said: "Why get upset . . . what can we do about it? And if we can't do anything, why get upset?" Sergio envied the few resolute anti-Fascists he knew, Communists and the like, because their attitude was as clear as that of the Fascists. But he was not able to distill his doubts and disgust into an unambiguous attitude, a plan of action. Even though he hated Fascism, he felt that it had wormed its way into his blood, not in the form of political allegiance, but rather as a kind of torpor and mortal passivity, like a poison that slowly intoxicates and weakens the body. He was confronted once again with his feeling of impotence, but this time it not only affected his personal life but encompassed the destiny of the nation and humanity as a whole. This thought paralyzed him and infused him with a kind of deadly inertia. Later he would remember this period as a nightmare he had experienced with his eyes open, like a dream where all is a blur and nothing happens and yet one is overcome by a sense of unjustified and terrifying oppression from which one does not have the will or strength to free oneself. In addition, for some reason during that period he was not commissioned to write any of the articles that normally kept him afloat; and to make matters worse, most of his few friends had left the city, either because they had been drafted or for other reasons. Sergio found himself alone and out of work and began to lead a solitary, monotonous existence, filled with uneasiness and anxiety. He lived at home with his father—an office worker of middling importance—and mother, and his two older sisters, unmarried and by now decidedly spinsterish. He spent most of the day in his small bedroom, reading and daydreaming, and went outside only to buy cheap cigarettes from the tobacconist across the street. Or else he wandered the streets, not daring to sit down at a café because he had no money. His daily cigarette runs and solitary meanderings filled him with a dull, subdued, deadening, airless melancholy, almost as if he were not living but rather dreaming that he was alive, in a world where the talk was increasingly of war and violence, a world that was plunging, like a rock down a steep hill, toward the abyss, an abyss that could be seen and measured. He was simply waiting, for events that he could neither avoid nor change in any way, not even within the narrow arena of his personal feelings. Every morning he bought a newspaper and cigarettes; he went home, read the front page, and then threw the newspaper aside, picked up a book, and tried to read. It was summertime and his room, facing a courtyard, was suffocating and hot.

Sergio lay on his bed, book in hand, half naked, and tried to concentrate. But he was only partly successful. He was easily distracted and would inevitably begin to inspect the few worn-out furnishings in his room, or gaze out the window at the little balconies hanging from the wall across the way, loaded with belongings. Even when he managed to read, it seemed to him, as when he took walks or did anything else, that he used only one part of his brain, almost mechanically, while the rest remained far away and preoccupied, though he could not quite say with what. He took a funereal, almost morbid pleasure in this solitary, silent, passive, wan existence, while at the same time reproaching himself for it, seeing it as further proof of his impotence and lack of self-confidence. At home, his parents—however timidly and discreetly—pushed him to work, implying that they could not continue to pay his way if he remained idle. He responded evasively that there was no point in looking for work under the circumstances, with war about to break out. But he knew that this response was inspired by the deep indolence he felt rather than by a sense of reality. There was work to be had, and it probably would not have been so difficult to secure a job. The truth was that he did not even have the strength to look.

[III]

He often bumped into Maurizio around town, and each time, he was struck by his friend's lighthearted mood. It seemed to him that Maurizio was

13

interested only in the pursuit of his own pleasures. He was usually in his car with one girl or another; the girls were constantly changing, and because of their slightly embarrassed, submissive attitude, Sergio knew that they were involved in a love affair with Maurizio. Maurizio often asked Sergio what he was up to but never seemed particularly interested in Sergio's response, which, it must be said, was always the same: "Writing, reading, and waiting." He seemed to consider Sergio a kind of sad sack, an idler, in other words an intellectual, and Sergio no longer cared to prove him wrong. He knew he was an intellectual of the worst sort, a man whose intelligence was neither creative nor useful and served only to poison and paralyze him like a subtle venom. Furthermore, even though Maurizio realized that war was about to break out, he did not seem to attribute any importance to this imminent threat. "None of this has anything to do with me," he commented to Sergio one day. "Do you know what history is? An excuse to do nothing and to let oneself go, maybe even to stop brushing one's teeth in the morning. After all, what's the point of brushing one's teeth?" Sergio was struck by this summary, which so perfectly encapsulated his own situation. With the excuse that war was about to break out, he no longer bothered to brush his teeth, or, in other words, to fight the effects of time. Like the destructive waters of a flood, time flowed over him, leaving him inert, like the corpse of a drowned man.

171   This condition of inertia, discomfort, and shame lasted until the end of the war. Sergio had not been called up, because he suffered from myopia, but he could not decide whether this was a blessing or

a curse. Though from the beginning he considered the war to be unjust and a lost cause, taking arms would have at least meant doing something or, better yet, letting himself be swept up in something. The war dragged on, month after month, as merciless and inflexible as an illness that must run its course and will end only after it has exhausted its virulence. Sergio felt this illness in his blood, like a poisonous fever that precludes any struggle. He waited, like many others, for the war to reach its foregone and predetermined end. At times he asked himself why he had never reacted in some way even though he was aware of the true reasons behind the conflict, as well as its absurdity and the baseness and incompetence of the men who had driven the country to war and were now conducting it. But always he came to the same conclusion: "I can do nothing but be aware of the fact that I can do nothing." His impotence was part of the air he breathed, a substance buried in the objects that surrounded him, in their appearance, in time itself. Later, he would remember those years—which after all had contained different seasons and climates—as one endless day, as when the scirocco blows and the colorless, cloudless sky weighs heavily on the rooftops. The air is opaque and stifling, without a whisper of wind, colors fade, and objects lose their shape and become part of an undistinguished morass, devoid of all potency or light, benign and disagreeable at the same time. He realized obscurely that for others, these years might have a quite different color: for example, for members of the regime, who had jumped into this increasingly desperate war; for its enemies, whose hope grew day by day. But he did not feel himself to be on one side or the other; even though he shared both desperation and hope, he could not find a real reason to chose one feeling over the other and join either side.

172   What tormented him the most, in addition to his impotence, was his awareness of its profound causes. The truth was that even as he wished with all his might that the regime would crumble, even at the cost of a total disaster, he was upset—without quite knowing why—whenever the regime or one of its allies was defeated on the battlefield. He realized that the regime's victories did not upset him as he would have wished them to. Quite to the contrary, each victory inspired an obscure, shameful sense of satisfaction. In other words, he both desired and did not desire the regime's downfall, both hated and did not hate it. What he said out loud was not always true, and what he felt in the shelter of solitude was often in contrast with his words. He asked himself what could be the reason for this unconquerable duplicity, but he was unable to pinpoint its source. At the time, one of his younger brothers had been called up and was fighting with the Italian army on the Russian front. Whenever he was gladdened by a German victory in Russia, he wondered whether his affection for his brother—with whom he was very close—was the root cause of this contradictory, painful attitude. But he had to admit that the real motives were deeper and more obscure. In truth, as he had often suspected, he did not want the German armies to be defeated, because such a defeat would lead to disaster, a disaster he was not prepared to confront. Deep down, he preferred to go on living in this deceptive,

bitter limbo, between disgust and impotence, and he knew that such a disaster would put an end to it, forcing him to take some sort of action. Yes, he thought to himself, he *was* this limbo, this malady, this ambivalence between one and another. This limbo, this malady, was his raison d'être, wretched and bitter as it was, but he had no other. And precisely because he knew that he could not find any other reason to justify his existence, he did not want the malady to end. All of this seemed to confirm Maurizio's careless comment. Sergio reflected: "I am nothing but an intellectual of the worst sort, in other words a man who is aware of all the reasons for action and yet is incapable of acting." Rereading Pascal's *Pensées*, he came upon the great philosopher's definition of man: That which distinguishes man from a clump of reeds is the fact that the reeds do not know that they are being crushed and a man does. "Man is a thinking reed." Bitterly, Sergio had concluded that there was no better description for him. But it seemed to him that Pascal was mistaken about one thing: a thinking reed, in Sergio's opinion, was far inferior to a simple reed. Not thinking was better than thinking without acting.

At home, everyone took him for a dyed-in-the-wool anti-Fascist. His family, who was not Fascist while at the same time not daring to be anti-Fascist, did its best to avoid political discussions, never referring to the war or the political situation in Sergio's presence. He knew that his mother and father and two sisters would have been saddened by any anti-Fascist declarations from him because they loved his brother, who was fighting in Russia, and feared for his life.

They simply wanted him to come home, and they knew that a defeat would impede his return. So he was silent. And still, he felt tossed around by his own impotent duplicity, like a fragile vessel buffeted by a tempestuous sea. On the rare occasions when he met with one of his very few remaining friends, he spoke of his desire for a German defeat. But as soon as he was alone, he realized with profound self-contempt that when he read the papers and saw that defeat seemed more and more inevitable and imminent, he felt a pang of disappointment and bitterness. This ambivalence vexed and disgusted him and inspired in him a gradual, funereal melancholy, as if he were suffering from an unnamable, mysterious disease for which there is no known cure.

174 Sometimes he asked himself, "So, then, does this mean I am on the other side? Am I a supporter of the regime?" He tested himself to see if his suspicions were justified. But as soon as he was in the company of Fascists, he felt something stronger than repulsion, almost hatred. Not a single one of their arguments was convincing—quite to the contrary. He was utterly incapable of cheering during military parades or speeches by Fascist officials; these displays felt like a bitter medicine, which nothing in the world could force him to swallow. When he spent time with someone who approved of or defended the regime, he experienced a deep, irrepressible discomfort, as if in the presence of a lie that must be combated at all costs. In other words, he was an anti-Fascist, at least in the presence of Fascists. But when he found himself in the company of a group of stalwart anti-Fascists, like the young men, around his age, who

met sometimes in a neighborhood café, he felt only a halfhearted enthusiasm for their declarations. He did not dislike them as much as he did the Fascists, or rather he liked them while at the same time feeling a mix of envy and discouragement. Though he agreed with what they said, he did not experience the kind of heartfelt ardor that melts away the many layers of intelligent thought to become a clear conviction. He tried to attribute this lack of conviction to external causes like the fact that his brother was fighting in Russia. But the truth was that this was simply his nature; he was convinced that he would have shown a similar lack of conviction no matter what the circumstances. His heart was frozen and his mind could express only doubts.

As time passed, the military situation worsened. Sergio noticed that the momentous, catastrophic news that appeared in the papers inspired no noticeable rumblings inside of him. The day Fascism fell, a day so intensely desired and awaited, he lay on his bed, as usual, with a cigarette in one hand and a book in the other. One of his sisters ducked into his doorway and gave him the news, dramatically. Sergio paused and collected his thoughts for a moment before getting up to join the crowds that, he was sure, were forming in the streets of the city. Then he changed his mind and gave up on the idea of going out. The next day, even after hearing about the celebrations, he felt no regrets for not taking part.

And then, suddenly, in the days that followed the fall of Fascism, he was finally presented with an opportunity to act, as if by miracle. This was the opportunity he had sought for so long, in vain. One day as he was crossing the sun-baked street, fiddling with a packet of cigarettes in his pocket, he heard someone calling him from across the road. He hesitated and then looked up, quickly recognizing the person calling out to him: it was Maurizio, this time on foot, no longer in an officer's uniform but rather in a civilian shirt and crumpled trousers. Sergio noticed that his friend was waving enthusiastically. With some hesitation, he crossed the street.

Maurizio said quickly: "I'm not an officer anymore . . . I threw my uniform into the weeds . . . What are you up to? You must be happy!"

"Why should I be happy?"

"You wanted the regime to fall, and now you have what you wanted!"

"Yes," Sergio said, distractedly, "now I have what I wanted."

Maurizio did not seem to be listening. Cheerfully, he said, "I'm getting out of here. This won't last. The Fascists will be back and who knows what will happen. It's better to get out of Rome. I'm going south . . . to Capri."

"Capri?"

"Yes, Capri . . . After all, it's an island . . . You never know . . . The Allies are already in Calabria . . . In a few days they'll be in Naples, maybe even farther north . . . Do you want to come?"

"With you?"

"That's right."

"But I . . ." Sergio began, buying time to reflect on Maurizio's proposal. "I'm totally . . . broke . . . and Capri is an expensive town."

Maurizio laughed; he seemed overexcited and unusually affectionate. "I'll lend you all the money you need . . . I'll pay for the trip . . . It'll be fun . . . There are lots of pretty girls there . . . They must be feeling uneasy because of the war . . . We can console them."

This time, Sergio said, without reflecting: "I don't think this is the time to be dreaming about pretty girls . . . People are dying . . . We're in the middle of a revolution. Don't you think your idea is a bit unseemly?"

His friend began to laugh: "I knew you would say that. You wouldn't be an intellectual if you didn't say such things. But my dear Sergio, what can we do? The things which are taking place around us are out of our control. Did they ask us if they should go to war? Are they asking us whether we want a revolution? The only thing I know is that we could die here, just like that, for no reason. You know what they say: every man for himself. Come on, let's go to Capri."

"No, I can't," Sergio answered, somewhat irresolutely.

"I knew it. Always the same. What are you doing here in Rome? Well, it doesn't matter . . . I'll call you tomorrow morning . . . I'm leaving in the afternoon. You have twenty-four hours to think about it . . . Good-bye." Maurizio shook Sergio's hand and walked off.

Sergio was in a state of anxiety, filled with indecision and disgust. Maurizio was right. For him, and others like him, the only option was to leave town and save his own skin. It was true that he too had no reason to stay, no cause to defend, no side to uphold. Maurizio, who, as usual, was more honest and clear than he, had come to the only logical conclusion commensurate with his circumstances, which were not really so different from Sergio's: he had decided to leave town, hide, and wait for the storm to pass. Maurizio joyfully, resolutely embraced that which Sergio felt forced to accept with regret, sadness, and indecision. On the other hand, somehow he had had the courage to utter those austere words in response to Maurizio's offer. They had slipped out of his mouth, without reflection or forethought, almost against his wishes. What did they mean? Perhaps simply that he had a conscience, vigilant though inert and inoperative, and that this conscience did not allow him to behave thoughtlessly and selfishly as Maurizio did, while failing to motivate him to do the opposite.

Finally, he reflected that he had twenty-four hours to consider Maurizio's offer, and with this prospect in mind he was able to momentarily quiet his doubts. But he realized on some level that if at first he had refused Maurizio's offer, it was mainly out of pique. All that separated him from his friend was an almost physiological rivalry, the desire to be different, to behave differently than he did. He felt contempt toward Maurizio, only barely mitigated by his involuntary sympathy and attraction. Maurizio was, in his mind, a typical representative of the society that had driven Italy to war, of the people who had sent the powerless into the battlefield and who, when danger approached, threw their uniforms "into the weeds," as Maurizio had put it. Of course, Maurizio was more charming, spontaneous, and, it must be said, more disinterested than the corpulent *commendatori* of the Via Veneto. But it was a question of age; one day, Maurizio too would become one of those pleasure-seeking fat cats, cynical and opportunistic. Sergio did not want to follow in Maurizio's footsteps or imitate his actions, even though in truth, he had no real reason not to.

That day, at the table, he could feel his family's sadness, bewilderment, and worry as they gathered around a spartan meal. Their anxiety felt like a reproach as he debated the question of whether or not to leave Rome. He knew that his family would not flee. More important, it was clear that they had no desire or thought of fleeing. His father, an aging public employee who for the last forty years had worked at one of the government ministries; his two spinster sisters, who were terrified by what was happening; and his mother, who understood nothing except that she had a son in uniform in a far-off land whom she did not know when she would see again, all seemed to consider the events around them to be a horrifying calamity, however inevitable. Sergio sensed that their vulnerable, frank unhappiness showed greater courage than his doubts and indifference. He told them that he had been invited by Maurizio to go to Capri and saw, shamefaced, how quickly they embraced the idea and begged him to accept this providential offer. Sergio's father sighed and said: "I would happily leave if I could. My place is at the ministry. But you have no reason not to . . . Why stay here?" His mother encouraged him anxiously: "Yes, you should go . . . go now . . . It's a good idea. That way you can have a little holiday; you need it, you're so pale." His two sisters said the same thing, although their arguments were tinged with envy, however innocent. Faced with their disinterested and, in its own way, courageous affection, Sergio felt even more guilty and disgusted with himself. He said he would consider it and retreated to his room.

179   As he lay on his bed he tried to reflect on the situation. It occurred to him that, given his family's courageous resignation, the option of accepting Maurizio's offer was not, after all, as contemptible as he had thought. But in truth he was not afraid of staying, and did not even know why he should be. His doubts were not born of a debate between courage and fear, but rather from his eternal feeling of inertia. As usual, he did not take action, or feel the impulse to take action. Maurizio, on the other hand, had taken action by inviting him to come to Capri with him, and this invitation forced Sergio to make a decision and to act. In other words, the choice was not between courage and fear, but rather between inertia and action. If he had not crossed Maurizio's path, it would never have occurred to him to leave Rome, just as it did not occur to his family. Because of his lack of reflection, Maurizio had been able to do something that the vastly more introspective Sergio was incapable of: he had put the options on the table, forcing him to make a decision, no matter what it was. In other words, he was shaking Sergio out of his apathy and inertia.

He realized that until bumping into Maurizio, he had simply followed his natural inclinations, without reacting in any way, and perhaps, deep down, this had given him a sense of self-satisfaction. But as soon as he saw his friend, everything changed. He could have simply rejected the offer out of hand, preferring his inertia. But this too would have been a decision, albeit one in consonance with his behavior up to that point. In any case, he had not done so; almost against his will, he had expressed his objections in terms of dignity and courage. His objection had replaced his previous state of inertia with something new, a choice between two temptations: cowardice and courage. In reality he was neither cowardly nor courageous but simply undecided. But because his response implied courage, it placed him in an awkward position. If he accepted Maurizio's offer and revealed his objections to be false, he would be behaving like a coward.

After much reflection, he came to the conclusion 180 that the one thing he was sure of was the fact that that his inertia could not last, and that when a man does not actively place himself at a crossroads which requires some kind of action, reality does it for him by confronting him with the need to act. In this case, the call to action had been Maurizio's invitation to come with him to Capri. Sergio had not sought out his friend, and their meeting had been the fruit of chance. But the casual nature of their meeting, and Sergio's lack of foresight, confirmed the impossibility of a continued inertia. Sergio was convinced that if Maurizio had not invited him to come along, something else would have presented itself, another external factor that would have forced him to make a choice: the Fascists, the Germans, the anti-Fascists, his family, or something else. Reality would not allow anyone to stand on the sidelines, even someone who was consumed by regret and anxiety. The time for intervention and action had arrived, inevitably.

The trouble was that his response to Maurizio, with its allusions to courage and dignity, had come to him without any previous reflection or basis in any particular sentiment. It had poured out of him, probably as the result of a conventional manner of thinking which he had engaged in without reflection, almost automatically. The proof of this was that once he was alone he realized that he had spoken without conviction, as if playing the role of the person he wished to be but was not. In a way, the words were simply an extension of Maurizio's, just as a color finds definition only when contrasted with another. Here, once again, was proof of how much stronger Maurizio was, in his careless way, than he. Either way the words meant little and did not represent any concrete reality, even one that was still imprecise and obscure.

181   That said, the next twenty-four hours, conceded by Maurizio—or rather accepted by Sergio—would have to lead to some sort of decision. Toward evening, just before dinner, a young man he had recently befriended came to visit. His name was Federico. He was delicate and very tall, with a wan face and red-rimmed eyes. Judging by his unhealthily purple cheeks, he might be suffering from tuberculosis. Unlike Sergio, he was, or at least seemed to be, enthusiastic and fully engaged in whatever subject concerned him at the moment. Although he stuttered nervously and lacked eloquence, Federico could communicate his ardor because of the vehemence and passion with which he expressed, or attempted to express, himself. When he arrived, Sergio was lying on his bed. Federico immediately confronted him with a proposal: he and a group of friends had taken over the offices

26

of a minor Fascist publication and were planning to continue publishing a newspaper reflecting the new political reality of July 24. What he was proposing was to publish anti-Fascist, anti-Nazi propaganda, under the very nose of the Germans who were still fighting on the side of Italy and practically occupied the country. Sergio wrote with ease and eloquence, as demonstrated by his occasional articles, and they knew where his sympathies lay; why not write for this newspaper, which could have an enormous influence, especially on younger people? Stammering, coughing, and periodically becoming distracted as he described the particulars of the project, Federico concluded in a peremptory fashion: "Before you answer, let me warn you that you can't say no. Otherwise, you'll be playing into the hands of certain people— and they are in the majority—who say you are indecisive, or worse."

"What do you mean, worse?"

"A coward," Federico said, without hesitation.

For a moment, Sergio considered trying to explain his inertia, his morbid fascination with ruin and decadence, and his inability to take vigorous, unambiguous action. But then he realized that such an explanation would have been interpreted as a pretext 182 to conceal that which his detractors called cowardice. Once again, reality had found him, taken him by the neck, and forced him to make a decision. "In essence," Sergio reflected during the short silence that followed, "I find myself faced with two proposals, Federico's and Maurizio's, equally extreme, and equally extraneous to me. I have no reason—no solid, profound reason—to choose one over the other, and my choice will inevitably be determined by extraneous, impersonal factors. The only thing I am inclined to do is nothing at all, but if I say this I will be judged falsely by both Maurizio and Federico. The first will think that I refuse to act because, as I inadvertently implied earlier, I want to be a hero; the second will believe that if I do not accept his proposal it is because I am a coward. Neither coward nor hero, I am nevertheless forced to choose, because the only attitude that comes naturally to me has been compromised by my imprudent comment. And given that I would rather not follow Maurizio's lead—though I'm not sure why—I am forced to do the opposite. Therefore, I will accept Federico's proposal."

These reflections lasted only a few seconds. Then, with a slight feeling of falseness, Sergio said: "You don't need to twist my arm . . . I accept, I'll do it."

Federico threw his arms around Sergio's neck, exclaiming that he had never believed that he would turn him down. The two young men immediately began to discuss ideas for Sergio's articles; Sergio proposed a subject, which Federico approved with his usual enthusiasm. Sergio promised to bring the article to the offices by midnight and, bubbling over with enthusiasm, Federico left him to his task.

As soon as he had left, Sergio went to the telephone to call Maurizio. He almost regretted his decision, which felt somewhat random.

183 Maurizio did not let him finish: "You'll come to regret your decision, you'll see . . . but do as you please, it's your business after all." But after saying good-bye and wishing his friend a good summer, Sergio noticed that he felt relieved. The fact that he had come

to a decision, no matter how little conviction he felt, still came as a relief, even if it should turn out to be a temporary solution. In any case, the complications would come later, since every decision leads to innumerable others.

After hanging up, he got down to work. The heat was suffocating in the little room, and the smoke of many cigarettes hung in the air, even with the window open; the cloud of smoke seemed to be pushed inward by a mass of air even more dense and foul than the air inside. But at that moment, for some reason, Sergio felt almost stimulated by his uncomfortable circumstances. He sat down at his little table and began to write the article on a rickety old portable typewriter. As he typed, he became aware that he was thinking obsessively about Maurizio and his trip to Capri. He imagined the immense expanse of blue sea, luminous and overflowing with freedom; he could see his life on the island, protected from the surprises of the war, an oasis of calm amid the drama. The life he imagined was that of an idle spectator rather than a man of action. He realized that as he pictured each additional detail, the tone of his article darkened, his accusations becoming ever more uncompromising and decisive. He thought: at last he was reacting. As always it was the rivalry with Maurizio that drove him. Their meeting in the street and the way Maurizio lived his life, his offer of an escape to Capri, now felt like a distant memory. Maurizio's ghost held out temptations to him which he had instinctively rejected—how else to explain his unaccountable, spiteful response? This idea calmed him, and after a pause, he continued to write without stopping until he had finished the article. Meanwhile, his sister had stopped in his doorway several times to ask, in the mournful, contrite tone his family always used with him, whether he would be joining them for dinner. Each time he told her that he was too busy. Finally, he put the article in his pocket and went to the dining room, where the table was empty except for his place. His mother and sisters were waiting for him. As he sat down, he said: "I've decided that I'm not going to accept Maurizio's invitation. I'm staying in Rome."

His sisters, who had barely been able to conceal their envy when he informed them of Maurizio's invitation, did not seem dissatisfied with the news. But his mother, who feared for his safety, pleaded with him: "Sergio, why are you doing this? What will you do in Rome? You need rest. They say the English will arrive in a week or less. Go to Capri, and when you come back it will all be over."

When he looked down at his plate, he saw it contained some greens and a can of sardines. He could not help but reflect that Maurizio would not be reduced to such meals for long. He picked up a sardine and answered: "That's precisely why I'm staying. In a week it will all be over."

"But what do you care? Go to Capri . . . Just this once, why don't you listen to your mother, who loves you?"

He looked at his mother, a small woman who resembled him in many ways. She had thick black eyebrows and a serious mouth that seemed designed for murmuring prayers in church, and her hair was gathered on top of her head. Suddenly he was irritated by her anxious expression, though he did not quite know why: "Do you really want to know why I'm staying? I'll tell you."

He picked up another sardine and went on: "I'm staying because the invitation came from Maurizio . . . Do you know what Maurizio represents to me? Through no fault of his own, perhaps, he reminds me of all the people who desired Fascism, who were eager to enter this war on the side of the Germans and who now flee, when danger is near, leaving others, like Sandro, to fight and die on their behalf."

"Die . . . Don't say such things, even lightly," his mother pleaded, fearing for her son in distant Russia. She had clasped her hands together, as if to invoke divine protection.

"Others die, or, in any case, fight, on behalf of those who run off to Capri," Sergio went on, angrily and with his mouth full. One of his sisters, the younger one, Gisella—a smaller and thinner, bird-like version of his elder sister, Carolina, who was shapely and tall but also had thick eyebrows and a pointy nose like a bird—observed: "It's true, you know: all those young men from good families who were my classmates at university avoided military service or at the very least were allowed to stay in Italy. But poor wretches like Sandro were sent off to war."

"But, *figlio*," his mother implored, "that may be true, but I already worry so much about Sandro . . . If I knew you were in Capri, it would reassure me . . . But instead . . ."

"No," Sergio said, taking the folded article out of his pocket. "I'm staying, and this is the first article I've written denouncing them . . . denouncing people like Maurizio and the Germans. I'm taking it down to the newspaper now. And I'll keep writing."

His mother clasped her hands: "But if you write such things you'll compromise yourself . . . What if the Fascists should return? Think about what you are doing, *figlio mio.*"

"That is precisely what I'm doing," he answered, with a slight feeling of falseness. "I'm thinking." The meal ended in silence. Then his mother and sisters, having given up trying to convince him to go to Capri, began to discuss the political situation as they often did, repeating neighborhood rumors and what was said in the papers. Now that he had rejected Maurizio's offer, their comments sounded less frightened and anxious. Evidently, the three women were reassured by his presence. Sergio felt almost annoyed: he had committed himself, more deeply than he had in his offhanded comment to Maurizio in the street. He finished eating in silence and, after announcing that he was going to deliver his article to the newspaper, went out.

Once he was in the street, he felt guilty for what he had said about Maurizio at the table. It was true that each day he felt more contemptuous of this easily defined group who, out of thoughtlessness, incompetence, avarice, selfishness, and corruption, had led Italy into catastrophe. They were the Fascist bosses, and the wealthy men of all stripes who supported them, along with their families and the society that for twenty years had allowed them to govern without opposition, doing exactly as they pleased. But now for some reason he felt that it was unfair to lump Maurizio with these people. Even today, almost two years after their argument, he felt attached to Maurizio by a strange emotion, a mix of infatuation and disapproval, of attraction and repulsion. For a few years Sergio had loved him above all others, with the strong, innocent, infatuated love of adolescence. Now, even though he was doing his best to destroy this love, enough of it remained to fill him with remorse and doubts about the truth of his accusations. He could not forget the time he had spent in Maurizio's home: happy years, full of deep, irreplaceable intimacy. After they had gone their separate ways, he had been almost alone; no friend, no matter how estimable, had taken Maurizio's place.

He knew that he was still attached to Maurizio because of the surge of emotion he felt whenever he bumped into him on the street or in a public place. He felt an almost invincible impulse to embrace him, a physical sensation that required some effort to control. Every time he saw Maurizio, his lips instinctually formed the question: "When can we spend some time together?" He had actually said this once, and Maurizio had stared back at him with an expression of surprise, responding evasively, without refusing entirely. Sergio had never again had the courage to repeat the question, but it was always on the tip of his tongue, ready to erupt at the slightest hint that his friend might accept.

With these thoughts circling in his mind, he began to realize that the resentment he had expressed at the table had metamorphosed into a stirring affection, filled with gratitude for all the good things he had experienced because of his friendship with Maurizio. He felt guilty about his current attitude toward his friend. He began to think that he had heard a note of disappointment in his friend's voice after he informed him that he would not accept his invitation. And he suddenly became aware of something he had not noticed before: by inviting him to Capri, Maurizio had taken the first step toward the reconciliation that Sergio had desired for so many years. After all, he had even offered to pay for the trip. This detail had escaped him until then, perhaps because it was so blatant and conspicuous. In other words Maurizio, after all those years, had shown himself to be a real friend, exhibiting the same generosity as when they were boys. In those days, Maurizio would bring out his toys, the toys of a rich boy, and say: "Take what you want . . . go ahead, choose." How had he not noticed this before? Perhaps he had been too lost in his own worries to be able to see the people around him.

188   He was moved by this realization and felt a touch of remorse. The truth was that Maurizio had wanted to help him; his invitation had been disinterested and friendly. Sergio, on the other hand, had responded harshly and ungratefully, almost with contempt. Now he wanted to change his friend's impression of him, and explain that he had refused not out of hatred—despite his earlier comments at the table—but for reasons that had nothing to do with Maurizio. Lost in these thoughts, Sergio had reached the headquarters of the newspaper. He decided that he would call Maurizio from the offices and ask him to come by before his departure so that they could say their good-byes.

< As Sergio left the house the next day he could feel
that though the temperature had risen, the sky had
finally cleared. There was a touch of freshness in
the air, as if caressed by a sea breeze. Sergio went to
the newsstand and bought a paper, with his article
on the first page; it was the lead story, as they call it
in journalistic circles. The previous evening, he had
called Maurizio, just as he had promised himself he
would; his friend had invited him to come by the
house on the following morning. As he walked toward the villa, Sergio felt much happier and lighter,
perhaps because he had decided to stay in Rome and
write for the paper, or perhaps simply because of the
slight breeze and less oppressive weather.

He could see that the paper was filled with bad
news, a familiar sight in the spiral toward disaster
that had begun months earlier. But the city felt normal; people were out in the streets; the cars glided
by, brass and nickel plating glistening in the sun; the
striped awnings of the shops were lowered to protect
the shop windows from the sun; the traffic police
waved their arms at street corners, directing the cars.
But as Sergio took a side street containing a morning
market, he saw that there were only a few food stands
selling meager provisions, a sign of the shortages to
come. A bit farther down, a huge throng of women
stood outside a grocer. A guard watched the crowd,
the women yelled, and a shop boy inside the shop
wearing a white smock surveyed the crowd indifferently. Sergio walked past the crowd at a brisk pace,

his mood still light and slightly aggressive. For some reason, a song from the Risorgimento, about the fall of Venice to the Austrians, came into his head: "*Il morbo infuria, il pan ci manca, sul ponte sventola bandiera bianca*" (the plague rises, we're short of bread / and over the bridge the white flag spreads). He had seen these words inscribed on a print that his father, faithful to the memory of the Risorgimento, had hung in their foyer. It depicted a bridge with a white flag fluttering in the wind and several uniformed men, some of them still fighting, amid groups of wailing women. Above the scene one could make out the profile of the city beneath a dark, scowling, tempestuous sky. But this time, Sergio reflected, Fascist Italy would fall, defiantly waving its black flags with childish gold skulls, beneath the serene, joyful summer sky. There was not enough bread, and what little there was had an unpleasant taste, but the only plague rising was skepticism and rhetoric. The truth was that it was the regime, not Italy itself, that was falling, along with the society that had ushered it into power twenty years earlier. He once again felt a wave of hatred toward the people he considered responsible for Fascism, the war, and Italy's defeat. And he was proud that he had published an article entitled "Who Is Responsible?" He would shake Maurizio's hand, but he was also happy that his friend would see the article and know what he really thought of the society to which he belonged.

Maurizio lived not far away, in a neighborhood of villas and gardens that, thirty years earlier, had been the newest and most elegant in the city. Now the wealthy families had emigrated to other, more outlying areas filled with houses built in the so-called Novecento style. Maurizio's neighborhood, which by now had practically become part of central Rome, was a bit shabby, with its large, dreary nineteenth-century houses. Walking toward his friend's house, where he had last set foot years earlier, Sergio suddenly felt a strange sensation, as if he were no longer himself but the poor boy who used to rush to his rich friend's house each day after lunch. He had walked past these houses every day for years, and recognized the oleanders with their lush pink-and-white flowers, the garden gates, and the stolid façades of the houses. How promise-filled, luxurious, and mysterious those streets had seemed to him, coming from his miserable neighborhood of office workers; how melancholy, mediocre, and lacking in real elegance they seemed now, on the eve of a historical catastrophe. He remembered that at the time he had felt intimidated, fascinated, and attracted by the people he met in Maurizio's villa, elegant women and girls and dignified, well-dressed men. He was sure that if he saw them now he would feel about them as he did about the streets of this neighborhood.

He was beginning to feel a resurgence of the hostility which he had experienced as a boy. At the time this sensation had been a mystery to him; he knew nothing of the people who lived in those houses, nor of why they lived there or how they were so different from his own family. The hostility had almost disappeared after meeting Maurizio, though part of it remained buried deep inside him, now transformed into a sense of unease and exclusion. He could see that in those distant years of his early childhood, he had had an accurate grasp of the relations between rich and poor, and that his friendship with Maurizio had been simply a parenthesis, after which Maurizio had returned to his world and he to his. In short, he had always been poor, with the thoughts and feelings of a poor man; only now was he becoming conscious of this important truth, which as a child he had perceived as an instinctive, obscure sensation.

Sergio walked to the end of the street and came to Maurizio's gate, which was ajar. On the sidewalk just outside sat a white angora cat. He knew the cat well, because, as a boy, he had seen Maurizio's father bring it into the house as a gift. The cat had the annoying nickname Puffi, and in those days it had always been affectionate toward Sergio, always mewing when he arrived and rubbing itself against him. But this time the cat didn't move; it sat perfectly still, on its hind legs, its fur shaggy, facing away from Sergio. He noticed that it had lost patches of hair and that beneath the dirty, ratty fur one could see its pink skin. Its expression was bewildered, almost blind. Sergio bent down, whispering the cat's name, his heart filled with a sudden sadness. The cat turned its head and stood up as if to walk toward him. But after taking one step it tottered and then fell on its side, after which it settled once again in its original position. Without knowing exactly why, Sergio felt his eyes well with tears; the cat was obviously sick, perhaps dying. But what a strange way to die; not curled up under a piece of furniture but sitting on the sidewalk, facing the street, as if waiting for someone to arrive, its fur shaggy in the burning sun. Sergio bent down, lightly caressed the cat—it did not move—and entered the garden.

192

In his memory, the garden was large and full of trees; now it appeared to be a small rectangle with a few medium-sized trees and two or three flower beds surrounded by gravel paths. But the gravel was dirty and the flower beds had been invaded by weeds which had begun to turn yellow in the summer sun. The trees had grown wild, but no taller. He noticed an air of neglect and age, which he could not pinpoint in any single element but seemed to affect everything. Just as old age exacerbates certain characteristics, this air of neglect was neither poetic nor atmospheric; it was not the melancholy, charming neglect of an aging castle, but rather the casual indifference that clings to something that is neither beautiful nor ornate. It merely confirmed the stinginess and lack of rigor of those flower beds, the useless paths, the trees planted here and there. The Risorgimento hymn returned to his mind and with it the recognition of all that Italy had once been and which, even now, amid the decadence and carelessness, still remained tragically magnificent. Majestic houses, enormous gardens, fountains, paths, shaded bowers. But the society of their day would leave behind only tasteless, ugly houses, measly plots of land, ornaments made out of stucco and industrially reproduced.

"What a shame, what a shame," he mumbled as he rang the doorbell. "This too will end, but without glory." These words, pronounced by the final secretary of the Fascist Party during a tearful proclamation, had stayed with him for days, like a refrain. Maurizio came to the door with a bright, open expression that surprised Sergio after all these funereal signs; it struck him as an indication of indifference bordering on ignorance. "Ah, it's you," Maurizio said, inviting him in. "There's no one home . . . only the cook, all the others have left." As he said this, he led Sergio from the foyer, through a series of anterooms, and, finally, to the living room. It was dark; Maurizio went to one of the windows and pulled aside a heavy drape. The room was just as Sergio remembered it; not a single object or piece of furniture had been changed. But it looked smaller, faded, not at all luxurious or magnificent as it had appeared to him many years earlier when he had first entered this room. It was of medium size with walls covered in red imitation damask and ugly, gold-framed paintings on the walls; the furnishings—antiques, many of them probably reproductions—were distributed here and there. The sofas and armchairs looked worn and dirty; it was evident that nothing had been replaced and that even the cleanliness of the room was questionable. In a corner there was a settee on which lay something long and white. Sergio looked more closely and saw that it was a dog, lying on its side with its mouth slightly ajar, its fur matted, reddish eyes half closed. Maurizio followed his gaze and said, in a jocular tone: "I don't know what's going on around here . . . The dog and the cat are both sick; I think they are dying . . ." Sergio looked at Maurizio, who did not seem to attach any importance to the agony of these two animals; he opened his mouth as if to speak, but then decided not to. Everything seemed to be in agreement: the neglected old house, the animals' suffering, the war, and the country's impending disaster. Maurizio saw none of this, or at least did not react to it, a sure sign that he too was part of this world that was sinking, not standing outside looking in like Sergio, if only as an impotent spectator. Maurizio was part of it, an actor in the events and at the same time a victim. With some effort, Sergio said: "So, are you off to Capri?"

"Yes, tonight," Maurizio said. "It's too late to catch the last boat. I'll spend the night in Naples and leave for Capri tomorrow." He paused, adding, "So, have you changed your mind? Are you coming with me?"

Sergio answered slowly: "No, I can't . . . I have work to do."

"What work?" 194

"I've agreed to write for a paper . . . Look here." He handed the newspaper to Maurizio, who took it reluctantly. On the way over, it had occurred to Sergio that he should show Maurizio his article in order to make clear what he thought of the events unfolding around them. But as he handed Maurizio the newspaper he realized that he had simply succumbed to vanity mixed with his old inferiority complex. He wanted to show his friend what he had written, to be admired by him. Maurizio glanced at the paper and set it aside. Sergio could not help remarking: "Why don't you read it? That way at least you'll know what I think, and why I'm staying."

With a bored expression, Maurizio opened the newspaper, read a few lines, and then set it aside. "It's useless, I don't feel like reading it. I don't care."

"How do you know?" Sergio said, irritated. "You haven't read it."

"I can imagine what it says."

"You can't."

"Of course I can. I know you."

"All right then, let's see," Sergio said, his irritation growing. "What do you think I wrote?"

"You haven't changed," Maurizio said with a half smile. "Always the same."

"Why should I change?"

"Anyway, you seem satisfied with yourself. You've written an article entitled 'Who Is Responsible?' So I'm sure you've done your best to indicate who is responsible for the war and for what is happening now."

"That's right."

"Well, I can imagine that your point is that those responsible are not the military but the Fascists and the government in general. How original . . ." He dug around in his pocket for his gold cigarette case, pulled out a cigarette, and lit it. Sergio watched as he smoked and repeatedly pushed back one of his blond curls, a familiar gesture. Just as he had when he saw the suffering of the two dying animals, Sergio felt the desire to speak up and explain his thoughts, or rather his feelings, but once again he lost his nerve. Maurizio was obviously a million miles away from what he considered to be the true path, and he felt an almost painful need to warn him and open his eyes. Maurizio did not seem to think that he too might be partly responsible. How could he, when even those directly and flagrantly responsible, the generals and the bosses, did not know it? Sergio felt a terrible sense of futility. He held out his hand, took back the newspaper, and said, somewhat falsely: "It doesn't matter . . . If you don't feel like reading it, I'm sure you have your reasons."

There was a long pause. Maurizio smoked, seemingly lost in thought. Then he said, "How long do you think the war will last at this point?"

Sergio answered, "I don't know, probably a long time."

"I'm convinced," Maurizio said, "that it will end very soon . . . I think the Allies will be in Rome in a week at the most, and then everything will return to normal. That's why I'm going to Capri; it's not worth giving up our vacation and even risking injury for something that is about to end."

He continued to smoke with an air of conviction, adding, after a short pause: "Considering everything, Italy will come out all right . . . We haven't been in the war for too long . . . As soon as it really got started, it's all over, at least for us . . ."

Once again, Sergio was tempted to contradict his friend's reasoning, which to him seemed so full of cynicism and skepticism. To Maurizio it was simply good sense. Once again, he held his tongue. Then he asked: "And then what?"

"Then, nothing," Maurizio said offhandedly. "The Allies will arrive and set up whatever government they please. Of course, they'll take away our colonies and our empire. After all, it's what we deserve. If we hadn't gone to war, we would have kept everything, 196 and Italy would have become the richest, most influential country in Europe. Mussolini was stupid."

"Only stupid?"

"I can't wait for it all to end," Maurizio continued, without noting Sergio's interruption. "I've wasted the past few years . . . I'd like to get a degree, even though it's late now."

"What kind of degree?"

"Maybe law," Maurizio answered, in an uncertain tone which reflected the uncertainty of his decision. "I must tell you that from time to time I think that you may be right . . . It's not good to hang around doing nothing . . . even people like me who have enough to live on. You were right when you told Emilia that I was wasting my life, do you remember? It made me angry at the time, of course, because no one likes to hear certain things; and the way she said it was so irritating . . . But I have to admit it: you were right."

Sergio said nothing and instead peered at his friend. He saw that Maurizio had changed, like his house and everything it contained. His face was still youthful and attractive, but it had a grim and tired quality that was new. His blue eyes, which had once been clear, limpid, and pure, seemed to have a dark halo around them, with a turbid, bored quality around the irises, a sickly glow. A line, as fine as a razor's edge, framed one corner of his mouth, making that side of his face look ten years older. And he was losing his hair, unevenly and in a manner that suggested dissoluteness and fatigue: a few blond hairs still stuck out of the middle of his balding pate, combed back, fine and trembling like bushes in the middle of a hillside full of mud, stones, and boulders. It was the face of a man who had enjoyed life to the fullest, and who still knew how. But when he spoke of wasted time and admitted to Sergio that he was right, his tone was unusually sincere and almost anguished. Sergio was moved by the idea that Maurizio was opening up to him, and realized once again that despite everything, his friend still occupied a place in his heart. As if guessing at his thoughts, Maurizio said: "I haven't been well for some time . . . I think I smoke too much." He threw away the cigarette he had just lit. "Or maybe I drink too much . . . And you know"—he hesitated for a moment and lowered his eyes almost shamefully—"the years go by and I realize I'm not young anymore."

Gently, almost as if fearing that he would interrupt the flow of Maurizio's confidences, Sergio said: "You're only twenty-seven."

"I know," answered Maurizio, "but, I don't know if it's the same for you . . . probably not, because your life is so different from mine . . . but even though I'm twenty-seven, I feel as if I were forty. I notice it especially in my relations with women." He stopped and was suddenly quiet, and seemed almost to regret having spoken.

"What do you mean, in your relations with women?"

"Well, you see," Maurizio said, uncomfortably, "I have a lot of dealings with women . . . Let's just say, I don't have many distractions . . . And for some time it has felt like it's always the same thing, and I'm bored." After a moment he continued, in an exasperated tone: "It's always the same—the meeting, the amusing repartee to show my interest, the invitation to go for a drive, dinner, or a day at the beach, the first kiss, then the second, then the third, and finally, the surrender. Every woman gives herself with the same gestures, the same words, the same objections, and the same impulses as the one who came before and the next one . . . You can see how all this could become a bore," he said, raising his voice slightly as if Sergio had contradicted him.

"I agree, of course," Sergio said, with a smile that he knew to be slightly false. The smile of a man who has never been in love with a woman.

"It's a bore," Maurizio went on. "It almost sickens me . . . When I put my hand on a girl's breast for the first time, it feels like the same breast as the last time, with another girl . . . And that goes for everything else, as well . . . Do you know what happened to me recently? After overcoming a woman's final re-sistance I sent her away. I told her that I had a serious venereal disease and did not want to infect her. She was horrified, but I knew that if I insisted, illness or no illness, she would still be willing . . . They're all the same, and I too keep repeating myself . . . All of this leads me to think that my youth is finished. What more is there to say?"

He seemed unhappy, but his uncomprehending, innocent sadness was like that of an animal that suddenly feels something amiss—a lessening or a change in its vitality—and cannot understand the cause. Maurizio did not understand the war or what was happening in his own house, just as he did not understand the illness of his cat and dog; in fact, he did not seem to understand even himself. After a pause, he said, "This is why I want to go to Capri. It's relatively quiet there because of the war. I want to spend a summer alone, without anyone around, so I can reflect a bit. Meanwhile, the war will end and then I will return to Rome and make a decision."

"What decision?"

"I don't know . . . maybe I'll find a job . . . or maybe I'll get married . . . I'll have lots of children and become a paterfamilias." He said this with a certain sour note in his voice, unsentimentally, with a kind of coarseness that Sergio envied, if only momentarily. "Why are you smiling?" Maurizio asked. "Don't you think I would be a good father?"

"I'm sure you would," Sergio answered, now smiling sincerely.

"After all," Maurizio said, more calmly, "this is more or less how things have always been. A young man would have a good time and then, later, he would get married. Why should I be different? I'll get married, I'll be faithful to my wife, I'll work . . . A wife, children, and a job—it's probably what I need."

"What do your parents think of your plans?" Sergio asked, not knowing what to say.

"Oh, nothing. They don't know . . . I am, as my father likes to say, his greatest worry in life. My mother behaves as if I were still seven years old . . . but they know nothing about my life." By now Maurizio was speaking with complete openness, in a voice filled with fervor. He got up from the couch, went to a cabinet in a corner of the room, and opened it, revealing a bar, bottles, and mirrors gleaming. He poured himself a generous portion of whiskey. "Would you like some?" he asked.

"At this time of day? No, thank you."

"It picks me up," Maurizio said, pouring some water into the glass. "I confess that I was almost afraid that you would accept, because it has become very hard to find and can only be bought at a very high price . . . I had a good supply at the beginning of the war but it's almost gone now."

"Did your family stock up on many provisions before the war?" Sergio asked, gently.

"I'm not sure," Maurizio said vaguely, slightly surprised at the question. "I think so . . . When the war began, and for months after that, my mother did nothing but accumulate things, as if we were under siege . . . I think we have enough clothes and food to last us several years." He returned to the couch and sat sideways, with one leg over the armrest, glass in hand. "Tell me the truth . . . You must see me as a kind of glutton: drinking, smoking, making love to women."

Sergio hesitated and peered closely at his friend before answering: in effect, the word Maurizio had chosen fit him quite well. His face, once so fresh and youthful, now clouded and impure, was that of a glutton. "No," he said finally, "I think you look tired."

"I am," Maurizio said in a tone that was suddenly innocent and plaintive, almost like that of a child. "You know, I hardly sleep. The doctor says there's nothing wrong with me . . . but I don't sleep at all, even when I take pills."

"You need to rest," Sergio hazarded.

"Yes," Maurizio answered with conviction, "I need to rest. In Capri I'll eat, exercise, sleep . . . it's exactly what I need. It's probably just this heat and this damned war."

"What are you saying? I thought you didn't give a damn about the war."

"That's right, I don't . . . and why should I? I didn't declare it and I have nothing to lose or to gain from it . . . But they just won't leave us alone, will they?"

"But you didn't fight in the war."

"I'm not crazy . . . I was an officer for a few months and then I managed to get myself demobilized . . . My father knows someone at the ministry of defense."

Feeling a wave of resentment, Sergio retorted: "My brother was deployed to the Russian front."

"You should have told me," Maurizio said, surprised. "We could have arranged for him to stay here."

"My family belongs to the class of people who do what has to be done and pay the price for the rest of us," Sergio said, darkly.

Maurizio did not react to his comment. "You know what troubled me the most? Emilia's death."

"Emilia is dead?" Sergio exclaimed in surprise.

"Yes, she died in tragic circumstances . . . I heard about it by chance from a German living in Italy . . . poor thing . . . She was Jewish, you know, and they came to arrest her . . . She jumped out of a window so they wouldn't take her . . . She must have been about fifty . . . What a way to die. At the time, it didn't affect me . . . I never really loved her and so much time had passed . . . But then I began to have trouble sleeping and I realized that whenever I lay in my bed I was thinking about her, or rather about the time when we were lovers . . . I suppose that my unconscious mind was marked by her death. In any case, perhaps it's a coincidence."

He had told this story in a casual, conversational tone. Evidently, Sergio thought, her death had not affected him too deeply; similar cases were quite frequent, even, one might say, normal. But Maurizio's unconscious, as he had said, adopting a term from psychoanalysis, which was all the rage, had been shaken. Sergio asked himself whether Maurizio's unconscious might be aware of other things, or at least sense them, and he concluded that perhaps his friend was not completely sincere, not only with Sergio but with himself. He was trying to protect himself, that was all. And if he felt the need to defend himself, perhaps all was not lost. Gently, Sergio asked: "I don't understand . . . what do you mean by your 'unconscious'?"

"You know," Maurizio said, awkwardly, "it's like when you fall and you think you haven't hurt yourself . . . Then a few days later it starts to hurt and you get a bruise . . . The unconscious . . . don't you know what it is?"

"You're the one who doesn't know," Sergio thought, changing the subject. "Maybe you should fall in love . . . If you could fall in love, everything would be all right. You'd be able to sleep, and all the rest."

"I can't fall in love," Maurizio said sincerely, with clear bitterness. "Either a woman jumps into bed with me too quickly, or something is missing . . . Either way, I soon lose interest. I have no illusions . . . It's been years since I've been in love."

"So how are you planning to go about getting married?"

"Finding a wife is a different matter . . . You don't need to be in love. I'll get married and we'll have four or five kids. I won't be in love with her but she'll still be my wife . . . No, love isn't for me."

Maurizio shook his hand and then lit another cigarette. Sergio insisted: "But wouldn't you like to fall in love?"

Maurizio was pouring himself another glass. Just as he was about to answer, he stopped, holding up one finger as if commanding Sergio to be silent. Sergio watched in surprise. Sergio could hear a low rumbling from outside, barely distinguishable from the silence, almost part of it. Then, like an airplane engine gaining speed, the noise grew, louder and louder, eventually becoming a howl. "The alarm siren," Maurizio said, calmly.

Sergio instinctively jumped up. These were the first air raids they had experienced, and the sound of the siren, linked to the idea of bombs falling out of the sky, inspired an agitation in him that was not quite fear but rather a sensation like being immersed in freezing water. It was the sensation of passing too quickly from a state of safety and calm to one of danger and tension. He bit his tongue as he looked over at Maurizio and saw that he was still sitting in his chair with an indifferent air. He began to pace up and down, saying: "I'm tense and this wailing irritates my nerves."

They heard doors slamming on the second floor and feet descending the stairs. The alarm began again after a short pause; it rose upward and spread out above them, evoking with its spiraling sound the immensity of the burning August sky over the defenseless city. The door to the living room opened and several people rushed in.

Sergio knew some of them. One was Maurizio's mother, a tall, fair-haired woman with cerulean eyes set in a red, swollen face; she was simultaneously bony and curvaceous, and it seemed as if the abundant curves of her breasts, hips, and thighs clung to her skeleton without concealing its great size and brittleness. Maurizio's father also appeared; he was a large, tall man with a reddish complexion and youthful appearance despite his completely bald head. He was elegant, taciturn, terribly calm, and slightly sly, just as Sergio remembered him. Maurizio's sister appeared; she did not seem to belong in that family, and in fact she was a daughter from the mother's first marriage. Maurizio's mother had been widowed at an early age and had remarried soon after the death of her first husband. This daughter, Marisa, could now be called an old maid; she was very beautiful, tall, with a limpid expression and a large nose, big, melancholy eyes, a dark complexion and delicate features. She must have been in her thirties. Sergio remembered her as a very elegant, worldly, but also sweet and gentle, young woman, whose many love interests were a constant subject of conversation, but who for some reason had never married. The fourth and final member of the group was an old woman whom he did not recognize. Her expression spoke of a great but almost pathetic goodness; she was thin, with a large nose and whiskers, with ashen skin and watery blue eyes. She must be a governess or a lady companion or perhaps a poor relation, or all three, Sergio thought, observing her servile attitude even at this moment of intense agitation.

Maurizio's mother seemed to be suffering from a panic attack. She was dressed in a summery, youthful outfit—a fluttering blue dress with white polka dots—and she clutched a small leather case. She rushed into the room and called out to her son: "Hurry, hurry, let's go to the shelter."

In response, not moving, Maurizio asked, "Why don't we stay here?" As if to accentuate his impassivity, he introduced Sergio to his mother: "Mother, you remember Sergio, don't you? Sergio Maltese."

"Good day, Maltese," Maurizio's mother said, in a rush. The wailing began again. She screamed, "Let's go to the shelter . . . That's the third alarm . . . Let's go!" She took Maurizio by the arm, as if to pull him out of the chair. Finally, Maurizio's father said calmly: "Get up immediately . . . You know that your mother can't find peace if you're not with us."

This reasonable request seemed to convince Maurizio. He got up from the chair and walked to the 204 door. "You come too," Maurizio's mother called out to Sergio as she went out, leading the group. "The shelter is in the Borghese Museum . . . come on, we mustn't waste time." As she reached the door, the old lady observed: "Madam, you dropped a hairpin," and bent down to pick up a tortoiseshell pin. Maurizio's mother arranged a lock of hair dangling in her face and answered, hurriedly, "Leave it there, dear, there is no time." Maurizio's sister, who seemed calmer, took the pin from the old woman: "You can give it to me . . . I'll keep it for her."

They walked through several anterooms, and finally out into the garden, feeling the sudden heat of the afternoon after the cool air inside the house. Maurizio's mother's high-heeled shoes clattered precipitously down the marble stairs of the main entrance. The others followed more calmly: besides the governess, who was obviously terrified, neither Maurizio's father, nor his sister, nor Maurizio himself seemed frightened. The front gate was ajar, and

53

the ragged cat was still sitting there, with its scrawny neck, dirty muzzle, and red eyes half shut in the sunshine. Sergio could not help reaching down to pat the cat softly. The animal turned toward him and seemed to look up at him almost gratefully, through swollen, hairless lids. Just then, the first burst of antiaircraft fire rang out, dry and loud in the summer sky.

"Oh God," Maurizio's mother cried, now running toward the entrance of the Villa Borghese, which was not far from their front gate. Without knowing why, Sergio also began to run, and he saw that they were all running, as if overcome, not so much by fear but by the urgency of the bursts. Maurizio's mother ran ahead, with her small case under her arm and her blue-and-white polka-dotted dress fluttering around her. She was followed by the elderly lady, running with great strides on her bony legs; just behind her came Maurizio's father and sister, who seemed to be running calmly, followed by Maurizio, who could not be said to be running but had accelerated his pace. He leaned forward, his face masked by large sunglasses. Sergio, who had been left behind when he paused to caress the cat, came last. Farther down the street he could see other people running in the same direction in the blinding August sun. The antiaircraft guns were firing consistently, with quick, angry bursts. When he had looked up at the sky before passing through the front gate of the villa, he had seen the white tufts of shells exploding in a straight line, then expanding slowly in the wind while others exploded, forming darker and denser areas here and there in the sky. They ran down an avenue, rapidly approaching the large whitish building of the museum. A little bit toward the right he could see the small door of the shelter, marked by a sign. The people ahead of them passed through the door and disappeared. Now the antiaircraft fire and siren stopped, and in the silence that ensued it was suddenly unclear why all these people were running. But just as Sergio was about to pass through the little door, he heard something that made him stop in his tracks and gaze up into the sky: a metallic, vibrating whir, surrounded by a duller, more insistent hum which grew louder and louder, threatening to fill the entire sky. "The planes," he thought as he went inside.

The shelter was simply the crypt, or basement, of the museum. The small group of fugitives was now precipitously descending a spiral staircase with marble steps and a low, vaulted ceiling, rushing between thick walls. Finally they entered a semi-dark cellar, seemingly vast, with low, unfinished, vaulted ceilings made out of a material that looked like concrete, supported by enormous, rough-hewn pilasters. The cellar seemed to be only partly occupied by a small multitude. Sergio noticed the presence of many women and children, and quite a few men. The arches and pilasters formed shadowy alcoves, corners in which it was impossible for the eyes to penetrate the darkness. He could see dark archways which seemed to open onto hallways leading into other areas. Sergio and Maurizio could no longer see the others in their group and began to walk around the dim basement, amid the anxious, frightened people. Far from reassuring, the heavy, muffled silence which seemed to emanate from the enormous arches augmented the 206 sense of imminent danger: those arches, however massive, did not appear at all solid, since they were built out of a crumbly material. He couldn't help thinking that a single bomb would send the whole thing crashing down on their heads. Maurizio, as if guessing Sergio's thoughts, pointed to one of the arches and said: "They call it a shelter . . . This stuff will collapse at the first impact . . . We'll be crushed, like mice . . . It's safer outside . . ."

"Do you come here every time the alarm goes off?"

"My mother comes, and when I'm at home, I come too to reassure her."

"What is that case she carries under her arm?"

Maurizio answered lightly: "Her jewels . . . She has several million liras' worth in there."

Sergio said no more. He saw that the rest of the family—father, mother, sister, and governess—were approaching. The mother, who had always treated him with a slight haughtiness, as if she felt that this son of a government employee was her inferior, anxiously asked: "What do you think, Maltese? Will the war ever end? Will it be over soon? What do you think?"

There beneath the arches, Sergio noted that her voice did not sound exactly terrified, but rather like the echo of words pronounced in some other dimension. Being in that place was like walking in the circles of hell, as if they had already died and their souls lived on, speaking in earthly tones. "It's impossible to know," he answered, "but of course, one day it will end."

With utter conviction, Maurizio's rosy, conciliating, discreet, well-mannered father mumbled—more to reassure his wife than to reiterate an obvious truth—"Don't worry, the war will be over soon . . . The Germans will win the battle for Russia; they'll occupy the rest of the country, and then they'll come here and drive out the Allies."

Sergio peered over at Maurizio's father and wondered whether he was joking. But he was quite calm and composed and didn't seem to be joking in the least. It was a case of complete incomprehension and deafness, Sergio reflected, similar to Maurizio's but more profound and almost comical in its absurdity. Sergio knew that Maurizio's father was a businessman, and he seemed to remember that his business was investing in stocks. He asked, cautiously, "Do you really think that the Germans can still win the war?"

"Of course," Maurizio's father said calmly.

"I'm not so sure," Maurizio's sister interjected, but it seemed to Sergio that her tone was even more unrealistic than her father's. By implying thought, her doubts gave her an air of obtuseness even greater than that created by her father's absence of doubt. Desperate and terrified, Maurizio's mother shifted her jewelry case from one arm to the other and said: "For all I care, the English can win, or the Germans . . . I just want someone to win so we can forget all this!"

"Don't worry, darling, the Germans will win the war and we'll all be fine . . . Don't worry yourself," Maurizio's father said, affectionately, patting her on the back. Maurizio, who had said nothing until then, asked suddenly: "What about you, *signorina*, who do you think will win the war?"

He was speaking to the elderly governess. She answered quickly: "Signor Maurizio, I don't understand such matters ... I don't even read the newspaper ... If you told me that neither the English nor the Germans, but rather the Chinese, were going to win the war I would have to agree ... After all, what can we do about it? It's not up to us ..." She went on; her tongue, which had been frozen in terror, suddenly loosened. Brusquely, Maurizio said, "Come on, Sergio ...," and turned to his family. "Sergio and I are going to take a look around."

"I'll come with you," Maurizio's sister declared. Sergio had noticed that she had been staring at him since their arrival, gazing at his face with a curiously intense, provocative gaze. He vaguely remembered rumors that circulated about her: that she was strange, perhaps crazy, and obsessed with only one thing, love. They set off down a corridor in silence. Maurizio walked ahead, his hands in his pockets, whistling quietly. Marisa took Sergio's arm and whispered: "You don't mind, do you? I'm so frightened."

Maurizio touched the wall. "They're oozing with moisture; they must be built into an embankment." Without turning around, he added, "Sergio, do you have a cigarette?" Sergio said no, somewhat uncomfortably.

"I'll go get some from my father," Maurizio said, heading in the opposite direction. As if she had been waiting this whole time for her brother's departure, Marisa pressed her body against Sergio's side, whispering, "Don't you remember me? I remember you perfectly ... You are a bit younger than me ... but you know ... back when you used to come by to see my brother, five years ago I think it was ... I fell in love with you ... but you never noticed."

They had reached the darkest point in the corridor. Sergio stopped, slightly agitated. Marisa touched his arm and searched for his hand: "You must be terribly unkind . . . You're always so serious . . . You never smile."

Sergio looked around. He had no feelings for Marisa, but the touch of her hand and the clear invitation it implied had an effect on him. A bit farther ahead there was a small red light, revealing a dark doorway. He stepped toward the light, but she held him back: "Wait a minute . . . I need to tell you something."

"What do you need to tell me?"

"I can't say it out loud . . . I'll whisper it in your ear."

He echoed her words, "In my ear," his voice filled with doubt. He could just make out a dark figure standing in the doorway, vaguely illuminated by the dim red light. It looked like a feminine form, but he could not make out the face. He could feel someone looking at him; the woman seemed to be watching them. Marisa whispered: "Come closer, and I'll tell you." 209

Mechanically, and still peering at the dark shape tucked into the doorway in the half light of the red bulb, Sergio leaned forward slightly. He felt Marisa's mouth glue itself to his ear with a circular motion of her soft, moist lips, like a suction cup. Marisa's tongue began to caress his ear, quickly and conscientiously. He felt aroused and at the same time embarrassed. Marisa kissed his ear until she was forced to come up for air. As she leaned back, she whispered breathlessly: "Got it?"

"Yes," he answered, in a daze, feeling simultaneously embarrassed and aroused.

"So, what do you say?" she asked, boldly.

They heard Maurizio's voice calling out to them as he returned, carrying a pack of cigarettes. "Marisa, Mamma wants you . . . She's afraid you'll get lost."

The young woman squeezed Sergio's hand conspiratorially and said under her breath: "Call me tomorrow." Then she let go of his arm and went off, exclaiming, "Why on earth would I get lost?" Her footsteps disappeared around the corner.

Maurizio walked over to Sergio: "Did you know that there are lots of little rooms down here where the museum's masterpieces have been hidden away? I just went into one. There was a Bernini statue in a kind of case." He lit a cigarette, adding: "Let's see what's in here," walking briskly toward the doorway where the dark, motionless figure stood.

Sergio felt embarrassed, as if the mysterious, dark figure were about to jump out of the shadows and accuse him: "I saw how you let Marisa kiss you." Maurizio, who was a few steps ahead of him, did not seem to notice the figure who had witnessed Sergio's embrace, or pretended not to. "It's so dark in here," he said, searching in his pocket for a flashlight to light the ground before him. As the beam illuminated the doorway, two small but sturdy feet appeared. They belonged to a woman. They looked like two small, fat doves roosting quietly side by side. Sergio noticed that the feet were clad in simple low-heeled shoes, almost masculine in design, and heavily worn. Then the beam slid up her bare legs, which were not quite fat but not slender either, with white, healthy-looking, hairless skin and a tender, child-like shape. The beam illuminated the edge of a simple red dress; it made the legs appear even more prominent, with their healthy, innocent air, more infantile than womanly. The young woman's hips were rather wide, Sergio noted, and her waist not particularly slender; like her legs and hips, there was something solid about her. And then her chest: two mounds protruding under the light fabric, high, solid, and at the same time soft. She had a lovely round neck, and a serious face, with a frank, straightforward beauty and a serene forehead hidden by a lock of brown hair. Her eyes were prominent, light-colored, and clearly outlined, and her nose was small and straight, with flared nostrils; she had pale lips like a fruit or a flower. It was a face with classical proportions, almost marmoreal and characterized by a dreamy, dignified serenity. She was a young woman, but could almost have been a prepubescent boy. She observed them with some diffidence; perhaps because of the light, her eyebrows seemed to express worry. Maurizio held the flashlight up to her face a moment longer, then shifted it slightly to the left. In the darkness of the small room, they could see a wooden structure. There, between two pieces of wood, a face was visible. It was very similar to the girl's, but made out of marble. It was a statue from the museum's collection, with a serene, pale expression and white eyes that stared out into the darkness. It was surprisingly similar to the real, human face that the flashlight had revealed a moment earlier. Sergio whispered: "Did you notice how much they look alike?"

"Who do you mean?"

"The girl and the statue."

"Do you know who that is?"

"Pauline Bonaparte," Sergio said. As if to evaluate Sergio's powers of observation, Maurizio aimed the beam of light at the face of the young girl and then at the statue, going back and forth until finally the girl called out, in an irritated voice: "Have you finished blinding me with your flashlight?"

For a moment, it seemed to Sergio that the statue, rather than the girl, had spoken. Maurizio beamed his flashlight in the girl's face once again, holding it there. "Forgive us, but we were noticing the truly extraordinary resemblance between you and the statue."

"What statue?" she asked. Her voice was neither sweet nor delicate. Like the rest of her, it was on the heavy side, and low, but still affectionate and caressing.

"Pauline Bonaparte," Sergio repeated.

The girl did not respond, as if she hadn't heard, or hadn't caught the reference. A moment later she asked, "Do you think the alarm has passed?"

"Usually there is a signal," Maurizio said.

The girl observed them with diffidence tempered by a touch of curiosity and a glimmer of hope. Finally she said: "Is the train station far from here?"

"No . . . why?"

"Do you know this address?"

212   In the light of the flashlight, she opened a shabby purse and proceeded to hand Sergio a scrap of newspaper. It was an advertisement for a furnished room near the train station. "So you're not from here," Sergio commented.

"No," she answered with a slightly embarrassed tone. "I'm from T.," a city in central Italy. "I arrived just yesterday."

"And why did you come to Rome?" Maurizio asked, boldly.

The girl seemed self-conscious: "I'm looking for work." She was shy, Sergio thought. She avoided looking at Maurizio but answered Sergio's questions, as if responding to something intimidating in his voice. Maurizio began to laugh: "What a time to be looking for work in Rome."

"Why, is it difficult to find work?" she asked cautiously, almost fearfully.

"It's impossible," he said, harshly.

"That's not quite true," Sergio said gently. "What do you know how to do?"

"Nothing, really," she said, simply, "but I thought . . ."

They heard voices just beyond the bend in the hallway. They could clearly hear Maurizio's mother calling out "Maurizio . . . Maurizio . . ." Then she appeared, with the small case still tucked under her arm, waving the other arm gaily. "It's all over . . . They've sounded the all clear. Let's go, Maurizio."

Beneath the vaulted ceiling, in the dark, Sergio thought her voice sounded like a ghost calling from the underworld, surrounded by other melancholy, incorporeal spirits. Maurizio, the girl, and Sergio all stared at her in silence. She too was still and silent, the case still under her arm, in the half light of the hallway. Finally, Maurizio said, dreamily, "All right, Mother, let's go." She seemed to finally take a breath, as if her son's words had released her from a spell and she had once again become a sentient being, no longer a ghost, as she had feared. As they walked silently behind her she went on about how frightened she had been, how long the alarm had lasted, and whether any bombs had been dropped. Maurizio walked slowly, as if trying to linger behind with Sergio and the girl. But his mother matched her footsteps to his and finally she took his arm, as if confirming her maternal role. Turning to Sergio, she said: "Of course, Maltese, you must understand the fears of a mother . . . In moments like these, I think principally of him." Sergio said nothing and instead gazed at the girl walking beside him with her eyes lowered.

They walked toward the exit with the rest of the people from the shelter, who were moving with the docility and deliberate pace of a multitude emerging from Mass or a cinema. One by one, they climbed the spiraling staircase and emerged into the blinding sunlight, across from the large square surrounded by trees and statues. Maurizio's mother turned to Sergio and said, in a worldly, detached, and somewhat disdainful tone: "Good-bye, Maltese . . . I hope to see you again in less extreme circumstances."

"Good-bye, Maltese," Maurizio's father repeated, smiling affably.

"Good-bye, Maltese," Marisa said. She squeezed his hand and as she let go, her fingers lingered on his with an air of complicity.

"Good-bye," the governess echoed, hurrying after her mistress.

Maurizio asked Sergio, "Where are you off to now?"

Sergio realized that the girl was still there, walking slowly nearby. He called out to her, suddenly decisive: "*Signorina* . . ."

"Yes?" she answered with a start.   214

"Would you like . . . may I walk with you?"

"Yes, thank you," she answered with complete frankness. Maurizio looked at her, then at Sergio, and said, "Call me after lunch. I'll join you."

"All right."

"See you later," Maurizio said, seemingly with some regret, before calmly joining his family, which was already some way off. Only after a little while, when he was already far away, did Sergio remember that Maurizio was supposed to leave early that afternoon. He felt a touch of surprise. The young woman asked, in her confident, trusting voice: "Where should we go?"

[V]

Under a burning sun, in the silent emptiness of the   215
park, they slowly approached the main path. The sun seemed fixed at a point directly above them, beating down on their heads. Time stood still, as if events were taking place outside of time, like figures beyond an impenetrable pane of glass. "Here I am," Sergio could not help but think as he gazed at the girl walking next to him and then at the path in the deserted park. "Here I am; all around, everything is disappearing, but I'm standing still . . . It's 1943 and this mysterious girl is here next to me . . . Many years hence,

65

if I survive this test, I'll remember this insignificant moment of no historical importance more than anything else in this clamorous, crucial period." It was true; he could feel that this moment, clearly delineated by his unhappy, fearful sensibility, was unique and would never be repeated, and that furthermore, it was important, though he couldn't quite say why. He felt a sensation that was deep, pungent, and intense and at the same time completely ineffable and indefinite. A feeling that encompassed not only the girl and himself but everything, all of reality, as if suddenly the dam holding back this wave of feeling had opened and the emotion flowed freely into the outside world, becoming one with it and staining it in its own hue. His eyes welled with tears. "So then, could there really be something beyond these important events taking place all around us . . . and is it possible that we are not just spectators or actors in these events?" He could not fully answer either of these two questions. He tried to define what he was feeling and understood that it was something terribly vast, a cosmic compassion that encompassed both the Fascists and the anti-Fascists, Germans and Italians, as well as the sky, the sun, the trees, and both himself and the girl walking next to him. She must have noticed his agitation, because she turned and asked, in her childlike voice: "Are you crying? Why?" [. . .]

221   She answered, firmly: "Please don't ask me [. . .]"
"But why?"
"Please."
"At least tell me why you left T."
"I can't tell you that either."

66

"Why this mystery?" Sergio asked. "Don't you trust me?"

"No," she said, staring at him with a kind of desperation. "Please don't ask any more questions, I beg you."

For a moment he sat perplexed, a flurry of ideas streaming through his mind: perhaps she was a spy or an adventuress, or a thief, or some other kind of criminal. But it was enough just to look at her, to see her innocent, almost childlike face, in order to know that this was impossible. There were doubtless dishonorable people in the world, but most of them were innocent victims, forced into crime by the war. Even if the girl's life was a mystery, it was sure to be a mystery in her image, innocent and simple. "Forgive me," he said, sincerely, "I didn't mean to be indiscreet."

She responded brightly, her voice betraying the slightest trace of a local accent: "Please don't apologize . . . it's understandable. You found me in this park, alone . . . it's normal for you to ask questions."

After a short silence, he said, "My name is Sergio . . . I'm a journalist. And I'm from Rome."

Again, she was silent, and after a moment he added, "Do you have a suitcase, or something else?"

"Yes, at the station."

"All right then," he said with some effort, "let's go get a bite to eat and then we can go to the station and pick up your bag. We'll take it to your room."

"All right," she said with a trusting docility that he found slightly jarring. "Let's go."

They got up from the bench and left the square, walking along a vast, empty avenue. Nella unexpectedly began to speak in a relaxed, trusting voice, as if they were old friends. Not only did she not attribute much importance to the war, but she did not seem to even understand its exact terms. After he asked whether she thought they had really been bombed that morning, she asked casually, "Were those German planes?"

Sergio stared at her in disbelief. "German planes? No . . . not yet . . . the Germans are our allies."

She turned away and said in a serious voice: "I don't understand any of it, you know . . . Germans, British, they're all the same to me . . . Now that the Fascists are gone, I assumed it was the Germans bombing us because we got rid of the Fascists."

"No," Sergio explained, "those were English planes . . . that is, if there were planes at all."

[. . .]

216 was not surprised by this request for a bathing suit. Nella looked at several different styles, measuring them with her eyes. The shopgirl stared out at the street rather than at Nella, and said: "This one is made of knitted fabric . . . This is a two piece . . . This is a one piece." Sergio could not help asking: "Do you sell a lot of these despite the war?"

"Yes, of course," she answered, "like every other year."

Nella asked, "Can I try one on? This one?"

"Yes of course," the young woman answered, picking up a bathing suit and taking it over to a folding screen. Now alone, Sergio looked around the shop nervously. For some reason he felt that he should pay for the bathing suit, and yet he wasn't sure that he had enough money and was afraid of appearing stingy. He said to himself, "I met her just three hours ago . . . she's nothing to me," and realized once again that his feelings, almost like a lover's, had no basis in reality. He was startled by Nella's voice asking, in a pleased tone: "Do you think it suits me?"

He turned around.

"It suits me, don't you think?" she repeated.

It was true: it fit her perfectly, Sergio thought, or rather, any bathing suit would have suited her. Without the red cotton dress that concealed and almost erased her shape, her body was revealed in all its luminous, firm beauty. Like her face, it was as appetizing as bread and as life itself. In her, nature seemed to express only candor, health, luminosity, and purity. He remembered a prostitute he had visited two weeks earlier, a young woman, dark-haired and ill-proportioned, dark-skinned and sweaty, and it seemed to him that this girl standing before him now was the exact opposite of that woman, as different from her as day from night. Nella's shoulders were plump and wide, her waist slender. Rising from this waist, her bust sloped upward, like two large round fruits about to burst. Her breasts were round and firm, and the wool of the suit stretched across them, almost painfully. Nella's hips were almost as wide as her shoulders, giving her body the singular appearance of a vessel, narrow in the middle and flaring outward at either end. Her legs touched, without the slightest space between them, and her thighs were full. The skin of her legs was hairless, amber-colored, and taut. Her legs were longer than he had imagined, and elegantly tapered. But most of all, the color, the healthy, innocent glow that her body emanated, made a deep impression: it was like the morning sunlight shining upon the objects in a room and the faces of those who have rested in a deep slumber and bathed in clear, fresh water. She had the sweet, limpid, healthy, and almost child-like flesh of a woman who had never known passionate love. But neither was she a virgin, he thought. Her virginity must have been taken almost by chance, perhaps in a single embrace by a fortuitous lover, an act of convenience, almost a means to release her vitality, so impetuous and fresh. Taken without pain and without love, as in nature, without a trace, without regret or shame, nor any other sentiment.

Nella strutted around the store, watched by the exhausted shopgirl. As a matter of professional obligation, she felt compelled to comment: "*Signorina*, that one really suits you." Finally, Nella said with conviction, "I'll take it." The two women returned to the folding screen, leaving Sergio alone.

Once again he felt the impulse to pay for the bathing suit and realized that if he did not do so he would feel shame and regret. When the two women emerged from behind the screen, Sergio pulled his wallet from his pocket almost without thinking and asked: "So how much is it?"

He was surprised to see that Nella did not protest and instead stood there calmly with a self-possession that did not exactly irritate him but troubled him more than if she had openly asked him to pay for the suit. As he paid he realized that he had only a few bills left in his wallet, just enough to pay for transportation. Holding the package under her arm, Nella said, "Thank you," in a simple, uningratiating manner that pleased him. They returned to the cab, which took off at a trot.

A few minutes later they arrived at the address on Via della Vite which Nella had pointed out before. She descended and waited calmly for Sergio to pay for the cab with his last remaining bills. Once again, she seemed ready to take her leave, and once again Sergio reacted by offering to carry her suitcase. Again, she accepted without any hint of embarrassment and preceded him up the staircase.

It was a modest old building, with a gloomy, steep staircase and vaulted ceilings. They climbed up four floors and Nella stopped at a door with the name Ginori written on a plaque and rang the bell. A scantily dressed woman came to the door, holding a baby in one arm; they could hear music from a radio and smell cooking. Nella said: "I saw a room this morning . . . I've come back with my suitcase."

Without a word or any sign that she had understood, the woman disappeared and then reappeared with a large key. It turned out that the room had its own entrance. The woman unlocked the door and said, "Here you are," and led them into a long, narrow room with a single window facing a courtyard. Someone called out from the apartment: "Adalgisa . . . Adalgisa . . ." She excused herself and ran out, closing the door behind her. Sergio and Nella were left alone.

Sergio realized that he absolutely had to leave. He had already paid for the bathing suit and the taxi, and if Nella decided that she wanted to go down to eat, he would be unable to pay for lunch. And yet the 219 thought of leaving made him unhappy. He wasn't sure whether he was attracted to her or not; he only knew that he did not want to leave. After a moment, he asked awkwardly: "Where should I put the suitcase?"

"Right here on the bed, that way it will be easier to un<pack>." He carried the suitcase over to the bed and s<at> down next to it, almost mechanically. Nella had retreated behind <a scree>n hiding the sink; he heard running water, and assumed that she was washing up. She reappeared, looking happy. "What do you think of the room?"

Sergio looked around. The place was utterly squalid; long and narrow as a corridor, with a bed at one end and a dresser and chest at the other. The heat was oppressive and the furniture was seedy, of the type found in most boardinghouses. With some effort, he said: "It's a bit hot."

"Yes, but it's in Rome."

She went to the window and opened it wide, looking out. She seemed so satisfied with her room and happy to be in Rome that Sergio could not help adding: "Well, at least it has its own entrance."

"Is that a good thing?" she asked, distractedly.

"Well, you can invite whomever you like."

She went over to the suitcase and said, in a dreamy voice: "I wouldn't know whom to invite . . . I don't know anyone here . . . You're the only person I know."

Almost teasingly, he said, "Well, you can invite me."

"I already have."

He held out his hand and said, as he held hers, "I'm sorry that this visit must end so soon, but I have to go."

220   "Why? Why don't you come have lunch with me?"

It seemed natural, he thought, to join her for lunch; and just as natural that he should pay. But he couldn't pay. He was about to say that he really had to go, when an idea occurred to him. They would go for lunch, and he would call Maurizio from the restaurant and ask him to join them. He would ask Maurizio to pay the bill, as a favor. He knew that Maurizio would not leave Rome that afternoon, and also that Nella was the reason, but for some reason he felt neither jealousy nor any scruples about asking him for a loan. "All right, then, let's go . . . but where?"

"Somewhere not too expensive and close by."

"We can go around the corner . . . to La Pergola."

"All right."

Nella locked the door with an air of satisfaction, holding up the key to show Sergio. He smiled and began to descend the stairs ahead of her. They sat down at one of the few empty tables at the trattoria. It was crowded, mostly with men, but, as they soon found out, almost nothing on the menu was available. Sergio explained to Nella that it was the same everywhere; between the bombings and the German occupation, food was growing increasingly scarce. They ordered rice and a focaccia with a bit of meat that the owner called steak. Nella eagerly ate this paltry lunch and Sergio, who wasn't hungry, nibbled on a bit of rice. He was thinking about Maurizio and realized he had begun to feel a kind of anticipatory jealousy at the idea of his friend's paying for lunch. But someone had to pay, and he had no money. He got up, mumbled an excuse, and went off to find a phone.

But when he dialed Maurizio's number, he had an unpleasant surprise: Maurizio wasn't home. Sergio returned gloomily to the table [. . .]

73

Version B

That winter, Sergio became friendly with a young 55
man his age by the name of Maurizio. In many ways,
Maurizio was Sergio's opposite. Sergio was poor; he
lived in a furnished room in central Rome and survived on a meager income from tutoring and writing
for various newspapers. Maurizio was well off and
lived with his parents in their villa on the outskirts
of town; he was slowly studying toward a still-distant
degree. Physically, Sergio was rather slight and very
pale, with a grayish complexion and a long, thin face
framed by black hair, small, intense eyes, a sharp
nose, and a large mouth with extremely thin lips,
curled at the corners. It was the face of a hunchback,
long-suffering and always on edge. Maurizio, on the
other hand, was tall and well proportioned, with regular, harmonious features, curly brown hair, tranquil,
open eyes, and a robust, slender frame. Sergio felt a
kind of attraction toward Maurizio and envied these
qualities—his serenity, his quiet sense of humor,
his pleasant nature or even goodness, his vigorous
good health—which seemed to augment his own
flaws. Sergio was a Communist and he considered
Maurizio bourgeois, even though he also had certain
non-bourgeois characteristics. But Sergio also realized that because he was poor and came from a poor
family, he envied Maurizio's comforts and wealth or
at least coveted them. He was attracted by the nonchalance with which Maurizio had become his friend,
unfazed by the difference in their social status and
their contrasting ideologies. Sergio was convinced

77

that this nonchalance was born not of indifference but rather out of a secret yet clear sympathy that Maurizio, despite his wealth and social station, felt toward Sergio's Communist ideals and toward people who were simple and poor and different from him. Sergio could not help expressing his thoughts to Maurizio. He told him: "You are bourgeois because you were born into a wealthy home, from wealthy parents. But your sympathies lie with us and underneath it all you probably share our ideas." Maurizio laughed but after further discussion he did not completely contradict Sergio's claim. A friendly struggle had emerged between them, a struggle which, in Sergio's case, had a precise goal. He wanted to convert his friend and convince him to join the Party. Maurizio, who still denied having the Communist sympathies that Sergio attributed to him, or even a hidden desire to adopt them, did not completely close the door. On the contrary, he lured Sergio on with an attentive attitude that was both facetious and evasive. That winter, Sergio felt particularly oppressed by a sense of inferiority toward life and other people, a feeling that had tormented him since childhood. Even more than in the past, he felt that he needed some sort of personal victory in order to believe in himself and in his own destiny, a destiny that had never seemed clear. Almost without realizing it, his desire to find affirmation became increasingly focused on one specific goal: converting Maurizio to Communism. To compensate for his own shortcomings, he had a tendency to consider the life of the Party as his own, its victories as his. While he felt that without the Party he would be nothing, he was continually reassured that at least

56

he could say to himself: "I am a Communist, and this is already a lot." The idea of winning Maurizio over to the cause pleased him to no end: firstly, because he was vaguely worried by his attraction to Maurizio and thought that once his friend became a Communist this attraction would become more licit and justified; and secondly, because Maurizio's conversion would reaffirm his own ties to the Party, which was an integral part of his life and had increasingly become the very matter of his life itself.

None of this was clear in his mind, however, and the only thing he was sure of was the obsessive, driving, and omnipresent desire to guide Maurizio toward his way of thinking. He felt that he needed this victory, or rather that the Party needed it—given that he and the Party were one and the same—and to this end, he carefully studied the best means to achieve his goal, with all the shrewdness and rationality he could muster. Even though he was convinced that Maurizio was ripe, like a fruit about to drop from the branch, he realized that it would not be easy, in part because of this ripeness. It was perhaps easier to convert an enemy in a moment of weakness, by simply vanquishing his point of view, than a sympathizer; a sympathizer could always defend himself from taking the leap with the comforting alibi of his sympathy.

Sergio's almost obsessive desire to convert Maurizio 57 to his fervently held ideas was no secret. Sergio had a girlfriend, Lalla, with whom he had been living for almost two years. Sergio had spoken to her about his aspirations regarding Maurizio from the very beginning of their relationship. As for Lalla, though she was not a Communist, she was able to comprehend and appreciate Sergio's ideas; all of their friends were Communists, and she herself professed to be a sympathizer. After a few discussions with Maurizio, Sergio told his lover that he felt that if he could not convince Maurizio, he could no longer consider himself a man. This desperate declaration expressed the anxiety and insecurity that Sergio felt at the time. One day, after going to see Maurizio, Sergio confidently told Lalla that he felt close to his goal. She observed, calmly: "In my opinion you're wasting your breath . . . He'll never come to a decision . . . Just wait and see."

"Why do you say that?" he asked, surprised. They were at a café downtown, just the two of them at an isolated table, after having dinner at a modest trattoria.

She did not answer him right away. "You know," she said, "sometimes a large boulder sits precariously on the edge of a precipice . . . It looks like it would only take the slightest push to send it tumbling down . . . but in reality it is so perfectly balanced that nothing in the world could make it fall. Maurizio is like that."

"What do you mean?"

"I mean," she said, "that Maurizio sympathizes with our ideas . . . he does not approve of the world he was born into . . . he can see its faults . . . he understands that there is no other way . . . and yet, he won't cross over to our side."

She seemed so convinced that Sergio suddenly had an inkling that she knew more about Maurizio than he did. Perhaps Maurizio had discussed the situation with her. After a short pause, he asked, "Why do you say that? Has Maurizio said something to you?"

"Of course not," she said calmly, "he hasn't said anything . . . it's just a hunch."

"I have the opposite impression."

"Well, I guess we'll see who's right."

She didn't seem to attribute much importance to the matter, Sergio reflected, but even so, he was irritated by his lover's tone. It was a sign that she lacked confidence in him and did not respect him. He changed the subject: "So, what shall we do? . . . Do you feel like going to the movies?"

Without looking at him, she answered: "No, I don't feel like it . . . In any case, we can't afford it . . . For once, let's just go to bed."

Once again he noticed the lack of enthusiasm and confidence reflected in the dryness of her tone. Again, he felt irritated, as he always did when she complained about their poverty, even indirectly: "You're mad at me because I don't make enough money . . . You wish I were rich, like Maurizio."

"That's not true," she said, with a note of resignation, "you know I like you just as you are . . ."

"So why are you using that tone of voice?"

She hesitated: "Well, yes, to be honest I'm a bit tired of it all: of eating half portions at Paolone's, of mending my own stockings, of looking for work and not finding it, of living in furnished rooms, of standing in line for the bathroom in the morning, of counting every penny . . . What's wrong with that? But it's not your fault."

Sergio said nothing. He was intensely irritated, but he realized that it was unreasonable to take it out on Lalla. After a moment, he said, "Let's go home."

"Yes, let's go."

They left the café and headed down the narrow streets of central Rome toward the alley where they lived. Sergio walked next to his lover, who was almost a head taller than he. She was wearing a light, threadbare brown coat, clutching her collar to protect herself against the wet, weak February wind. He looked at her legs. He could see the spots where she had mended her stockings. Her calves were plump and round. She hadn't mentioned the state of her shoes, but it surely annoyed her even more than her stockings; they were worn out, deformed, muddy, and extremely old. Lalla walked briskly, crumpling her face in the wind. She had a mane of fine, frizzy hair; beneath it her face looked tiny, with a delicate nose, childlike lips, and big, <. . .> eyes under a prominent forehead. Her neck was long and her whole body was strangely proportioned; she was not beautiful, but there was something expressive about her. Her shoulders were narrow but she had a large, sagging chest, a thin waist accentuated by a wide, shiny belt, and ample, even opulent hips. Once again he said to himself that she reminded him of a strangely elegant, awkward reptile from a prehistoric age, with a
59 long, rippling neck, a tiny head, and a powerful, massive lower body. Rather than beautiful, he reflected, she was profoundly attractive. Lalla walked a step ahead of Sergio and he observed her, until finally they reached the doorway. Sergio pushed open the door, which was always unlocked, and they climbed up four dark, dank floors in silence. Lalla moved quickly, undulating like a reptile, and he could not help thinking of all the staircases he had climbed in his young life, walking behind one prostitute or another. This

thought vexed him; he was often vexed by his own thoughts when they were not as he wished them to be. He wanted to respect Lalla and was convinced of his affection and esteem for her. Sometimes he suspected that such thoughts were precisely what Catholics referred to as the Devil: thoughts, feelings, reflections that rise to the surface despite our better nature, against our will and unworthy of us. When they reached the landing Sergio reached forward and opened the door as Lalla waited, out of breath. The foyer was illuminated and they tiptoed down the hall to their room, as usual. Lalla went first and turned on the light. Sergio walked to the corner where the coatrack stood and removed his raincoat and shoes, and then sat down on a rickety armchair near the yellowing curtain.

Lalla began to undress in silence. First she removed her little brown overcoat and carefully placed it on a hanger in the closet. Then she pulled her dress over her head. As she stood there in her short green slip, the strange proportions of her body were even more apparent: the large thighs, outlined with heavy muscles under the fabric of her slip; the almost painfully slender waist that looked as if it had been compressed by some sort of contraption since infancy; the low, ample chest; and finally the long neck topped by a small head. Every time he saw her partly dressed or nude, Sergio could not help being aroused; this was one of the things he did not approve of in himself and would have liked to change. Usually he said nothing and tried to avoid looking at her. But on that night he felt discouraged and unhappy and he could not resist, just as a drunken man cannot resist a bottle whose contents promise release and oblivion. Now she was fussing around the room, opening the bed, checking her hair in the mirror. As she passed him, he reached out his hand: "Come here . . ."

60

She paused, saying in an indecisive, plaintive voice: "Why should I? What do you want from me?"

"Come here . . . I need to be near you."

"I'm too big to sit on your lap," she said, mournfully. "You're too small for me . . . I'm too heavy . . . Don't you agree?" But she too was a bit aroused and perched willingly on his lap, sitting sideways with her arms around his neck. The armchair creaked under their combined weight, and she whispered: "Am I too heavy?"

Sergio didn't answer; instead he sought her lips. They kissed, in silence, for a long time, as if silently agreeing to seek consolation for their unhappiness and discouragement in the joys of the flesh. It was always the same, he thought to himself, not without a certain melancholy satisfaction: she would hesitate, struggle slightly, and then give in and indulge him. It was a sign that she loved him and that he still pleased her. They kissed once, and then pulled apart and kissed again; this time Sergio pulled her head slightly away by the hair. They separated again, still looking at each other, and Sergio rested his head on the back of the armchair. She kissed him, this time pressing down with the full weight of her chest and body. After the third kiss they separated and Lalla said, caressing him with her long, shapely hand: "This is what poor people do when they can't afford to go to the movies or the theater or a café . . . Love is our entertainment, isn't that right?"

He grumbled: "Why do you say that? We love each other . . . that's all."

"Poor people love each other too . . . That's why they have so many babies . . . because they don't have anything else to distract them at night."

"Do you want to have a child with me?"

"Of course . . . I love you," she answered, seriously.

"Do you really love me?"

"Very much."

She still seemed dejected and unhappy, and yet filled with passion. Her body pressed against his, and she wormed her hand into his shirt, between two buttons, and caressed his chest, not so much to please him, he thought, as for the pleasure of feeling his skin beneath her hand. He could not help thinking about the fact that she was beginning to weigh heavily on his legs, making his knees ache. They kissed again, and he shifted slightly. She noticed and said, with a melancholy laugh, "I'm too heavy . . . You're too small for a big woman like me, Sergio."

He did not respond. As she retreated to the other side of the bed to undress, he too began to undress in silence. He was not as neat as she was and usually threw his trousers, jacket, and shirt on the floor. They were both naked now: she on the other side of the bed, and he by the armchair. She tiptoed toward him, picking up his clothes piece by piece, murmuring censoriously, "What a mess you make . . . Strange; after all, you didn't grow up with servants to put your clothes away, iron your shirts, and present them to you the next day, like Maurizio." He said nothing, feeling slightly annoyed; Maurizio's name reminded him of his task and the difficulties that faced him. As she leaned down to pick up his shoes, he pulled her toward him, pressing her firm belly and the warm, soft flesh of her breasts against his meager, skinny frame. Still holding his shoes, she allowed him to embrace her. Then she pulled away, placed the shoes beneath the armchair carefully, and said, "Let's go to bed."

The bed was typical of furnished apartments, wide but also very low, with an iron frame and a thin mattress. "I don't have a decent nightgown . . . they're all torn or dirty," Lalla said, sighing as she parted the bedcovers. "I'll have to sleep in the nude." Sergio lay down next to her in silence. She turned off the light and pressed her body against his. In the dark, she asked, "Do you love me?" "Very much," he answered quickly, reaching around her waist to pull her close. "Make love to me," she said in the dark, turning so that her back was pressed against his body, her buttocks against his groin, her legs slightly open. She pulled his arm around her and guided his hand to her breasts. He sought her sex with his own; with her hand, she guided him inside her, amid the hair and the profound, burning moisture of desire. Once inside her, he remained still with his arms around her, attached to her back like a baby Eskimo or a member of one of the nomadic tribes who carry their young on their backs. They always did this, holding each other in a tight embrace, joined together, motionless, until sleep overcame them, merged and amalgamated into one flesh, perhaps more out of a need for consolation and togetherness than desire. Later, in the dark of night, they would pull apart involuntarily. The following morning Sergio always awoke on his

side of the bed, with a wide expanse of cold bedsheets
between them.

[11]

A few days later, Sergio and Lalla visited Maurizio at
home. They had called him that morning, as usual.
During that period, their friendship had reached
its apogee; they saw one another almost every day.
Maurizio, who did not like cafés, where one was uncomfortable and had to share space with other people, had invited them to his house. It was the first
time they would meet there. Sergio's goal of converting Maurizio to his political ideas had not changed.
He also knew that Maurizio was aware of this and
had invited them over with this in mind. In short,
there was between them, in addition to their mutual
sympathy and the obscure attraction Sergio felt—and
which Maurizio also seemed to feel—the matter of
Maurizio's conversion to Communism. It hung there,
silent but clear to both of them, like a game whose
rules they both knew and played day after day. Sergio was convinced that deep down it was a struggle
for power: the power of an ideology, whose truth and
validity he wanted to impose upon his friend, as well
as his own personal power. And the power of a social
reality which Sergio felt his friend would eventually
have to accept, if the ideology itself and his personal
authority were not enough. He was convinced that
Maurizio was simply weak, afflicted by a lassitude
that was the result of a lack of ideas and the personal

87

deficiencies of a man with less fortitude than himself. A weakness born of a social situation whose hopelessness Maurizio himself admitted and condemned. 63 Under such conditions, Sergio reasoned, there was no alternative for Maurizio but to convert if he was a man of good faith and good intentions. And since he had no doubt that Maurizio was a man of good faith and good intentions, he was convinced that in the end he would convert.

He mentioned none of this to Lalla. Nevertheless, for some reason he sensed that she looked upon his plans with some skepticism. They set out for Maurizio's in the early afternoon. That afternoon, Sergio was in a hurry, as if impatient to lock horns. Lalla seemed to intentionally take her time in preparing for the visit. Sergio sat for a long time in the armchair by the window, waiting for her to finish brushing her hair. Lalla had a very limited wardrobe, but she made a conscious effort to dress as well as possible, applying herself to her toilette with a care that irritated him even more than their lateness. First she went to the bathroom wearing her old, tattered dressing gown, and stayed there for a good half hour. Then she sat at her dressing table. He waited in silence, angrily chain-smoking in the dark room, which looked even smaller and shabbier in the gray light of the rainy afternoon. With exasperating care and deliberateness, she brushed her hair and applied face cream, lipstick, powder, eyeliner, and mascara. She sat on a low stool, her powerful hips spreading over the edge of the chair; her dressing gown hung open, revealing two dark, oblong breasts, delineated by a pink fold that formed on her belly because of her hunched posture. Peering into the mirror with her head inclined, she presented her small profile and elongated neck. From his position, he could just make out her face in the mirror, embellished by the shadows and her contemplative air. Each time he looked over as she combed her hair with careful, slow strokes, his irritation grew. But then he would catch a glimpse of her reflection in the mirror, and his irritation would pass and he would feel content to wait, almost as a way to prove his love for her. In the end, however, his impatience won over, and he broke his silence: "Couldn't you move a bit more quickly? We're already half an hour late."

"Why are you so worried about being on time?" she said, without turning around. "He can wait . . . You'd think he was your lover."

"What nonsense . . . I can't stand being late, that's all." 64

"But sometimes you make me wait for hours," she said slowly, still combing her hair.

"That's different."

"You should always be on time . . . The truth is that your feelings for Maurizio are different."

"What do you mean by that?"

She paused for a moment and then said, distractedly: "If I weren't convinced that you love me and that you are normal, I would think that you were a little bit in love with him."

"What a stupid thing to say."

She finished arranging her hair in silence and went over to the bed and sat down, pulling a plastic bag out of the dresser drawer. It contained a pair of new stockings. "I bought them just this morning," she said, leaning over to pull on one of the stockings. "You can't say that I'm not doing my best to do honor to your dear Maurizio."

Sergio said nothing. Lalla finished putting on her stockings, then a slip, and finally picked out her best dress, the one she wore on special occasions. For some reason, this irritated Sergio, and he protested: "Why are you wearing that dress?"

"It's the only decent one I have."

"You usually wear it to parties," he said, bitterly. "This isn't a party . . . Why don't you dress normally?"

"Why should I?" she said, staring at him. "Maurizio has invited us to his house . . . I should do my best to look presentable."

"He'll get the impression that you're intimidated and honored by his invitation."

She looked at him for a moment with a dreamy expression. "Why do you say that?"

"Because . . . I don't want to give the impression that this is a big event . . . an honor."

"Who wants to give that impression?"

"You, with all your fineries and that dress."

"Do you know why you're saying this?" she said, sharply.

"Why?"

"Because despite your Communist ideals, you feel socially inferior to Maurizio . . . That's the truth . . . and you're trying to project your feelings onto me. But I don't feel inferior in the least."

Her answer irritated Sergio even more, almost as if it contained a grain of truth; but he quickly examined his conscience and concluded that she was wrong: "Don't be silly. Why should I feel socially

65

inferior? What kind of Communist would that make me?"

"I don't know . . . that's your business."

He paused. Then, in a precise, almost scientific tone, he explained: "As you know, we are very poor, and he is very wealthy. I don't feel inferior in any way, please believe me . . . but it's important to me that he not feel superior to us, and if he sees you arrive all gussied up for a simple, friendly conversation . . . If it were a party, at his house or elsewhere, I would be the first to say that you should make an effort . . . Elegance is important, and dressing well for a festive event is a serious matter . . . I'm not as stupid as you think . . . but I don't want him to get the wrong idea about us . . . that's all. I'm also thinking of him, because I have great affection for him, not only about us."

Lalla listened carefully, and answered, somewhat bitterly: "You think he's stupid, but he's not . . . All right, I'll take off this dress and wear the oldest, most worn-out one I have . . . the one I wear when I teach."

"No need to go overboard . . . Then he'll think we want to make a spectacle of our poverty, and that would just be another way of revealing a feeling of inferiority."

"What dress would you like me to wear, then? The selection is quite limited, after all. I only have three dresses."

"Just wear the one you're already wearing," he said, moodily. "Do whatever you want . . . but let's go, shall we?"

This time she said nothing and simply shrugged. 66 She put on her usual brown coat. Drily, she said, "Let's go."

They traversed the dank cooking smells lingering in the hallway and came to the foyer. When they were on the stairs, he felt a wave of disconsolate passion and took Lalla by the waist: "Are you still angry with me?" he asked.

She looked up at him. "No . . . why?"

"Because of what I said about the dress."

"Of course not, don't be silly."

Sergio felt mortified, though he did not quite know why. His eyes welled with tears. He whispered, "I'm at a difficult time in my life, you know that . . . I need you to love me very much."

"I do."

They separated and began to go down the stairs. Now that the turmoil of the moment had passed— a turmoil he could not explain—Sergio had become his lucid self again. He knew that this invitation was important and realized that in the duel he was about to fight with his friend, every false step could be fatal. He reviewed his arguments in his mind, as he did before speaking at Party meetings, reexamining his logic and approach, and anticipating his friend's counterarguments. Just as when he prepared to speak in public, he felt lucid, determined, cool, and self-assured. He knew that this coolness and lucidity, mixed with a touch of cynicism, formed a kind of streamlined, utilitarian structure planted squarely upon a deep foundation of enthusiasm, hope, and faith: his enthusiasm, his hope, and his faith in the Communist Party and its destiny. One could build any kind of edifice upon such a foundation, he reflected, no matter what materials one worked with. The foundation was solid and sound.

He was so distracted and lost in thought that he almost forgot where they were, standing at the bus stop, waiting for a bus to carry them through the city. His actions had become almost automatic; his mind was submerged in thought, like an atmosphere that did not thwart action but nevertheless impeded his awareness of his actions. A while later they were 68 walking down an empty boulevard with villas and gardens on either side, in an elegant neighborhood, one of the oldest in the city. "Here it is," Lalla said, pointing at the number on the gate.

"You've been here before," Sergio said with a start, surprised by her certainty.

"No, I just know the number," she responded simply.

It was a black iron gate, bolted with an iron bar on the inside. Tall, robust trees, revealing the garden's age, protruded above the pillars of the boundary wall, which were surmounted by decorative urns. Lalla reached out a gloved hand and pressed the button of the gleaming brass doorbell. Sergio looked at her and then turned to gaze into the street. It was truly an elegant street; all around there were high walls with tall trees looming over them, and the façades of a few imposing villas. Cars were parked here and there, all of them luxury models. It was a gray, cloudy day, and humid; it had been raining, and there were large puddles on the sidewalks. The dark, looming sky seemed to threaten more rain. "A mild, average day," he thought, mechanically, and for some reason he could not explain, he shuddered, as if struck by a bad omen. He realized that the sangfroid he had enjoyed during their long walk, and which had made him almost forget his task, was now submerged beneath a feverish, dreamlike ardor. His cheeks were burning; his heart was pounding. "What the hell is wrong with me?" he wondered.

"What did you say?" Lalla asked, coming closer.

He had said these words aloud. This vexed him. "Nothing . . . I didn't say anything."

"Yes you did . . . you said: What the hell?"

"I didn't say anything. I was just thinking aloud."

The gate opened and a butler in a striped jacket invited them in, stepping aside to let them pass. Sergio and his lover followed the butler through the garden. As they could guess from the tall trees looming over the wall, it appeared to be very old, filled with mature bushes, trees, and thick creepers. Once they were actually in the house, Sergio's heart began to beat normally again, and his cheeks no longer burned. He was glad: once again, he felt cool and in control. They entered a vast anteroom decorated with wooden chests and weapons mounted on the walls, then another, and finally, they arrived in a large sitting room. It was dark inside: the walls were hung with rich fabrics; heavy velvet curtains covered the windows. Like the two previous rooms, this one was furnished in a style that had gone out of fashion twenty or thirty years earlier. There were carpets, clusters of dark armchairs and couches—many them old and threadbare—a multitude of paintings on the walls, large vases, and imposing bric-a-brac on every surface. The room had an air of stale, worn-out luxury, empty and tired, as if it had been decorated according to tastes and a way of life that no longer existed. The air was murky, even though it was still early in the day. "It's too dark in here, I can't see," Lalla exclaimed, traversing the room confidently and switching on the central chandelier, a bronze object with three arms. Sergio noted her self-assuredness, finding it disagreeable, and once again suspected that Lalla had been in this house before. Again, he banished the thought, convincing himself that it was impossible and absurd.

They sat across from each other in two deep armchairs positioned in a corner of the sitting room and waited, without speaking. The house was immersed in silence. The walls were thick and insulated; they could hear nothing from the tree-filled garden, except a vague scraping which seemed to come from downstairs. Perhaps someone was poking around in the cellar. It was hot, almost too hot, and, like the house, the heat felt old, stale, impure.

After a long wait they heard steps, and Maurizio appeared in a doorway at the other end of the room. Sergio observed something he had never noticed before: Maurizio had a slight limp, almost imperceptible but just pronounced enough to catch the eye. Even so, his gait was not without grace. He was tall, as Sergio noted bitterly, with wide shoulders, and a strong, dynamic presence. His face appeared slightly older than that of a twenty-eight-year-old man: it was somber, with large black eyes, a prominent nose, a dark mustache, and very white teeth. His features were striking, vigorously outlined. He had large hands and feet, and emanated an air of simplicity and energy. But underneath he was actually extremely reflective, prudent, and cautious, as well as extraordinarily pleasant, affable, and polished in his manner. This mildness was surprising in a man with such a vigorous, almost brutal appearance. He was like a giant who is able to hold a butterfly between two fingers without hurting it, Sergio reflected. He knew that he was attracted to these contrasts in Maurizio, that they were perhaps the principal reason for his attraction. Maurizio greeted Sergio and Lalla in a loud, 71 booming voice that was also perfectly courteous, like a bear who has been trained to bow to guests. "Please forgive me for asking you to travel all the way to this gloomy old house. I thought we might be more comfortable here than at a café."

"We're very comfortable!" Lalla exclaimed, in a friendly tone.

"You're limping," Sergio said, out of the blue, as Maurizio crisscrossed the room, moving chairs so that they could sit more comfortably.

"Yes, I've had a limp since '43," his friend answered, casually. "I was shot in the leg."

"Where?"

"In Africa . . . I was a Blackshirt," he said, watching Sergio, as if to judge his reaction. Sergio couldn't help crying out: "You were a Blackshirt?"

"Yes . . . I was eighteen . . . you know . . . the errors of youth," Maurizio said, in a flippant tone that seemed in stark contrast with his rich voice. "I've never mentioned it . . . I was a true believer . . . and then I was a prisoner of war . . . I was held for three years."

"Where?"

"In the United States."

"So you were a Fascist," Sergio repeated, almost in disbelief.

"A rabid Fascist . . . as Fascist as one can be . . . I idolized Mussolini, and I even admired Hitler."

He invited them to another area of the sitting room: "There's no light over there . . . it feels like one is being punished . . . Come sit here." They moved to another group of armchairs and couches. Sergio sat in an armchair, and Lalla on the couch next to Maurizio. He crossed his legs. Sergio noticed a small detail: Maurizio was wearing a dark blue suit with pinstripes, like a stock character in a movie. Which character? The international swindler, the sharp-dressing shyster, the professional seducer.

Soon after they sat down, the butler returned with a large silver tray carrying a bottle of whiskey, a si-phon, and an ice bucket, as well as olives and some crackers. In silence, he placed everything on the coffee table in front of them. Sergio noticed the massive, an-tiquated design of the silver tray. This was a bourgeois household, he reflected, but of the old-fashioned kind, typical of the Fascist period: wealthy, opulent, solid, massive. "I asked the butler to bring us some whis-key," Maurizio said, pouring a glass. "I know that you and Lalla enjoy it, and I do too . . . but if you prefer cof-fee, tea, or a sweet liqueur, don't hesitate to ask."

"No, whiskey is fine," Lalla said, smiling.

Maurizio poured the whiskey, picked up a few cubes of ice with the tongs and dropped them into the glasses, adding some seltzer water. Sergio noted that he did this with a surprising grace for such a bear-like man. He also noticed that Maurizio had poured himself a small amount of whiskey, about half what he served them. "Don't you drink?" he asked.

"Not much. I drank too much as a young man, and now I have to be careful . . . I have trouble with my liver."

He took a sip, refusing the cigarette that Sergio offered: "I don't smoke."

"You have no vices, it seems," Lalla said in a frivolous tone that irritated Sergio. "You don't drink, you don't smoke . . ."

Maurizio did not respond. Sergio lit a cigarette in order to give himself a more nonchalant air. He felt that he had to move the conversation as quickly as possible away from this generic chitchat to the subject he had come to discuss. But he realized that his cheeks were once again burning and his heart was beating furiously. He picked up his glass, took a big gulp to steady his nerves, and said, looking straight into Maurizio's eyes: "Shall we pick up our discussion where we left off the other day?"

Lalla began to laugh: "How single-minded you are . . . You haven't even given him a chance to catch his breath . . ."

"No, no," Maurizio said, in a friendly voice, "by all means, let's talk . . . after all, isn't that why you've come? Let's continue where we left off the other day."

Sergio took another gulp of whiskey and realized that he had almost finished the glass. Maurizio filled it again. Sergio thanked him in a vexed tone and began, "We had reached, shall we say, the negative side of the question . . . You were saying the other day that your social circle, which you have always been a part of and which you belong to by birth and by wealth—in other words the bourgeoisie—disgusts and bores you, and that you find it insufferable."

"Exactly," Maurizio said, very serious. "I find it empty, incompetent, corrupt, stupid, and quite worthless . . ."

"And you said that you've felt this way for a long time, but that you used to believe that all people were the same. Then, you realized that these defects were not human defects but rather social defects, and this realization led you to distance yourself from these people."

"Yes."

"And you said that this social circle does not deserve to survive . . . not because it is unjust for a few to control so much wealth but rather because it is unjust that these few, who have so much wealth, should be so contemptible."

"Yes."

"And what did I say to you?"

"You said that I was a Communist even if I didn't know it."

"Exactly," Sergio said, somewhat taken aback by his friend's calm. "That's exactly what I said."

"But then," Maurizio interjected, fiddling with his glass, "I said that it wasn't true . . . I know everything about Communism that a person like myself can know . . . Didn't I say that?"

"Yes, it's true."

There was a pause. Sergio's cheeks were still burning. He attributed this to the whiskey. Even his sight seemed to be obscured by the tension he felt. He couldn't see Lalla, and could only barely make out Maurizio's face. Sighing, he continued: "Yes, that's where we were when you suddenly stood up and walked off. Actually, I must admit that it crossed my mind that you left because you had no more arguments with which to defend yourself and wanted to escape our discussion. But then I changed my mind when you called the next morning."

Maurizio said nothing. Lalla was sitting very close to Maurizio, smoking, looking at each of them in turn. She had unbuttoned her coat. She got up abruptly. "I hope you don't mind if I take this off. It's very hot in here." And without waiting for a response, she removed her coat. Maurizio poured more whiskey into her glass. He returned to his seat and once again faced Sergio, who took a puff of his cigarette and said: "In other words, looking at the issue from the negative side, you yourself have said that you are dangling from the branch of the bourgeoisie like an overripe fruit, about to drop . . . Nothing keeps you there, not even money . . ."

"Least of all, money," Maurizio said, completely calm.

Lalla interrupted: "Wait a minute . . . Are you saying you would be willing to give up this house, your butler, your old habits, and go to work?"

"I already work," Maurizio said, without looking at her, "in agriculture."

"You mean, you manage your properties."

"Actually, I'm a land surveyor and assessor . . . ," he said, calmly. "But of course I also manage my properties, which are quite vast."

Sergio felt impatient. He waited for this parenthesis to close before continuing. "As we were saying, from the negative point of view, you are ripe, about to drop from the branch . . . so let's move on to the positive side of the question: you claim to understand our ideas, our aspirations, our doctrine, and all the rest."

"More or less, yes." There was a moment of silence. "Well enough, anyway," he added in an ambiguous tone. "You don't need to repeat them . . . it would be pointless."

Sergio had not expected this last comment. He had prepared a series of arguments, based on his readings and on the enthusiasm he felt for the cause. With this comment, Maurizio rendered all of this irrelevant. "Are you so sure?" he asked, somewhat vexed. "Many people think they understand Marx, without ever having read his writings."

"Don't worry, I've read Marx."

"And you can't stop there . . . You have to read Lenin, and Stalin . . ."

"I've done that as well." Maurizio paused to reflect for a moment, and then went on: "You see, I'm very conscientious, even pedantic . . . When I have doubts about something, I leave no stone unturned, I try to find out as much as I can . . . I read and study. As soon as I saw that I did not approve of the bourgeois way of life, I turned to your beliefs, of course . . . But I wasn't satisfied with the marches, the militant songs, and the red flags. I began to read and study. I've done little else the last five years."

"Five years?"

"That's right . . . I also read about Russia and the 76 Soviet state, in English and in French."

"You also speak English?"

"I learned when I was a prisoner of war."

"So you're sure I can't tell you anything you don't know?"

"Forgive me for saying it, but I don't think so." He took the whiskey bottle and, after asking "Would you like another drop?" poured more into their glasses without waiting for a response. Sergio noticed that it was the fifth time Maurizio had filled their glasses, while his own remained untouched. He leaned forward. "Well, then . . . I have to ask: What effect have your readings had? Did they convince you that we are on the right path?"

Maurizio paused to reflect. "They convinced me that Communism is a serious matter and that unless something dramatic happens, the world will most likely become Communist."

"You think so."

"Yes, I do," Maurizio said, calmly.

Sergio felt a question on the tip of his tongue, but he resisted asking it, saying instead, "On paper, after reading about our doctrine, you have no arguments against Communism."

"None."

"You think the Communists have it right."

"Yes, of course . . . certainly they do."

The moment had come for the crucial question: "So, since you are practically a Communist already, why don't you join the Party?"

Lalla began to laugh out loud, which irritated Sergio intensely. He turned to her angrily and snarled, "What is there to laugh about?"

"Nothing, it's just that I've been expecting this question, and you finally got around to asking it."

"I don't see what's so funny."

"You're right, there's nothing to laugh about," Maurizio said, and then paused for a moment. "I'm not going to join the Party . . . that's all there is to it."

"But why?"

"For no reason. I'm just not going to do it."

"But that's not a reasonable answer."

"I know."

There was a long silence. Sergio realized that he was almost drunk, but he didn't mind. He felt a powerful affection toward Maurizio and would have liked to embrace him. Finally, he said, warmly, "I'm still waiting for your answer . . ."

"I've already given it to you."

"That's not an answer."

Maurizio laughed, showing his white teeth. "Listen," he said, "try to follow my logic . . . There are rational arguments that can be countered with other, equally rational arguments . . . right? If one does not have a rational argument, it means that one is in the wrong. Don't you agree?"

"Of course."

"But then there are irrational arguments . . . Do you agree that such a thing exists?"

"Of course."

"Well then . . . rationally, I have no response to your arguments. You're right, I agree, I should be a Communist. But irrationally . . . I have many objections. You yourself admit that such irrational objections exist. Well, for irrational reasons, I cannot become a Communist."

"Fear is one example," Sergio said, with some bitterness.

Maurizio waved away Sergio's words. "No, I don't mean contemptible reasons like fear, money, or self-interest . . . don't worry."

"So what is it then?"

"I already said it . . . no reason . . . What does it matter?"

"It does matter, it matters a lot . . . I may be able to respond, explain, argue . . ."

"But you would respond with rational arguments, and reason has no power to refute its opposite . . . You would need to find an irrational argument that is more powerful than my own."

"Perhaps I can."

Maurizio reflected for a moment. "If you did, you wouldn't be a Communist."

"Why?"

"Because Communists argue with reason and not with irrational arguments . . . It is the Fascists who use irrational arguments."

"By now, Communism has incorporated even the irrational arguments of Fascism."

"But I don't believe in Fascism anymore."

Sergio realized that there was nothing he could do, at least for now. He suddenly became aware of how tired and drunk he felt. His head was spinning, his throat was dry, and he had no arguments left. Or rather, the process of converting his feelings into rational arguments was no longer possible because his thoughts had been frozen by the alcohol and his exhaustion. Still, he felt he had not done quite enough to try to convince Maurizio. He said, in an exasperated voice, "What you say sounds clever, but I'm telling you, if you, who claim to be a Communist in every way except for a few irrational objections, keep living like this, going against your true nature, stifling what is best in you, you will end up in a bad way . . . That's what I think . . ."

Maurizio smiled. "But if I were to become a Communist, I wouldn't be following my true nature but rather denying it . . . The irrational part of me is who I really am."

"Those are just words."

What exasperated Sergio more than anything was Lalla's silence. He imagined her to be full of skepticism and irony. He turned to her. "Why are you so quiet? Say something, speak."

She laughed. "I'm not saying anything because I'm drunk . . . Maurizio has made me drunk."

"And besides," said Sergio, picking up where he had left off, "there aren't as many irrational arguments as you claim . . . The only irrational obstacle that counts is a lack of courage . . . You're afraid to take the leap . . . that's all."

"*Hic Rhodus, hic salta* . . . What you say is nothing new . . . it's the Rubicon all over again . . . ," Maurizio said, quietly.

"That's right, it's just like the Rubicon," Sergio said, becoming impassioned. "People like you don't have the courage to cross."

"People like me?"

"Bourgeois types like you, who are convinced of the decadence and corruption of the bourgeoisie . . . A working man would leap over the abyss, but not you."

"For the working man there is no abyss . . . that's why he jumps."

"So you admit," Sergio exclaimed, in a loud voice, "that what holds you back is your social class, your butler in his striped jacket, your silver trays, your whiskey bottles."

Maurizio did not respond directly to this attack. He seemed to reflect for a moment, and then smiled. "If you look carefully, it turns out that Communism does not seek to persuade through rational arguments, though it makes much of rationality and pretends to base itself solely upon it . . . The Party apparatus is rational, but its means of persuasion is absolutely irrational . . . Even the worker cannot be seduced through reason, though you insist that it is so. The truth is that it takes something other than reason."

"And what is that?"

"I don't know . . . hope for a better world . . . the hatred of injustice . . . the will to struggle, and to vanquish . . ."

"And?"

"The same is true of people like me," Maurizio laughed; "even a debased bourgeois like me needs an irrational argument to be won over."

"What do you mean?"

"I mean that man is not a rational animal . . . or rather that man is rational only when he speaks, not when he acts . . . In order to make him act, one must call on something beyond reason . . ."

"Such as?"

"Well, it's different for each person, for each group . . . I wouldn't presume to tell you how to complete your task . . . you know better than I."

"What task?"

"Do you deny," Maurizio said, in a calm voice, "that you came here specifically to win me over?"

80   "I don't deny it, no."

"Well then that is your task."

There was a long silence. Maurizio played with his glass, peering up at Sergio with his dark, perfectly limpid, calm eyes. Lalla's laughter broke the silence:

"Sergio, you've been defeated . . . time to throw in the towel."

"Perhaps I've been defeated, at least superficially," Sergio said, bitterly, "but he is the true loser . . . He admits that he is in conflict with his nature."

"Yes, but still, you've been defeated . . . ," she said, laughing drunkenly, "at least today. Your plans for today have been foiled."

Lalla laughed again, and Sergio looked at her, as if for the first time. It was as if a fog had suddenly lifted. She was sitting very close to Maurizio with her powerful legs crossed, her chest protruding beneath her dress. There was no more than a palm's width between her and Maurizio on the couch. Sergio could clearly see that their hands were touching, or rather that Maurizio was holding her hand. It all happened in a moment; then, like a fog that is momentarily lifted by the wind but returns once again, he could no longer see anything at all, and even doubted what he had seen before. For the first time, he thought: "What if all these discussions about Communism are simply a pretense? What if Maurizio is simply trying to seduce Lalla?" He noted that he was not jealous, perhaps because of his affection for Maurizio or perhaps because the alcohol made it seem quite natural for the two of them to be holding hands on the couch. As if guessing at his thoughts, Maurizio asked: "Why do you care if I convert to Communism? Why does it matter to you?"

"Because I like you."

"Thank you . . ." Maurizio looked down.

"Yes," Lalla exclaimed drunkenly, "Maurizio is very nice." She pressed herself against him, squeezing his arm.

Somewhat dazed, Sergio went on: "I feel a real friendship toward you . . . and I'm convinced that it would not take much to make a good comrade out of you . . . That's why it upsets me that you don't want to join."

There was a pause. "Well," Maurizio said in his calm voice, "I'll join . . . that is, if you can find an argument that will convince me."

"But arguments are connected to reason, and you just said that you can't be won over by reason."

"I said argument, but I meant 'the thing.'"

"What do you mean, 'the thing'?"

"The 'thing' that will convince me to join."

"And what is that?"

"It's up to you to discover it . . . You're the one who wants to convert me."

"Do you know what it is?"

Maurizio hesitated for a moment, and then said, "Yes."

"So," Sergio said, as if to summarize their conversation, "there is something that would convince you to become a Communist."

"Yes."

"And this thing," Sergio hesitated, "belongs to me . . . It is at my disposal . . ."

"I think so."

"Is this thing a means to an end?"

"Yes, or at least it could be."

"Is it legitimate?"

"For a Communist, all means are legitimate, are they not?"

Sergio considered this statement for a moment and then said: "Yes, as long as they are truly justified."

"But doesn't Communism justify anything and everything?"

"This is not a joke," Sergio said, suddenly becoming angry. "Communism aims to change the face of humanity . . . And to improve the lives of millions of people who are suffering and cannot express themselves . . . It aims to aid in the progress of humanity, to bring happiness . . . It's not a joke."

"I'm not laughing," Maurizio interjected. "Don't you think that such goals justify any means?"

"Of course."

"What I can't understand is what difference my joining the Party would make."

"Every person counts," Sergio exclaimed. "We want the best people, those who have something to offer, to join our side, one by one . . . And then the other side will be extinguished, it will perish . . . You yourself are not important . . ."

"Well, thank you."

"No, listen . . . you're not important, but still, you're something . . . Our victory will come in small increments . . . One more . . . People like you will help us reach our goal . . . Until people like you decide to join us, we cannot be victorious . . . Our strength does not lie in force or violence, but in persuasion and numbers . . . When everyone of value is on our side, the battle will be won."

The image of Maurizio holding Lalla's hand returned to him. Suddenly it all became clear. "I know the argument that will convince you to join our cause."

Maurizio looked at him with a slightly surprised air. "What do you mean?"

109

Sergio felt drunk, and was afraid that he would reveal what he had seen: "You want to know too much . . . I'll only say that I know."

"?????"

"I will use this knowledge when the time is right . . . but not now."

"When the time is right but not now . . . ," Maurizio repeated, as if reflecting on Sergio's words. He picked up the bottle. "Would you care for some more whiskey?"

Sergio said no with a firm gesture. "You've already given me far too much . . . You deliberately made me drunk."

"What do you mean, deliberately?"

"Yes, you made me drink . . . and Lalla too . . . Look at her, she's completely drunk."

Lalla got up, as if she could take no more of this perilous discussion. "Where is . . . the bathroom?" she asked casually. "I'd like to powder my nose, as they say."

"How crass of you, Lalla," Sergio said languidly, without moving.

She stood up completely. "What do you want me to say, that I need to pee?"

83 "Nothing, I don't want you to say anything."

Maurizio also stood up. "Please," he said, with his usual gentle, relaxed courtesy, "Come with me." Lalla followed him out of the sitting room.

Now alone, Sergio stood up and stretched his legs. He felt overexcited, drunk, and at the same time amazed at his lack of jealousy, given what he had just seen. It was clear; Maurizio was trying to seduce Lalla, and at that very moment they were probably kissing in some dark corner, perhaps in the bathroom, between the sink and the toilet. He walked briskly to the door through which they had disappeared, and looked out. He did not know whether what he felt was curiosity or jealousy. He saw a wide, dark hallway, with three doors on either side and a glass door at the end. There were elegant carpets and cabinets with bibelots, as well as paintings and arms, all of them immersed in the sumptuous, dusty, somnolent atmosphere of the house. He took a few steps toward the glass door, which he assumed led to the bathroom, but halfway there he discovered a staircase up to the second floor. As soon as he looked upward, he saw Maurizio descending with his light step.

"Are you looking for something?" he asked.

"I'm looking for my argument," he wanted to say, intoxicated not so much by the wine as by the illusory, almost feverish lucidity he felt. But he said nothing and instead made a vague gesture. Maurizio insisted, with a touch of irony: "Perhaps you too would like to . . . ?" Sergio laughed, putting his hand on Maurizio's arm. "No, I'm fine. I'm not in the mood to inspect your house today."

Maurizio did not respond, and they returned to the sitting room together. Without sitting down, Maurizio said, "Sergio, you haven't convinced me, but we must discuss this again in the future . . . as soon as possible, in fact."

His tone was serious and solicitous, but Sergio could not help laughing. Patting his friend on the shoulder, he said: "You don't give a damn about Communism . . . You have other things on your mind."

"What do you mean?"

Maurizio sounded so serious, almost threatening, that Sergio took a step back. "I was just joking . . . I know that you mean what you say, and that one day you'll become a good Communist, maybe even a better one than I."

84

"That would be impossible."

Lalla returned, walking toward them. She was clearly drunk, and moved with difficulty, pausing languidly and swaying her hips, which she did not normally do when she was sober.

"Let's go, Lalla," Sergio said.

"Yes, let's go."

They shook hands in the foyer. "See you soon," Maurizio said, opening the door.

"See you soon," Lalla replied.

Sergio said nothing. They traversed the garden and went out into the street, arm in arm.

[III]

They were silent during the bus ride home. Sergio was still drunk but could already feel the alcohol receding little by little. Lalla seemed lost in thought; he couldn't tell whether she was still drunk. But as they were getting off the bus, she tottered, whispering: "Hold my arm; I really drank too much."

Sergio took her arm and led her down the crowded sidewalk. "Shall we go to the café?" He too was whispering.

They almost never spent time at home; their rented room was just a place to sleep, and when they weren't with friends, they were at the café. But she answered: "No, I feel almost sick . . . let's go home."

Sergio said nothing and led her in the direction of the rooming house. The small street where they lived was close by. They walked slowly, and when they reached the door, Sergio asked, "Don't you want some dinner?"

"I told you I feel sick . . . and it's a good thing too. That way we can save some money."

Sergio noticed that as soon as they were alone, Lalla gave up her worldly, flirtatious attitude and adopted the disappointed, bitter, and irritating tone he knew so well. Annoyed by her constant complaints about their poverty, he decided to tell her that he had seen everything: the hand-holding and the rest of it. They climbed the stairs and went into their room. Without removing her coat, Lalla walked over to the bed and lay down.

Sergio watched her for a moment and then lit a cigarette as he settled into his usual armchair, by the window. From there he could see the whole room: the screen concealing the washstand, which was decorated with little red circles, each of which contained a tiny black devil; the table in the middle of the room, made out of crude wood, with four round legs, beneath a lamp with a white shade; the low, wide bed in the corner with its iron headboard decorated with curlicues and knobs; the chest at the foot of the bed, made out of the same crude wood as the table, with a marble top; the tall, narrow armoire in the other corner, which, because of the meagerness of their wardrobe, contained more than a few empty hangers. The room was large but cold and depressing as a tomb despite the central heating. It was the furniture, Sergio reflected, that emanated this coldness; the furnishings were dead, their souls departed long ago in the warehouse of some secondhand dealer. Lying on the bed, amid all this dead furniture, Lalla projected an irreducible, aggrieved vitality, a silent but steady protest against the poverty and penury that surrounded them. She lay on her side without moving, and the round mass of her raised hip seemed to conceal the rest of her body, which was invisible from where Sergio sat. He focused his gaze on this part of her body, so prominently displayed. After a moment, he asked: "What's wrong? Can you please tell me what's wrong?"

"I don't feel well. I drank too much," the hip responded.

Quickly, as if bringing up an inconsequential subject, he said, "I saw you holding hands with Maurizio . . . Don't think I didn't see you."

86 There was a brief pause. Then: "I wasn't holding his hand; he grabbed my hand and held it tightly, against my will," the hip said.

"I don't believe you."

"Fine, don't believe me," the hip answered, indifferently.

As his mind cleared, Sergio began to feel the first pangs of jealousy. It was almost painful, like what a man might feel if he possessed only one thing in the world and feared he might lose it. Lalla's indifference was proof that she no longer loved him, and that she was in love with Maurizio. Unable to control himself, he asked: "Are you . . . do you like Maurizio?" He could tell that his voice was strained and anguished.

"I do like him."

"Do you love him?"

"No"

"You're lying."

The hip did not respond. Sergio waited a moment and then said in an exasperated voice: "If you love Maurizio and you want to be with him, don't hesitate . . . go . . ."

The hip responded hesitantly, slowly: "You've taken leave of your senses."

"No, I haven't," he said angrily, "you *were* holding his hand . . . I saw you pressing up against him . . . And you had already been in that house . . . I could tell."

The hip answered quickly, simply: "It's true, I had been there before."

"You see . . . you're lovers."

"That's not true."

"But you say you've been to his house before."

The hip was silent for a moment and then, slowly and quietly, said: "I've been there twice . . . Maurizio is in love with me and he invited me to his house to talk . . . so we talked . . ."

"And then?"

"Then nothing."

"What do you mean, nothing?"

"Nothing . . . I told him that I love you and that I couldn't love two people at once."

"What did he say?"

"Nothing . . . He was unhappy, of course."

"But do you really love me?"

As he uttered these words he felt his throat tightening, almost as if he was about to cry. There was a pause, and then the hip said, "Come here."

Sergio obeyed and went over to sit next to the hip on the bed. The hip said: "Give me your hand."

Sergio obeyed. He stretched his arm over the hip, in the direction of the invisible head. He felt her take his hand, and then the slight pressure of her lips against his skin. She gave him an awkward, drunken, indolent kiss. "I love you," she said, "but if you don't believe me it's all right. I feel sick."

"But why did you go to his house? And why didn't you tell me?"

"Why should I tell you? I wanted to know what he had to tell me . . . If I had told you, I wouldn't have been able to go."

"In short, Maurizio asked you to betray me . . . to visit him in secret and make love to him."

After a brief pause, she said: "No, he's a decent person. That's not what he wanted."

"So, what was it then?"

"He asked me to marry him."

"Marry him?"

"Yes."

"And you said no."

"Right."

"Why?"

This time she did not answer. Sergio shook her shoulder, alarmed. "Why?" he repeated, and the same steady voice said: "Because I know I would end up loving him . . . I don't love him now, but if I agreed to marry him, and I knew that I could have all the things that I needed, and live a better life, I know that I would end up loving him . . . I would love him out of gratitude . . . Many women love out of gratitude, and I would be one of them."

"So you don't love me."

"I do love you . . . I love you because with you there's no question of gratitude; it's just love and nothing else . . . I prefer this love to the kind that springs from gratitude, that's all."

Sergio could not stop himself from expressing disgust: "You're a whore."

"Yes, I'm a whore . . . you said it. I like Maurizio, I like his house, I like his money, his comfortable life . . . If I think about this, I can't help feeling that I'm a whore . . . and that's why I won't marry him . . . because I don't want to become a whore . . ."

Sergio said aloud what he was thinking: "You're either a whore or you're not . . . If you are a whore, there's no point trying not to be."

"Why not?" the voice continued. "It's a question of temptation: I could become a whore, just as you could become a thief, for example. But if I'm with you and I love you, then I'm not a whore . . . It's a question of what one does. We are what we do . . . If I don't behave like a whore, then I'm not one."

"So you're with me because you don't want to become a whore."

"Precisely."

He did not respond. After a brief pause, the voice said: "Could you go to the sink, and bring me a moist towel?"

He did as she asked: picked up a towel, dipped it in cold water, and returned. A hand reached out and took the towel. The voice said: "I feel better now. I'll tell you another thing. I'm a whore, it's true, but how could I not be?"

"What do you mean?"

"I mean that my way of life goes against every instinct, every desire in my body . . . I am mortified, disgusted by poverty. I want a house of my own . . . I think about it day and night. Even a small house, but full of my things, my clothes, my chair, my kitchen, my sitting room. I'm tired of going from furnished room to furnished room, from boardinghouse to boardinghouse, eating half portions at the trattoria.

89 I'm tired of being poor . . . can't you understand that?"

He touched his face and realized that his eyes were filled with tears. In a pained voice, he said: "I'll find a job and buy you a house."

"You'll never be able to buy me a house," she said, "only Maurizio can give me that . . . So you see, when I think about all the things that I need, that I want, that I would like to have, I feel like a whore, just as you said, from the soles of my feet to the top of my head . . . a whore . . . and I feel that if I married Maurizio I would truly become just that. I would love him because he can give me the things that I so desperately, desperately need."

Sergio began to cry. Tears streamed down his cheeks. "You've never said any of this before," he said, after a short silence.

"I hinted at it . . . but I didn't want to make you suffer. Poor little thing," she said, in a tender voice, "you're already so agitated that I didn't want to add yet another thing to worry about. But what do you think? When we make love and I have to go wash myself with cold water in a dirty old bucket behind that grimy screen, don't you think I wish I could have a nice tiled bathroom, with a big tub full of boiling water? I'm constantly mortified by our miserable existence, constantly . . ."

"If you feel so mortified, why don't you accept Maurizio's offer . . . Why don't you marry him?" Sergio asked, with a note of desperation.

"Because then I would feel humiliated in another way . . . I would feel like a whore, as I said. I wouldn't be able to help loving him passionately, if only because I would feel bound to him by my comfortable life. But it would be at the cost of my dignity. I would feel like a whore, and I would be humiliated."

Sergio desperately searched for something solid within himself, something to hold on to in the midst of the dejection brought on by these cruel words. Then, like a man who sees a dim light in the shadows and realizes that, no matter how faint, it is still a light and the shadows are merely shadows, he said: "One day all of this will change . . . That is what we're fighting for . . . so that everyone can live comfortably and no woman must feel like a whore."

She answered in a measured tone: "Yes, that is what you Communists are fighting for . . . it's true . . . but by the time you reach your goal, I'll be long gone."

"Don't you believe in us?"

90

"How can you say that, after I've chosen to stay with you rather than accept Maurizio's offer?"

She sat up on the bed and removed the wet cloth from her forehead, dropping it on the floor. She looked over at Sergio. "So, shall we go down for our usual half portion, or shall we just stay here and continue humiliating each other?"

"Let's go," he said.

She looked at him. "Come here. Kiss me."

He leaned forward and his lips touched hers. She smelled of alcohol, and it was clear that she was still drunk. They kissed. "Love matters to me," she said, "more than a house, money, or anything else . . . Don't you know that?"

"Yes," he said quietly, looking down.

"Let's go."

[IV]

For about a week they did not see Maurizio. As their visit receded into the past, Sergio began to feel increasingly unsure of his love for Lalla, and more obsessed by the idea of getting his revenge by convincing Maurizio to convert to Communism. His feelings were complex and difficult to explain. On the one hand, he felt something like contempt for this woman whom he possessed and who loved him; on the other, he felt a strong attraction toward his friend, whom he had not been able to win over and who seemed to be slipping through his fingers. He was also afflicted by a more recent and deeper crisis of self-confidence. He felt excessively ambitious, neurotic, like a mediocre salesman who, after a touch of whiskey, becomes excited about his dreams, while his friend, Maurizio, remained calm and sure of himself, lucid, unmoved. He often thought back to their visit and realized that he could not remember it without feeling an unpleasant, burning sense of humiliation. He was ashamed of his earnestness, of his candor, and of his zeal, which now seemed weak

and cowardly. He wanted to prove to Maurizio—but
mainly to himself—that he still held some cards, perhaps the best ones. He felt that they were fighting a duel, though a hidden one, undertaken with nonlethal weapons. He could not shake off the shame of having lost the first round. For some reason, the fact that Lalla had chosen him over Maurizio and his flattering, seductive offer did not console Sergio in the least. In truth, Lalla was superfluous, insignificant to his struggle, which was not about love but about politics. In the realm of love, he was victorious, at least for now, but this victory meant nothing. In the realm of politics, he had been defeated, and he was unable to conceal the sting of this defeat.

His relations with Lalla had not improved; to the contrary, they had eroded even further. She still complained about their lack of money; in fact, her grumbling had become more bitter than ever. She seemed increasingly mortified and angered by their precarious financial condition. This real, concrete inability to satisfy his lover made him hate her at times, as if she had become the personification of his impotence and his inability to take control of the situation. When he had been drunk at Maurizio's, he had imagined that he knew what would happen and felt that he held the strings, controlling his own destiny and that of others. Now he realized that he was just a poor wretch, incapable of making a living or of imposing his will on others. He had believed himself to be a maker of destinies, but instead he was simply a man without a job, though still a Communist. His political beliefs seemed to him the sole positive element in his life, but even this required some sort of proof, a victory, a confirmation of his self-esteem. In other words, even this positive could become a negative if he was unable to accomplish that which had become his constant obsession: Maurizio's conversion to Communism.

He did not mention any of this to Lalla. She had never been privy to his innermost thoughts, and now less than ever. She knew that he wanted to convert Maurizio, but she did not know—nor did he want her to—just how important this conversion had become. It was a constant, vital, irrepressible need. Reflecting on how much he concealed from Lalla—and how little he revealed—he realized that in fact he considered her an inferior being and treated her accordingly; to him, she was a beautiful, lovable object. He knew that this was a cruel attitude, filled with contempt and indifference. Sergio could see this clearly, but it never occurred to him to modify his behavior by opening up to Lalla partly or even completely. The truth was that, while he made his plans to convince Maurizio and thus to control him, his relationship with Lalla, despite its one-sidedness, gave him a certain sense of power and superiority. But he did not know how to use this superiority, because it lay in the arena of love, which he considered unimportant and unworthy, rather than that of politics, the only arena that counted. And yet, it was still a kind of superiority.

As these thoughts went through his mind, he continued to live the same unhappy existence which was so repugnant to him. One morning, after eating at a simple trattoria in the neighborhood, Sergio and Lalla returned to their room. As she led him up the stairs, she asked, "What shall we do today?"

It was Sunday. Sergio hated Sundays, and was annoyed by his hatred for them. He hated the fact that the city was crowded with poor people ambling slowly down the streets, staring at the windows of the closed shops. But these were the very masses he was supposed to love, and so he did not like to admit his aversion, even to himself. "I'm staying in," he said in an irritated tone.

"All day?" she asked, dubiously.

"Until the evening."

Lalla did not seem unhappy at the idea. For some time, almost as if her renunciation of Maurizio had increased her love for Sergio, she had seemed happy whenever he planned to spend time with her. This attitude caused him a slight, insinuating irritation: "There you have it," he thought, "women can think only of this animalistic emotion called love, and are not interested in anything else." He was silent as they went up the stairs. When they reached the top, she stealthily took his hand and almost furtively brought it to her lips and kissed it. "Do you love me?" she asked softly, passionately.

"You know I love you," he answered, with bittersweet sincerity.

She kissed his hand again and they went inside. They walked straight through to their room. Lalla closed the door and began to undress. She always did this, mainly to protect her clothes, but on that day Sergio felt that there was another reason, one that vaguely annoyed him, a kind of obscure erotic impulse. Silently, he sat down in the armchair next to the window. Lalla undressed completely and put on her dressing gown, which had once been Sergio's.

She completed a few tasks, with a calm, serious air: she combed her hair, removed her lipstick with a handkerchief, pulled down a window shade, and smoothed the bedcovers, which were still messy from the morning. Then she came over to where he was sitting and asked, awkwardly, "What's wrong?"

"Nothing. Nothing at all."

She did not notice his irritated tone and carefully sat on the armrest of his chair, with her legs across Sergio's chest. The robe hung open, and Sergio could see her breasts pressing against the deep crease in her belly. It excited him but at the same time, for some reason, he felt irritated by his feeling of arousal. As she often did, Lalla began to touch his face with her large hand. She caressed his face slowly, pausing at the temples, and then, still slowly, ran her fingers through his hair. Then, with a graceful, hungry gesture, as if leaning down to take a bite of a piece of fruit dangling from a tree without pulling it off the branch, she kissed him on the mouth. They began to kiss, and Sergio felt the burning heat of her love melting the stingy, hard metal of his repulsion. He also noticed that her love diminished his feelings of frustration and impotence, and this too vexed him. But still, he responded to her kiss. Every so often she interrupted the long kiss and began to cover his face with tiny, dry kisses that tickled pleasantly and made him smile, almost despite himself. Then she would once again begin kissing him on the mouth, with the same inextinguishable avidity and quiet fervor. Their mouths continued to twist and overlap, passing in and out of each other, biting, rubbing, sucking, opening and closing. Their faces were bathed in saliva as their desire grew stronger. They had stopped speaking, and Lalla began to remove her lover's clothes, with the clumsy eagerness typical of women in such moments. Now she was undoing his tie, unbuttoning his collar, and introducing her hand into his shirt, placing her palm against his chest. Now the hand moved downward, unfastening his belt, unbuttoning his trousers and his underwear. His clothes were completely undone from his neck to his groin; he sat, with his legs open, head tilted backward. Lalla kneeled on the floor and kissed his belly.

He did not know how much time passed. The room was silent and steeped in shadows as they embraced, switching positions every so often. Lalla sat on his knees, then on the ground with her head against his groin, then on an armrest, leaning sideways to kiss him, then on both armrests, then again on his knees, heavy and full of desire. Sergio realized that as time dissolved, so too did his anxieties: his sense of inferiority, his irritation, his repugnance, rage, feelings of impotence and frustration. But even though they dissolved almost magically beneath the prodigious caresses and tenderness of her powerful, indefatigable body, he realized that it was only an illusion: his anxieties did not disappear, they were simply pushed aside. As he thought this, he returned her kisses and caresses until he found himself lying naked on the bed with his lover. "I love you so much," she whispered as she pressed herself against him. "What else matters if we love each other?"

He did not respond, realizing that if he spoke he would reveal his dissatisfaction at this carnal, affectionate resolution. He held her close. But at the same time he knew that he was not satisfied; he knew that they would make love and that after their embrace Lalla would press herself against him and fall asleep, content. And that later, still tired and lazy, they would get out of bed, wash, dress, and go out. And that the streetlamps would shine on them as they walked side by side to their usual café, down the muddy streets of their neighborhood. This predictability cast a bitter pall over their embrace, and yet, as Lalla had said, what else were they to do? Lalla led his movements, pressing her body against his, trapping his legs between hers, teasing and tormenting him with her tireless, restless hands. "It's still early," he thought, "I need to slow things down, otherwise what will we do later?" This thought seemed to capture their situation more completely than all his subtle, complex conjectures. He was like a man with only a few coins in his pocket; once they were spent, there would be nothing left. "Not yet, Lalla, wait," he said.

She did not respond, pressing against him even more tightly, breathing heavily through her nose and mouth. For a long time, they remained locked in a tight embrace. Then she began to move again, rubbing her body against his restlessly and insistently. Believing enough time had passed, Sergio decided to take her, as Lalla clearly desired. They drew out their lovemaking as long as possible—they embraced, rolled around, intermingled on the bed. Finally, he moaned deeply. She responded from the shadows, with a long, satisfied, loving, dolorous moan. They lay there in a heap, one on top of the other, and then, like two lifeless bodies separated by frost, fell away from each other and lay side by side on the bed.

Later, Sergio shook off the somnolence brought on by their lovemaking and got up. Lalla was asleep, or so it seemed, but the shadows made it impossible to see whether her eyes were open or closed. He looked over at the clock on the dresser: six thirty. Four hours had passed. Four hours, he could not help thinking, that another man might have spent going to the movies or the theater or the stadium. He remembered what Lalla had said: "Love is our entertainment . . . like all poor people," and he could not help thinking that she was right. Making as little noise as possible, he quickly got dressed, still ruminating on her words. He asked himself whether he really loved Lalla, and could not help thinking that if love means creating an idealized transfiguration of the beloved, then what he felt was certainly not love. Sergio had very precise 96 notions about love; one could even say he had a theory. To his mind, every epoch had a central concept, an idea upon which man focused his attention. In the past, love had been the focus, and for this reason it had been imbued with man's best most varied qualities. Like a flood, love had spilled into areas that were not, strictly speaking, its purview: politics, art, death, war, and peace. But now the central idea of life was politics; love, deprived of its embellishments, reduced to its essence, and humbled, had wasted away, lost its mystery and richness, and been reduced to its barest form: the sexual encounter. Nothing could be done about this, he thought as he watched Lalla sleeping. Man's imagination, intelligence, and fervor had moved elsewhere, and what had once formed the

very fabric of life had been reduced to an isolated dec-
oration laid over a pattern of an altogether different
nature. "I'm going out," he said, softly. Lalla moaned
in assent. "I'll be back in a couple of hours." Another
moan. He left.

The street was already dark. He went directly
to a bar nearby and, almost automatically, dialed
Maurizio's number. He had not planned to make this
phone call; in fact, when he entered the bar he had
no idea he would go to the phone. He had planned
to have a coffee. The telephone had drawn him like a
magnet, and that was it. Like an automaton, he heard
himself responding to Maurizio's greeting, "I need to
speak to you right away." Maurizio answered that he
could meet him wherever he liked. After agreeing to
meet at a café downtown, Sergio slammed down the
phone.

What an amusing spectacle, Sergio thought as he
walked toward the café. He did not know what he
needed to discuss with Maurizio but was sure that
as soon as he saw him, the words would come spontaneously, just as the desire to call him had come.
He realized that, had he wanted to, he would have
easily deciphered the reason for this meeting, but he
did not want to analyze his reasoning too closely. The
spontaneity of his actions made them feel more inevitable than any dogged analysis and planning could.

97   He waited for Maurizio at the café, an old place
frequented by writers and painters. It was crowded
as usual. But in the back, down a corridor lined with
Empire-style divans upholstered in red velvet, there
was a newer room, sparsely furnished and somewhat
cold, and usually quite empty. Sergio sat down at a

table in the back and ordered some tea. He did not wait long. Soon, Maurizio appeared and strode over to his table.

Sergio realized that once again his heart was racing. As before, he asked himself: "Why did I ask him to meet me here? What do I want to say to him?" He did not know exactly what he would say, and Maurizio's calm, controlled, self-assured expression as he removed his coat, hung it on the coatrack, and sat down at the table, slightly pulling up his trousers as he bent his legs, deeply disconcerted him. How could Maurizio, who was not a Communist and had come quite unprepared, be so calm while he, who was a Communist and should have known in advance how the meeting would end, was in such a state? Maurizio did not give him a chance to gather his thoughts. As soon as he had ordered some tea, he confronted the issue at hand: "Can you explain to me why the devil you are so adamant about my becoming a Communist?"

Somewhat taken aback, Sergio was barely able to mumble: "I gave you my reasons the other day."

"Yes, and they were very convincing . . . I mean, they make perfect sense. But I don't think they are your true reasons."

"And what do you think my true reasons are?"

"It's simple: you want me to become a Communist because you are one," he said, with some brutality.

"So?"

"So, according to your own words, since you hold me in high esteem . . . it bothers you that someone whom you esteem could prefer not to be a Communist . . . To you, the fact that a person might be worthy of esteem without being a Communist is a rebuke, an insult."

"I don't understand what you're getting at."

"It's obvious," Maurizio said, "we all want to improve, perhaps even become the best version of ourselves ... but the Communists believe that it is impossible to improve without joining their cause ... The fact that I—a person whom you hold in high esteem—am not a Communist makes you question your own faith ... It feels like a contradiction. You've admitted as much yourself. You say: we want the best people to join us, so that only the dregs, the refuse, will be left behind. Since you don't consider me to be the dregs, you want me to become a Communist ... If I don't, you might begin to wonder whether in fact it is true that Communism contains an infallible truth ... In other words, my very existence as a man worthy of esteem who does not embrace Communism could foment doubts which you fear more than anything and would like to avoid at any cost."

Sergio drew a deep breath. After all, Maurizio was a reasonable man, and it should be possible to have a discussion without becoming overly excited. He said: "Perhaps you're right ... but from my perspective it simply means that I want to illuminate you and show you the error of your ways, or rather help you take the leap and make up your mind."

"Thank you," Maurizio said with an odd look, adding: "Actually, I'm prepared to take the leap and sign on to the cause if you are willing to employ an irrational argument, as I mentioned the other day ... Rational arguments won't win me over. But we are made of flesh and blood and where rational arguments fail, irrational ones can drive us to action. Signing up is not simply a question of being convinced, it's a call to action . . . therefore if you employ the right argument I'll sign up."

Sergio's heart was beating fast. "What is the right argument, then?" he asked, softly.

"I thought you already knew."

"I don't know what you're talking about."

Maurizio removed a cigarette from the pack and played with it, leaning forward. "Well, there's no use beating about the bush. It's Lalla . . . If you let me take her to bed, I'll sign up the next day. I'll become a Communist for good."

Sergio's heart stopped racing. He felt completely calm and coolheaded. It was just as he had thought. The reality of knowing what argument would convince Maurizio, in other words discovering Maurizio's weakness, changed everything; instead of feeling unsure of himself and inferior to Maurizio, he now felt confident and superior. Suddenly he was happy and completely lucid. Finally, he said to himself, Maurizio was in his power, after their many enervat- 99 ing arguments in which he had always—rightly or wrongly—come up short. "I already knew," he said, after a brief silence. "I saw you two, or rather I saw how you grabbed her hand the other day."

"I knew you saw us."

"And now," Sergio continued, still calm, "I should get up, insult you, and leave."

"But you won't," Maurizio answered, calmly.

"No, I won't," Sergio said, trying hard to emulate his calm demeanor. "Why would you want such a thing?"

"It's simple," Maurizio said, and for the first time since Sergio had known him, he became agitated. "I feel, shall we say"—and here his voice became a whisper, as if oppressed by the weight of his feeling—"I feel a very strong attraction to Lalla . . . I desire her violently, that's all . . . It's stupid, but there it is . . . I'm attracted to her, it's in my blood. I'm completely contaminated by this feeling and I can't stop desiring her . . . I even offered to marry her."

"She told me."

"Since she doesn't want to marry me, I don't see any other way to get what I want . . ."

"But why do you desire her so much?" Sergio said, knowing that it was a stupid question.

"I just do."

Sergio pondered the question for a moment, or rather pretended to. This feeling of power—after being powerless for so long—made his head swim, and it was difficult to formulate precise thoughts. "Why do you think I can get something from her that she has already refused? She'll refuse me as well."

"She won't refuse. If you tell her, 'I want you to go to Maurizio and do what he asks,' she'll do it."

"You're a creep, you know that?"

Maurizio answered calmly: "Why do you feel the need to insult me? I'm not forcing you . . . There's nothing reprehensible about my feelings for Lalla . . . You can simply turn down my offer and I'll never mention it again."

Turn down the offer? Nothing would be simpler, Sergio reflected. But that was not what he wanted. In a certain sense that was his least attractive option. Turning down Maurizio's offer would mean returning to his earlier, primitive state of insecurity and mistrust. He already had Lalla's love, but it was no good to him. Holding on to that love, refusing Maurizio's offer out of love for that love, would not help his situation. He needed to overcome Maurizio's resistance, to convince him, to make him do what he wanted. "If I were to do what you ask . . . and I'm not saying I will . . . would you then do what I want?"

"Immediately . . . The next day, I'd request my Party membership."

"But can't you see," Sergio said, realizing that the question was directed more to himself than to Maurizio, "that if I did this, your Party inscription would lose much of its value? Or even all of it?"

"Why?" Maurizio smiled. "What connection is there between Communism, which is a sociopolitical and economic theory, and my love for Lalla? None . . ."

"Your conversion would be neither spontaneous nor disinterested."

Maurizio laughed. "Perhaps it would no longer be spontaneous, but is there really such a thing as a disinterested conversion? There is always a motivating interest of some sort."

"And what if I refuse?"

"Then it would mean that Lalla matters more to you than the Party . . . in other words, you would be a bad Communist."

"According to whom?"

"According to you Communists," Maurizio added, harshly. "You're just like the Christians. Christ said one should leave one's family and follow him."

"What would you think of me if I refused?"

"That you're a bad Communist but a good lover."

"And if I accepted?"

"That you are a bad lover but an excellent Communist."

"And why would that make me a bad lover?"

"I think it's obvious . . . What kind of question is that? What you want is reassurance."

"What do you mean?"

101 "You want me to say that you can be both a good lover and a good Communist."

"Go to hell."

Once again, Sergio was annoyed. He needed something to help him regain his feeling of superiority. "Sorry . . . You may not believe me, given the subject of our discussion at this little café table, but I love Lalla."

"I don't doubt it," Maurizio answered, completely serious.

"I find it hard to control my feelings."

"I can understand that."

"What would you do if you were in my shoes?" Sergio asked, abruptly. Then, realizing how naïve his question sounded: "No, don't answer me. It's a silly question."

"Why do you think it's silly? I can say that since I'm not a Communist, the conflict does not present itself. I don't have to choose."

"There are other factors that might force you to choose." Sergio wanted to discuss the matter further: "For example, I don't know, your fortune, your inheritance."

"Money means nothing to me . . . I wouldn't give a square inch of a woman I love for all the wealth in the world."

"Your freedom, then."

Maurizio laughed. "Don't you see that, not being a Communist, the question simply doesn't apply, unless I was a coward or a miser or some other despicable being? Unless Communism is the prize, one simply is what one is by not giving up Lalla, even for a good cause . . . You Communists have invented the reason for giving her up, it is a reason created by you Communists over the course of the last fifty or one hundred years . . . or at least that is what you believe, and what you have convinced yourselves of. By which I mean a reason that does not put those who adopt it in an unfavorable light."

"What you're saying is that it would not be judged unfavorably," Sergio said bitterly, "if I were to say to Lalla: spread your legs and let Maurizio have his way with you."

Maurizio laughed. "Why do you have to put it that way? But no, you would not be judged unfavorably . . . at least not by me."

There was a long silence. Maurizio observed Sergio with his bright, alluring eyes. Finally, he said: "I want you to know that I understand . . . listen . . . Are you listening to me?"

"Yes."

"All right, listen . . . You yourself said that bringing even a single person to the cause is an important achievement. Especially if that person is worthy of respect, staunch, and mature . . . So, on the one hand you have nothing less than Communism, the greatest dream of freedom and happiness man has ever conceived, a dream that the Communists are dedicated to realizing, in order to ensure the well-being of millions of human beings, the betterment of their lives, to give them the capacity to express themselves, to free their minds and fulfill their destinies. And on the other hand? Not much . . . a woman, like so many others, an ordinary woman, who has the misfortune of being desired by me . . . a human body that I desire . . . and yes, I want, as you said, for her to open her legs, as all women do, for love, stupidity, money, and for millions of other reasons . . . There is no comparison between these two things . . . Tell me if I'm wrong."

"No," Sergio said, quietly, "you're right." He was struck by Maurizio's inspired, sincere lyricism when he spoke of the Communist cause. He would have liked to sound like that.

"If I'm right," Maurizio continued, now with a slight tremor in his voice, "then why do you hesitate?"

That was the long and short of it: he wanted Lalla, Sergio could not help thinking. His whole being was contaminated by this desire. Sergio abruptly got up. "That's enough, I'm leaving. I'll make a decision soon."

"You'll make a decision?"

"Yes," he answered, with a hint of rage, "don't I have to?"

"In a sense, yes," Maurizio said.

"What do you mean 'in a sense'?"

"Well, you don't really have to."

"What do you mean?" Sergio said, hopefully.

"Well," Maurizio said, quite deliberately, "you could ask Lalla what she wants."

Sergio looked over at Maurizio. "Lalla isn't a Communist . . . she doesn't really believe in the cause . . . so it's obvious what her answer would be."

"Meaning?"

"Meaning that she would say no."

"True. But if she were to say yes, then you would not be involved."

"And?"

"And then it would be a matter between Lalla and me . . . and I wouldn't have to join the Party. I would marry her, or she would simply become my lover."

Sergio once again stood up. He was irritated. "In other words, you'll only join the Party if I am the one who forces Lalla to sleep with you and she accepts out of love for me . . ."

"That's right."

"Well in that case you wouldn't be signing up because you desire Lalla, but rather because you want to obtain her consent through my efforts . . . That's a different matter altogether." Satisfied with the subtlety of his reasoning, Sergio sat down again.

Maurizio seemed perfectly calm. "Perhaps I'm a degenerate . . . Perhaps I can only derive pleasure from obtaining Lalla through your efforts . . . What difference does it make?"

It appeared that Maurizio had an answer for everything. "But you're not a degenerate," Sergio retorted.

"How do you know? There are men who are attracted to little girls . . . Maybe I'm attracted to women who love Communists and give themselves out of love for their Communist lovers, in other words, out of love for Communism . . . so what?"

"That's a very modern kind of perversion."

"Precisely . . . Who says that love doesn't change through time?"

Sergio got up again, intending to leave. "Good-bye," he said, holding out his hand.

"Good-bye."

104 After this meeting, Sergio sank into a kind of oblivion. It was like the theater, when the curtain falls at the end of an act, and the audience has no idea what is going on backstage. He was a spectator, watching himself from the outside. This feeling of oblivion distanced him from the darkest zones of his own conscience so that he had no idea what was going on there. At first he decided to discuss Maurizio's proposal with Lalla, but then, for reasons he did not fully understand, the whole matter slipped from his mind. From time to time he sensed an encumbrance where before he had felt only emptiness; but this encumbrance, which was caused by the decision that loomed before him, remained obscure and unspoken, though at times he felt oppressed by it. But he continued to do the same things as before, aided by his feeling of oblivion.

They continued to see Maurizio; now that spring had arrived, he often picked them up in his car and they drove to Ostia or into the countryside for lunch. Deep down, what surprised Sergio was that Maurizio did not seem to remember his bold proposal. He was as courteous, irreproachably friendly, and thoughtful as ever, almost ceremonious in fact, and it seemed to Sergio that their rapport had returned to its previous ease, when neither he nor Lalla, nor even Maurizio, knew that both of them desired Lalla.

One day in March, Lalla told Sergio that she needed a new dress. She stood in front of the armoire in her bathrobe, pointing at the only summer dress she had from the previous year. Sergio could see that it was worn and threadbare, and discolored under the arms. But he had no money. "I can't do anything about it . . . I won't get paid until the end of the month." Lalla said that she would rather stay at home in bed despite the increasingly sunny weather than go out in such a dress. Now in a bad mood, Sergio told her to do as she pleased, and went out.

As soon as he was in the street he thought of Maurizio and decided to ask his friend for a loan so he could buy Lalla a dress. On some level, he sensed that there was a connection between this decision and the one he still had to make regarding Lalla and Maurizio, but he refused to follow this line of thinking. He called Maurizio and told him that he wanted to meet, and Maurizio, in his usual polite manner, said Sergio could come over whenever he liked.

Sergio did not wait long in Maurizio's sitting room. It looked shabbier than ever in the morning light, with the sun streaming in through the curtains. As soon as his friend appeared, he said: "Listen, I need to ask you a favor."

"Please have a seat," Maurizio said. "What can I do for you?"

After a pause, Sergio continued: "I'm broke . . . Lalla desperately needs a new dress . . . Could you please lend me the money? I'll pay you back in a month."

Maurizio betrayed no emotion. "How much do you need?" he asked, in a calm voice.

"Twenty thousand lire."

"That will only buy a very modest dress," Maurizio said, fixing him with his gaze.

"Well, we're modest people," Sergio said, almost angrily, "and we dress modestly."

Maurizio reflected for a moment: "Modesty is fine of course . . . but if I may be frank, Lalla dresses like a beggar."

Sergio pressed his lips together, offended. "Why do you say that?"

"Because it's true," Maurizio said, with a cruel calm. "She wears rags . . . shapeless skirts, worn-out shoes . . . Her gloves are dirty and full of holes . . . The other day she was wearing a blouse that was discolored under the arms from sweat . . . Her stockings are darned . . . Perhaps you haven't noticed, but she looks like a beggar. If I were you I would be ashamed to go out with her."

Sergio was so disconcerted by this attack that he did not respond immediately. His heart was heavy. After a long pause, Maurizio continued: "Listen, instead of twenty thousand, I'll lend you two hundred thousand . . . It's very little, even for a woman who dresses moderately well, and almost nothing for Lalla, who owns no clothes at all. At least she'll be able to buy a dress, stockings, a blouse, some shoes, and maybe a few other things . . . like a slip or a camisole; I'm sure hers are in a terrible state, if she has them."

As he calmly said these words, he pulled a checkbook and a pen out of his pocket. He wrote out the check, saying, "Don't worry, you can pay me whenever you like."

"But I . . . ," Sergio began, still taken aback.

"Don't worry," Maurizio said, holding up his hand, "and anyway, you can't deny her these things that will make her so happy. It makes her deeply unhappy, as it would any woman, to go about dressed in rags.

After all," he said, staring at Sergio, "I'm happy to give you this money . . . I'm very attached to Lalla, as you know, so it gives me pleasure."

Without paying any more attention to Sergio, he finished writing the check. Sergio watched him, staring at the dark, shiny hair on his head, the head of a courteous, well-brought-up man bent over the checkbook at the small table. He wanted to protest, to stop him, but he knew that he would not, though he was not sure why. He had a strange feeling, a kind of gratitude mixed with humiliated attraction, and at the same time, a bitter sense of powerlessness, of irredeemable inferiority. Once again Maurizio had shown him up and was imposing his will; he towered over him with his money, as he had before with his intelligence. Sergio felt a violent desire for revenge, though he was not sure what form this revenge would take. He saw his hand reaching for the check, bathed in a ray of sunlight that came in through one of the windows. As in a dream, he heard himself say "Thank you." He peered at the check. It was in his name, and suddenly it occurred to him: "He doesn't want Lalla to know . . . This is between Maurizio and me . . . Either he really loves her, or he wants to humiliate me, or both."

As if hearing his thoughts, Maurizio said nonchalantly, "Of course you shouldn't tell Lalla that I gave you the money . . . Tell her you were paid to write a screenplay or something along those lines . . . You've written for the movies in the past, haven't you?"

"No."

"Well, think of something . . . then after a while I'll give you more money . . . for the next installment of your screenplay . . . That way Lalla will be happy . . . Clothes are important to women."

"But I'll never be able to pay you back."

"It doesn't matter," Maurizio said.

Without knowing why, Sergio blurted out, "You think that, with the excuse of this lie about a screenplay, I'll accept more money from you."

"Well," Maurizio said, shrugging, "if you are willing to take this money I don't see why you wouldn't take more."

"Have I accepted?"

"Well, you put the check in your wallet."

"And how much will you give me later?"

"As much as you need," Maurizio said, calmly, "so that Lalla can dress decently."

"And you're happy to give me this money?"

"Yes, very . . . As I said, I feel great affection for Lalla."

"Or is it because you want to humiliate me?"

Maurizio pretended not to hear his rebuke. He walked over to a small bar on wheels and asked, invitingly: "Would you like an aperitif . . . a cocktail?"

"Yes, thanks."

"A martini, then," Maurizio said. He mixed the gin and vermouth in a large glass, then rang a bell and asked the butler for some ice. As soon as the butler left the room, he asked, in the same calm voice as before: "Regarding our earlier conversation . . . have you come to a decision?"

Sergio's heart jumped. "What do you mean?"

"Our conversation about my possible conversion to Communism."

In a voice that did not feel like his own, and with the same spontaneity that had led him to ask Maurizio for money, Sergio heard himself respond: "I accept."

There was a sound of broken glass. A small glass 108 had crashed to the floor; it was not clear whether it had fallen out of Maurizio's hand or had simply tumbled from the bar. "How nervous I am," Maurizio said. His voice was agitated, polite, and intense. The butler returned with the ice. "You can put it there, Giovanni," Maurizio said in his usual voice.

Maurizio picked up the pitcher containing the mixture of gin and vermouth and returned to where Sergio was sitting. He dropped in some ice with a spoon and, pouring the mixture into a small glass, said, with some nervous anticipation, "Not only will I sign up, but I'll donate two million lire to the Party . . . on the day you fulfill your promise."

He looked almost upset, overcome by a powerful, long-repressed happiness. Sergio could not help thinking that he seemed happy to join the Communist Party, and to obtain Lalla in the process. In other words, he had killed two birds with one stone. Sergio felt weak, and slightly faint. The blood drained from his face. In order to steady his nerves he gulped down his drink. Maurizio insisted: "So, how will we go about it?"

"You're very impatient," Sergio said, looking at his friend.

"You know I'm head over heels for her," Maurizio said.

"I'll speak with her today . . . but I'm not sure she'll agree."

"If you really want to, I'm sure you'll convince her."

Sergio stood up, abruptly. "I'm leaving," he said, adding, "don't get up . . . I know the way." He rushed out without waiting for an answer.

[V]

109 Two questions went round and round in Sergio's mind. Why had he taken the money? And why, once he had taken it, had he accepted Maurizio's proposition to convert to Communism?

He could answer the first question with relative ease: out of love for Lalla. But he knew that this was not the real reason. The truth was that he had accepted the money for reasons that were deeper, and more obscure. He felt the need to thrust Lalla into Maurizio's arms, and this money was simply a means to that end; he had sold Lalla to Maurizio, like a piece of merchandise. Why did he feel this need to thrust Lalla into Maurizio's arms? The obvious answer was that he wanted to convince Maurizio to become a Communist, but the second, more subtle, was closer to the truth: there was a struggle for power going on between them, and he wanted to vanquish his opponent. If he convinced Maurizio to join the Party it would be his victory, the proof of his power. Each of his actions had two motivations, one more generous and more noble, the other darker and more selfish. He had accepted the money so that Lalla would be able to look more presentable, and so that she would become Maurizio's lover. He wanted her to become

Maurizio's lover so that he would join the Party, and in order to feel superior to him. Which was the true reason? Probably both, just as all our actions tend to be both disinterested and selfish.

These were his thoughts as he waited impatiently for Lalla to come home. He had expected to find her there, but when he returned, the room was empty. The landlady could tell him only that Lalla had gone out shortly after he had. It was odd; he knew that she did not like to go out alone, and she was lazy. He also knew that she had no money, not even enough for a coffee.

He waited for a long time until finally there was a knock on the door and the landlady told him that Lalla was on the phone. He picked up the receiver.

"What are you doing?" she said.

"What do you mean, what am I doing?" Sergio asked, surprised. "I'm waiting for you."

Her voice wavered: "I'm here at . . . I've been waiting."

"Where?"

He could hear voices, as if Lalla were asking for the address. She said: "Listen, take a taxi for once in your life . . . Come to Via Sisto Quinto, number twenty-seven."

"Where?"

"I can't explain . . . I'm drunk . . . Just come." She hung up.

Feeling annoyed, Sergio took his overcoat from the coatrack and went out. He found a taxi in the piazza around the corner. From the look on the driver's face he surmised that the address lay quite far away. The taxi traversed the entire city, went down a few suburban streets, and then up a hill, and finally turned onto a new road lined with a few very modern buildings. On one side of the road lay these new constructions, each set quite far from the next, while on the other, the lights of Rome glimmered in the darkness. The taxi stopped. "Number twenty-seven," the driver grumbled, pointing at one of the new buildings, six or seven stories tall, looming in the darkness.

Sergio paid and went inside. The foyer smelled of lime and recently waxed wood. It was not a luxurious building, but rather one of the new apartment complexes being built for the middle bourgeoisie, on lots that had until recently been farmland. As soon as he was inside, he realized that in her drunken state, Lalla had forgotten to tell him the apartment number or the name of the person she was visiting. "What now?" he wondered, looking around. He began to climb the stairs.

On the phone, he had heard voices and music. As soon as he encountered noise coming from one of the doors, he stopped. The pale, blond wood door had a plaque with the name Moroni. He hesitated and then knocked.

A young-looking maid came to the door. The shapely, almost elegant girl had blonde hair and wore a lot of makeup; her mouth was wide and red and she had blue eyes. Somewhat taken aback, Sergio asked if a young woman by the name of Lalla was there. There was a clamor of voices and a record player. The foyer, compact and bare except for two or three small objects, was empty. "There are so many people," the maid answered, "I don't know . . . Wait here a moment and I'll bring the master of the house."

146

She disappeared, and after a few minutes a man appeared; he looked to Sergio like a prosperous farmer or country merchant. "You must be Mr. Sergio," he said, as soon as he saw him; "come in, come in, we've been waiting for you."

He looked about forty years old, a short man with a large head and a prominent brow, and extremely regular features, almost like a sculpture. His face had a rustic, serious air. His large nose and wide mouth—which curved upward at the corners—seemed to belong on a larger, more vigorous frame. His tousled, messy hair revealed a pale bald spot, and he had a wide, yellowish, hard, and pensive forehead. He introduced himself—"Moroni"—and led Sergio into the other room, the source of the music and voices.

This room, which was rather small and almost empty of furniture except for a few chairs and a sofa in one corner, contained about twenty people. It was filled with smoke, and a record was playing; a few people danced. Sergio spotted Lalla in the arms of a young man with blond hair; he looked like an office worker, with thick glasses. As soon as she saw Sergio she walked up to him and exclaimed, "Sergio, you're finally here," embracing him emphatically. Sergio noticed that her breath smelled of alcohol. He took her in his arms and, pretending to dance, maneuvered her into the foyer. After releasing her arm, he asked: "What on earth are you doing here? Who is this Moroni, and who are the rest of these people?"

She laughed: "Moroni is an angel."

"And you're drunk," Sergio said.

"Yes, I'm drunk," she said, "and you know why? Because our life is depressing . . . because we're a pair of sad cases ... When I drink, I can forget about it."

"Who is this Moroni?"

"He's one of my students," Lalla answered, slowly. "I've mentioned him to you before ... one of my English students."

It was true. He remembered Lalla's mentioning a certain Moroni, but had forgotten the name. He looked at her: "You didn't mention this little gathering."

"I didn't know about it. He called at the last minute ... You were gone ... so I came and then I called you."

"I'm hungry," Sergio said, firmly; "I haven't eaten."

"There's food in the other room," Lalla said, pointing to a small room off the foyer. As if there was nothing left to say, she turned around and returned to the sitting room.

Sergio went into the little dining room. Lalla was right: there was an abundance of food, and the room was empty. He picked up a plate, served himself some meat and vegetables, and sat down in a corner to eat. He began to feel contempt for Lalla, as if she had somehow become worthless in his eyes. He realized that this feeling was simply part of the preparation for what he was about to do: inform her of Maurizio's proposition. He felt neither love nor affection for her, only a kind of impatience and incomprehension, as though her thoughts and complexities did not touch him in the least. What bothered him was her vacillating, exalted, inconsistent, irrational, and frivolous attitude toward life. She lived in a state of constant romanticism, based on nothing. In the end, he reflected, he would leave her, even without Maurizio's intervention. As he sank into these cruel thoughts, Moroni entered the room.

"I see you've eaten . . . Would you like anything else?"

"I would like some wine," Sergio answered abruptly, without looking up.

Moroni went to the table, poured a glass of wine, and offered it to Sergio. "So, you are Signora Abbiati's boyfriend."

Sergio was quietly surprised at the description, but did not comment: "Yes."

"The young lady," Moroni continued, with a warm respect in his voice, "tells me that you will be getting married soon."

Sergio snapped to attention. Not only had he never asked Lalla to marry him, but it had never even occurred to him. And yet Lalla had mentioned marriage to this man who was her student. This proved that marriage was something she hoped for, that their situation made her uncomfortable, and that she would have liked to be his wife. He felt a sudden wave of compassion, mixed with irritation. "Yes, we should," he answered vaguely.

"Well," Moroni continued, emphatically, "I must say that it makes me happy to hear it . . . Miss Lalla is a lovely girl, sweet, genuine, and intelligent. She will," he added, "be a lovely bride."

Sergio started at the word "bride," with its old-fashioned, provincial air. Moroni continued: "I would like to be one of your witnesses. I've known Miss Lalla for over a year and I feel great affection for her . . . Please remember."

As he said this, his voice quivered. Sergio looked up and answered as kindly as he could: "Thank you . . . As soon as we've set the date we'll let you know, of course."

Moroni seemed to be in the mood to trade confidences: "Do you know why I like her so much? I lost my wife, and Miss Lalla resembles her . . . I lost her when she was still young, more or less Miss Lalla's age . . . The resemblance is quite strong . . . See for yourself." He pulled out his wallet and removed a photograph, which he handed to Sergio. It was an old ID photo of Moroni's late wife. The face—which was all one could see—looked as if it had been touched by death. One could barely make out the features. Sergio noted a slight resemblance, especially in the irregularity of the face, the large forehead, small nose, and wide mouth. But little else. He returned the photograph to Moroni: "It's true, there is a certain resemblance."

"You see?" Moroni said. "It is truly extraordinary . . . I find it very moving," he added, touching his face and looking, as he said, quite moved. Sergio peered up at him but said nothing. He had finished eating. Finally, he stood up, leaving his plate and glass on the table. Moroni rushed over: "I'm so sorry . . . I'm a bit upset; you see my wife was everything to me."

Sergio poured himself another glass of wine, in silence. "I would love to invite you to the country," Moroni added, "I have a little house in Olevano . . ."

"We would love to," Sergio said, firmly, and headed toward the living room.

114 Lalla was dancing with a young man with a great mop of brown hair and thick glasses. Sergio noticed

that she seemed very drunk: she shifted her feet clumsily and grasped her partner tightly, her hips moving
awkwardly, like an animal whose lower limbs have
been affected by a strange paralysis. He sat in a corner,
trying not to look at her: seeing her move so clumsily
and with so little grace made him feel a wave of contempt and almost hatred, as toward something vile
and almost worthless. After the song ended Lalla did
not leave her partner; the two stood side by side in the
middle of the room, talking. Then the dancing began
again; there were more couples now, and Sergio saw
that her shaggy-haired partner was casually leading
Lalla toward another room, through a half-open door.
They twisted and turned awhile longer near the door,
after which the dancer lightly pushed the door open
with the same hand he used to encircle Lalla's waist,
and they disappeared into the next room. The door,
which the man had pushed from inside the room,
was now in its original position, slightly ajar, and no
one had noticed their disappearance. For a moment,
Sergio did nothing as feelings of rage and jealousy
washed over him. Finally, he pushed through the
throng of dancers and opened the door to the other
room. He stood in the doorway.

As he had suspected, they were no longer dancing. The room contained a bed, an armoire, and a
few other pieces of furniture. There were coats and
hats everywhere. Lalla was sitting on the bed with her
back to the door, struggling clumsily in the arms of
the shaggy-haired man. She did not seem to be fighting very hard; one of her shoulders was already exposed and her blouse was sliding down her arm. The
young man was insistently trying to twist her head so

that their lips met. Lalla was still struggling, but just as Sergio came into the room she was beginning to put up less of a fight. Sergio went around to the bed and violently yanked the shoulder that was still covered. "Get up. Let's go," he growled.

The young man let go and Lalla pulled away slightly, clumsily fixing her hair. "Who are you?" the man asked Sergio.

"That's none of your business," Sergio replied. "You were right to bring her here . . . That's how it's done, isn't it? After all, the *signorina* didn't put up much of a fight, did she, so your conscience is clear. But now the *signorina* is coming with me, because I am who I am."

"Listen here," the man objected, standing up. Lalla was sobbing: "Sergio . . . stop it . . . leave me alone . . . go away." As she said this, she rose lazily from the bed.

"I'll go, but you're coming with me."

"Don't move," the other man said, in a more confident tone, as he walked up to Sergio. "Who are you?"

"That's right, who are you?" Lalla said in a drunken voice.

Sergio stared at Lalla's cheek. The skin was dark and covered with a fine down which, at the temples and around her ears, gradually merged with her hairline; her hair was combed up in a bun. He was tempted to become violent, but with a cold, almost experimental aggression. He raised a hand and slapped his lover, saying: "That's who I am, and now let's go."

She bowed her head, as if in defeat. "Stop that," the bespectacled young man objected, but Sergio pushed him out of the way and he fell backward onto the bed, into a pile of overcoats. Gripping Lalla's arm, Sergio pushed her out of the room, through the crowd of dancing guests and into the foyer, where they were joined by their host. "Are you leaving?"

"Yes . . . Lalla's not feeling well."

"I'm sorry to hear it." Moroni mumbled a few more niceties, and repeated the invitation to his villa in Olevano. He held the door open for them. Lalla stared down at the floor as she dressed mechanically and said good-bye to her student. Sergio continued to grip her arm as they descended the stairs. Once outside, Sergio hailed a taxi and they got in. As the taxi drove away, Sergio turned to Lalla and said, "You whore."

Lalla did not respond and simply sat in silence with her head down, as if lost in thought. As they passed a streetlamp, Sergio noticed that she was crying. For some reason, this rekindled his contempt, and he said, with conviction: "You're just a whore . . . Anyone can have you . . . They don't even have to pay you . . . Never mind your feelings of gratitude toward Maurizio . . . some whiskey is enough. Whore."

Still in silence, she shook her head and continued to cry. As the taxi sped along, Sergio felt his rage increasing. Suddenly unable to control himself, hc said again: "You whore," and hit her awkwardly on the back with his fist. Lalla moaned and hid her face in her hands.

When they arrived, the taxi stopped and they got out. As Sergio paid, the driver observed: "That's no way to talk to a woman." He was almost an old man, with the air of a paterfamilias. Sergio stared at him for a moment and then silently grabbed Lalla's arm, pushing her toward the door.

They climbed up the stairs four by four, practically running. Lalla kept tripping, covering her face with one hand. Once they reached their landing, Sergio dragged her toward their room. He pushed her violently onto the bed. She fell heavily, making the bedsprings creak. Then he closed the door and turned on the light.

Lalla was lying facedown on the bed with her face in her hands, sobbing loudly. Sergio sat down on the bed and said, furiously: "I can't leave you alone for a moment without you doing something stupid . . . What's wrong with you? What kind of a woman are you?"

Without looking up, still sobbing, she replied: "Why are you so cruel, Sergio? I'm drunk, I already told you . . . and I'm so tired of this life, of being poor, tired of everything . . . That's why men can do what they want with me . . . But why are you so cruel? Why don't you try to understand?"

An enraged lucidity had replaced everything else in Sergio's mind. "So you're tired of being poor?" he said, furiously. "Well look what I have here. I have money for you, look here . . . Get up and look." He removed Maurizio's check from his wallet and grabbed Lalla's hair, pulling it until she was sitting upright. "Here's your money, look at it. Two hundred thousand lire."

She stared at the check in astonishment. Despite his rage, Sergio took care to conceal Maurizio's signature on the check with his thumb. "Now you can buy clothes and everything else you want . . . I signed a contract to write a screenplay for two hundred thousand lire . . . Later I'll get another eight hundred . . . so you can stop complaining about how poor we are."

He put the check back in his wallet and pulled Lalla toward him, until their faces were almost touching, and stared into her eyes: "Listen to me . . . you were about to sleep with that lout just because you had a few drinks in you . . . so it seems that such things are not difficult for you. Now, listen to me . . . Maurizio is planning to join the Party within the next month . . . Do you hear me? He's going to sign up. But in return, he wants you . . . Listen, now . . . I want you to do what you were about to do with that dancing monkey for nothing, you whore, but with Maurizio instead, to ensure that he keeps his promise. Do you understand me?"

She stared at him, bewildered. "You want me to become Maurizio's lover?" she said, finally.

"Yes," Sergio answered angrily, although with less conviction.

"Do you know what you're asking?"

"Of course . . . I'm asking you to do this for a good cause, instead of doing it for no reason at all."

She touched her face and said in a muted tone: "I feel awful . . . I really drank too much."

She said those words in a languid voice. She got 118 up from the bed, walked to the door shakily, and disappeared. Sergio remained on the bed, still furious, wallet in hand.

Lalla was gone for a long while. Finally, when she returned, she closed the door behind her and went over to the mirror. Sergio stared, waiting for an answer and hating himself for it. The answer never came. Lalla undressed, walked around in the nude for a few minutes, put on her tattered old nightgown, and returned to the bed, without a word. Sergio wanted to press her for an answer, but could not find the strength. Meekly, Lalla said, "Move over so I can get in." He got up and she climbed into bed. He too undressed and climbed under the covers, suddenly exhausted, and fell asleep at once. During the night, he thought he saw a light and the outline of Lalla leaning on one elbow, one breast visible through the holes in her nightshirt, with a lock of hair dangling in her face as she contemplated him in silence. But perhaps, he reflected the following morning, it had all been a dream.

[VI]

A few days later, the three of them decided to go to Olevano. Maurizio had a dilapidated old car that he hardly ever brought out of the garage where it sat rusting away. Moroni, Lalla's pupil, was expecting them. Sergio and Lalla had not returned to the subject of Maurizio's political conversion and the condition he had placed for it. Lalla's silence was so ambiguous that Sergio sometimes had the strange feeling that the subject had never been broached at all. Other times, he felt that the issue hung in the air and that even though none of them mentioned it, they were all thinking about it. It was present in their spirits if not on their lips, fermenting, growing, becoming increasingly real. But none of them discussed it. Sergio felt that one day it would explode, like an illness lying dormant in an apparently healthy body.

They left early. Lalla sat in the front next to Maurizio, with Sergio in the back. During the trip they laughed and joked, intoxicated by the thrill of the road, the beautiful spring weather, and the change of scenery after so many months in the city. Lalla was, it seemed to Sergio, particularly affectionate toward him. She was wearing a new skirt, a new blouse, and new silk stockings, all bought with Maurizio's money. She glanced back at Sergio several times and said: "Sergio is making money now . . . Maurizio, you wouldn't believe it . . . everything I'm wearing, from my hat to my shoes, was bought with Sergio's money." Maurizio answered calmly: "How lovely . . . So what happened?" "Sergio is writing a screenplay," she said proudly; "the hard times are over." Her happiness and the new clothes made her look even prettier. Every so often she turned to Sergio, gazing at him affectionately with her large, dark eyes or quickly caressing his hand, which lay on his knee. Sergio felt a strange emotion, a combination of guilt and surprise: Could she really still love him after his proposal? How could she not realize that he did not love her and considered her an object, precious perhaps, but inanimate, to be used as a means to an end? He knew of course that she could not have forgotten his proposal. And he wondered, almost cruelly, what her decision would be now that the problem was in her hands, with all its humiliating weight and mortifying ambiguity.

They drove for a long time through the countryside in the warm spring sun. After they passed Zagarolo and were driving through terraced hills and small forests, the car suddenly came to a stop. "Something must be wrong with the motor," Maurizio said; "this damned car is always breaking down." He got out and invited the others to do so as well. While Maurizio peered at the motor, Sergio and Lalla began to walk down the empty, sunny road.

It was a beautiful day. Lalla pointed out a few tiny white clouds, clearly delineated against the pure, luminous blue sky. Sergio suddenly turned to her: "Why did you tell Moroni that we were getting married this year?"

"How do you know?"

"He told me."

"I know we'll probably never get married, but I love you . . . Perhaps you won't understand this, but a woman always hopes to marry the man who loves her. I'm a woman just like any other. I would like to be your wife."

"But I don't want to be your husband," he said, harshly.

Without seeming to notice his tone, she took his arm. "Let me at least have my illusions . . . Why are you so cruel? What have I done to you?"

"Nothing."

"You see? So why not just let me say whatever I like? Another person might say that they hope to win the lotto, and I say that I would like to marry you . . . What harm is there? There was a good reason for me to say it."

"What was that?"

"Moroni is in love with me. He says that I look exactly like his dead wife. He has asked me to marry him several times. So, just to shut him up, I told him we were engaged."

Sergio said nothing.

"Sergio, why are you always so cruel with me? I had started to hope, these last few days after you gave me all these gifts . . . but now you've reverted to your cruel ways."

Maurizio called out: "Shall we go?"

"Let's go back," Sergio said; "we can discuss this later." Lalla followed him in silence.

They were not far from Olevano; the town was visible on the horizon, at the summit of a rocky hill. When they reached it, they caught a glimpse of a man leaning against the parapet of a bridge over a small stream, beneath the shade of a leafy tree. He walked toward them, indicating that they should stop. It was Moroni. He went over to the car, exclaiming, in his loud, boisterous voice: "Welcome! Welcome to my town, *signorina*." He stepped onto the running board of the car and guided them toward his home, which was built on a terrace cut into the hill, below street level. The car descended a narrow road with vineyards on either side and finally came to a stop in a court-yard in front of the simple, square façade of a white three-story house with green shutters. Moroni helped Lalla out of the car. When they had all emerged, he asked: "No bags?"

"Why should we have bags with us?" Sergio asked.

"I was hoping you would stay today and tomorrow, Sunday, and perhaps even Monday," Moroni said, clearly disconcerted. Lalla laughed: "It's true, he told me, but I forgot."

Sergio was intensely irritated, though he was unsure why. The place was pleasant, and he was tired of the city. The idea of spending three days in the country pleased him. Furiously, he turned to Lalla: "You only think about clothes. You forget everything else."

"Don't worry," Maurizio said in a conciliatory tone, "Moroni can give us some soap . . . We'll make the best of it. Perhaps we could even stay tomorrow night as well." Lalla did not seem happy about this solution, but did not contradict him. They followed Moroni into the house.

It was lunchtime, and Moroni invited them into the dining room without delay. Even though the house was bathed in sunlight because of its position on the side of a hill overlooking a vast, sun-baked valley, it was still cold inside, as country houses with no other heating but a fireplace tend to be. A chaste, stale smell of dusty worm-eaten furniture and simple cooking filled the shady rooms, decorated in a heavy, rustic style tinged with bourgeois pretensions. The house had been built in the nineteenth century, Moroni explained, and no changes had been made since then. This was obvious from the large, dark furniture and the heavy drapes, the oval mirrors framed in walnut, the chairs upholstered in ribbed fabric. Their little group sat down at the dining table, and a servant—a local peasant woman with red cheeks and frizzy hair—carried in an enormous platter of pasta. There were several carafes of wine on the table, enough for a much larger group to become drunk. Everything was abundant, heavy, and countrified. They ate in an uncomfortable silence. Maurizio, who seemed to be in a good mood, served himself an ostentatiously large portion, but Sergio and Lalla barely touched their food. Sergio was still annoyed about the suitcases, and Lalla explained that pasta was fattening and that she had to "watch her figure." Their host, who had served himself a large portion, observed: "I had forgotten that women today never eat pasta. Of course, my wife ate everything."

"When did she pass away?" Sergio asked, almost distractedly.

Moroni looked at Sergio. "Less than a year ago," he answered simply.

"Oh, so it's still very recent."

"Yes," Moroni said, putting down his fork and looking straight ahead. "Very recent . . . and nothing has changed," he sighed, adding: "If it were just the house, that would not be a problem . . . but nothing has changed in me either. Everything has stayed exactly the same." He seemed upset as he said this, and did not pick up his fork again. But it was also clear that he did not mind discussing his pain, and even that he needed to discuss it. Sergio asked: "What do you mean when you say that nothing has changed?"

"Nothing," he repeated, looking unhappy. "A deep love like the one I felt for Laura does not go away from one day to the next . . . I feel that something which occupied an enormous place in my life has disappeared, but at the same time I'm living as if it were still here."

"You and your wife had a good marriage," Maurizio said, looking up at him.

Moroni shook his head. "Quite to the contrary." He began to eat again, and then pushed away his plate and poured himself a glass of wine. "We didn't get along at all . . . Laura was a difficult woman . . . or perhaps I was the difficult one . . . Our life together, at least while she was alive, felt like a torment."

Sergio, who had not expected this response and had until then taken Moroni for a typical inconsolable widower, began to pay closer attention. Maurizio asked: "Why didn't you get along?"

The peasant woman returned with clean plates. Moroni drank some more wine and then dried his mouth. "Why? It would take too long to explain . . . but we just didn't see eye to eye . . . We fought almost every day. If I said white, she said black, and vice versa." Moroni looked at each of his guests in turn. "You won't believe me, but many times I wished, not that she would die, but that she would go away and leave me to my own devices."

"Well," Sergio said, with a slightly mocking tone, "that's what happened . . . You should be glad."

"I imagined," Moroni continued, without acknowledging Sergio's interruption, "that once she was gone, or dead, I would feel as if a great weight had been lifted and I had recovered the freedom to do whatever I wanted. I imagined that day as the most beautiful day of my life. But instead . . ."

"Instead?" Maurizio asked.

"Nothing . . . Not only did I not feel liberated, but I realized that I loved her and that I couldn't live without her." Moroni made a desperate gesture with his hand and then served himself some meat from the platter the servant had brought in.

The topic was so intimate that there was nothing to do but wait for Moroni to go on. After eating a piece of meat, he continued: "For you to understand, I would have to explain many things . . ."

Lalla said affectionately, "Go ahead, why not?"

The other two also insisted, assuring him that they would not be bored. Moroni was convinced. He drank some more wine and continued: "To explain what I feel, I must say first of all that I still love my wife and that I now realize that I was always in the wrong. But in order to understand this, I must tell you about myself."

"Go ahead," Lalla said. 125

Moroni hesitated, then proceeded: "I was born right here in Olevano. My family was large, we were three boys and two girls. We own land and several houses in town. We're not rich, but well off. No need to describe what my family is like, what would be the point. Let's just say, they're typical of their social class and background. As insensitive and unsympathetic as they come."

He spoke with vehemence. After a short silence, he continued: "My grandfather was a farmer and worked hard to be able to stop laboring in the fields. My father was not wealthy, but he earned his fortune through hard work. They're farmers. Behind my life of comfort lie centuries of working the land. We all know what such families are like: mean, hard-hearted, stingy, selfish, insensitive, ignorant . . . You get the idea."

"That's not always true," Maurizio said. "I have known farming families who did not have these defects."

"Perhaps," Moroni said quickly, "but my family had all of them and I was no exception. I was mean, hard-hearted, selfish, ignorant . . . and I continued to be this way for as long as I lived with my family . . . In other words until the day I got married."

"What was your wife like?" Lalla asked.

"She was the daughter of a government employee from Rome . . . well-educated, with a diploma in music. She was studying to be a pianist . . . Then she gave up music, and for the last few years she stopped playing altogether. But there's no point in my talking about my wife," he exclaimed, his voice strained.

"Why?" Sergio asked, surprised.

"Because she's dead, and telling you what she was like explains nothing . . . Any woman would have been unhappy with me, that's the truth . . . no matter what her origins. Simply because she was a woman, that would have been enough. And it's true, she was unhappy with me."

Sergio asked, "But did she love you?"

"Yes, of course," Moroni said, almost offended, "otherwise she wouldn't have married me . . . In my coldhearted way, I sometimes accused her of marrying me for my money. But it wasn't true, and I knew it."

"Was she poor?" Sergio insisted.

"Very poor," Moroni said. He was quiet for a moment, and then continued in his strangely afflicted, contrite tone: "When she was alive, I believed that I was in the right . . . Sometimes I even hated her because I thought she dragged me down . . . Then, as soon as she died, I realized that I had always been in the wrong, always, every moment of our life together . . . and I realized that by fighting against my mean-spiritedness, stinginess, and ignorance, she had changed me . . . I was no longer mean, ignorant, or stingy, or at least I had become less so . . . But by the time the transformation was complete, she had died, perhaps because she had depleted her strength in her effort to change me . . . and I was left alone. I realized too late how she needed to be loved. If only I had not been such a monster."

There was an embarrassing silence. The private subject matter and Moroni's sincere, emotional tone combined with his strange objectivity and humility had left everyone shamefaced. After a long pause, Lalla asked: "What would you have done if she hadn't died?"

"But she did die," Moroni said, bitterly, shaking his head.

"But what if by some miracle she could come back to life?"

Moroni stared at her. "I would treat her differently," he said, very seriously; "I would shower her with the affection I now feel, too late. Love, passion . . . She would be the most beloved woman in the world."

"Are you sure?"

"Yes."

After another pause, Lalla added: "What a shame that she's gone. She did not get to reap the benefits of her efforts."

"It's true."

"So now you would truly love her, for the first time," Lalla insisted as if to convince herself of Moroni's sincerity and seriousness.

"Yes, I would love her . . . No one has ever loved a woman as I would love her if she came back to me."

There was a long silence. Finally Maurizio asked, cautiously: "Why have you told us these intimate things? We barely know each other."

Moroni's response was disconcerting in its sincerity: "I told you this story because of the young lady," he said, looking at Lalla, "because she looks so much like my wife that when I'm with her I can't help talking about her. Please forgive me . . . I've burdened you with my personal suffering. I'm a bad host."

Lalla said in a gentle tone: "Not at all. To the contrary, it was very interesting . . . If we hadn't talked about this, what would we have talked about? This and that, as they say."

Lunch was finished. They went to the sitting room, which was decorated in a very similar style to the dining room. A sense of abandonment and widowhood seemed to emanate from the very slipcovers on the furniture. Moroni was contrite and slightly ashamed of what he had revealed at the table. He circled around his guests, showing an almost overwhelming attentiveness, offering coffee, liqueur, and cigarettes, and asking again and again if his guests needed anything. After finishing her coffee, Lalla said, "I think I'll take a nap. Since we're not leaving until tomorrow . . . I think I'd like to lie down for a moment."

Sergio said that he too would like to lie down. Maurizio took a book from a small bookcase in the sitting room and said he would read. They did not have to ask twice. Attentive, ceremonious, and kind, and still contrite, Moroni led them up to the second floor. There were three rooms, one for Lalla in the middle, with a room on either side for each of the men. Moroni wished them a good rest and went off. Maurizio rushed into his room, book in hand. Lalla pretended to go into her room, and then slipped into Sergio's through a door connecting the two rooms.

Sergio was lying on one of two large walnut beds.
The room was small and filled with large, heavy furniture. Lalla sat down next to him. Raising his head slightly, he saw that she seemed close to tears. After a moment, she took his hand awkwardly. "How do you feel?" she asked.

"Fine."

"Are you angry with me?" she asked, surprised by his curtness.

"Not in the least."

As if trying to start a conversation, she said: "I feel so sorry for Moroni . . . Imagine, after spurning his wife while she was alive, now that she's gone, he loves her so much . . . It must be terrible . . . like what one feels after committing a terrible crime."

"Yes," Sergio said, indifferently, "it must be terrible."

After a moment, she continued: "I'm sure that if he remarries, he will love his wife and be an ideal husband . . . I'm sure of it."

"You're probably right," Sergio said. Then, after a moment: "He seems set on you . . . Why don't you marry him?"

"You must be joking," she said, adding in a tremulous voice: "Do you know what I was thinking as he spoke? That his experience could be a lesson for anyone . . . People should love each other when they are together, because afterward it's too late."

"You're saying this for my benefit, of course."

"Yes," she admitted, frankly, "because you are ruining our love with your resentment and complications. Why don't you just relax, Sergio, why don't you just love me, simply, as Moroni would love a new wife if he had one?" She began to cry and held Sergio's hand, bringing it to her lips and kissing it repeatedly.

Sergio did not withdraw his hand. "But I do love you."

"Maybe you do," she answered, "but you don't show it. You treat me horribly. That day you were drunk, you made a proposal that I don't even want to repeat. I haven't answered you, as you might have noticed . . . and I've been trying to forget it. But you should never have made it, if you love me."

129 "What proposal?" Sergio asked, surprised. He did not remember being drunk, and did not understand what she was referring to.

"You said I should become Maurizio's lover . . . so that he would join the Communist Party."

Sergio knew he was blushing. He was annoyed with himself. He said, drily: "I wasn't drunk . . . and that proposal was serious. I'm still waiting for your answer."

"I refuse to answer," she said, still crying, "and you are a better person than you pretend to be. I truly hope that we will love each other and that our relations will improve. After all, it was all just a question of money. I was unhappy about being so poorly dressed and you were irritated by my complaining. But now you're making money and you've shown your love by giving me money from your advance. My love, if you really love me, why does it displease you so much to show it?"

At first, he did not respond. Then all of a sudden, and almost despite himself, the words poured out: "It was all a lie . . . It's not true that I'm writing a screenplay . . . It's not true that I'm still expecting a second payment . . . Do you know who gave me that money?"

She stared at him, her eyes wide open, as if she couldn't see him: "What do you mean, it's not true?" She pulled her hand away and touched her own face.

He hesitated, and Lalla said: "Whoever it is, why are you telling me?"

"Because I don't feel like lying. The truth," he began, sitting up and looking over at her, "is that Maurizio gave me that money . . . I went to him to ask for a small loan of twenty-thousand Lire so I could buy you a dress . . . and he offered me two hundred thousand, saying that it was shameful for a beautiful woman like you to go around so poorly dressed. And I accepted . . . but I don't want to brag, he's the one who gave me the money and suggested the story about the screenplay. You owe your new clothes to him. I don't make any money and I'm still the same miserable soul I've always been."

Lalla sat motionless, watching him. She seemed almost happy at the revelation: "So Maurizio made up the story about the screenplay . . ."

"Yes."

"But why? Wasn't it simpler to just tell the truth?" 130

"He didn't want you to know."

"He loves me too," she said, in a reflective tone, looking at Sergio. "If he didn't, he wouldn't have been so circumspect." She caressed her dress: "So I owe all of this to Maurizio."

Sergio remembered what she had said earlier: "I'm a whore . . . If someone gives me presents and treats me well, I can't help loving him." And suddenly he became furious; he was overwhelmed by a wave of contempt and a powerful desire to hurt her. He shouted: "Yes, you owe it all to him! So now you will love him, you can't help it! You said it yourself, you can't help loving a man who gives you presents . . . Go ahead and love him, you whore . . ." He leaned over and grabbed Lalla's arm, slapping her several times. He kept repeating "whore," and striking her again and again. Lalla tried to protect herself, but at the same time she seemed to offer her face for him to slap. After two more blows, she turned away on the pillow. Sergio began to pace up and down.

Lalla continued to cry. Then she got up and stood in front of the mirror on the dresser. Sergio was surprised to see that she did not come to him and try to gain his forgiveness for a crime she had not committed. "The other day," she began, slowly, "you asked me to do something and I chose to try to forget and never bring up the subject again. But after the way you've treated me . . . I've decided that I'm going to go to Maurizio's room and do as you ask . . . Afterward, you can make a deal with Maurizio, he can join the Party, or not . . . but if I go, I won't come back . . . Maurizio gave me these clothes, he loves me, he'll treat me well. Why should I stay with you?" As she said this firmly, she walked toward Maurizio's door.

Sergio watched her with a bitter feeling of impotence and jealous rage. He wanted to stop her, to tell her that it wasn't true, that he loved her and did not want her to give herself to Maurizio. But he found that he could not utter a single word. Perhaps Lalla expected, or even hoped, that he would call her back.

131

So it seemed to him from the lassitude with which she walked toward the door. Sergio swallowed hard but remained silent. Lalla slowly opened the door, and Sergio could hear Maurizio's surprised voice asking, "Who is it?" The door closed behind her.

Sergio waited a few moments, almost hoping that she would return. Now that Lalla had done what he had asked, he felt an anguish very much like jealousy. It was an acute, impatient anxiety that came in waves, like the edge of a saw against a tree trunk, or a pendulum: for a moment it would become overpowering, then less intense—a kind of torpor, but still painful. Then another pang, like a loud noise ringing out in the silence, or a wisp of fog lifting to reveal a forest; the pain would rise again, and then die down. He realized that perhaps for the first time in his life, and certainly for the first time with Lalla, he was jealous; until then he had considered her a kind of object, contemptible and without value. He was surprised at his emotions, so unlike the pattern of his relations with her. He could not admit to himself that his jealousy was quite natural, almost humiliatingly so. What disturbed him most was the idea of the sexual act, the notion that the most intimate, hidden part of Lalla's body was now at Maurizio's disposal, revealed for his pleasure. Like all betrayed husbands and lovers, the furor of his jealousy was focused upon the sexual act, upon the cavity that Lalla would offer up to Maurizio's sex. This coarse, objective, barbaric fetishism was unpleasant to him, but he could do nothing to control it: the act, the sexual coupling, tormented him. He was like other men: farmers, workmen, the simplest of people. As he lost himself in these reflections and images, he strained to hear what was happening in the next room. As yet, he had heard no sighs, no creaking springs, nor any other sound that might accompany lovemaking. Almost involuntarily, he got up and pulled a revolver from one of the pockets of his overcoat, where he had put it that morning. Like a sleepwalker, he opened the door to Maurizio's room.

He expected to see them naked on the bed in an embrace. Instead, the room was bathed in a white, tranquil light that streamed in through the window, which was filled with the white afternoon sky. Maurizio sat in his shirtsleeves, completely dressed, on the bed next to the dresser, smoking. He barely raised his eyes toward Sergio as he entered the room. "What's wrong?" he asked, calmly.

"Lalla's not here," Sergio muttered.

"No, clearly, she's not," Maurizio answered, simply. "Unless she's hiding in one of the closets . . . You may look if you like." His tone was sarcastic; it was clear from his expression that he knew what had happened between Sergio and Lalla.

Sergio felt ridiculous. The revolver, symbol of his conventional, vulgar jealousy, weighed heavily in his pocket. He sat down. "Wasn't she here?"

"She came in for a moment, but then she ran off."

Maurizio paused before going on: "I could hardly believe it but she did what you promised . . . She came in here to offer herself to me . . . just as we had agreed."

"She offered herself to you?"

"Yes," Maurizio answered, with a kind of cruelty, "she sat right here on the bed, embraced me, and offered me her lips . . . just like that."

Sergio bit his lip: "What did you do?"

Maurizio laughed. "I'll tell you . . . I hadn't expected her to come so soon, or perhaps I just wasn't ready . . . but I turned her away."

"You turned her away?"

"Yes, I felt that my freedom was worth more than her love or her person . . . Faced with the choice of possessing her and becoming a Communist, on the one hand, or not joining the Party and giving her up, I chose the latter."

Sergio observed him in silence. He felt like a man who has long desired an object and decides to buy it at any price, but then overhears another customer who declares it to be of no value; suddenly Lalla, who a moment earlier had seemed irreplaceable, lost all her value and uniqueness. He felt his image of Lalla deflating, losing weight, becoming hollow and deconsecrated; she became a valueless object, like before. As the scale tipped away from his love for Lalla, it tipped more and more toward his political beliefs and Maurizio's conversion. Lalla had been turned away, and Maurizio would not join the Party; Sergio would once again feel inferior to his friend. This thought loomed over him. He remembered the feeling of insecurity and impotence that had taken hold during his first conversations with Maurizio, and his desperate will to overcome his friend's arguments. He saw everything clearly now: on the one hand, there was Lalla, a woman like any other who had been willing to give her body to the dancer at Moroni's party, who was insufferably sentimental, and whose beauty meant nothing, like everything that is not the product of reason; on the other hand, everything he had fought and struggled for. Suddenly he said, in a trembling voice: "But you said you loved her."

Maurizio said calmly: "I did love her . . . or rather I desired her intensely . . . I still do."

"So why did you turn her away?"

"No reason."

"No reason is not an answer."

"Well, it seemed to me that you were getting the better deal."

"Why?" Sergio asked, sincerely intrigued.

Maurizio spoke calmly and slowly: "I'll explain it to you . . . I desire Lalla . . . but if you look closely, what is Lalla? A woman like so many others . . . I have a strong desire to make love to her . . . but this love is not so different from what I could experience, for example, in a brothel . . . I would make love to her on this bed, and then she would get up, return to you, and I would be left with the memory of an embrace which was no different from any other. We're no longer children . . . only children believe that women are irreplaceable . . . But the truth is that women are all interchangeable." He laughed, adding: "I remember something that happened long ago . . . I went to a brothel . . . I was eighteen . . . My cheeks were burning, with a mixture of shame and desire, and I was as nervous as if it had been a romantic assignation. It was the first time I had been to such a place, and I felt intimidated . . . Perhaps because of this, I turned away one woman after another; none of them lived up to my expectations . . . Finally, the madame came over and said, almost affectionately: 'Women are all the same, one is just as good as the next . . . Take it from me, my boy, they're all the same.' I remember she said this with deep conviction, and after that I no longer had the courage to refuse and took the next one who came along . . . I can't remember whether or not I was satisfied with my choice."

"What are you trying to say?"

"I'm trying to say that you are like the Devil in an old fairy tale: you want to buy my soul with Lalla, who is beautiful, yes, but hardly unique . . . But my soul is truly unique, if perhaps not beautiful, and once I've sold it . . . that's it . . . I don't have another. The truth is, everything happened too quickly, but no matter, it just reinforces my conviction that Lalla holds little value compared to what you want in exchange . . . I refuse your offer."

"You refuse . . . ," Sergio mumbled.

"Yes."

Sergio felt that he was going mad. "Don't you real- 135 ize that you desire Lalla intensely? I warn you, you may regret your actions."

"Why should I?"

"Because . . ." Sergio suddenly felt perfectly lucid and eloquent, despite his agitation. "I'll explain that in a moment . . . You said that you were willing to join the Party, isn't that so?"

"Yes."

"And this hasn't changed?"

"No," Maurizio said after a moment.

"Well," Sergio said, triumphantly, "I offered you the chance to join while gaining something for yourself, in other words Lalla . . . That way, you would become a respectable man, and to top that off, you would have the pleasure of possessing Lalla . . . But if you don't accept, your desire to become a Communist

goes unfulfilled, your disgust in your current life-
style continues, and on top of everything else, you
will have to live with the regret of letting Lalla slip
through your fingers. Are you sure you're making the
right choice?"

Sergio felt strong and lucid; he was convinced that
he had Maurizio in a bind. He thought he saw a hint
of worry in Maurizio's eyes. His friend was silent for
a moment, then asked: "What do you mean? I can
change my mind?"

"Whenever you like."

"If I were to ask you to call Lalla back to my room,
you would do it?"

"Yes," Sergio answered, feeling almost drunk.

Maurizio seemed to debate something in his mind.
"All right," he said in a low, hoarse voice, "call her."

Sergio did not hesitate. As if transported by a
magical breeze, he floated out of Maurizio's room
and into Lalla's. Maurizio's analogy, equating Sergio to a Devil who expects a soul in exchange for
earthly gifts, exalted him and freed him from his
last remaining scruples; it endowed him with a kind
of clear-sighted, demonic lucidity. "Yes, I want his
soul; it is the most important thing in the world to
136 me . . . What do I care about Lalla?" He burst into
her room and closed the door behind him. Lalla
was in bed; only her head and one arm were visible above the covers. But she was awake and she
watched Sergio, her eyes open wide. "Come on,"
Sergio said quickly, "go to Maurizio."

"Why?" she asked, surprised.

"He has accepted the deal," Sergio said, almost joyfully; "come on . . . he said yes."

She did not seem to understand. "What do you mean, he said yes?"

"He will convert to Communism if you give yourself to him."

"And what about you?"

"I want you to do it," Sergio said. He paced around the room. Then, hurriedly: "No, don't move . . . I'll call Maurizio. I'll have him come here, it's better." He had the impression that Lalla wanted to say something, but he didn't give her the chance. He opened the connecting door and said to Maurizio, who was still sitting on the bed: "Please . . . come in."

Maurizio smiled slightly as he entered the room. Lalla stared at him, then at Sergio, and remained willfully silent, as if waiting to see what would happen next. Sergio said to Maurizio: "Go ahead . . . I'm leaving," pointing at Lalla, who still lay under the covers with her eyes open wide and one bare arm next to her head. Still smiling, Maurizio went to the bed and slowly caressed Lalla's face. Lalla watched him, still saying nothing. Sergio took a step toward the door, but Maurizio raised one hand and said, in a clear voice: "Don't go."

Sergio felt his heart skip and stopped in his tracks, his hand still on the doorknob: "Why?"

"I want to say something," Maurizio said. "Sit there." He pointed to a chair near the headboard.

Sergio sat down. His heart was beating furiously, and his face was burning. "You fell for it," Maurizio said, slowly.

"What do you mean?"

"You fell for it," Maurizio repeated, sitting at the foot of the bed, his legs elegantly crossed: "I've been 137 waiting for this moment for over a month . . . You fell for it and there's no going back."

"But what do you mean?" Sergio asked once again, in an agitated voice.

Calmly, Maurizio explained: "I'm not in love with Lalla, nor have I ever been. Even though I find her very beautiful and very desirable, I have never desired her and don't desire her now . . . but I wanted to prove something to you. In other words, I too wanted your soul . . . and I knew it would be mine if I convinced you to do certain things . . . You wanted me to become a Communist, and I wanted to show you what Communism can lead to. And one more thing . . . I have no intention or desire to become a Communist . . . I never have . . . Not only do I have no desire to do so, but I have always hated Communism . . . In other words, I am and have always been an anti-Communist. And that is why I became involved in this whole ruse."

"What does that mean?" Sergio asked, aghast.

"It means that while you did your best to convince me to sell my soul for an hour of lovemaking with your woman, I was trying to manipulate you into selling yours . . . by doing something which, when you look back, will make you deeply ashamed . . . In simple terms: I wanted to see whether, in the name of Communism, you would sell the woman who loves you and whom you love. And I succeeded. Judge for yourself which one of us has lost his soul to the other."

"So none of it was true. You weren't tempted by Communism . . . You didn't love Lalla . . ."

"All lies."

"Why did you give her the money?"

"In order to trick you . . . A man who accepts money from his wife's lover is lost . . . And that money was not easy for me to obtain . . . I'm not as rich as you think . . . I had to sell some of my mother's jewels."

"You wanted so desperately to prove me wrong?"

"At least as desperately as you wanted me to sell my soul," Maurizio said, coldly.

"But what have you gained?"

"Just as I said . . . I have proved that you Commu- 138 nists are not as clever as you think . . . You are willing to give away what is real for an illusion . . . and you are capable of dishonorable behavior . . . In other words: I am now in possession of your soul . . . It's almost as if I had it here in my pocket . . . and you will never have my soul."

"So you were always my enemy?" Sergio asked in a breathless voice.

"On an ideological level, yes . . . Of course you are an intelligent, pleasant person . . . but this is quite a debacle for you, isn't it?"

"A debacle?"

"Well, you've done the following," Maurizio said, counting on his fingers; "you've accepted money from me for the woman you love, you attempted to sell her to me, and, when I rejected her, you desperately tried to make me reconsider . . . all of this in order to secure a political conversion that will never take place."

"Perhaps," Sergio said, exasperated, "but you'll be the loser in the end . . . You'll go on living without a positive purpose."

"To the contrary," Maurizio said. "The positive purpose of my life is the opposite of the base actions I have pushed you to commit: a respect for humanity and a rejection of the idea that a person can be used as a means to an end, even a noble one; respect for oneself; and the freedom to choose, a freedom that all men and women possess . . . a freedom which, in Lalla's case, you did not respect."

They heard a scream. Lalla was now sitting upright on the bed, half naked, tired, upset: "Finally, one of you has said something that is true . . . Neither of you has shown any respect for my right to choose . . . You have done so in the name of Communism, and you in the name of anti-Communism . . . You've both treated me like an object . . . but I've had enough."

They stared at her in bewildered silence. She pulled up the strap of her dress and continued, now in a low voice, rendered hoarse by the power of her emotions: "I want to reclaim my freedom . . . I've come to a decision . . . The two of you should go back to Rome today . . . I will stay here with Moroni."

"With Moroni?" Sergio asked, sarcastically.

"Yes, Moroni," she said, suddenly angry. "At least I know that if I decide to marry him, as he wishes it, he will love me . . . without getting mixed up in debates about Communism and anti-Communism . . . He'll hold me in his arms, love me, say sweet things to me, take me, make love to me, make babies with me, and make me feel like I am living with a man made of flesh and blood and not with a marionette like the two of you. You may not realize it, but you're just like two marionettes."

"And what about Moroni?"

"Moroni is different . . . Even if the Communists take over and he loses everything, he will be a man;

the two of you are just puppets without a drop of blood in your veins. Your heads are full of words . . . You're just the same, the two of you . . . Even if things change, for me nothing would change."

Sergio stood up. He realized he had offended her and was suddenly terrified of losing her. "Lalla, please forgive me," he began, "I'm so sorry . . . from now on I'll love you and think of nothing else . . . Of course you're hurt . . . I promise I will never do it again . . . We'll live together and I'll love you forever."

"It's too late," she said bitterly. "Why don't you just go to bed with the Communist Party . . . and he can go to bed with his political party . . . I, on the other hand, will go to bed with a real man . . . Giacomo . . . Giacomo . . . ," she called out, in a loud voice. The door opened and Moroni entered, as if on cue. Lalla called out to him: "Giacomo, come here," and he went to her, standing next to the bed. "From this moment, he is my *fidanzato*," she said. "Take a good look, and then please do me a favor and get out."

Maurizio stood up. "Let's go, Sergio. It's best," he said, with an almost satisfied air. But Sergio insisted, "But, Lalla . . ."

"You don't believe me," she yelled, with a kind of fury, "but I will make love to him right here in front of you, and you can't do anything about it . . . Come here, Giacomo, make love to me," she said, making space for him on the bed, and then bending over to unbutton his trousers. Moroni looked embarrassed. Then she threw her arms around his neck and kissed him, still saying, "Come here, make love to me."

Now feeling less awkward, Moroni began to caress Lalla, with a strange smile on his lips. Sergio could

140 see it was all over for him. He took a step toward the door as Lalla repeated, "Make love to me, make love to me." She was naked to the waist, with Moroni next to her, already half undressed. Sergio and Maurizio left the room; Maurizio walked ahead, with a haste that seemed almost triumphant, merciless. They went downstairs, still pursued by Lalla's voice crying out "Make love to me, make love to me," and finally they stepped outside. Her voice still rang in their ears as they stood in the courtyard. The car was there. Maurizio got in. "It's really better if we leave," he said. In shock, Sergio tried to say something but did not have the strength to oppose him. He climbed into the car, and they left.

[VII]

141 For a long time, Maurizio drove in silence. They had taken the tree-lined road out of Olevano, shaded by leafy, old plane trees, and now they were descending quickly toward the valley. The town loomed higher and higher above them, with its houses perched on the rocks, their stone sides indistinguishable from the smoky gray hillside, punctuated here and there by bushes of capers and broom. As soon as they were on the open road, Maurizio sped up. The speedometer rose to fifty, then to sixty miles per hour. Sergio did not speak; he was still trying to understand the catastrophe that had befallen him back at Moroni's provincial manor. Finally, Maurizio asked, "What are you thinking about?"

Sergio struggled to speak. "I was thinking that I should have stayed in Olevano . . . Why did we leave in such a rush?"

Maurizio answered slowly: "We left because we had no business there . . . Lalla will marry Moroni, and he'll love her, just as she said. We were superfluous."

"I should have insisted," Sergio said, in a desperate tone; "maybe I could have persuaded her."

"Yes, but then you would have returned to Rome and life would have gone back to the way it was, and you would have started to hate and despise her once again. She would have left you in any case."

He was silent for a moment, then added: "It's better this way . . . A woman cannot go on forever in a situation like yours . . . At a certain point the cord breaks . . . I think it happened at just the right time."

"But you never loved her," Sergio said angrily. "I did, and I still do."

"Nonsense . . . You never loved her either . . . You only loved yourself . . . or rather, you loved the Party, which was just an extension of yourself."

"That's not true."

"Yes it is . . . You became a Communist because you weren't strong enough to live on your own merits . . . And then once you became a Communist, you became disenchanted, because you realized that your weaknesses had not changed. So you tried to prove to yourself that Communism is the most important thing, your raison d'être. You had only one way to prove this to yourself . . . by sacrificing Lalla on the altar of your political credo. And that's what you did. Why are you complaining?"

Sergio wanted to say that he was complaining because he felt an acute, powerful, unbearably bitter pain, where just a few hours earlier he had felt security and a conviction of his dominion over Lalla. And that his pain had taken the shape of an unfillable, gaping hole, as if the spot in his heart which until now had been filled by Lalla had suddenly suffered a terrible spasm, revealing its emptiness. But he knew he could not confide in Maurizio. They were not friends. In fact, as Maurizio had said earlier, they were enemies, and there was nothing he could do about it. As if guessing his thoughts, Maurizio added: "You would be less disappointed, or perhaps not at all, if you had a new convert to the cause sitting next to you rather than a complete enemy of your ideas . . . Isn't that right?"

Sergio rebelled against Maurizio's insightful comments. But he knew that his friend was right. He objected: "Even if it were true, I would still love Lalla and be hurt by the idea of losing her . . . I would still lament my loss."

"Perhaps, but not the way Moroni laments the death of his wife . . . If one loves a woman, one must love her as he does . . . One must love her above all else . . . What do you think? Lalla left you because she knew that you did not love her more than the Party, and because she knows that Moroni will love her more than anything . . . Women cannot accept becoming secondary, second fiddle."

Sergio angrily retorted: "Well, at least you're satisfied . . . You think you've won the match . . . You forced me to act dishonorably, you made me lose Lalla, and now you're feeling triumphant, isn't that right?"

"Not at all . . . I'm just as defeated as you are, don't you see? The victory consisted not in defeating one another but in being loved by Lalla . . . She is humanity in its rawest state, the masses, the weak, vulnerable flesh that both of us sought to conquer . . . But we employed arguments that were interesting only to us . . . Meanwhile, we completely forgot the one true argument: love, affection, respect, passion . . . It is Moroni's only argument, and that's why he won."

"What does all of this mean?"

"It means," Maurizio said, once again displaying his pleasant, dreary logic, "that our arguments are interesting only to us, as Communists or anti-Communists . . . but women—in other words, the people—want to live in peace and to be loved for who they are, to fuck and to be fucked. It means that we are predestined by history to be the cuckolds of humanity . . . She betrayed us because we did not love her for who she is, without ulterior motives."

"How clever you are," Sergio said, sarcastically.

"I'm not philosophizing . . . I'm just observing reality . . . I think that when these wars of religion that currently divide the world finally come to an end, someone else will come along and reap the spoils, as the saying goes . . . People want to be loved for themselves . . . When they feel used, they only pretend to believe what we say, and then they run off with the first person who really loves them."

"Do you think Lalla will be happier with Moroni than she would with me or you?"

"Of course . . . Moroni has a very precise, very neat little story, and Lalla fits into it perfectly: he did not love his wife as he should have, Lalla resembles her, he will love her as he was not able to love his wife ... Meanwhile, you were dreaming about the Party, and I had my own cold-blooded business to think of."

"Such as?"

"Myself, my own precious self ... I had myself, and you had your Party ... But for Moroni, there is only Lalla."

He said these words in a calm, definite tone, as the car went faster and faster. The car [. . .]

Version C

As soon as the war ended, two important events 226
happened in my life. The first was that I joined the
Communist Party. I suppose that every man acts for
reasons that are both selfish and disinterested. My
disinterested reasons for joining the Party—from
now on I'll call it "the Party," which is how we refer
to it—were not very different from those of count-
less others who took the same step at that moment,
whether farmers, factory workers, or people of means.
It seems pointless to discuss these reasons, because
the story I want to tell is a very personal one, one that
will allow me to reveal who I am to the world and to
myself. Disinterested reasons, as such, reveal little or
nothing about the self. Quite to the contrary, they are
the patrimony of all men. Suffice it to say that I joined
the Party in good faith, with the requisite sentimental enthusiasm and knowledge of doctrine. As to my
selfish reasons, they were many, and now that I ex-
amine them, I see that they all lead back to Maurizio
and my friendship with him. But let us proceed in
an orderly manner; the subject is rich and, in its way,
full of surprises. I must proceed carefully, in order of
relevance, if I hope to unravel it. So I will go back to
the beginning. One of the many things that Maurizio
accused me of, in his condescending, sarcastic way,
was being an intellectual. He would say: "Intellectuals like you," or "You're a typical intellectual," or even
"Oh, you're nothing but an intellectual." Maurizio's
attitude was not the only thing that made me hate the
word. Like the word "bourgeois" and so many others,

its meaning has deteriorated over time, taking on negative connotations that it did not once have. Today it is almost an insult to call someone an intellectual, and there is no one who, hearing himself referred to in this way, does not feel the impulse to protest. But what bothered me the most was to hear Maurizio utter this word. I felt an unjustifiable attraction toward Maurizio and held him, also unjustifiably, in high esteem and wanted to be his friend. I realized that, despite his maliciousness, he was right: I was, without a doubt, what is normally referred to as an intellectual. In other words, I was an educated person of limited means, unable to enjoy culture as a mere ornament or pastime, forced to write movie reviews for a third-rate newspaper, to translate mystery novels and write articles for the society pages. I was idle and constantly busy, eternally unemployed and always occupied. Even physically, as he often noted, I resembled the perfect intellectual: slight, with a mop of unruly hair and glasses, dressed in casual pullovers instead of collared shirts, in muddy shoes and frayed trousers, my pockets always overflowing with bits of paper. I was an intellectual from head to toe, inside and out, and I knew it. So why did it offend me to hear Maurizio say it? I have already mentioned that the word "intellectual" has become an insult; in addition, I felt hurt that by describing me in this way, Maurizio revealed that he had no doubts about my nature, that he had pigeonholed me forever and ever. In other words, I no longer held any surprises for him: I was an intellectual, and no matter what I did in life, I would never be anything else. What this denied me was the freedom, the margin of autonomy in human relations, that allows us to escape from the mortifying tracks of habit and routine. This hurt me more than the insulting connotations of the word "intellectual" itself. I suppose that one of my self-interested motives for joining the Communist Party was so that I could retort: "You think I'm an intellectual? Well, you may be surprised to hear that I've joined the Party . . . I'm a Communist now. What do you think about that?"

Some will say that becoming a Communist is not 228 the only alternative to being called an intellectual. It's true, I could have gone to work in an office, or become an explorer, a factory worker, a pilot. But we mustn't forget that Maurizio's attitude toward me, his condescending, obstinate contempt, was part of a superiority complex with clear overtones of class: he was rich and I was poor; he came from a powerful, established family and I from an obscure, petit bourgeois background; he was well dressed, elegant, and worldly, while I was unkempt, introverted, and awkward. Perhaps I also joined in order to feel morally superior to Maurizio, so that I could say: "Not only am I not an intellectual, but I can tell you that you are doomed, that you belong to a doomed class, that all your money, your worldliness, your elegance, and your airs will not save you on judgment day, and that day is near. On that day you will be judged and found wanting, and you will be thrown to the curb, like a piece of trash." I didn't think this so much as feel it, with great intensity but always combined with the strange and unlikely attraction that Maurizio inspired in me. Be that as it may, this was certainly my second reason for joining the Party, by which I mean my second, more personal and self-interested reason.

229   There was also a third and final reason, connected to the others: I did not feel my strength to be equal to Maurizio's. And by this I mean my physical presence, because morally I considered myself to be vastly superior to him. I could not change my physical presence; even if I stood on my tiptoes or puffed out my chest, I did not become taller or more robust. But more than height and robustness I felt that I lacked another, more important element of physical presence, the magnetism, energy, and aura of vigor that lead to success in life, more than intelligence or desire. In Maurizio's presence I shrank and shriveled; my breadth, consistency, and energy were diminished. I became small, weak, lacking, empty. His step was surer than mine, his gaze made me avert my eyes, his voice was stronger, and his presence obscured and obliterated mine. In other words, I was a typical intellectual. So it seemed to me that by joining the Communist Party, which was powerful both in numbers and in ideology, I would feel stronger in comparison with Maurizio; I would absorb some of the Party's strength, and it would bolster my own. In the Middle Ages, wretches like me became monks in order to be able to look the arrogant landowners in the eye; well, I became a Communist for the same reason, in order to successfully face off with the arrogant bourgeoisie, as embodied by Maurizio.

I've gone on long enough about the first important   230
event in my life during the postwar period. Now I'll
move on to the second. Up to that point I had never
experienced a great love, only brief affairs with girls I
met here and there, whom I did not love and who did
not love me. But as soon as I returned to Rome from
the countryside where I had been hiding—at the
time, half of Italy was still occupied by the Germans
and the front lay somewhere near Florence—I met
a woman whom I believed myself to be in love with,
and who certainly loved me. Her name was Nella and
we were almost the same age—I was twenty-seven,
and she twenty-three. I met her at Allied Headquarters, where I had gone to inquire about work. Nella
was a typist there. The moment I entered, I was
struck by her appearance. She had a large head with
a great mane of shiny red hair, pale skin with freckles, large golden-brown eyes the color of chestnuts, a
small button nose, and a wide mouth. Her arms and
shoulders were narrow, like a young girl's, but she
had firm, upturned breasts, well pronounced beneath
her thin dress, like an ancient statue. I was struck by
her appearance, but what intrigued me even more
was a certain quality about her that I noticed right
away: her shyness. This shyness was as evident as innocence on the face of a six-year-old; it revealed itself in the apprehensive, almost alarmed look in her
eye, in the care with which she sat at her small desk
in front of a typewriter, and in the embarrassment,
even discomfort with which she responded to my

simple questions. She kept repeating, "I don't know, I really can't say, I have no idea," after which she would turn away to face her typewriter, though her body remained slightly turned in my direction and she lacked the courage to actually go back to work. Finally I said, somewhat impatiently: "*Signorina*, I see that you are not able to answer my questions, but could you please let your boss know that I'm here?" She hesitated. "The major told me that he should not be disturbed." I responded, somewhat aggressively: "The major and his orders can go to hell; I was told to come here, and I want to speak to someone." She blushed deeply, got up without a word, and walked to the door of the British major's office. I could see now that she was quite petite, almost like a young girl, except for her well-developed, womanly chest. Her hips and legs were girlish and thin, and she wore child-like, low-heeled shoes. She traversed the room, went to the major's door, and knocked lightly. The sound of her knuckles against the wood was almost like a bird scratching in its cage. She listened for a moment and knocked again, more loudly now, then disappeared behind the door. A moment later she returned, looking relieved and almost sympathetic. "He will receive you in just a moment," she said with her head down as she returned to her desk. I sat across from her. As she was about to return to her task, I reached across the typewriter and touched her cheek, driven by some unknown demon and strangely attracted by her intense shyness. She sat completely still, staring at me, lips trembling slightly. Meanwhile, I could see that she was blushing from the nape of the neck, up over her pale cheeks, and up to her forehead; the blush

238

shifted like the shadow of a cloud passing above the earth. She continued to sit perfectly still. I reached out to touch her eyes with my hand and felt them beneath my palm, her eyelashes fluttering with a willing, submissive gentleness. Then I touched her forehead and dug my hand into her thick mane. I pulled her head toward me over the typewriter until our lips met. At first she resisted, then, after I held her insistently, she gave in with a moan, her shapely chest pressing against the typewriter keys. Her mouth was slightly ajar and eager, her eyes wide open and filled with a look of anxious, unhappy submission. She looked like a small animal, silent despite my strange, almost violent behavior. I took my time before kissing her, watching her watching me, breathlessly, torso pressed against the typewriter, her head twisted uncomfortably to one side. Her enormous brown eyes looked overwhelmed by this wait, beseeching me as she breathed heavily; more than ever she looked like an innocent, timid animal caught in a trap, waiting anxiously for the coup de grâce. I observed her for a moment longer, deriving an almost cruel satisfaction from her expectant attitude, and then finally I kissed her. At first she struggled, but then her dry, tight mouth relaxed and softened; she separated her lips and returned my kiss with a passion and intensity that amazed me. It was truly as if she had been waiting for this kiss for years, expecting it despite the fact that she had never laid eyes on me before that day. Her impulsiveness 239 revealed a powerful force capable of overcoming her shyness, and something else that I could not quite identify but which moved me intensely. a kind of anxious unhappiness, a tenderness assuaged, a total, passionate devotion. As we kissed, the door behind me opened. The British major's voice rang out; breathlessly, we pulled apart. Calmly, he announced, "*Signorina*, your services will no longer be required." Then he closed the door.

Nella got up from her chair and I followed, feeling dejected and embarrassed. She gathered her belongings in silence: a threadbare purse in which she placed a half-empty pack of cigarettes and some matches, an umbrella no larger than a fan, and a wide straw hat. Apologetically, I said, "I'm so sorry," to which she responded, "It doesn't matter," without looking up. She said this shyly, without the slightest impudence, and yet, there was an almost victorious note in her voice. As I stood there, unsure of what to do, she said simply: "Let's go." She walked beside me, head down, hat in hand. Then she looked up and said: "There is some lipstick on your lips . . . come here, I'll wipe it off." She led me to a half-open door. It was the bathroom; as she closed the door behind her, she went over to the mirror and peered at her reflection. Then she turned around, with the water running, and said, "Come here, let me wipe that off." She pulled a handkerchief out of her bag, moistened it, and, standing on her tiptoes, gently rubbed my lip. I pulled her toward me, and we kissed a second time. I grabbed a corner of her dress and violently yanked it up above her knee. She pulled away, as if trying to break free, but without removing her lips from mine. The anxious, submissive unhappiness I had seen on her face during our first kiss had spread to her whole body, which twisted and pulled in vain as she tried to liberate herself from my grasp. In the end she gave in, as she had before. I turned her around so that her back was to me, and pushed her head down toward the sink, as if to wash her face. I pulled up her dress and took her from behind, standing up, just as a bull takes a cow or a stallion penetrates a mare, except that we were not standing in the middle of a beautiful field, but rather in a narrow space in front of 240 the sink; instead of the sun shining overhead, there was a lightbulb above the mirror; instead of a bubbling brook, the gurgling of pipes. But the feeling was the same: an irresistible, blind, full-bodied impulse, more animal than human. I remember that, as I penetrated her, holding her firmly and pushing up against her back, I pulled her hair and kissed her face and neck with an animal-like gratitude and tenderness, just as I imagine a horse licks its mare while mounting her. Afterward, we ended up in the street almost without knowing how we had arrived there, as if the cloud of desire that had overcome us had also borne us through the building's thick walls and deposited us on the sidewalk, far from the place where our encounter had occurred.

I have described this first encounter in some detail, not in order to indulge in the questionable pleasure of describing such a scene, but to point out something, an aspect which subsequently became an important element of our relationship: contempt. Nella was shy, sweet, chaste, and lacking in vulgarity or impurity, and yet, mixed with my desire, I felt something for her that was very close to contempt. It was this contempt that led me to take her in this manner, in these circumstances, without consideration, respect, or even pity, as if wishing to hurt her rather than love her. Why did I feel this way? I did not know at the time, and have never been able to understand it fully. My contempt had no justification, either in her physical person or in her personality as I came to know it. This mysterious, inhuman, blind emotion, so profoundly unsympathetic, poisoned our relationship from the start and kept me from loving her with the same abandon with which she loved me. When all is said and done, the story I intend to tell is the story of this contempt.

[III]

241 I accompanied Nella to her room in a modest boardinghouse, and then returned to my own furnished room downtown. Once I was alone, I reflected on what had happened, but after only ten minutes, an impulse drove me to leave my bed and telephone Nella. Without hesitating I told her that since I had caused her to lose her job, it was only right for me to try to repair the damage. Why didn't she come and stay with me, live with me? Timidly, hesitantly, she asked whether I wanted her to come right away. Not only had she accepted my offer, but I could tell that she feared I might change my mind. This humble, submissive, and anxious eagerness moved and excited me. As I stood in the hallway speaking to her on the telephone I felt the same powerful, animal-like desire that had led me to make love to her in the bathroom. I answered that yes, of course, this was what

I desired, and that she should pack her clothes in a suitcase and come as soon as she could. "I'll be right there," she answered, her voice so happy that even her shyness seemed to evaporate. I went back to my room to wait for her, and as the minutes passed, my excitement and desire grew. After a wait that at times seemed almost unbearable, the door opened and Nella appeared wearing her wide-brimmed straw hat and carrying a fiberboard suitcase. I took her by the waist and threw her down on the bed. She struggled to remove the hat which, like a child's bonnet, was attached with an elastic under the chin. But I simply couldn't wait and took her again then and there, with her head arched back in the straw halo of her hat, like a modern saint. She entreated me quietly not to hurt her. I collapsed on top of her, my cheek against hers, and slowly removed the hat and spread her red hair on the pillow, kissing her ardently. She stared at me with her big brown eyes full of tenderness, and said nothing. Finally she broke free and began to put away her few belongings, coming and going quietly, diligently, in a way that was both childlike and domestic. Thus began our life together.

We were poor, so poor that after paying the rent or buying something to wear there was practically nothing left over for food. No matter how hard Nella looked for work as a typist, she found nothing, and I had to support both of us with the scarce income from my obscure journalistic efforts. In those tumultuous, miserable years, newspapers popped up and disappeared like mushrooms after the rain and I went from one publication to the next, always searching for work, indifferent to political affiliations. The deep division between the Communists and other political groups had not yet taken hold. I performed the most diverse tasks, from writing for the crime pages to correcting proofs or, most often, writing film reviews. I became the movie critic for a morning daily, which meant that I had to stay up late into the night writing reviews after a premiere. My life became more ordered, though this regularity felt false and unwelcome because I did not love my work and considered it merely temporary. But temporary in comparison to what? This was a question I could not answer; I did not realize at the time that my feeling of transience was an extension of my intellectual nature. And my work was not the only thing I considered temporary; so too my living conditions, my daily routine, and, more than anything, my relationship with Nella. The only thing that felt definitive was my Party affiliation, which was merely symbolic after all and had caused no real change in my life or even altered my manner of thinking or my anxieties in any way. I had expected more, perhaps a kind of complete renewal, but was forced to accept that everything had remained the same and, furthermore, seemed inalterable. This idea disillusioned and tormented me. I told myself that sooner or later I would have to do something to prove that I had become a real Communist, not only by affiliation, but also in spirit. But what? I had no answer, at least for the moment.

I said earlier that this was a difficult period in my life, but in truth it was probably the happiest time I had known up to that point. As is often the case I was quite unconscious of my happiness. In fact, I considered myself to be deeply unhappy. Now, with the benefit of hindsight, I can say that I was mistaken, and can even describe the source of my happiness, a happiness I have never felt since that period. Principally, it was a product of the very poverty that afflicted me, of the challenges in my daily life and the bitterness of my struggle. My happiness consisted in being in touch with myself, bound to myself in the way that soldiers are bound to one another in battle. Solidarity exists not only between two different people, but also within oneself. Well, in those days, I felt in full solidarity with myself. I was in touch with the essential and most intimate part of my being, the part that life, fortune, and comfort tend to lead us away from until we lose awareness of it completely. I lacked purpose and hoped that this purpose would be provided sooner or later by the Party and that one day, when I could clearly grasp the purpose of my life, I would find happiness. I didn't realize that, quite to the contrary, the purpose of life is to be close to oneself, united and in touch with the truth about oneself, and that even the Party, with all its means, could not provide me, or anyone else for that matter, with another purpose than that. Accidentally, I had already attained my aim in life, but I did not know it.

My happiness, which I have only recently become aware of, had another, less inward source. It was also derived from my relations with Nella, relations which from the beginning had been tinged with contempt. My contempt for Nella's clumsy and submissive nature not only impeded me from seeing her many qualities, but also inhibited me from understanding that we were actually very close, that we loved each other. Alas, man spends his life chasing shadows, like the dog in the fable, we often drop a slab of meat already in our possession in order to chase its reflection. My first encounter with Nella at the offices of the Allied radio service had been a rare occurrence: a complete and instant physical understanding, but I was unable to see this and instead considered it a vulgar, easy encounter which under different circumstances would have had no consequence. Our relations continued in the same manner, but I insisted on seeing them as a kind of mortifying, disheartening situation to which I submitted out of weakness and which I hoped to liberate myself from at the earliest opportunity. My wrongheadedness blinded me to the true nature of our relations, which in fact grew out of a pure and healthy love, so seldom experienced in life, and the synonym of happiness.

Our life was monotonous and I remember that this monotony also tormented me. I dreamed of a more varied existence. Later, I realized that boredom and routine constitute the solid, regular backdrop upon which we embroider our actions. We lived in a large, squalid furnished room looking out over a dingy alley in the old quarter. I was always the first to get up in the morning and after washing and dressing as best I could, I would sit down at a table in front of the window, with my back to the room. There, I would work on various translations, mostly from English, boring, ill-paid work with which I rounded out my small income as a film critic. Nella stayed in bed; she needed many hours of sleep and it was not unusual for her to sleep through the morning. I worked in silence, with the book on one side, the typewriter in front, and the dictionary on the other side. The room was quiet and

Nella slept. With the windows closed I could barely hear the street noise—voices from a nearby market, a few cars, the sputter of a motorbike. I worked without pleasure, with a feeling of impermanence and an exaggerated disgust for this impermanence. I worked, I reflected angrily, *just to get by*. In the late morning I would finally hear Nella's sleepy voice wishing me a good morning, and I would answer her casually, without bothering to turn around. I kept working as I heard her rise from the bed, yawn—I imagined she was stretching—and walk around the room picking up clothes, brush her hair in front of the mirror, step out of the room to the bathroom, and return. Finally, I would see a bare arm reaching around my shoulders and her loving eyes would appear, sparkling and tender, beneath a mane of messy hair. She offered me her lips, saying "You haven't kissed me yet today." I kissed her and with that my morning would come to an end, because one kiss would lead to another and another until finally, almost despite myself and not without a certain sense of annoyance, I ended up back on the bed with her. Nella was always willing to make love, at any time of day; but the morning, after she had taken a shower and was still fresh from the soap and water, her body vigorous after ten hours of sleep, was perhaps her favorite. Her childlike face still free of lipstick or powder, her hair still frizzy from vigorous brushing, her naked body solid, muscular, smooth, and clean, she made love with a strong appetite, as if eating a piece of freshly baked bread. Despite the stuffiness of the room and the threadbare, ugly furniture and messy sheets, her cool, healthy body reminded me of the countryside, touched by the

245

spring sun, leaves covered with dew, earth still moist, bathed in the fragrance of stonecrop and mushrooms. We made love for a long time on the cold, messy bed, and then Nella returned to the bathroom, followed by me, after which we usually went out for lunch.

As I've said, I had very little money and was terribly conscious of my poverty. In fact, I was almost obsessed by it. Walking next to Nella I could not help but notice how shabby she looked. She wore little faded blouses like a child, with sweat stains under the arms, and flimsy skirts, deformed and worn-out with use; her stockings had long runs in them like scars, mended with needle and thread. Her shoes were ragged, with worn-out heels that tilted inward or outward. Nella seldom complained, but when she did, it was with a painful intensity that carried the echoes of endless sacrifice. Sometimes I caught a glimpse of her standing in front of a shop window in dreamy silence, gazing at a blouse, a handkerchief, or a skirt. It pained me to see her so poorly dressed, but at the same time it annoyed me slightly when she complained or drew attention to the state of her wardrobe. I was even more disheveled than she; women have a mysterious talent for making clothes look presentable. My trousers were always shapeless and frayed, my jackets had grease spots, and my shirts were filthy and covered in stains. It was just after the war and clothes were hard to come by. I did not have an overcoat; instead I wore several sweaters under a dirty raincoat. Nella had her threadbare little coat. Whenever we passed an elegant shop window and I caught a glimpse of our reflection in the glass, I thought, "There go a couple of bums."

My lack of funds was a constant torment, like a thorn in my flesh that I could not dig out. When we went out to eat, it became a cruel nuisance, not so much because I wanted to spend more, but because it forced me to make humiliating choices: If Nella ordered this or that item, would I be able to order fruit? Could we afford two main dishes? I must say that Nella always tried to spend as little as possible. But her restraint also felt like a complaint or a reproach. It would almost have been a relief to have her order what she really wanted instead of worrying about whether I would be able to pay.

We ate at very modest trattorias, frequented by other people like us—in other words, to use the term I detest, intellectuals, as well as factory workers and lowly office employees. As we sat across from each other at a table lined with paper, with worn-out cutlery and simple earthenware dishes, Nella would smile at me tenderly and happily, holding my hand in hers. I could sense that she knew how to fully enjoy the good moments in life, as well as how to forget life's challenges and the larger questions that make us suffer deprivation even more intensely. I envied her and told myself that I should try to imitate her, but I simply couldn't. I could always feel something hard, painful, irremovable coming between me and happiness: lack of money, or the Party and my lack of purpose, or the fact that Nella did not understand me and never would, beyond the basic level of love and tenderness. I sulked in silence, scowling, unresponsive to her touch, irritated with myself and with her. She would ask what was wrong, why I was so preoccupied, and I would give vague, insincere answers, mumbling something about work, or being tired, or anything else that came to mind. She believed me, or 247 pretended to, realizing perhaps that she would not be able to penetrate the real reasons for my ill humor. Then the waiter would bring our food and we would eat in silence.

After lunch we would walk home slowly down the narrow, ancient streets of central Rome. She threw herself on the bed and I lay down beside her. We slept in each other's arms, Nella relaxed as always, and I, as usual, beset by the nagging sense that such intimacy was a betrayal of my true self and my goals. But who was I, and what were these goals? At the time I did not know, and even now I could never admit it openly, but my main goal consisted simply of rejecting the present, including my love for Nella, and my fixation with underlining the impermanent, incidental nature of my circumstances. I never let myself go completely; even in moments of abandon, a part of me kept its distance, observing the scene, holding back. This constant effort, the irrepressible impulse not to give myself to Nella in the way that she gave herself to me, was so clear that even she, so blinded by her love, eventually noticed. "Why can't you just love me as I love you? You don't want to love me, that's the truth . . . You can't let yourself go." I would assure her it wasn't true, but I knew I was lying. She would sigh with resignation and almost a kind of foreboding: "One day you'll realize that you've ruined everything . . . but it will be too late."

Later I would get up and return to my table, to my translation work. Nella would stay in bed a bit longer, dozing, or pick up a book and read, resting on one elbow. Every so often she would stop and say something, as if to reassure herself that I hadn't forgotten her. It was difficult for her to resist coming over to kiss or caress me. After a while she could no longer hold back; she would come up behind me and ask: "Haven't you finished yet?" in a sulky, unhappy voice. Or she would tiptoe up and kiss me hard, making my ear buzz for the next five minutes. "Don't you know that you have to leave me in peace when I'm working?" I would say, roughly. "I'm sorry," she would say, humbly, "but I couldn't resist." Then she would climb ²⁴⁸ back onto the bed and read while I continued with my work. Later, she would get up and begin to carefully prepare her toilette. Finally, when her patience had run out, she would say, "I'm going down to the café," and disappear. I breathed a sigh of relief—somewhat insincere, I knew—and worked for another half hour. Then I too went out.

I would meet her at the café, a squalid little back room at a neighborhood spot. Sometimes she would be there alone, sitting in front of an espresso, more often she was joined by friends and acquaintances, intellectuals and their girlfriends. They passed the time discussing, debating, and commenting on the day's events, until dinnertime. In the evening at the trattoria, I felt the same anxiety and ill humor as I had earlier at lunchtime. We did not eat much in the evening, and sometimes we skipped dinner altogether and ate sandwiches and beer at the bar on our street. When I had money, Nella accompanied me to the movies, otherwise she would go home and I would go to the movies alone. I sat and watched the film with a growing sense of futility, frustration, and irritation: nine times out of ten the movie was a worthless waste of time. Even so, I had to write a review, if only to point out its shortcomings. I would run to the newspaper offices and quickly scribble a review on any available surface. Then I went home, where I would find Nella half-asleep on the bed with her thick mane of hair spread out over the pillow and her slender shoulders. I undressed quickly and climbed under the covers, and she immediately turned over and pressed herself against me with all the strength of her youthful, fresh body. That was the moment when I loved her the most, or rather gave myself most fully to my love. I was tired, worn out, disgusted with myself, more uncertain than ever about my future, and sickened by my work. These embraces were like a refuge and a consolation after an absurd, hopeless day. In the dark, I encircled her tightly in my arms, dug my face into the firm, feverish tenderness of her breasts; I bit her and caressed her with a feeling of sweetness mixed with rage. It felt as if by embracing her I became a child again and found a lingering trace of maternal consolation in her trembling, exposed flesh. Sometimes as I embraced her my eyes welled up with tears; I was thankful that the darkness concealed my weakness. With those tears I expressed the bitterness accumulated throughout the day. With a sort of sixth sense, Nella often asked me, tenderly: "Why are you crying? Why are you crying?" Then she would hold me tightly in her child-like arms, pressing my face against her soft, womanly breast. After a long pause, when she felt she had consoled me, she would turn around and press her hips against my groin; I would encircle her waist with one arm and her chest with the other, and penetrate her slowly in the dark. I remained inside of her, pacified, and fell asleep. We stayed there like this, locked in an embrace, until morning.

I have described in detail a day in my life in order to paint a picture of my daily existence at the time; every day was the same, and this monotony was one of the reasons for my unhappiness and my dissatisfaction. As I have mentioned, at the time I was waiting for something to change, even, if necessary, for the worse, but I did not know what, and I had the vague suspicion that nothing would change if I did not decide to take action. But why and how was I supposed to act? I did not have the answer, and so I waited. As I said before, my sense of expectation gave me a false impression of my life and hid its true, positive reality: Nella, my love for her, her love for me. I was fascinated by the mirage of a remote oasis where I would finally be able to drink from a bubbling but as yet unreal spring, and I did not realize that I was already standing in a corner of this oasis, with palm trees all around, surrounded by cool shade and with a spring at my feet, full of limpid, cool water.

[IV]

I had forgotten about Maurizio, or rather I never thought about him explicitly, but in the deepest corner of my consciousness I knew that our paths would cross sometime in the future and that the silent battle we had been fighting since childhood would continue.

This certainty had become almost an unconfessed desire: the truth was that I wanted him to reappear and for our battle to resume. I felt that my membership in the Communist Party, which had been triggered mostly by feelings of inferiority, would reveal its true meaning only when I had achieved victory over Maurizio, or at least engaged in a confrontation with him. As I've said, I still felt impotent, mortified, aimless, and uncentered, despite my Party membership. And I had a sneaking feeling that this impotence, mortification, aimlessness, and uncenteredness would be dispelled if I found someone or something to fight against. In theory, this was true, and perhaps not only in theory. Even those who, like me, were not activists and whose political activities were limited to joining up and socializing with other Party members, even we imagined a world in which the conflict between Communist ideals and the various forces that opposed them was a question of life or death. But we do not live on ideals alone; in any case, I could not do so. I felt that this struggle must become something personal and compelling, something direct and specific, in order to be truly transformative and constructive. I also felt, for some reason, that Maurizio embodied everything I was struggling against in this dark, challenging moment we were living. Perhaps it was my own strange and very human rivalry with Maurizio that led me to believe this. We will never know what comes first, the idea or the human impulse; this question does not intrigue me. I felt the struggle to be real, powerfully so, and that was enough for me.

I did not seek him out. For some reason, I was sure that he would reappear, in the way that certain profound, important things in our life often do, at regular intervals. What was the basis for my certainty? The equally unspoken, hidden knowledge that without Maurizio I did not fully exist, that he was my other, negative and baleful half, without which everything that I considered positive and good for humanity could not exist, neither in myself nor in the world.

One evening after dinner Nella and I went out to a 251 café where we usually met with our friends to engage in the same discussions until past midnight, night after night. But for some reason on that particular evening the café was empty; our friends had apparently made other plans. We stopped at two or three other cafés in the neighborhood, but they too were empty. I was in an especially surly mood—I can't remember why—and Nella, who tended to react to my ill humor with tenderness and caresses, was getting on my nerves. Finally we sat down at a café with a few iron tables and chairs, illuminated with tubes of blinding neon light. We were the only people there. It was a small room with high ceilings, a dirty floor, and empty tables. After a mediocre coffee, I began to pick on Nella, as usual. The point of departure was always the same: for one reason or another, I would start talking about politics and the Communist Party, and my conviction that the Party would soon come to power. But instead of reacting enthusiastically to my revolutionary dreams, Nella received them, as usual, with innocent, uninformed indifference. I had convinced myself that a revolution was imminent. In my state of befuddlement, mortification, and impotence, this idea was the one source of light I could see for the country as well as for my own personal existence. It was practically impossible for me to accept that my conviction and sincere, almost mystical hope for change, inspired by my resentment toward the political leadership that had brought Fascism to power and forced Italy into war and catastrophe, was not shared by Nella. My noble ideals sailed right over her head, like a cannon shooting into the air. She, on the other hand, attached herself tenaciously to the only real thing that existed between us, our love, and, as was becoming increasingly clear, she could see nothing beyond this love. I tried to explain to her, with abundant ideological, psychological, moral, and political arguments, why revolution was inevitable and desirable, but I could see that she was distracted. Her attention was focused only on me, no matter what I said. If I had been discussing idle gossip rather than pouring out fervent arguments for revolution, it would have been exactly the same to her. I could sense her lack of interest in the way she nodded, saying "yes, yes," as one does to a child whom one loves and has no intention of contradicting. She did little things that revealed what really mattered to her at that moment: loving me, being close to me, living with me. As she assented to my arguments, she would take my hand and kiss it, still pretending to listen. Or she would gently provoke me by pressing her leg against mine, seeking a more intimate, distracting contact. I would exclaim: "You don't care about what I'm saying." To which she would answer, with almost mystical abandon: "I always agree with you, no matter what you say." This irritated me even more. "Come on, Nella, what if I'm wrong? You have to contradict me if you disagree." She would confess, humbly, "You are so much more intelligent than I am . . . of course you're right." "So you agree that the revolution is coming?" "Of course, if you think it is," she would say, taking my hand and kissing it passionately. "Don't kiss me . . . Why don't you think for a moment?" "I'm sure it will come . . . and no matter what happens, I'll always be beside you, always . . . I'll never leave you." "But that's not the point!" I would finally exclaim, exasperated. "You have to reason, use your brain, think!" "I do, I think I love you." "You're an idiot, a stupid, silly thing," I would say, brutally detaching my hand and pushing her away, "you're nothing but a piece of meat, a sex, a being without dignity, without autonomy, without freedom." "Don't be angry with me," she would implore; "why are you so cruel to me?" These last words were said in a strange, cloying voice tinged with surprise. Even now that we are no longer together, I can still hear her: "Why are you so cruel to me?"

I remember that on that evening, as I was explaining for the hundredth time why I believed that a revolution was imminent, she took my hand and began to press it against her cheek, kissing my palm passionately from time to time and gazing up at me from beneath her red mane with her big brown eyes, full of love and admiration. It was clear that the emptiness of that little room excited her and awakened in her a desire to make love in some dark corner, just steps from the door. What irritated me even more was that I too was becoming excited at her touch and was beginning to have trouble following my own complicated reasoning. Suddenly filled with fervor, I asked: "Don't you agree?" She pressed my hand and put her face close to mine, saying, "To me, you're always right . . . but now, kiss me . . ." Earlier, I described Nella as timid and passive, discreet, and extremely demure. But when it came to love she was brazen and quite unashamed, though her manner remained innocent and awkward. I must admit that these were the qualities I most admired in her, and which excited me the most. But at that moment, after the effort I had put into explaining my ideas to her, her insistent talk of love and kisses filled me with rage. "Enough!" I said, in a loud, trembling voice. "I try to talk to you and all you do is rub against me . . . Leave me alone . . . You're like an animal . . . Leave me alone!" She held my hand tightly and, not paying attention to my furious words, pulled me very close, offering her lips. At the same time, she slipped one leg on top of mine, almost climbing on my lap, revealing one knee and part of her thigh. As I pulled away, I slapped her, brutally giving release to the discontent I had felt on that and many other evenings. She stared at me in surprise, still holding my hand. Finally she let go, wide-eyed, but still rested her leg on mine. Two enormous tears appeared, filling her eyes and pouring down her cheeks. Now furious at myself for my brutal, stupid action, I tapped the plate with my spoon and called the waiter. Nella pulled away her leg but continued to cry quietly without drying her tears, sitting still and straight with her eyes wide open. After paying the astonished waiter I got up as if to leave. "I think it's best if we go to bed," I said curtly. She followed me in silence, still crying.

As we walked out into the narrow street, just a few steps from our door, a slow-moving car almost hit us, and we were forced to step aside and press our backs against one of the buildings. As the car rolled by I turned to protest, still furious from the scene in the café, and the car came to a stop. It was a large model, old-fashioned but quite luxurious. A figure leaned out of the window. I heard a surprised voice: "Sergio, is that you?"

I was still so angry that I found myself at a loss for 254 words. I stared in the direction of the voice; a man leaned his head out of the car but I didn't recognize him and could barely make out his face. "Don't you recognize me? It's Maurizio," he said, and suddenly, like a shipwreck victim who finally catches sight of a ship on the horizon after staring into an empty, pitiless sea, I called out, "Maurizio!" I don't know if I felt happiness or relief, or something even more profound. In any case, my reaction was involuntary and automatic.

"Finally!" Maurizio said, in a tone that was already less intimate and bore a trace of irony. He opened the car door, saying, "Get in, get in . . . I haven't seen you in ages! Get in, we'll talk."

"I'm not alone," I said, not moving.

Maurizio answered calmly: "I can see that . . . Well, why don't you both get in?"

I took a step as if to get into the car. But Maurizio's voice, now completely sarcastic, stopped me in my tracks: "I see you haven't changed . . . head still in the clouds . . . Why don't you introduce us?"

I thought to myself: "Here we go, right from the start, putting me in my place and making me feel inferior. He can go to hell." I gave Nella a little push and said: "Nella, this is Maurizio."

"Pleased to meet you," Maurizio said, taking Nella's hand. Timidly, she mumbled a few words. "Here, climb in next to me," Maurizio said, pointing to the front seat, "there's enough space for all of us." Without a word, Nella climbed in next to him and I followed. Maurizio shut the door and we set off.

Maurizio drove a short distance without saying a word. Nella was sitting next to him in an embarrassed, almost fearful position, pressed against my side, as if afraid that he might touch her. I had placed my arm on the headrest and could almost touch Maurizio's neck. As we turned onto a larger, more brightly illuminated street, I glanced over at him, scanning his profile as he drove. I hadn't seen him in four years, but at first he did not seem changed. His face was still pale and perfectly smooth beneath his dark hair, which was not exactly curly but, just as I remembered, had a slight undulation and a kind of liveliness, falling in long, graceful waves at his temples and on the nape of his neck. His eyes were black, deeply set and slightly hollow, and there was a look of concentration and sharpness about him, oblique and fierce, like a predatory bird. But something had changed: his mouth, which I remembered as having a particular, almost contemptuous, even slightly cruel expression, was now partly hidden by a short mustache that almost completely covered his upper lip. There was something slightly unreal about it; in my mind I continued to see Maurizio's mouth as I remembered it, without the mustache, and the two images did not quite coincide; instead, they seemed superimposed. It was almost as if he were wearing a mask which I could see, while still remembering his real face underneath. The dimple in his willful, shapely chin seemed to underscore his domineering, obstinate nature. As if sensing my gaze with his highly developed awareness, he was silent and still as I watched him. As soon as my curiosity was satisfied and I turned away, he began to speak. "Let's go to the Gianicolo," he said; "it's a beautiful night . . . We can talk in peace . . . unless the *signorina* would rather go to a café . . ."

The car turned off of the Corso and sped down Via del Plebiscito toward Largo Argentina. It was still early and the streets were illuminated and full of cars. The car turned onto Via Merulana; we crossed the Ponte Garibaldi and took the Viale del Re. "You keep staring at me . . . do I look so different?" he asked.

Somewhat disconcerted, I said: "Not at all . . . except for the mustache."

"Left over from the war . . . I had a beard when I was with the *partigiani*."

So he had been with the *partigiani* and he was letting me know, I thought to myself. It was almost as if he knew that I had done nothing, that during the civil war I had stayed in Rome and hadn't even bothered to hide, since I wasn't on any list. Once again I sensed the feeling of inferiority that had so deeply marked my relationship with Maurizio. I wondered whether I should tell him that I had joined the Party, but decided to wait. He added: "I'm sure you haven't changed . . . I don't even need to look at you; I'm sure you're still the same."

"Well, I've changed too," I couldn't help saying, with a touch of irritation in my voice. "I haven't grown a mustache, but I've changed."

"In what way, I'd like to know? When I spotted you, I thought you looked exactly the same . . . still that intelligent look . . . always the intellectual . . ."

I felt a sense of profound exasperation; once again, he was accusing me of being an intellectual. "I see your opinion hasn't changed."

"What do you mean?"

"You still think that intellectuals are good for nothing."

"Why do you say that?" He feigned surprise. "I only said that you looked like an intellectual, not that you looked like a good-for-nothing."

Once again he was right, and once again I had revealed my own weakness. I bit my tongue out of exasperation and said, "I know that's what you believe."

"No, actually, that's not at all what I believe," he said, quite seriously.

Meanwhile, we had turned onto Via Dandolo and were speeding up the spiraling road, swerving around each turn in the shade of the tall trees. I felt Nella's hand reach for mine, and once again, I became irritated with her. It seemed to me that she had noticed Maurizio's effect on me and wanted to console me with her gesture, and assure me of her solidarity and affection. Almost violently, I pulled my hand away and said with ill-concealed bitterness: "So neither of us has changed . . . that's the truth of the matter."

After a long series of uphill turns, we finally arrived at the square in front of the Fontana dell'Acqua Paola. Maurizio drove up to the stone parapet and turned off the motor. For a moment we sat in silence. Then Maurizio said, "Let's stretch our legs," opening the car door. We climbed out and went over to the stone wall, gazing down at the sparkling lights of the darkened city. I was eager to reveal that I had joined the Party; it was the most important news in my life, and also the newest weapon in my struggle with Maurizio. But I wanted to approach the subject gradually: "So," I asked in the dark, "do you still live in your old villa on Via Bertoloni?"

"Yes," he answered, distractedly.

"With your parents?"

"My father is dead. I live with my mother."

"And your sister?"

"My sister?"

"Is she married?"

"No."

"Do you still give parties with music and dancing?"

"Sometimes."

"And cocktail parties?"

"Yes." He was silent for a moment. "We had a party just the other day in honor of my Allied friends . . . If we'd crossed paths earlier, I would have invited you."

"Do you still have a butler and staff?"

My tone had become clearly sarcastic. Still he answered with the same calm confidence. "Yes, that's right."

"Do you still live off of your annuity?"

"More or less. But I also work."

"What do you do?"

"I work in the movies."

"In what way?"

"Oh, it's not much . . . I'm in business with a small producer."

Cautiously, I asked: "So you were with the *partigiani*?"

"Yes, in the North, in the Veneto."

"What party were you affiliated with?"

I was so used to having him slip through my fingers that for a moment I was afraid he would say that he had been with the Communists and that my secret weapon would be obliterated before I had even had the chance to use it. But he said, with the same calm air: "Oh, no party in particular . . . I'm more or less a liberal, if you must know my political allegiance."

I hoped he would ask me about myself, but he didn't. Instead, he said, "Let's talk about other things . . . It's such a beautiful night, and this is such a beautiful view." I detected a decidedly ironic note in his voice. In fact, after a moment, he added: "You're just being your usual intellectual self . . . you can't relax even for a moment."

"I'm not an intellectual," I couldn't help saying. "The reason why I like to discuss such matters even while gazing out at the view on a beautiful night is that I'm a Communist. I joined up after the war."

He said nothing. "The revolution is coming," I blurted out, "and when it does, there will be no place in it for people like you."

He did not respond to my attack. Instead he turned to Nella, unexpectedly, and asked her: "*Signorina*, are you a Communist like your boyfriend?"

I was surprised to hear her respond, shyly but firmly: "I haven't joined the Party, but I agree with Sergio, naturally." I felt her hand squeeze mine, and again felt irritated by the gesture, taking it to mean that she thought I was weak, despite my political affiliations, and needed her help. But I also felt a tinge of gratitude, and could not help squeezing her hand as well. Maurizio insisted: "Do you also believe that soon it will be the end of the road for the likes of me?"

"Yes."

"I see," he continued, "so we're class enemies."

"That's right," I said triumphantly.

"Well," he said, after a short pause, "that shouldn't keep us from being friends, at least until the revolution comes."

I detected a sincere, friendly tone in his voice, and all of a sudden, as if pushed by an unexpected inspiration, I said: "We've always been friends . . . and I hope that before that day comes, we will become even more so."

"What do you mean?"

259

"I hope that eventually you will feel the same way I do . . . Then we will not only be friends, but also comrades."

He was silent for a moment. I hoped he would say "perhaps"; I had never loved him as I did at that moment. But instead, after a long silence, he said, slowly: "Unfortunately, at least for the time being, I'm not looking for comrades . . ."

"Go to hell," I thought, with some disappointment. Instead, I said, "You never know."

As if struck by my good sense, Maurizio answered, "Yes, that's true, one never knows."

We remained there, gazing silently at the panorama. Finally, just as I was thinking, "Now I'll tell him that I need to go home . . . He shouldn't get the idea that I enjoy his company," he suddenly took the initiative, saying brusquely, "I'll take you home . . . It's late."

I bit my lip and followed him to the car. We did not speak during the drive. At a certain point Maurizio asked Nella, "Where do you live, *signorina*?" With a slight note of satisfaction, she said, "with Sergio."

When we arrived at our destination, he got out of the car and helped Nella to the curb. "Listen," he said, "I have a few friends coming over on Sunday. I'd love it if you would join us . . . That is, if you don't mind spending time with a bunch of capitalists."

I answered that we would love to come and thought I detected a happy note in Nella's voice as she said, "Of course, we'll be there." Once again, I became annoyed with her. Then the car drove away and we went inside.

[V]

260 In order to make clear how important this meeting was to me at the time, I should reiterate how firmly I believed in the imminence of a revolution in Italy. I was as convinced of it as I am of writing these words today. It seemed impossible that the disorder, poverty, corruption, and social disintegration which had befallen the country in those years would not lead to a revolution. I had no doubt that as soon as the Allied forces left, a revolution would break out, destroying everything in its path. But even more than the conditions in the country, what drove me to believe this was something that lay in the deepest recesses of my soul, something that I considered to be the only firm, luminous reality in my life, buried beneath the contradictory passions, the impotence, and the darkness. It was my rapt, ineffable, almost mystical hope for a

better world, one where I would finally feel happy and at peace. It is impossible to explain in words what this hope meant to me; such feelings can be understood only by those who have experienced them. I can only say that my hope, which rendered the day-to-day reality that surrounded me almost unbearable, conjured a not-too-distant mirage of an almost perfect human society; it was my firm belief that the cruel imperfections of the present world were the result of social ills which the revolution would eliminate. Depending on one's point of view, this mirage could be described as deceptively utopian, or as an achievable goal. I suppose that those who find pleasure in the world as it is, who love reality and do not believe that things can improve except in certain limited circumstances, would see this hope as a pipe dream. And those who do not see it as a mirage in the true sense, or who prefer this mirage to reality—because it creates a goal that is not immediate or material and allows them to project the best part of themselves upon that goal—fall into the category that is vulgarly referred to as idealists. I was an idealist, a concept which has become quite ridiculous in our time but which originally had a very precise meaning. I did not approve of the world as it was, either socially or personally; in other words I loved neither the world nor myself, and thus it was logical that I should believe in something that seemed to promise both a better world and a better self.

I imagine that such sentiments might drive a more simple man to religious exaltation; in the past, they might have driven even a cultivated man to such religious zeal. But I was not a simple man; as Maurizio liked to say, I was an intellectual, and

261

we were no longer living in the Middle Ages, but rather in the twentieth century. Communism, whose theories I had studied in depth, seemed to provide a blueprint which, through mathematical calculations and hypotheses based on real-life experience and concrete, undeniable values, would lead to the construction of a solid edifice in the near future. I had examined Communist theory from every angle, and I was increasingly impressed by how closely enthusiasm and calculation, psychology and statistics, theory and practice, history and utopianism, means and ends, were bound together. Communist theory was like a marvelously well-built machine, in which moral and human factors fit together perfectly. In a century marked by scientific progress, Communist theory, which was ultimately as dependent on faith as Christianity, had the advantage of being expressed in the language of our time, which was not religious but scientific. In other words, Communist theory represented the embodiment of the ancient dream of total palingenesis, if one believed—as I did—that science was man's truest path toward pulling himself out of the dark ages.

There was something else, in addition to my exalted, mystical hope and my confidence in science, which confirmed both my hope and my confidence: my acute, absolutely real sense of the decadent, faded, empty, spent, worn, tired state of the world that Communism intended to banish, by which I mean the world of which Maurizio was an amiable but typical representative. I felt that this world was irreparably doomed, not only in the vague future—one can say this about all living things—but now, in the very near future. The corruption and stultification of Maurizio's world, which I sensed not only intellectually but even physically, could not go on for much longer. The world that blocked the way toward Communism was to me like a majestic old tree which has been devoured from the inside by insects, sustained only by its bark, so weak that it could be knocked over by a child despite its enormous size. Of course I realized that not everyone could see the internal corruption of that world, but it seemed to me that it would soon be apparent to all. I was simply more informed and more prescient. But soon, everyone would know that the tree was only a pile of dust. And then the revolution would erupt, as they say, spontaneously.

It is likely that my state of mind, which was more one of certainty than one of expectancy, rendered me particularly insensitive to the small complications of daily life. Maurizio's invitation gave me the sense of once again entering into a dialogue with him, a healthy exchange of ideas, but it also forced me to face certain challenges that I normally tried to ignore by losing myself in dreams of total palingenesis.

The invitation was for seven-o'clock—in other words, it was a cocktail party. Nella and I spent the afternoon at home; I worked on my translation while Nella lay on the bed reading as usual. She was a bit agitated; several times she interrupted her reading to kiss me behind the ear, or to speak to me from the bed, or to complete some small task or walk around the room. I knew what was bothering her: our visit to Maurizio's. I knew it because I also felt the same agitation, and for the same reason. Thus, after she had listlessly picked up and laid down her reading several times and I had listlessly forced myself to continue working, we finally reached the end of the afternoon. I glanced at my watch and shut the dictionary, covered the typewriter, saying, as I rose from the table: "I think it's time to go to Maurizio's."

There was no answer from the bed. I turned toward Nella and saw that she was lying on her back with one arm under her head, staring up at the ceiling. She was wearing only her slip, her breasts and arms bare. I said quietly: "Come on, get dressed . . . it's time to go."

Finally, she answered me in an obstinate tone I had never heard: "You go . . . I'll stay here."

I went over to the bed, surprised, and asked: "Why don't you want to come? He invited you as well."

"I don't feel like going . . . You go . . . I'll wait here."

263   Now more irritated than surprised, I asked: "What's wrong with you? Why don't you want to come?"

"I just don't."

"That's not an answer."

"It's the only answer I can give you."

I sat on the bed and took her hand. "But why? Don't you like Maurizio?"

"No, that's not it," she said, breaking free almost rudely. "I don't have anything against him . . . I don't mind him at all."

"So what is it?"

"You go . . . I'm not coming."

I realized that I would get nowhere with this indulgent tone, and instinctively switched to a more heavy-handed approach. I leaned over the bed where she lay with her head resting on one arm, and grabbed her by the hair, demanding, in an irritated tone: "Why are you being so stubborn?"

Now she seemed to realize that she would have to give me an explanation for this mysterious attitude. She broke free, jumped up from the bed, and walked, barefoot, to the closet containing her few clothes. She opened it and pulled out a hanger with a dress, practically throwing it in my face: "This is the only thing I have to wear to your friend Maurizio's party . . . a dress from before the war . . . Look, the armpits are discolored by sweat . . . It's been mended many times over and it's completely out of style. I don't want to be embarrassed in front of the women who will be at the party, dressed up in new clothes. I'd rather stay at home . . . that's why I'm being so stubborn." She said this in a tone of almost painful relief. Then she pulled up her slip and showed me her leg: "Look at these stockings . . . They're full of runs . . . It's the only pair I own, or rather I have another pair but they're in even worse condition . . . They'll all laugh at me . . . No thanks . . . I'd rather stay home."

She said these words in a childishly spiteful voice which would have made me laugh if I had not already been so irritated with her. She came back and placed one knee on the bed, as if she was about to climb in. This obstinate gesture pushed me over the edge. Once again I grabbed her by the hair and pulled her toward me. "You're coming," I said, furious.

She twisted her face, staring at me angrily, as I held her in an uncomfortable position, twisted sideways. "No, I'm not," she said.

"Yes, you are."

"I won't go," she repeated, still talking out of one side of her mouth as I pulled her uncomfortably toward me. "You want to humiliate me . . . That's your aim . . . You want to humiliate me in front of your friend by making me look like a beggar at his party. I won't go."

I don't know why, but this trumped-up accusation made me even more furious. As I reflected later on the scene, I realized that there was a grain of truth to what she said. My aim was not so much to humiliate her but rather to use our poverty—so clearly denoted by our clothes, especially hers—as a challenge and rebuke to Maurizio's wealth. But I did not realize this fully at the time. To the contrary: I felt the accusation to be completely false. "You idiot!" I yelled, "why would I want to humiliate you? What would be the point?"

"I don't know . . . but you do, you want to humiliate me and you don't realize that it will be worse for you if I come . . . People will think that you don't care about me when they see that you let me walk around dressed like this."

"What do I care what they think? You know it isn't true . . . I can't make any more money than I do now . . . and that's all there is to it."

For some reason, I was filled with a terrible rage. Deep down I admitted to myself that, just like my inscription in the Communist Party, I saw Nella as another weapon in the arsenal I was building against Maurizio. She reinforced my position by loving me, and sustained my presence with hers. Now she was denying me this weapon. But it is possible that my rage contained a premonition of what would come later, that my consciousness was playing a kind of trick to keep me from offering Nella to Maurizio in exchange for . . . his defeat. But I'm getting ahead of myself. All I know is that, in the grip of rage—and at the same time ashamed of this rage—I raised my hand and struck her face, which was turned toward me as I pulled her head by the hair toward my knees. I hit her once, twice, striking the hand she had raised 265 to shield herself. I struck her again, trying unsuccessfully to reach her other cheek; then, disgusted and still furious, I wrenched her body to the ground, still holding her by the hair. She fell onto the rug at my feet, her head in her hands, moaning deeply in a tone that sounded more pleasurable than aggrieved. With renewed fervor I kicked her back and her flank, violently at first and then more weakly, already repentant, surprised at the soft, delicate pliancy of her flesh. Then I got up and began to walk almost mechanically around the room. She remained where she had fallen, curled up with her face turned toward the bed and buried in her delicate hands, as strands of her great mane of shiny red hair escaped between her fingers. I could see the light copper-colored fuzz on her neck, against the diaphanous skin, and suddenly felt a wave of tenderness. In order to avoid having to look at her, I went to sit at my table in front of the window with my back to the room.

I was disgusted with myself. I had behaved in a brutal, cruel manner and I felt ashamed. But the darker, more profound reasons for my behavior—which I did not completely comprehend, nor want to—disgusted me even more, and disconcerted me deeply. I knew that Maurizio was the real source of my anger, and that I had become angry at Nella only because the situation involved Maurizio. If she had complained about our financial situation and her lack of decent clothes in other circumstances, I would probably have been hurt and mortified, but I would not have become so infuriated. I would have been able to see that after all, she wasn't completely mistaken; women like to be well dressed, even ones who live with Communists. The reason I had struck her in this brutal, savage manner was that Maurizio was involved, and, though I could not yet make out the exact cause, I sensed that it did not put me in a good light. This brutality seemed to belie a kind of jealousy, as if I had been upset that Nella wanted to dress up for Maurizio. But at the same time I realized that beyond this jealousy lay the same feeling of social inferiority I had always suffered in Maurizio's company. I had beaten Nella because on some level I felt that her behavior reflected my own hated weakness. But there was something more: when I had struck her and ordered her to go to Maurizio's party even though she had no decent clothes, I had felt a kind of disgust with myself, almost as if I had wanted not merely to force Nella to take part in a banal cocktail party, but rather to gratify Maurizio in some other, deeper, more unmentionable way. Like everything else, this suspicion led back to my sense of social inferiority. I was almost like a man who feels so inferior and is so hard-pressed to make a good impression that he is willing to throw his wife in another man's arms, just to please him. I also felt, in some vague and undeveloped way, that my relations with Nella, and the very existence of Nella—in other words the fact that I had a lover—placed me in a position of strength in relation to Maurizio and supplied me with a weapon in my struggle against him. So no matter how I looked at the situation, Maurizio was involved, and this disgusted me, humiliated me, and made me feel angry.

I sat on my little chair lost in thought and staring obstinately out of the window with the shutters ajar. Finally, I decided that the only way to mitigate the feelings of disgust and shame that were washing over me was to apologize to Nella, to admit that I had been wrong, and perhaps even to tell her that I understood her concerns and no longer wanted to go to Maurizio's party if she didn't want to go. This decision immediately improved my mood; suddenly I wondered why I had ever felt so strongly about going to the party. I had behaved like a fool. Nella and her love were worth more than all the parties in the world, and my main priority was to protect this love; nothing else mattered. These thoughts gave me a sense of relief, like a man who has climbed a mountain and gazes down at the mire where he had once struggled for survival. From this perspective I could survey the person I had been and the actions I had taken just a few minutes earlier with a certain understanding and compassion. But my sense of well-being did not last; at the very moment I was preparing to go to her, to take her in my arms and say, "You were right . . . we won't go to the party," two bare, child-like arms encircled my shoulders. Nella's hair and cheek were pressed against my face, and her submissive, imploring voice said the words I had heard so many times before: "Why are you so cruel to me?" Then she said, "I'll get dressed and we'll go to Maurizio's . . . It's all right, we'll go." I could still save the situation by answering, "No, no, I don't want to go anymore . . . You're right . . . Let's stay home."

But the gratitude I felt at her sudden capitulation kept me from speaking. I realized that despite the loving, clearheaded conclusions I had come to just moments earlier, what I truly wanted was for her to give in and agree to go to Maurizio's. Now that she had agreed, I felt no desire to dissuade her. I did not have time to dwell on this new change of heart. Nella's mouth sought mine and soon her sweet, insatiable lips were on mine. We embraced and then Nella broke free with a laugh: "I have to get dressed or we'll be terribly late." Feeling flustered, I turned my chair to face the room.

She went over to the bed, still wearing nothing but her little slip, and sat down. With her curly head bent forward in the weak light of the ceiling lamp, she sewed two patches under the armpits of her old brown silk tea dress. I watched her with a mixture of guilt and satisfaction. Guilt over the brutal scene that had just ended, but satisfaction at having reaffirmed my will over her and bent her to my wishes. She sewed happily, lightheartedly, making large, loose stitches, as if in a hurry to leave for Maurizio's. Her demeanor had changed completely, and once again I felt a prick of jealousy and was tempted to say that I no longer wanted to go out and would rather stay at home. As a precaution, I asked: "Earlier, you didn't want to go to the party . . . Now, it seems as if you're almost happy to . . ."

She did not look up from her sewing: "I don't care at all whether we go to your friend's party or not . . . I'm just happy that I was able to overcome my resistance and make a sacrifice for you, to do what you want me to . . . I'm happy because I know that you're happy, and I'm happy to be happy that you're happy . . ."

Her answer disarmed me completely. I watched in silence as she finished sewing and got dressed. She was wearing a greenish slip, mended in several places, under which her pale white breasts blossomed tenderly, with childish, innocent sweetness. Beneath the frayed hem, her legs were as thin as a child's; her arms too were thin and pale, as was the top of her bony chest. Her skin was pale, with freckles here and there like most redheads, and more freckles on her face, giving her a slightly impish air, despite her innocent expression. But it was the impish look of a child who is fundamentally naïve and innocent, not that of a devious full-grown woman. I watched her with a mixture of affection and shame, remembering that just a moment earlier I had struck those freckled cheeks, brought tears to those eyes, and kicked her slender, graceful back. Nella came and went, carefully inspecting many pairs of stockings in a drawer, all of them with runs repaired many times over. Two were in slightly better condition. She pulled her dress over her head, emerging with messy hair and glancing over at me for the first time. Finally, she put on her shoes, hopping up and down in front of the mirror on the armoire. The dress was old-fashioned and had long ago lost any shape it might once have had. She looked tattered but still fresh and desirable, despite everything. I was happy to be going to Maurizio's, and this time my motivations were quite natural and good-natured: Nella was beautiful and I was proud of her beauty and wanted Maurizio to see her and admire her as I myself admired her.

Finally we left the house and climbed onto a jeep transport to go to Maurizio's. It was still the early days of the Liberation, and public transportation did not yet run regularly in Rome. On the jolting platform on the back, exposed to the wind, Nella tried to stand next to me despite the crowd pushing from all directions. I stood still, holding on to the simple iron railing that could barely contain the crowd of passengers, like a string holding a bundle of asparagus. Nella, in her innocent, provocative way, pressed her back against me, and every so often she would shoot a loving, malicious glance over her shoulder. As I've said before, she had a young, fresh, solid, muscular body, and she knew that her body pleased me, and that I could not help being excited by it. It was obvious that she was trying to obtain forgiveness, or at the very least to win me over through the warm contact with her body. In other words, even as I regretted my brutal, insensitive behavior toward her, she feared that I was still angry and was trying to obtain my forgiveness with this innocent, sensual provocation. She wanted to be near me and to press her body against mine, with the insatiable ardor of her love, an ardor that had been awakened from the moment our eyes met on that day at the offices of the Allied Forces and which had continued to grow, despite my coldness, brutality, and lack of sensitivity. Excited by her innocent, tenacious passion—even more than by the warm contact of her body—I stood perfectly still as she mischievously took advantage of each jolt of the jeep to press her solid, bold, youthful body against my chest, belly, and legs. Finally, pressing against me even more closely, she whispered, "Do you love me?" As she said this she gave me one of her most intense, radiantly moist glances. For once

I was won over; I put my arm around her waist and pulled her close.

The jeep rushed recklessly through the streets in the refreshing summer breeze. At each stop the young man in short sleeves who was driving would announce the name of the street in a hoarse voice. My earlier disgust and ill humor completely forgotten, I held Nella in an amorous embrace as I so seldom did even in the intimacy of our room. Our argument had dissolved, and I realized, with a shadow of annoyance, that in a way Nella had won with her tenaciousness and the intensity of her passion. Because of the internal conflict I felt between my passion and the impulse not to give in to this passion, I was at a disadvantage to Nella, whose strength was like that of a child or an animal. A small child or an animal is able to devote all its energies to overcoming a man's doubts; for this reason, an infuriated child or an enraged cat can inspire fear in grown men. Like a child, or an animal, Nella was capable of only one feeling at a time, to which she would give herself completely, without hesitation or reserve. At this moment, she was filled with love for me. Normally such thoughts would have made me reject her insistent physical presence— innocent and sensual, naïve and mischievous—which so doggedly sought out my own. But perhaps because of the warm breeze, or the strange and awkward circumstances that imbued our proximity with a sense of adventure, or my slight remorse for my earlier behavior, I felt at that moment that I loved her almost in the same way that she loved me, in other words without reserve or fear, with total abandon.

The jeep came to an abrupt stop and the same coarse, breathless voice announced: "Via Bertoloni." At that moment, without warning, all the excitement, desire, and love I had been feeling disappeared, as if a charm had been broken. I knew that in a moment I would be in Maurizio's company, not only physically—not such an ominous prospect—but in the sense of our struggle, which would inevitably begin again. Our battle, which had been suspended for many years, would be fought even more ardently than before. I was excited, not by love or desire but rather by a pugnacious and troubling fear of not being up to the challenge. I felt that Nella's flirtatiousness in the jeep had disarmed me and distracted me from my struggle with Maurizio and the means by which I meant to overcome him, and from the results I so desired. Suddenly, like a boy on his way to an exam who has been momentarily distracted by the traffic or the spectacle of nature and then is forced to come back to reality at the sight of the schoolyard, I felt almost a sense of panic. I tried to assemble in my mind all the points of contrast between Maurizio and myself: my membership in the Communist Party, his association with a class of people whom I considered doomed, my firm belief in the imminence of revolution, my desire to turn my inferiority complex into a lasting and powerful sense of superiority . . . As I went through this list in my mind, I tried to recover my earlier aggressive, decisive mood, which I considered more favorable to the execution of my plan. I could feel that my heart had begun to flutter and that I was out of breath. I saw a gate with the number sixty-four and whispered to Nella, "We're here."

It was a large gate with two pilasters topped by two massive pots filled with luxuriant ivy. I felt so overexcited that I decided to pause for a moment to look around before pressing the bell. We were on a pleasant street in an elegant, almost deserted neighborhood lined with gardens. Behind the garden walls, one could make out leafy trees and the aging façades of mansions and large houses. There were cars parked on both sides of the street, many of them luxury models. Many probably belonged to Maurizio's guests. Nella peered at me, surprised by my hesitation. "What's wrong? You look pale . . . Don't you feel well?"

I answered steadily, "I'm fine."

"Why don't you ring the bell?"

"Yes, of course," I said, pressing the brass button on the pilaster.

The gate opened, and a butler in a striped jacket 273 appeared and invited us in. We followed him through the garden and to the door, which was set on one side of the house, protected by an old glass-and-iron roof. Ten years earlier I had often visited Maurizio's house, and I suddenly realized that everything looked smaller, more modest, older, and less luxurious than I remembered it. In those now distant days, I had always felt an intimidating impression of luxury and wealth whenever I entered that house. Now I realized that this luxury and immense wealth had existed only in my imagination. Of course it was a large, comfortable house, I said to myself, looking around as we passed through the foyer and an anteroom leading to the main rooms of the ground floor, but nothing more. The décor was nothing special, without style or taste; one could even call it nondescript. Everything that had seemed so impressive ten years earlier was now revealed to be much less so to my cold, informed eye: the shabbiness of the furniture, which was old but not valuable, of the kind one finds at second-hand stores; the ugliness and excessive profusion of vases, firearms, and knickknacks distributed on every table and cabinet; the old-fashioned tapestries made out of simulated damask silk on the walls, and the dark, heavy curtains that obscured the windows. The house, I saw immediately, was poorly maintained; it was clear that an insufficient staff cleaned those vast, poorly lit sitting rooms, and did so only superficially. There was the sense of debris left in dark corners, of unwaxed floors hidden beneath ragged carpets, and of dust spreading like an impalpable veil over everything. I also saw that nothing had been replaced in the last ten years and that everything looked visibly worn: the velvet couches were stained and tatty, the damask on the walls was faded, the curtains were dusty and limp. This tired quality struck me as a concrete symbol of a moral condition: that house was, as they say, stale; nothing had been renovated or improved upon for many years, just as ideas, convictions, feelings, and taste grows old; in other words the entire inheritance of the family that lived in that house, and more generally of the social class to which this family belonged, was antiquated and tired. Needless to say, I felt almost a sense of victory as the decadence and modesty of Maurizio's home were revealed to my eyes, as if I hoped to find the same qualities in him, a decadence and modesty which would render him less formidable. I hoped that he would no longer carry the air of superiority which in the past had so tormented me.

The first two rooms were empty, and the doors and windows were all open to let in the night air from the garden. We could hear music coming from a smaller drawing room at the rear of the villa; as we entered we saw that most of the guests were in this room, crowded around a bar near the far wall. There was a radio playing and some of the guests were dancing, both inside and also on the terrace outside. There were about thirty guests and they were exactly the kind of people I had expected to find: men and women belonging to the Roman bourgeoisie, many of the men in blue suits, neither young nor old, a bit corpulent, a bit bald, dressed to the nines with pomaded hair and clean-shaven cheeks, and wearing an expression, also typical of their class, that seemed to combine contentment, skepticism, and irony. The women were not terribly young, and I noticed that most of them were attractive and dressed with a kind of fussy elegance, with lots of bracelets and jewelry and a profusion of color; they seemed vivacious, excited, enthusiastic. In the small crowd, I could make out a few brown and green uniforms, and the stolid faces and blond hair of Allied officers. I also noticed that among these bejeweled ladies—who with their high heels and fancy clothes reminded me of festive statues of the Madonna—Nella looked like a little servant girl who had wandered in from the kitchen to ask the master a question. Her simple, ankle-length 275 dress and low shoes made her look small, and the lack of jewels or décolleté added a modest air that made her look even smaller. Only her hair, which in the semi-darkness of the room was tinged with copper and gold from the light of the few lamps, looked precious. It seemed to reveal an equally precious moral quality, a naïveté, a purity, and a child-like simplicity.

No one there knew us, and we knew no one. Paying no heed to Nella, I navigated among the groups sitting and standing around the room, talking, laughing, and dancing. I was looking for Maurizio. Nella followed my footsteps with a tenacious fidelity that I found both irritating and touching, without leaving me for a moment, her steps matching my own. She seemed intimidated by the small crowd of elegant strangers and for some reason I became annoyed with her and whispered: "Don't make that face." "What face?" she asked, surprised. "Stop looking so bashful . . . Your toenail is worth more than all of them combined." She stared at me again and said: "I don't feel the least bit intimidated . . . It's just that I don't know anyone." "I don't either," I said, "what of it?" We had reached the bar. I climbed onto one of the stools, feigning an awkward ease, and invited Nella to do the same. She obeyed, but perhaps because she was too petite, or because she was not accustomed to being perched on a stool, she slid off the first time and was able to climb back on only after pulling her dress up over her knee. Once again I felt annoyed by her awkwardness. Attempting to hide my ill humor, I asked if she wanted something to drink.

"I don't know . . . I suppose so . . . Whatever you say," she said, unsure of herself.

Behind the tiny bar, a chubby, indolent-looking young man was amusing himself serving drinks to his friends, imitating the gestures of a bartender. Smiling, he said, "At your service . . . What can I get you?

Brusquely, as if he were really a bartender, I said, "A whisky for me . . . Nella, what do you want?"

"I . . . ," she said, vaguely, "I'll have whatever you say."

"Whatever you say." This was invariably her answer when I asked her "What do you want?" no matter what the subject.

I repressed my irritation at her passivity and said, "Another whiskey for the *signorina*."

The young man was no longer smiling, and stared at me with a look that was both mocking and annoyed. Nevertheless, he picked up a bottle of whiskey and two glasses, poured some liquid, held out the glasses, and said: "Here are your drinks . . . but just to be clear . . . I'm not really a bartender."

I felt myself blush and grew even more irritated. I held out my hand across the bar and said: "Please excuse me . . . The name is Maltese."

He held out his hand: "Giacinti." And then, looking at Nella, "and the *signorina*?"

"Nella," I said.

"Just Nella?"

For some reason I wanted to say, "Yes, just Nella." But instead I muttered: "Nella Ciocchi."

Some dance music came on the radio. Giacinti put the bottle back on the bar and turned to Nella. "Would you like to dance?"

Again I felt a surge of irritation as Nella turned to me before accepting his invitation. "Go ahead," I said, "that's what we're here for."

With the same docility as before, she reached toward the young man as he approached her. For a moment I watched them dance. The young man was stiff and upright, smartly dressed in his blue suit, like a mannequin; every so often, he moved his shoulders in a way that seemed both ridiculous and typical of a man of his particular social circle. As I watched I realized that it hurt me to see Nella, usually so awkward and unskillful, pressed up against him, her chest against his chest, her belly against his belly. It wasn't exactly jealousy, I thought, but almost a feeling of profanation and absurdity. I gulped down my drink, still watching the two of them, then drank Nella's as well. The dance concluded, and another began. Nella glanced over at me with an anxious expression as she accepted another dance in Giacinti's arms. Now, feeling uncontrollably nervous but trying to simulate calm, I stepped around the bar and stood in the bartender's spot. First, I poured myself another glass of whiskey, twice as much as before. But soon a couple came up to the bar and said, as if speaking to a bartender, "Two whiskeys, please."

They had mistaken me for a bartender. For some reason, a little devil led me to try to imitate the much more self-possessed Giacinti. I poured two glasses of whiskey, added some soda water from a siphon, and was about to offer the drinks to the two guests. The young man, who was sitting sideways at the bar and talking, said, without looking at me: "Some ice, please."

My head was spinning. I could feel the whiskey I had drunk rising to my cheeks with an unpleasant ardor and my eyes clouding over with its fumes. I managed to find a bucket of ice at my feet, dropped two cubes in each glass, and placed them on the bar, just as Giacinti had done: "Here are your drinks . . . but I just want to make something clear . . . I'm not the bartender."

But here things took a confusing turn. Instead of introducing himself, the young man stared at me for a moment, surprised or perhaps simply distracted, after which he took the glasses and placed them between him and the young woman and went on talking as if nothing had happened.

I forced myself to put out my hand: "Allow me to introduce myself . . . Maltese."

This time, the young man behaved with more propriety. Coldly, with a hint of annoyance, he introduced himself and his companion. I can't remember their names, and perhaps I did not even hear them; by then I was feeling bleary, irritated, and scattered— in other words, drunk. After this quick introduction, the young man went back to his conversation. Desperately, I leaned over the bar and repeated Giacinti's move: "Excuse me, *signorina*, may I have this dance?"

She was quite young, very thin and pale, wearing a red velvet dress. She had a long neck, a small, bird-like head, round eyes, and a small mane of frizzy hair. She stared at me for a moment and then, without looking to her companion as Nella had, answered coldly: "Thank you, but I don't dance."

I felt my face burning with a sudden, absurd wave of embarrassment. I knew I had a disconcerted look on my face, and with much effort I tried to modify it with a smile that attempted to be slightly ironic and at the same time indifferent. But I realized that

278

243

my efforts were unsuccessful and that I had managed only to render the stiff, embarrassing mask of bitterness and awkwardness on my face even more uncomfortable. The two went on talking, the radio went on playing dance music, and I began to look around for Nella, unsuccessfully. Was it the whiskey that clouded my eyes or my sense of embarrassment that obscured my sight and ability to reason clearly, making me feel drunk? In order to regain my dignity, I turned toward the bar and once again filled my glass—which I had already emptied four times—and then walked around the room with unsteady steps, as if looking for someone. Finally, I headed toward the French doors that led out into the garden, which were wide open.

I say "as if looking for someone," and in fact that was precisely what I had been doing from the moment of our arrival. I was looking for Maurizio. As I walked toward the garden, I thought vaguely that I might find him outside, given that I had not seen him in the house. I now realized clearly that I was drunk, and that this drunkenness had unleashed, as the saying goes, my "true self": the scene at the bar, my awkwardness, my sense of shame, all revealed, more powerful than ever, my old inferiority complex. For a moment, I had felt free. Yes, I thought as I walked unsteadily out of the sitting room, I was still the same person I had been ten years earlier, at least where Maurizio was concerned. The intervening years, my Party membership, my relationship with Nella, and my resolution to be strong and aggressive had all come to nothing.

Stopping every so often to take a sip from my glass, I affected a blasé, worldly attitude as I stepped through the French doors onto the terrace. Outside, there was a paved courtyard surrounded by trimmed hedges with lights hidden inside, illuminating the open space. A few couples danced, others sat on benches, iron chairs, or on the low garden walls. Beyond the hedges one could make out the soaring silhouettes of tall, leafy trees, rising up toward the limpid May sky. The garden, which from the road looked like little more than a slender strip, was in fact quite large. After gazing at the couples and small groups to see if I could identify Maurizio, I began to walk down a small lateral path in the garden. My glass was almost empty, and suddenly I felt very silly walking through the garden clutching an empty glass. My drunken state, however, kept me from carrying this observation further. I continued down one path, took another, walked a good distance, and found myself standing in front of a small fountain consisting of a small basin and a mask which spat out a small dribble of water. The fountain was built into the garden wall and illuminated by the moon; the path ended there, and I was forced to turn back. I took another path. I reflected that if I met Maurizio, I would take the offensive; I would tell him exactly what I thought of him, of his house, of the people he frequented, and I would remind him once again, but this time more brutally, that he and the class he belonged to were doomed and destined to imminent destruction at the hands of the revolution. Meditating on the "writing on the wall" with which I hoped to confront Maurizio once and for all, I was filled with a violent hostility and an aggressive desire for victory. As I walked down another long, meandering path, I suddenly came to an abrupt stop. I could see Nella and Maurizio sitting on a nearby bench in a twist in the path. They were talking; Nella was closer to me, with her back turned, but I could see Maurizio's face. Nella stood up and said, in a clear voice: "I'm going home," and walked away. She seemed unsteady, and it occurred to me that she too was drunk. Maurizio was still sitting on the bench, smoking, staring straight ahead. As I approached him, I said, "Ah, there you are . . . I was looking for you."

280   He said nothing as I approached him unsteadily. I thought I noticed a look on his face that I had never seen before, one of boredom, disgust, and irritation which, for some reason, I attributed to the party. As I said earlier, I was moved by the aggressive desire to attack and defeat him with a few cutting words. But when I saw the look on his face, I thought: "He knows that the people he has invited to his party are stupid and contemptible . . . He knows that his social circle is doomed . . . He is better than they are . . . He could be one of us." All of a sudden, my hostility disappeared, replaced by an unexpected, intoxicating feeling of affection and solidarity. As I sat on the bench beside him I asked almost timidly, "Am I disturbing you?"

He started, looking up at me as if seeing me for the first time. "Not at all . . ."

"What are you doing here, all alone in the garden?" I asked. "I thought you were dancing."

He looked at me and said, slowly, "I'm smoking a cigarette . . . as you can see."

"You're bored . . . ," I said, my voice full of hope and understanding. "You needed a break . . ."

He looked at me again with some surprise. "I was dancing with Nella," he said curtly, "and then we came here to talk for a moment."

I noticed that he said her name casually, and also that he mentioned her before I did, as if to protect himself. But strangely, perhaps because of my drunken state, this observation did not inspire any particular reflections. At that moment, Nella was the furthest thing from my mind; even if I had caught her kissing Maurizio, I would not have reacted in any way. Making no reference to his response, I said, "Maurizio, why can't you be sincere for once in your life?"

He shuddered and stared at me in silence. Then, slowly, cautiously, he said, "What do you mean?"

I told him I was drunk. Up to that moment my drunkenness had manifested itself only physically: an unsteady walk, clouded vision, confused logic. But as soon as I opened my mouth I realized that my drunkenness would also be revealed in my speech. As usual, this knowledge did not stop me; quite the contrary: "Even if you refuse to be honest with me," I said, vehemently, "I'll be honest with you . . . The time has come to speak openly."

I wanted to shock him, but at the same time, because of the typical confused logic brought on by drink, I also thought that what I said was true and just, and that what I was about to say was even more so. "There is a kind of silent, wordless war going on between us," I said, stumbling over my words with a fiery impulsiveness, "I know it and you know it . . . but at least I have the courage to admit it."

"A silent . . . wordless war?"

"For as long as we've known each other," I went on, unflinching, "we've been engaged in a battle, and each of us wants to declare victory over the other . . . One could say that our struggle began on the day we first laid eyes on each other . . . I don't know why, really . . . Perhaps because of the social chasm between us . . . You're rich and I'm poor, you come from an established family, and my roots are obscure . . . Or perhaps the real reason is that you feel more powerful and want to impose your strength, and I cannot help but react to this imposition . . . But at the same time," I continued in a triumphant tone, "even though we hate each other, we also love each other . . . It's useless to deny it . . . I am mysteriously drawn to you, and you to me . . . We avoid each other and seek each other out . . . I don't know what you feel, but I know very well what I feel."

"What do you feel?" he asked slowly. If I had been less over-excited and more sober, I might have noticed a sudden coldness in his voice, almost like a clinical curiosity.

"I feel a sort of attraction," I said, "and I know why . . . I consider you to be an extraordinary person, highly intelligent, with great charm. These are rare qualities . . . At the same time I hate to see these qualities go to waste, not be put to any good purpose . . . You lead a useless life, among useless, or worse, contemptible, people"—I made a vague ges-
282 ture in the direction of the house—"and you don't realize that your strength, which is already consider-able, would be increased many times over if it were put to use."

"By becoming a Communist?" he asked, quite serious and without the slightest touch of irony, now observing me with real curiosity.

"That's right," I said confidently, "why not become a Communist, like me?" As I said this I put my hand on his arm. "Don't deny it, you know that the people here tonight are empty, contemptible, awful . . . You know that the social class you belong to is doomed . . . You know it . . . so why don't you draw the logical conclusion?"

He was studying me closely. With a slight effort, he said, "Yes, I know . . . What about it?"

If I had been less drunk, I would have noticed that he was not looking directly at me but rather above my head, dreamily, at the trees. His distracted state was significant. I noted it without reflecting on its significance. I went on, ardently: "If you already know this, then why, why . . . "

"Why don't I follow your example?" he said, casually finishing my sentence.

"Yes, why?"

He was quiet for a moment. "We'll discuss it another time . . . Tell me more about this battle we've been waging . . . How do you see it?"

I felt a wave of aggravation and anger, and yelled out: "See? You don't have the courage to look squarely at the logical conclusions of your feelings and thoughts . . . Nevertheless, the battle between us will end with my victory . . ."

"Why is that?" he asked, smiling slightly.

"Because after being the weaker combatant for a long time, I am now in a position of strength, that's why . . . Because you insist on untenable positions, while I have the courage to overcome them . . . Because I am no longer the useless little intellectual that you used to make fun of . . . I am a new man, and you are a relic of the past, like all the people you know. Everything around you is old . . . this house, the furniture, the fabrics, the chairs . . . the people . . . everything is old . . . and if you don't watch out, you'll suffer the same fate . . . you'll die."

283   "Everyone dies," he said, lightly.

"Don't pretend you don't understand," I said, violently; "you're an intelligent man, Maurizio, very intelligent, and you know better than I do what I mean . . . Don't pretend not to."

He peered at his cigarette and then flung it into the bushes. "Let's go inside," he said, "it's time."

"But, Maurizio," I cried out, running after him and grabbing his sleeve, "why don't you answer me? Why can't you be honest? I've been open with you."

He stopped. "You have been honest with me," he said, uttering each syllable clearly, "and you've told me that there is a silent, wordless war between us . . . Well, thank you for the warning . . . I suppose we will continue to do battle."

"That's it?"

I don't know what I had expected: perhaps that he would strike me, or concede defeat and pronounce himself ready to join the Party. "That's it," he said with a smile, "and it's already quite a lot . . . I didn't know that you were my enemy."

"But, Maurizio, why do you say 'enemy'? Why do you pretend not to understand?"

"And I will act accordingly."

I grabbed his sleeve desperately. "How can you call me your enemy? Only a friend, a true friend, could speak to you as I have."

He began to laugh, almost like a child. "Of course," he said, tapping me on the face almost affectionately, "what do you think I am, a fool? I understand . . . We're friends, all right? And you're drunk, that's also a fact."

I did not have the strength to react. He walked off, leaving me standing there as he receded from view. Once he was gone, I sat down on the bench mechanically. I realized I had behaved like a fool. What had I done since arriving at that house? Not only had I let myself blurt out an absurd, ridiculous declaration—almost a declaration of love—but I had spoken of our struggle and my plans to vanquish him, to achieve a final victory. Now I was ashamed, and I understood that once again I had surrendered to my drunken state and, more important, to my ever-present sense of inferiority. For a moment I felt such regret and anger that I almost gave in to the impulse to run after Maurizio, strike him, and say, "This is what you deserve . . . This is how I really feel about you." But I realized that such a scene would be inopportune at the very least. Since there was no question of taking back my words and repairing the gravely compromised situation between us, I could only hope to put them in the context of a new plan of action. I felt comforted by the thought that he had admitted to feeling contempt toward the people at his party, and had almost promised to continue our conversation in the future with the words "We'll discuss it another time." I reassured myself with the thought that perhaps my drunken honesty had not yet ruined everything, and that I might return to battle with weapons that were not yet completely blunted.

Meanwhile, despite my thoughts of regrouping and second rounds, I was still drunk and I knew that my drunkenness would not pass anytime soon and might still lead me to say or do something regrettable. I decided it was time to leave the party which inspired such contempt in me and where I had managed to behave so contemptibly. I headed down the path toward the villa. I was very drunk and realized that I could neither walk straight nor think clearly. My drunkenness insinuated itself into my thoughts, clouding them with the very idea that I was drunk. I walked a bit farther until suddenly I found myself in front of the wall with the little fountain and the mask spitting water from its mouth, beneath the light of the moon. Instead of walking toward the house, I had gone in the opposite direction, toward the back of the garden. The mask seemed to jeer at my deflated, unhappy state and my sense of defeat after so many dreams of victory. I dunked my head in the cool water and held my breath for as long as I could. I came up to draw a breath and dunked my head again. I did this several times until I was convinced that I felt more clearheaded, and then began to walk quickly toward the villa.

285 This time I found my way without difficulty. The first thing I saw on the terrace in front of the French doors was Nella, dancing with Maurizio. I went up to her with a decided step and took her arm abruptly. They stopped dancing and stared quizzically at me. "We have to leave," I said, suddenly realizing that my

tongue, blunted by alcohol, was moving with difficulty: "We've got to go now."

"But I'm dancing," Nella said. I looked into her face and realized that she too was drunk. Her hair was messy and her eyes more beautiful than ever, filled with the vague, drowsy, uncertain, tremulous beauty of drink. Despite her naïveté she wore a somewhat infatuated expression on her flushed face: "I'm dancing," she repeated uncertainly, her voice plaintive as she looked toward Maurizio, pleading for his help.

Maurizio intervened: "Yes, we have to finish this dance," he said, once again taking her in his arms. "Come on, Sergio, be nice, sit on that chair," he said, pointing to a small wicker chair against the wall and preparing to continue dancing.

I felt a stubborn, drunken desire to have my way: "I want you to come with me now," I said angrily to Nella.

Nella faced me: "You go . . . I'll catch up with you," she said, quite seriously, and not a little drunk.

"But you're drunk," I retorted angrily, trying to grab her arm.

"Oh, and you're not?" she answered, childishly. Maurizio began to laugh. "Come on, don't be angry, wait for me," she continued after a brief pause, stumbling a bit over her words. "I only have, let's see, five dances left," she said, looking at me tenderly, "one with Maurizio, and four more."

"And then a last dance with me," Maurizio added, clearly amused by my disgruntled air.

"And then a last dance with him."

"But I don't feel like staying," I began, "I want to go home."

Maurizio, who seemed to be enjoying himself, suddenly called out: "Gisella . . ." I turned in the direction of his words. In the doorway of the sitting room stood a tall, shapely, and attractive girl, with a great mane of hair that descended from her small head down to her shoulders. She was watching us uncertainly. "Gisella," Maurizio said again, "come dance with my friend Sergio . . . He's dying to dance, and I can see that you are also looking for a partner."

A word from Maurizio was all it took. As docile as a harem girl responding to her master's instructions, the tall, shapely Gisella approached me and, with her arms extended, said, "Here I am, shall we dance?" and I found myself pressed against the elongated body of this horse-like girl, my nose buried in her hair. Over her shoulder, I looked at Nella. She too was watching me, and as soon as she saw that our gaze had crossed, she stuck her tongue out at me mischievously, like a street urchin, as if to say: "Serves you right." Her gesture disarmed me, because once again it revealed Nella's deep, inalterable innocence, which was perhaps the quality that most drew me to her. The tall Gisella was speaking: "You know, I have no idea who you are."

"A poor wretch," I said emphatically.

She peered at me and said: "You couldn't possibly be as wretched as I am."

"Why is that?" I asked.

"Because I am in love with a man who does not love me," she said, with impudent sincerity.

"Who is he?"

"That man over there," she said, looking at Maurizio.

Suddenly, I forgot my desire to leave the party; such was the power of Maurizio's name. With feigned coarseness, I asked: "What do you see in him? I know him well . . ."

"Really?"

"We went to school together . . . So what do you see in him? He's a hollow, selfish, arid, vain, heartless man . . . a useless person."

As I said this, she observed me with her round, bird-like eyes. Suddenly she said: "Do you know why you say those things?"

"Why?"

"Out of envy."

I blushed, knowing she was right. I said, violently, "And do you know why you say that?"

"Why?"

"Out of stupidity."

She too blushed, but with anger. Pushing me away, she said: "Listen, I think we should stop dancing. I don't feel like being insulted." She began to walk down the path toward the little fountain. I ran after her, taking her arm: "Don't be angry . . . I was just joking."

"I don't find that sort of thing amusing."

"Come on . . . let's dance."

"I don't feel like dancing anymore . . . It's too hot . . . Let's sit over there," she said, no longer angry, but instead with a kind of flirtatiousness. She pointed at the bench where Maurizio and Nella had been sitting earlier.

We walked over to the bench, and the girl sat down. Fanning herself with a handkerchief, she said, "Tell me about yourself."

For some reason, perhaps because of my drunken state, it occurred to me that she might be attracted to me and want to be alone with me. In an insinuating voice, I asked, "Why do you want to know?"

"No reason . . . because we've never been introduced."

"It's true . . . Well, my name is Sergio Maltese, and I'm a journalist and a film critic . . . and a Communist."

This last word surprised her: "A Communist?"

"Yes."

"Let me warn you that I can't stand Communists."

"Why is that?"

"Because they want to eliminate rich people."

"Are you rich?"

"No . . . but I like the idea that there are people out there who are."

She said this with such an air of obtuseness and obstinate conviction that I could not help thinking, with equal conviction, "How stupid she is." "Perhaps that is why you love Maurizio, because he's rich," I insinuated.

"That's one of the reasons," she said, with animal-like sincerity. "I don't like poor people: they're stingy and small-minded . . . You can tell Maurizio has always had money . . . Can't you see how generous and gentlemanly he is?"

She was clearly a stupid woman. And yet it seemed to me that her vapid affirmations had more weight than all my well-formulated philosophical ideas about the coming revolution. With sudden aggression, I said, "People like you and Maurizio will soon be swept away . . . You won't even have eyes to cry."

She stared at me in complete bewilderment, eyes wide open. Only now did I realize that she too was quite drunk. Her round, sky-blue eyes seemed to wander and were filled with uncertainty. "What do you mean?"

"A revolution is coming," I said, feeling twice as stupid as she, but unable to stop myself. "And all this," I said, waving toward the house, the garden, and the young woman, "all this will be confiscated and placed at the service of the people."

Something completely unexpected happened. The girl began to cry: "Oh no . . . please . . . please don't hurt him," she cried out, her head in her hands, "please don't."

And then, after a moment, she turned her anger toward me. "It's all envy . . . People like you want a revolution because you're envious . . . because you don't have money and you prefer that nobody else have it if you can't have it too . . . You're just envious, that's all."

I felt defenseless, drunker than ever, and quite ridiculous. And yet I could not help defending myself: "You don't know what you're saying."

"Oh yes, I do." 289

"No, you don't . . . and this time I really mean it: you are a stupid woman."

I had stood up, and she looked me up and down. "Get out of here," she said, angrily.

"I'm leaving," I said, flustered; "it was you who brought me here."

"Go away . . . Can't you see I want to be alone?"

I walked away without arguing. I was angry and flustered, and even more ashamed of the way I had behaved over the course of that terrible evening. What had I been thinking, talking about Communism and revolution with that silly girl who could think only of Maurizio and her feelings of rejection? I had reduced these profound issues in my life to mere bourgeois chitchat at a bourgeois party, and for this I was terribly ashamed. I knew that all this had happened because I was drunk; but what was this drunkenness but an expression of my feelings of inferiority and weakness? I did not like to drink, nor did I enjoy being drunk; I had drunk only in order to have something to do and to overcome a moment of awkwardness and embarrassment. No matter what I did, I returned to the same point of departure: when I had planned to go to the party my intention, like a piper, had been to force Maurizio to dance to my tune, but instead it was I who had been played.

Still unsteady, and drunker than ever, I returned to the terrace. Couples were dancing on the paving stones in the light of the lamps tucked into the hedges. Nella and Maurizio were no longer there. Vaguely, I thought, "Maurizio is courting Nella . . . He wants to steal her away from me," but as before, this thought did not elicit any particular reaction. Where Maurizio was concerned, I noticed, I was neither jealous nor suspicious. I went inside; here too couples were dancing, while others crowded around the bar. I saw Maurizio dancing with a slight girl with puffy hair, and felt something like disappointment, as if I had hoped rather than feared to find him courting Nella. Despite my drunkenness and confusion, I tried to decipher the reason behind this sense of disappointment as I stepped into the next room, which was almost empty. Nella was there, sitting on a couch with 290 a man I did not know. The man, who looked to be in

258

his fifties, was large, with a wide chest, a big head of gray hair, and a striking, aristocratic face, with a pronounced nose, mouth, and chin, and sideburns down to the middle of his cheeks. When he stood up, however, he did not seem to grow any taller. In fact, he was quite short, with very short legs and tiny hands and feet. Drunkenly and without moving, Nella said: "This is Maurizio's business partner . . . I'm sorry, what is your name?"

"Moroni," he said, holding out his hand.

"He says I should be in the movies," she said loudly; "he says I could make a lot of money . . . Isn't that right, *signor* Moroni?"

"We would need to do a screen test," he said, seriously, with a slight accent. "In truth, I'm not an expert, but at first blush I would say that the young lady is quite photogenic."

"And I could make a lot of money, isn't that right?" Nella asked loudly.

"Well of course, yes."

"I could make lots of money and buy myself lots of clothes," she said loudly, sounding very drunk. "Because we're very poor, *Signor* Moroni . . . He can't even buy me a pair of stockings . . . Just look at them," she said, stretching out her leg and pulling up the hem of her dress to expose a white thigh; "look at how many times I've had to mend these stockings."

Moroni, with a discretion for which I was quietly grateful, barely glanced at Nella's shapely, tapered leg, though I could tell he would have liked to gaze at it for longer. "Yes, of course," he said, with some embarrassment, "you could buy all the stockings you like."

"And clothes too," she said, loudly. "Do you know when I bought this dress? Ten years ago . . . Look how discolored it is under the arms . . . and how old-fashioned it is . . . I was ashamed to wear it, but then he slapped me."

Moroni sat in embarrassed silence. Annoyed, I said: "Come on now, why should Moroni care about such things?"

She leaned toward me and took my hand: "But I love you . . . and I'm glad you slapped me . . . Bless your hand," she said, kissing it fervently, "bless this hand, which slapped me over and over again!"

291 "Stop it," I said, impatiently, trying to pull my hand away.

But Nella did not mean it in this way. "You know, Mr. Moroni, I love him, and I always will, even though he treats me terribly . . . I would do anything for him . . . Don't you believe me?"

"Oh yes," he said, without looking at her.

"I love him . . . but we're poor, and I want to make money so I can support him . . . He's a Communist because we're poor . . . but if we had money, he would change his mind."

Moroni looked at me with some curiosity. Suddenly angry, I said, "You're saying stupid things, and to make matters worse, they aren't even true . . . I already told you: my political loyalties and our private life are of no interest to Mr. Moroni."

Moroni sat down again. "Are you," he asked, turning to Nella, in a courteous, almost shy voice, "are you a Communist as well, *signorina*?"

"No . . . I mean yes," she said loudly, "I am everything that Sergio, my love, wants me to be . . . I love him, and if tomorrow he asked me to kill you because you are a capitalist, I would do it without hesitating."

"You're drunk," I said, contemptuously. Then, turning to Moroni: "Don't pay her any mind . . . she's had too much to drink."

"What a coward you are," she shouted. "I may be drunk, but I would say the same thing even if I were sober . . . It's true, Mr. Moroni . . . I love him and I would do anything for him . . . anything."

I expected Moroni to get up and leave, or at least to show embarrassment and irritation. But instead, much to my surprise, he said, with a sigh: "You are a lucky man, Mr. Maltese, to be loved in this way."

"Yes, we love each other," she said loudly. "Or at least I love him . . . we loved each other from the very beginning. He came to the office of the Allied Command, where I was working, and kissed me, and the British officer saw us kissing and fired me on the spot . . . so we left, and would you believe it, Mr. Moroni, we made love there, in the bathroom . . . not the most comfortable place to make love, is it, Mr. Moroni? And yet that's how our love began."

Once again I felt ashamed; in fact, I had never felt so mortified, and for so many reasons, as that night at Maurizio's party. Moroni watched us, not, as I would have thought, with embarrassment or distaste, but with a clear expression of benevolent, almost affectionate envy. Finally, he said, "Signorina, you are right to love him . . . and your sincerity does you honor . . . many men would be proud to have their lady friend make such declarations, even after a few glasses of wine . . . but please excuse me, I must go . . . pleased to meet you, Mr. Maltese . . . remember, *signorina*, the name is Moroni, at your service." He got up and walked away slowly and, I thought, with some regret, as if sorry to leave us.

Nella and I were alone again, sitting on the deep velvet couch in the darkened sitting room. "You've said enough silly things," I berated her, angrily; "I think it's time for us to go home."

She put her arms around me. "Are you angry with me?"

"Yes."

"Why?"

"There are things one doesn't talk about in front of strangers."

Still embracing me, she looked at me with a serious air. "I said those things because Moroni was teasing me, treating me as if I were someone to be taken lightly . . . I wanted him to know that I love you and only you . . . What do you think? Do you think I really believe that he will offer me work in the movies? He only said that in order to entice me."

293   I was struck by how serious she seemed, despite her drunk, exalted tone. "But you also told him that I joined the Communist Party because I don't have any money," I said.

She held me even more tightly. "I said that just to make you angry . . . I know it's not true."

"And why," I asked, won over by her tenderness, "do you want to make me angry?"

"For no reason . . . because I'm silly . . . Forgive me."

She held me in a tenacious, violent embrace that seemed to emanate not from her thin, child-like arms, but from the very source of her passion. I could not help but give in, but even at that moment I felt the contempt which I now know was the thing that ruined the best moments of our love. I kissed her and she returned my kiss with tumultuous avidity, her passion rendered almost chaste by her ardor and the fragrance of alcohol on her breath, usually so fresh and pure. As we kissed, I heard a familiar voice: "How they love each other, those two." Instinctively, I pulled away. 294 Nella, who was less modest, barely moved or even turned her head.

Maurizio was standing in front of us and an Allied officer stood next to him, observing us with his hands in his pockets. I noticed the officer's quizzical expression. Slightly irritated, I got up and said: "Yes, we do love each other . . . what about it?"

Maurizio did not answer, and instead approached Nella and said, in a gently ceremonious voice, "I just wanted to tell you that if you'd like something to eat, a cold supper has been served in the dining room."

"With pleasure," Nella said, jumping up and taking Maurizio's arm with a spontaneity that surprised me. "Let's go, I'm terribly hungry." She turned toward the officer and said, "Are you coming too, Major Parson?" and without waiting for a response, led us into the next room. Involuntarily, I wondered how she could possibly know the officer's name, and came to the conclusion that she must have danced with him earlier in the evening. The officer turned and followed them, and I tailed behind, feeling unhappy and vaguely insecure.

The dancing had stopped and the guests crowded into a small room I had not noticed before, adjoining the room with the bar. It contained only a long table, which was covered with food, served by three waiters. Gisella had been right, I thought, when she said that Maurizio was a generous host and a real gentleman. This *buffet froid* was truly magnificent, not only for the stomach but also for the eyes, with a variety of colorful and fragrant food laid out elegantly on a beautiful embroidered tablecloth, with china plates and crystal glasses. I wasn't hungry, however, and after watching Maurizio prepare a plate for Nella I made my way through the crowd to the bar. The only other person at the bar was Major Parson—the Allied officer Nella had spoken to earlier in a familiar tone—who sat there drinking with one foot resting on the brass railing. Staring into his pink, stolid face, which was almost repulsively virile, with two reddish whiskers like tiny brushes, I suddenly realized where I had seen him before, and why his expression had seemed so strange when he saw me kissing Nella. He was the Allied officer who had caught us kissing that day long ago at the offices of the Allied Command, and who had fired Nella on the spot. I felt a violent wave of aggression; I had often hoped to cross paths with him one day and give him a piece of my mind. With a trembling hand, I picked up a glass, poured myself some whiskey, and said, trying to sound very calm, "I believe we've met."

He looked up with his blue eyes and peered into my face, "I don't believe so, at least as far as I can remember."

Somehow he and Maurizio had merged into one. I felt that if I had the courage to confront the officer, I would also know how to vanquish Maurizio. I realized fuzzily that the greatest obstacle I faced was a certain superiority they both had, a physical magnetism and self-assurance that I lacked. They were made of the same cloth, while I, despite my intellectual and moral superiority, felt fragile and yielding in comparison. With barely contained aggression I said: "Six months ago, you saw us, Miss Poggi and myself, in your office."

"Ah yes," he said. He spoke Italian slowly but correctly. "I remember. The two of you often kiss in public, I see?"

With an effort to sound forceful, I said, "You did not behave very honorably on that occasion . . ."

Something completely unexpected happened. Instead of reacting aggressively to my aggression, the officer put his arm around my shoulder almost affectionately and said, in a warm, almost imploring tone of voice: "Let's not mention that deplorable incident . . . I assure you that I was very sorry to do what I did to Signorina Nella . . . But my hands were tied . . . I caught you in the act, and certain things which in another context would be inoffensive are simply not permissible . . . Let's not speak of it again . . . To your health." He held out his glass for a toast to our reconciliation.

I felt at first that I should respond aggressively, rejecting his conciliatory gestures, perhaps by throwing my drink in his face, as I often had in my revenge dreams. But my thoughts were slower than my actions; I had already raised my glass and clicked it against the major's. Almost automatically, I said, "To your health . . . and to the Allies."

"To your health," he said in a cordial, sincere tone.

I had nothing left to say; in my drunken state, I

260*

265

could now see two Major Parsons, with two noses, two mustaches, and four eyes. But perhaps the second face was not Parson's but Maurizio's . . . In fact, I now saw that the second face was pale, with dark eyes and a dark mustache. Suddenly I realized that indirectly and by proxy, Maurizio had once again scored an easy victory, taking advantage of my weakness. Brusquely, I said: "Excuse me, major . . . I need to go see what Nella is up to," and without waiting for his response I ambled off, "like a whipped dog," I reflected, with my tail between my legs.

The crowd in the dining room had thinned and Nella was gone. I went back to the sitting room: no sign of Nella. I went out into the garden, scanned the terrace and the adjacent paths, but she was nowhere to be seen. As I returned toward the bar, Gisella, the woman who was in love with Maurizio, grabbed my arm: "Are you looking for your girlfriend?" she asked.

"Yes."

"Well then, no use looking for her on the ground floor; you should check upstairs . . . in Maurizio's bedroom."

I took her response squarely, like a slap in the face; and just as if she had struck me, I was stunned for a moment, my mind blank. The meaning of her words was clear, and yet I was incredulous. Then I remembered that Maurizio had accepted the challenge I had foolishly made in my drunken confession, and I realized that he intended to humiliate me by courting Nella and stealing her away from me. It was coarse and vulgar to attack me in the private realm, since he could not do so on an ideological level. And though I knew that Maurizio was neither coarse nor vulgar, I also knew that he would not have hesitated to stoop to such measures to humiliate me. Cuckoldry, I thought 261* with little reflection, was one of the preferred methods for proving one's strength in bourgeois society. It seems strange to say, however, that even as I thought this I felt no pangs of jealousy. While Maurizio perhaps hoped to humiliate me by stealing Nella, I perceived in this cuckoldry an opportunity to humiliate him. In other words, though I did not yet know when or how, Maurizio's potential desire for Nella was a possible point of weakness which might lead to my victory. I thought this as I climbed the stairs in the front of the house up to the second floor. Once I was upstairs, I did not hesitate: one of the doors was open, and I was convinced that it was the bedroom Gisella had alluded to so maliciously.

The room was almost dark, except for a small lamp next to a large, low bed that almost filled the room. I could just make out a figure lying on the bed—Nella—in the light of a small lamp which illuminated her chest and arms. Maurizio was not lying next to her, as Gisella's jealous words had implied. He was sitting beside the bed and pressing a white towel, probably moist, to her forehead. I realized immediately what was going on and said in an unsteady voice: "What happened? Are you feeling sick?"

Without looking up, Maurizio said: "It's nothing . . . she just drank too much."

Out of the darkness, where her head lay buried in the pillow, I heard Nella's hesitant, halting voice: "I thought I was hungry . . . but as soon as I ate I felt sick."

Once again I felt ashamed: for having thought ill of Maurizio and for having assumed that he had behaved basely. But I still suspected him of attempting to turn the tables in order to make me appear ignoble. Drawing closer, I said, "What a disastrous evening . . ."

"Why?" Maurizio asked, now looking up at me. "Are you bored?"

"Quite to the contrary . . . but Nella and I both got drunk, and we've made fools of ourselves."

Maurizio said nothing. Nella's voice rang out: "I feel better now . . . I want to go home."

As she said this she tried to sit up, but as soon as she did so she emitted a groan and fell back on the pillow. "Uff, I feel awful."

Maurizio, now standing, said to me, across the bed: "I think it's better if we leave her alone for a moment."

I reflected on the evening, which I had described a moment earlier to Maurizio as disastrous; I thought back to the downstairs rooms, filled with odious party guests. And suddenly I said, quite forcefully, looking at the clock: "I want to leave . . . It's terribly late."

"You go," Nella moaned, "I'll come later . . . as soon as I feel a bit better."

"All right," I said, almost shocked at my own words, "I'll go . . . Maurizio will bring you home." I felt sincere. I truly could not stand to stay at the party, or in Maurizio's house, one minute longer. Maurizio walked around the bed and pushed me gently toward the door: "Let's leave her alone . . . Listen, if you need anything, just ring this bell." He said these last words in a gentle, quiet voice, and then, still pushing my arm slightly, led me out of the room.

"So you'll bring her home?" I asked, uneasily.

"Don't worry."

We returned downstairs. For some reason, when we reached the ground floor, I turned to Maurizio and said, "We need to talk, the two of us."

"Whenever and as often as you like," he answered. We shook hands and I left, walking with determination.

As soon as I was outside, my self-assurance abandoned me. I felt lost. As I walked down the street, the events of the evening returned to me, like a row of disheveled actors in the glare of the footlights. I saw myself ringing the doorbell, aggressive and convinced of my inevitable victory; and later, at the party, careening between the extremes of my own suspicion and the unpleasantness of others, uncertain, angry, and awkward, thrown about like a cork in the tempestuous seas. Once again I told myself that I had gone to Maurizio's house planning to make him dance to my tune, but instead had been played. As I examined everything I had done that evening I realized angrily that there was not a single action I was not ashamed of. In addition, every action was connected to the one that came before and the one that followed by a common thread, a common theme: my own confusion, impotence, and inescapable sense of inferiority. This was particularly notable given that in every case I had been the one to become enraged and to take action, but each time my actions had been misguided. Meanwhile Maurizio, the undisputed victor, had not become the slightest bit upset nor been pushed to

263*

act in any way; he had simply behaved like a polite, generous host. In other words by doing nothing he had come out victorious, while I had spent the evening running around and growling like a nervous, unhappy dog, accomplishing nothing. I became even more dejected; this was the reason why I considered Maurizio to be superior, though his superiority was neither moral, intellectual, nor rational, but rather something physical and truly inalterable, something that seemed to emanate not from his humanity, but from his very nature, something, in other words, which I sensed but could not explain, just as one can feel the power of an animal even before seeing it, or feel the magnetism of a particular personality without understanding its cause. Had this superiority been merely a social, moral, or intellectual issue, I would have felt calmer and would have been able to blame my defeat on the alcohol I had consumed. I had faith in the revolution; I was convinced of Maurizio's ethical weakness; I felt intellectually superior. I understood, however, that Maurizio's superiority was a material question; despite his defects, his unpleasant social position, and his intellectual limitations he was made of sturdier metal than I, and that was the long and short of it. To extend the metaphor, he was made of tempered steel, like a sword, while I had been fashioned out of vulgar cast iron, the kind that stoves are made of and that breaks under a heavy blow.

264*

As I've said, this sense of irredeemable and ineffable inferiority caused me great suffering. I did not know why this ancient rivalry had now become mixed with my political aspirations, intellectual ambitions, and moral hopes, but it seemed to me, deep down, that if I could not triumph over Maurizio, then the revolution too would fail; I would continue my life as a miserable, mediocre intellectual, and all my actions would continue in the same negative, abnormal vein as they now seemed to. Maurizio was the symbol of everything I sought to defeat within and outside of myself, and our struggle was the testing ground, as they say, of my personal strength and of all the ideas and principles I embraced. I don't know which made me more unhappy: my awareness of the fact that we were built from different metals, or the importance I attributed to my stake in this after all quite modest rivalry. I knew that I suffered as only an impotent man can suffer, like a man who leaves a woman he has intended to deflower intact on the bed, sheets crumpled in vain.

Immersed in such bitter reflections, I walked mechanically in the darkness to the end of Maurizio's street. Mechanically—almost without realizing it—I boarded a bus, got off at my stop, walked the rest of the way, climbed the stairs, entered the boarding-house, and shut the door. Perhaps shaken by the sight of the empty room, a silent yet eloquent witness of my defeats and torments, I felt a sudden wave of rebellion well up inside me. Yes, it was true that Maurizio was made of a harder metal than I, but it was only partly true, and only in a world where men were judged as metal bars or cogs in a machine. In the real, human world, and beyond all poetic metaphors, this question of metals meant nothing, and the truth remained that Maurizio was a man like me and like many others; in other words, his strength lay only in my weakness. It was only because I thought 265* or felt, or in any case had convinced myself, that Maurizio was stronger, that he in fact acquired this strength. I could now see that what I had to do was convince myself of the contrary, in other words arrive at the inalterable conviction that in reality Maurizio was weak, very weak, and that I, for a host of reasons, was vastly stronger. I had already expressed this conviction in abstract form, theoretically, by objectively examining Maurizio's situation and establishing its weakness in comparison to my own. When he and I had spoken in the garden, I had argued: "I am the new man, and you are a relic of the past." But even as I had exclaimed these precise, true words, I had felt that Maurizio, despite belonging to the past, was still superior. Why? Now I realized that it was because I believed in this new man only with my head, but not with the deepest fibers of my being, the part of us that allows us to hold and return the gaze of a rival, that lends authority to our voice and decisiveness to our gestures, and forms the basis of the true strength of powerful men. I needed to release this conviction from the antechamber of my mind and send it to the deepest recesses of my being, into my blood, my flesh, my true matter. But I realized that by a circuitous route I had returned to the question of matter, to the evaluation of man as metal, substance, chemical makeup. In desperation, and still drunk, I turned out the light and threw myself facedown on the bed fully dressed.

I'm not sure how long I lay like this, with my mouth pressed into the pillow and my body spread across the bed. I must have slept for about an hour, a sleep without dreams, dark and deep. When I awoke, my hand went automatically to the light switch; I saw that the clock on the dresser said it was four in the morning and realized that Nella had not yet returned. It occurred to me that perhaps she was really sick, to the point that she could not leave Maurizio's villa, but then it occurred to me that her sickened state might only have been an excuse to spend the night at the villa. I did not have any deeper thoughts on the issue; this final hypothesis did not awaken worry, jealousy, or any other particular feeling. I began to undress, pulling off my clothes and throwing them on the floor far from the bed. I climbed under the covers and once again turned out the light. I think I fell asleep almost immediately, but this time my slumber did not last long. Little more than a quarter of an hour had passed when a light came on and I caught a glimpse of Nella between half-open lids swollen with sleep as she entered the room carefully, on tiptoe, try- ing to avoid making noise. I closed my eyes again, feigning sleep, and watched as she went back and forth, undressing quickly, putting her clothes away in the closet—carefully, as always—and placing her slip, stockings, and shoes on a chair at the foot of the bed. When she was completely undressed, she went over to the vanity table, sat down on the narrow stool in front of the mirror, and began to comb her hair with quick, energetic strokes. From the bed I could see her torso, almost adolescent and boyish except where it widened and grew paler in the discreet but clearly feminine width of the hips. Her mane of red hair, tinged with a metallic hue in the light of the lamp, made her shoulders appear even more narrow and her arms more child-like as she brushed her hair. Every so often she turned her head slightly, energetically brushing the hair to one side, and I could see, beneath her outstretched, raised arm, the round, heavy, buttery whiteness of her breast with its pink tip. As I gazed at her, so chaste and innocent, it occurred to me that I loved her and that I was lucky to have such a lover. Then, as she got up from the stool and tiptoed over to the bed, I closed my eyes quickly. She put one knee on the bed and leaned over me, her breasts hanging over my face. I could smell her breath, innocently soaked in the ardent fragrance of alcohol. She whispered, "Are you asleep?" I pretended not to hear her, and she repeated the question one more time, in a slightly more audible voice: "Are you sleeping?" She clearly wanted to wake me, but at the same time wanted to let me sleep, a childish contradiction which suddenly made me smile. "No, I'm awake," I said, rousing myself and putting my arms around her waist. "I thought you were sleeping," she said, panting, pressing her cool, solid, smooth, slippery body against me. As I kissed her, I stretched out one arm to turn out the light and then embraced her more tightly, with both arms. She returned my embrace with infantile, awkward ardor, murmuring: "Do you love me? Do you love me?"

After we made love we lay side by side, my arm still around her slender waist and her hand languidly resting on my groin. For a few moments, in the dark, it seemed that we were both remembering the events of the evening. In fact, after a few minutes, Nella began to speak; her tone was that of a person who is unsure of her interlocutor's reaction: "You remember that man, Moroni, who said he would find work for me in

267*

274

the movies? He was serious . . . He's Maurizio's partner . . . After you left, I went back downstairs and the
two of them looked after me and told me that soon
they will arrange a screen test for me."

"Well, I hope it goes well for you," I mumbled in
the dark, with a touch of sarcasm.

She thought I was jealous, and immediately embraced me and planted a kiss on my cheek, saying
quickly: "I'll always love you, and only you . . . even if
I become a movie star and make lots of money . . . I'll
give it all to you . . . You can do what you like with it.
I won't keep even a penny for myself."

"You want me to become a kept man," I said, with
the same sarcastic tone.

"Don't say that . . . I want you not to have to work
for money, so you can focus on your studies . . . They
both like you very much and, you know, Maurizio
told me that deep down he more or less agrees with
your political ideas."

She was clearly saying these things so that I would
accept Maurizio's favors, which, I suspected, were
self-interested. She wanted to gain my consent. But I
did not linger on Nella's intentions. Instead I asked,
eagerly, "What do you mean?"

"I mean that he too is a Communist, even if he's
not an actual Party member. Aren't you glad?"

It was clear that she was attempting, with innocent
feminine resolve, to render Maurizio more sympathetic to my eyes in order to convince me that the
offer was an honorable one. Even with this knowledge, my mind had already set off in pursuit of yet
another mirage. I asked Nella: "Are you sure that's
what he said?"

"He definitely said it . . . Maybe he was drunk, but I don't think so."

268*   I was no longer listening. My mind was already lost in myriad reflections, like <a hunting dog> following a scent in the forest and through fields. This tangle of thoughts became more obscure and dense as I lost myself in its possibilities. Eventually, I fell into a deep sleep, lying next to Nella in silence as she continued to talk into the night.

[VI]

I awoke late the next morning with the firm intention of returning to Maurizio's house to confront him man to man, without the distracting presence of guests or alcohol, and, I hoped, unburden myself of my feelings of inferiority. It was as if my mind had been hard at work through the night and had come to this decision without my knowledge. I had two new weapons, in addition to the ones I already knew of: his probable feelings for Nella—or at least his obvious interest in her—and his confessed sympathy for the Party. I would have to insert these new weapons or levers into a crack in his shield in order to destroy it completely. I intuited deep down that these were very powerful weapons, and, though I did not know exactly how I would use them, I had a feeling that I was on the right track and that if I was careful, I might finally attain my much-desired victory. It may seem strange, but the idea that Maurizio might also hold his own weapons, or even the same ones, did

276

not occur to me. And yet I should have suspected that Nella and the Party could also be turned against me. But that is how we men are made: we see everything from our own point of view and have great difficulty imagining another perspective.

This time I did not want Nella to know about my visit, so I did not share my plans with her. She was still asleep when I snuck out of the room to use the telephone in the vestibule of the rooming house. After asking for my name and giving an ambiguous answer regarding Maurizio's whereabouts, Maurizio's butler went off to look for him. After a few minutes, I heard Maurizio's voice on the line. I said drily that I wanted to see him, and he answered quickly that we could meet whenever and wherever I liked. We made an appointment for that afternoon at his house. Then I said impulsively, "Thank you for bringing Nella home last night."

"You should thank Moroni," he answered; "he was the one who took her home."

"In that case, please thank him for me."

"I will."

Quietly, I returned to our room without awakening Nella, who was lost in a child-like slumber. I sat at my table and worked on my translation until almost two in the afternoon. Meanwhile, Nella had awoken. She said good morning as usual, coming up behind me and kissing me, taking me by surprise. She got dressed and we went to eat at the usual trattoria, where we paid on credit. Nella kept yawning and I too felt tired, but at the same time I was unnaturally awake, filled with nervous energy rather than physical vigor. When we returned home Nella threw herself on the bed. She said, "I'm going to sleep for a bit"; I had already picked up a book and was reading, stretched out on the armchair. She added, absentmindedly: "What are you going to do today?" For some reason I answered, "I'm going to see a producer . . . Maybe he'll ask me to write a screenplay, who knows." "That way we'll both work in the movies," she said, yawning. She fell asleep almost immediately. The appointment with Maurizio was not until the late afternoon, so I continued to read for a while longer. Then it occurred to me that it would be best not to show up at Maurizio's tired and nervous, and I decided to take a nap. This again proved that I assigned a great importance to my meeting with Maurizio, yet another sign of my inferiority complex, which I was anxious to rid myself of at any cost. Ruminating on these thoughts, I stretched out on the bed, my feet against Nella's shoulder and my face against her feet. I fell asleep almost immediately.

270*   I awoke suddenly with a heavy head and a bitter taste in my mouth, as if I had not rested at all. As I sat up and looked around, I realized that Nella was no longer lying next to me, nor was she in the room. There was a piece of paper on the typewriter: "I had an appointment with Maurizio to discuss working in the movies . . . I'll be home early, before dinner." I was taken aback; Maurizio had said nothing about this and he was not in the habit of hiding things. Of course, it would have been useless to hide Nella's visit since I too was supposed to see him that afternoon. I reasoned that Nella must have called him and that Maurizio had invited her to his house at the same time I was supposed to be there. But why hadn't Nella waited for us to go together? With these questions circulating in my head I quickly got dressed and left the rooming house.

I was now in a rush to "surprise" Nella at Maurizio's; this way, I reasoned, I would have yet another weapon to use against Maurizio. I could prove that he had hidden something from me, and this would be useful when I decided to confront him about his feelings for Nella. Deceptiveness and lying, whatever the reason, were signs of weakness, and I was glad that Maurizio had finally cracked. Reinvigorated by these thoughts, I decided to take a taxi to Maurizio's house, and once there I did not hesitate to ring the bell; instead, I rang it with a kind of aggressive impatience.

The butler came to the door and wordlessly led me into the largest sitting room. The house, which the night before had been crowded with people and full of light, was now silent and dark. There was no sign of Nella. I sat in an armchair and almost involuntarily thought that she was probably somewhere upstairs. This thought was surely caused by jealousy; I knew of course that the bedrooms were upstairs and that Nella could be there for only one reason, in other words if something had happened between her and Maurizio the night before and an amorous relation had begun between them. But, though jealousy was the cause of this train of thought, I did not feel the corresponding emotions. I was calm and almost hopeful. I was locked in a struggle with Maurizio, and if Maurizio wanted Nella that would give me the upper hand.

A few minutes later the door opened and Maurizio walked in. Standing up, I asked, "Where is Nella?"

279

I must have looked visibly perturbed, because Maurizio seemed almost alarmed. Calmly, he asked: "What do you mean?"

"She told me she was coming here."

At first he looked surprised, but then he seemed to remember something and said in a measured tone: "I made an appointment with her, but not here, at the offices of Aquila Film, our production company . . . My partner, Moroni, will talk to her. I decided to stay here so that you and I could meet."

Once again I had betrayed myself and allowed my thoughts to lead me in a direction that did not fit my tortuous reality. I sat down, annoyed. "I'm sorry . . . I fell asleep and when I woke up I found a note from Nella saying that she had an appointment with you."

"That's right."

He went about the room opening windows and shutters in order to allow in the late afternoon sun. I took advantage of this pause to pull myself together and watch him. Even though this was our third meeting, I had never observed him closely; I now had the opportunity to see whether he was still the Maurizio I had always known and against whom I felt compelled to do battle. Our recent meetings had taken place in exceptional circumstances which were not conducive to close observation. The first had been in the dark, in Maurizio's car and in the square on the Gianicolo. The second was in a crowd of guests, after too much drink. I now observed him with great curiosity, as if seeing him for the first time.

272*

I was struck by a detail I had never noticed before: Maurizio had a limp. There was nothing disfiguring about this slight, halting movement; to the contrary, it gave him a mysterious, distinctive air. Comparing the man I had before me to my memories from five years earlier, I now saw that there were subtle changes. Back then, there had been something adolescent about him, whereas now one could say that he was almost too manly. He was tall, well built, with wide shoulders and big hands and feet; his face was pale but not wan, and rather full and well-fed; he had a bristling mustache beneath a pronounced nose and a willful chin and jaw. The overall impression was of physical strength; at first glance, he seemed hampered and embarrassed by it. He also seemed almost awkward or clumsy, as if he might knock over a table or step on someone's toes at any moment. But as I observed him more closely I realized that this first impression was misleading. In truth, as he moved about the sitting room his gait and gestures revealed a singular skill, prudence, and agility. By analogy, it occurred to me that the apparent simplicity and coarseness of his personality might conceal a similar agility and cunning. His face, for example, radiated an air of great simplicity, without subtlety or indecision. His brow was square, his eyes clear and well-outlined, his nose pronounced and mouth completely lacking in sinuosity. But then, if one looked more closely, one could just make out a slight air of prudent, cautious concern. His mouth had a tight cast to it, his eyes were shaded and slightly evasive. Behind the somewhat brutal mask lay a clever, cautious spirit.

He carefully regulated the position of the curtains 273*
so that the soft late afternoon light would shine evenly throughout the room. Then he came and sat down across from me. I felt much calmer and more lucid,

as if this chance to observe him had reassured me. He asked: "Would you like something to drink . . . a whiskey, perhaps?"

"No, thank you!" I said, with alacrity. "I think I drank enough last night to last me all year."

"As you like," he said, serving himself half a glass from a bottle on a small table and then mixing it with mineral water. After a brief pause, I spoke: "Last night I drank far too much, and I'm afraid I behaved deplorably."

He said nothing. It occurred to me that silence was probably one of the tactics he used to embarrass people who, like me, were impatient and overly earnest. So I decided that I too would remain silent. I would say nothing until he spoke, even if this meant that we sat in silence until the end of my visit. I pulled a pack of cigarettes and some matches out of my pocket, slowly lit one, and began to smoke. I reasoned that if Maurizio had no hostile intentions toward me, he would be surprised by my silence, and after a few moments, he would say something, or at least point out my strange behavior. But if, as I believed, he was hostile toward me and was animated by the same rivalry that I felt, he would remain silent, in an attempt to force me to speak first. In that case it would be obvious that he too saw us as rivals and enemies, as two people locked in struggle, however unspoken and unspeakable that struggle might be. A few minutes passed. I smoked in silence. Every so often, Maurizio took a sip of his drink. After a while I glanced at my watch and saw that seven minutes had passed. I waited another three minutes, and still, neither of 274* us spoke. Now I knew that I was right. Maurizio and

I saw things the same way; he did not consider us to be friends or acquaintances, but rivals, perhaps even enemies. This discovery encouraged me. The previous evening he had maintained a slippery, evasive attitude, hiding his intentions and leading me to wonder whether my interpretation of our rivalry might be simply the result of my own twisted logic and the fruit of my feelings of inferiority. But now I thought to myself: "So it's true . . . you too have a desire to conquer me, to put me at a disadvantage, as they say." This was a heartening thought: better a confessed enemy than a false friend. I decided to wait another five minutes, still hoping to make him talk. But after five minutes I had to confess that in this silent test of wills he was surely, if not necessarily the stronger party, at least the most disinterested. In other words, he emanated a complete indifference, whether sincere or excellently simulated I did not know. If I departed without speaking, I would be left with a nagging curiosity about what he might have said and how I might have responded. I would leave with the suspicion that he had nothing to say to me, and no desire to hear what I had to say. As I thought this, lucidly and objectively and in silence, I was once again forced to recognize that he was the stronger of the two. Suddenly I became annoyed and blurted out, in a cutting voice: "Fine, I'll speak . . . I'll speak first . . . but only to say that I can see your tactics; I know that by remaining silent you are presenting me with a kind of challenge, and I refuse to rise to the challenge. After all, we're not children anymore . . . staring in silence and waiting to see who will crack . . . That's a kid's game."

"That may be true, but still, you spoke first."

Evidently he felt strongly about his methods and was congratulating himself on the results: he had forced me to break the silence. I pretended not to understand what he was insinuating and continued: "Why are you limping? I don't remember you having a limp five years ago."

238* He answered indifferently: "I broke my leg fighting with the *partigiani* . . . jumping off a boulder in the mountains."

There was another silence. I stared at him and finally gave voice to a thought that had been bouncing around in my head for a while: "You know, you've changed."

He looked at me with some curiosity: "In what way?"

"You used to be more sure of yourself . . . and more arrogant, at least with me . . . Now you seem more prudent."

Almost with humility he confessed: "Yes, it's true."

"Why is that?"

He reflected for a moment: "I imagine it's because of everything that happened . . . We suffered quite a blow."

"You suffered quite a blow."

"Fine, *I* did."

He seemed strangely docile, even a bit sad. I asked, sympathetically: "What do you mean to do now?"

"Me? Nothing . . . I came back to Rome, I set up this movie business with Moroni . . . We're trying to make a movie . . . Hopefully, we'll succeed. That's all."

Finally approaching the topic I had come to discuss, I said: "Nella tells me that you agree with my ideas."

He looked at me and asked, "What ideas?" though it was clear that he knew what I meant.

"My political ideas."

"Well, yes," he muttered, hesitantly, "all in all, I think that you Communists are on the right track."

"So?"

"So, what?" 237*

"What are you waiting for? Why don't you take the leap, as they say?"

"You mean become a Communist?" he asked, gravely.

"Yes."

"I'm not waiting for anything," he said, with sudden conviction. "I just don't want to, that's all."

"Why not? After all, we're on the right track, as you yourself have said."

Instead of answering directly, he asked: "Why do you care? Last night, when you were drunk, you said the same thing."

"I care because, despite everything, I feel close to you," I said, slightly embarrassed.

He laughed. "You're being insincere."

"Why do you say that?" I asked, taken aback. At that moment, I felt that we were truly friends. My friendship with him seemed like a solid, immutable, poignant fact.

"Because it's not true . . . As they say, 'in vino veritas' . . . Last night you said that we were enemies, or at least rivals . . . and that you had always felt yourself to be my enemy . . . God knows why." And as he said this he chuckled, pouring himself another glass of whiskey.

I felt embarrassed. It was true, he was right; how could I have forgotten? "Well," I tried to explain, "I feel that I am both your friend and your enemy . . . I'm your enemy because in a way you are mine."

"Am I?" he said, staring at me. "Not at all . . . I don't understand you . . . Why would I be your enemy?"

"Come on, now," I said, with some effort, "you don't claim to be my friend, do you?"

I awaited his response with a deep, painful sense of uncertainty. For some reason that I did not understand I hoped that he would respond affectionately: "Of course I'm your friend." I knew that if he said that I would throw my arms around his neck and embrace him. Instead, he said, with insulting detachment: "I'm neither your friend nor your enemy . . . We're mere acquaintances."

I felt profoundly mortified, and at the same time angry at myself for feeling this way. I cared about his friendship and was hurt to hear him deny it. But his excessive indifference also confirmed my belief that he was not sincere, at least not completely, and made me think that his indifference was simply a new side of the obstinate hostility I had always attributed to him. "You say that," I could not help exclaiming, "because you know that it is the answer that hurts me the most . . . It is the answer of an enemy."

"I assure you," he said, looking at his glass with his head bowed, "that you are quite mistaken." He was silent for a moment, then continued: "You did not answer me sincerely . . . Why is it so important to you that I become a Communist?"

"I already told you," I began. Then I changed tactics: "Let's say it's because of my enthusiasm for

236*

Communism . . . When you believe in something, you want others to believe in it too."

"Fine. But why don't you try to convince Moroni, for example, or someone else?"

"Because I don't care about Moroni."

"Why do you care about me but not about Moroni?"

I did not answer. Nothing I could say would serve my argument. No matter what I said, I felt obscurely, it would lead me away from the subject and facilitate Maurizio's arguments. "Don't you have anything to say?" he insisted after a short pause.

"I've said everything there is to say," I answered, spitefully. "Do whatever you like . . . If you want to stay in your swamp, stay there . . . But I'm warning you: time passes . . . and soon it will be too late." As I said this I got up excitedly.

He remained sitting and said calmly, "I want to be clear with you . . . Even if I had no other reason, it is enough to see how much you want me to do this to convince me not to."

"But why?"

"Because your motives are not disinterested . . . that's all. No one believes the words of a man who speaks out of self-interest."

APPENDIX

1) Version A, typescript p. 188 (see p. 35)

[*In this version, when Sergio reads his article for the newspaper, he feels disappointed. This is quite different from his feelings in the revised version.*]

When Sergio went out the following day he realized that though the heat had intensified, the sky was now completely clear and the air was clean and crisp, with a touch of sea breeze. Sergio went directly to the newsstand across the street and bought a copy of the newspaper containing his article. He saw that it had been placed on the second page, with the local news, in small type. He felt disappointed; he had hoped that the editors would print it on the first page, as they had promised. He took the newspaper and crossed the street once again, to wait for the bus that would take him to Maurizio's. He had called his friend the previous evening as planned, from the newspaper offices. Maurizio had said that he would expect him early the following morning, because he was leaving at noon. It was nine o'clock, so there were still three hours left.

As Sergio waited for the bus, he read the first page of the newspaper. It contained news from the front, all catastrophic despite the euphemisms used in the military communiqués, as well as several articles denouncing the war and the dangerous dualism of the incongruous alliance between the anti-Fascist government and the Germans. Everything seemed to be in order and the sun was shining; people calmly walked to and fro and a few cars circulated in both directions, brass and nickel plating gleaming in the sun. Even the faces of the other people waiting for the bus

2) Version B, typescript p. 117 (see p. 156)

[*In this version, when Sergio asks Lalla to gratify Maurizio, she accepts, unlike in subsequent versions.*]

She said these words in a plangent tone, then got up and tottered to the door, opened it, and disappeared. Sergio lay on the bed, still furious, wallet in hand.

He did not wait long. Less than five minutes later, Lalla returned, closing the door behind her, and went to the mirror. Her words broke the silence: "All right, I'll do it . . . I will decide what day, and in what manner . . . but you can tell Maurizio that I accept."

She spoke calmly and seemed less drunk than before. Sergio got up and said, "I'm going to bed, I'm tired."

3) Version C1, typescript pages 229, 158–160, 242 (see p. 193)

[In this variant, the meeting takes place in the offices of the Allied radio services. The female character appears quite different from the one who will later go by the name of "Nella."]

I've spoken enough about the first important event 229 that took place in my life during the period following the end of the war. It's time for me to touch upon the second. Until that point, I had not experienced a great love; instead I had had brief, casual relations with several young women whom I did not love. But as soon as I returned to Rome, when half the country was still occupied by the Germans and the front line still lay near Florence, during that terrible, dark, anxious time, I met a woman whom I thought I loved and who surely loved me. Her name was Nella, and she was more or less my age; I was twenty-seven years old and she was twenty-five. She was tall, taller than I, with a thin, ardent, lean face and two flaming black eyes, a pointy nose, and fleshy lips. In profile, there was something almost animal-like and thirsty about her expression. Her body was also thin and equally ardent, lean, and highly strung. This ardor 158 and muscular slenderness were her principal characteristics; she reminded me of a gamecock with long, muscular legs, alive with nervous energy, veins filled with dense blood flowing at a temperature much higher than that of most people. She had a small head atop a muscular, stiff neck, an almost flat chest, and large, coarse hands and feet. Her legs were also coarsely shaped, not fat but strong and muscular and inelegant, with thick ankles and knees. Everything about her denoted rough origins, though she did not seem to be of peasant stock, for country folk often have a sweetness and grace about them. Her roughness was more typical of the petite bourgeoisie, or shop class, and in fact she came from a family of merchants in a small town in Lazio, Anagni I think, where they sold pots and pans.

I met Lalla in the offices of the Allied radio services, where I had gone seeking work. I had been involved in radio before the war, and now that I had no work, I had been told I might be able to find something there. She was a secretary in one of the offices. After I introduced myself, she said: "Please take a seat . . . I'm afraid you'll have to wait a while." I was struck by the frank, direct, almost aggressive tone of her voice and the look that accompanied her words, which I can only describe as provocative. It was Lalla's normal expression, which she used with all men, but I did not yet know this; I assumed that it was meant for me and only for me. After I took a seat, as she suggested, I began to talk to her. She was very relaxed and forthright and had no problem telling me her name and age, and she soon began to tell me about the town where she was born and about her parents. We were alone in the office, a small room facing a courtyard. She sat at her desk, and every so often she would return to her work and type a few lines very quickly, after which she would again pause to answer my questions. She spoke sarcastically about her superiors who were American and British officers. Finally, as if resigning herself to the fact that she would get no more work done while I was there, she turned toward me on her chair and crossed her legs. I remember that I noticed for the first time how heavy and strong her legs were, like the rest of her body. With her large, coarse, and somewhat impure hands she opened a pitiful, threadbare purse, pulled out an American cigarette, and lit it. When she 159 noticed that I was staring at her legs, she pulled the hem of her skirt down below her knees. We continued to talk; I can't quite remember what we discussed, nothing in particular. It was the kind of conversation dictated by desire, roughly equivalent to certain kinds of birdsong or animal calls. The substance was not important, and perhaps she did not even hear what I said, but my tone of voice came through and she must have felt it beating down on her like a ray of sun through a window. Finally she stood up. "I'll go find out if the major can see you," she said. As she walked across the room, I stared at her again and confirmed my first impressions of her. I could not help thinking that she was a woman of the people, down to her fingertips: provocative, vulgar, coarse. She was wearing ugly shoes with heels that were too high, an ugly, stretched-out skirt, and a loose sweater over a worn blouse. But in those threadbare clothes, the animal-like, aggressive quality of her beauty was almost more powerful. Her clothes surrounded her without touching her, it seemed; they were meant to be torn off, violently, in the fury of an amorous passion. As soon as she returned, saying "Not yet, you'll have to wait a bit longer," I grabbed her by the skirt, baring her thigh as I pulled her toward me. She did not pull away, and instead twisted her head to one side, rubbing her lips against mine, hard. Then she said, softly, "Let go . . . not here." Her lips were covered in a dense, thick lipstick, and this was what got us into trouble. At that very moment, the door opened and the British major looked out. He saw me sitting, my mouth covered in lipstick, and Lalla standing in front of me, her skirt still in my hand and slightly raised, exposing part of her leg. Calmly, he said: "*Signorina*, your services are no longer required." He said the words in an objective tone, without reproach, as if dismissal were the automatic result of the lipstick on my lips. Then he closed the door. Lalla was upset, I suppose, but showed it for only a brief moment as she stood facing the door with a surprised expression. Then she shrugged. "Well, let's go," she said, heading straight for the coatrack, from which she took her hat and a small umbrella the size of a fan. Somewhat dejected, but still feeling excited and stimulated by her proud, aggressive attitude, I followed her silently as she gathered her things, picked up her bag, and put on her jacket. "Sooner or later I was going to have to leave this dump," she said, almost as if to console me and diminish my sense of guilt. When she was ready she opened the door. But before leaving, she took one final look at the office and said, "Good riddance." We walked out into the hallway. I was still following her, feeling guilty and embarrassed, but also darkly aware that there was something strange, abnormal going on inside of me. She turned to look at me and began to laugh, almost ostentatiously, arching her shoulders and pushing her belly forward, in an almost provocative gesture. "Where do you think you're going looking like that?" she asked. The hallway was empty, and the door that led to the bathroom was ajar. She opened it, pulled me inside, and closed it behind her, pushing me against the mirror. I saw then that my mouth and cheek were still covered in lipstick; it looked like a kind of ridiculous, obscene red mustache. "Were you planning to walk around the city like that?" she added, laughing. Now she was near me, and I could not help grabbing her skirt once again, pulling her toward me as I had earlier in the office. This time she did not protest. She stretched out her hand and shut the door, locking it from the inside. With her other hand she assisted me, unzipping her skirt, shimmying out of it and leaning forward, lifting her hips and opening her legs, grabbing hold of the edge of the sink and lowering her head, as if to rinse her hair with water. I took her like this, from behind and standing up, like a bull taking a cow or a stallion a mare, except that we were not standing in a field of flowers but rather in a narrow bathroom, in front of a mirror and a sink. There was no whispering brook, only the gurgle of pipes. But the sensation was the same, that of a concrete, sensual impulse, a physical communion so perfect that it transcended the limits of blood and the senses and touched our souls. I remember that even as I stood there, still holding her firmly, I kissed her face humbly, full of gratitude, and she did the same. Later, we walked in the street, and it felt as if we did not really know how we had ended up there, as if we had been walking in a dream or had flown out of the window.

Later that same day, Lalla went to her rented room, 242 gathered a few belongings in some boxes tied with twine, along with a tattered old suitcase, and moved into my room at the boardinghouse, where there were two beds. I had proposed the idea, almost timidly, and she quickly accepted, saying simply: "You made me lose my job . . . You ruined me . . . now you have to take care of me." And thus began one of the most difficult, and also one of the happiest, periods of my life.

4) Version C, typescript p. 270 (see p. 233)

[These lines describe Nella's and Sergio's feelings as they ride the bus to Maurizio's house.]

[. . .]I was proud of her and of her beauty, and I wanted Maurizio to see her and admire her, just as I admired her at that moment.

Finally, when it was already quite late, we left the apartment and took a bus to Maurizio's. He lived in a neighborhood which, twenty years earlier, had been one of the most elegant and modern in the city. Now other, newer neighborhoods had sprung up around it, so that what had once been practically a suburb had become almost part of the city center. On the bus I noticed that Nella seemed uncomfortable and avoided looking me in the eye. It occurred to me that as she reflected on what had happened earlier at home, she felt hurt, and I suffered a pang of guilt. As soon as we stepped off the bus, she said:

Finally, when it was already quite late, we left the apartment and took a bus to Maurizio's neighborhood. Recently, new neighborhoods had sprung up around it, so that what had once been practically a suburb had become almost part of the city center. As the bus drove along, I became distracted thinking about Maurizio and our visit. Examining my feelings, I realized that I felt driven by an aggressive, pugnacious impulse, and at the same time I was tormented by a fear of not being up to the task at hand. It never occurred to me to think that this was just a simple visit, without particular significance, like so many others; I knew that this was not the case, and in a sense I was preparing myself

296

for what I thought awaited me. But instead of analyzing my own feelings of inferiority toward Maurizio and consciously replacing those subjective feelings with objective goals—as one often does in such cases—I tried instead to analyze his superiority, which was all in my mind, and to discover his points of weakness. As I have said before, to me it seemed that Maurizio's superiority sprang from his vitality, a quality that was mysterious and impossible to pin down, something I sensed but could not define. At the same time I believed that his social status was his greatest weakness; in other words, I believed that he belonged to a social class which I considered to be irreparably doomed. I realized that if I could impart this sense of doom, this fear [. . .]

NOTE ON THE TEXT

I. MATERIALS

The typescript pages of the three unpublished drafts of Sergio and Maurizio's story are in the archives of the Fondo Alberto Moravia in Rome. They consist of 258 typescript pages, on Fabriano Extra Strong paper measuring approximately 28 x 22 centimeters (11 x 8½ inches), unnumbered by the author. The numeration, provided by the archive, reflects the order in which the pages were discovered. Many pages had been damaged over the years and were recently restored.

A REDISCOVERED SUITCASE

The pages were found in a suitcase which was discovered, in poor condition, in the spring of 1996. According to Moravia's heirs and the directors of the Fondo, it was in the basement of Moravia's home on the Lungotevere della Vittoria. Another suitcase—which can be seen in photographs taken by Serafino Amato in the special edition of the *Quaderni del Fondo Moravia* (journal of the Fondo Moravia) dedicated to the exhibit *Moravia and*

Rome (November 2003, pp. 2–3, 201–203), had been discovered, in better condition, a few months earlier, in September 1995. The two suitcases contained various pages written by the author, including materials relating to several novels, such as *La ciociara* (*Two Women*), *La noia* (*Boredom*), and *L'attenzione* (*Attention*), as well as stories which were later included in *Racconti romani* (*Roman Tales*), *Nuovi racconti romani* (*New Roman Tales*), and *L'automa* (*The Fetish*). Thus all of these papers date from the fifties and early sixties, and certainly before 1963, the year Moravia moved out of his home on the Via dell'Oca and into his new home on the Lungotevere. It is possible that the writer, or someone else, filled the suitcases during the move in a somewhat disorderly fashion, packing recent and relevant texts and documents, not to be confused with material Moravia was actively working on at the time. It is also possible that these papers remained in the suitcases, untouched, from 1963 until they were discovered thirty years later.

This may explain their survival. As has been noted by several sources, the writer was known to destroy his preparatory materials once a book had been published. We recall the account of Sebastian Schadhauser (a German sculptor and friend of Moravia's), transcribed from a video at the Fondo Moravia. Schadhauser accompanied Moravia on several trips during the seventies and eighties, and assisted him during his convalescence from a hernia:

> During that period I often lit the fireplace in order to burn manuscripts. When [Moravia] finished writing something, he was in the habit of burning the manuscripts. He didn't keep manuscripts, he burned them. Also the corrected proofs. When he

received proofs from a newspaper, he would correct them, and then when they came back from the editor, he would burn them. There is a fireplace in the corner of his house on the Lungotevere della Vittoria. It's set at a diagonal, like this. He would light a fire there and burn papers. During that period, I did it because he couldn't get up. But he burned all of his manuscripts. I don't think there are many manuscripts in circulation. He had this habit. For him, the finished work was the published work. The rest, he burned.

Up to the present, no other drafts or notes related to Moravia's novels from before the seventies have been found; there are only a few clean proofs, kept by his editor, which reflect the final version of the work (there is one typescript of *La romana* (*The Woman of Rome*) and one of *La noia*). The situation with the more recent novels is somewhat different; the Fondo Moravia has several drafts that survived in the writer's home. Of course, it is possible that in the future other lost typescripts or manuscripts will be found, especially if they were given by the author to friends, relatives, or editors, as in the case of a typescript of *Il disprezzo* (*Contempt*), that was discovered in 2002. This was an almost final draft of the novel, and it is now in the collection of the Fondo Moravia. But until now the only texts that have survived from the writer's office are those discovered in the suitcase at the house on Lungotevere della Vittoria, which escaped the flames thanks to the vicissitudes of the move.

In order to understand the dimensions of Moravia's directive and to evaluate the typescript pages that have survived, we must pause to reflect on the very small number of pages that have been discovered.

It is of course impossible to quantify the total number of typescript pages produced by the author over the course of preparing a novel, but based on the meager resources—letters and interviews—to be found in the "Notes on the Texts" in Bompiani's Classici edition of *Opere complete di Alberto Moravia* (*Complete Works*), volumes 1–4, we could estimate the number to be around one thousand pages, over two thousand in the case of the longer novels. For example, the typescript pages relating to the composition of *La ciociara*, *La noia*, and *L'attenzione* found in the two suitcases represent only a small fraction of the total preparatory materials relating to those works (about a fifth). This would mean that the 258 pages relating to the three versions of this unpublished novel would have been only one small part of the complete preparatory work. If they represent early versions of the novel, that would mean that there was still much work to be done before the completion of the final version.

The pages found in the two suitcases were immediately handed over to the Fondo Alberto Moravia, which was new at the time. The Fondo, in turn, passed them on to the Gabinetto Vieusseux in Florence (directed by Enzo Siciliano) in September of 1995 and April 1996. There, they were numbered, indexed, and partially restored. In April 1999 they were returned to the Fondo Moravia, where they still reside, and where we were able to refer to them during the preparation of the multivolume "Classici Bompiani" edition.

Even if further study of these pages relating to the story of Sergio and Maurizio might have suggested the possibility of an alternative order, we decided to keep the original numeration provided by the archive because it documents the order in which the pages were originally found (in the suitcase). If in fact this order was determined by Moravia himself, we can derive useful information from it, as we will see, in the task of identifying the texts.

The "Due Amici" Typescripts

Among the pages found in the first, more battered, suitcase were those related to an unfinished project. In the absence of a title, they are identified in the Fondo Moravia under the heading "Sergio Maurizio." For this edition, we decided to use the title *I due amici* (Two friends). These pages date from the period 1951–1952 and are the oldest example we now have of Moravia's compositional methods. The aforementioned typescript for *La romana* (*The Woman of Rome*), in the collection of the late Valentino Bompiani, is different: it is in a completed draft, ready to be be sent out to readers.

Before reconstructing the biographical and narrative context, we must describe these texts carefully, pointing out the details which are most useful for dating them and determining their internal order.

Version A

The first group of pages, which we have called Version A, consists of sixty-two typescript pages, unnumbered and unmarked by the author, plus nine more abandoned, rewritten, or substituted by him. According to the current numeration in the archive, this corresponds to pages 162–225 and 231–37 in Dossier 6 (Incartamento 6). Many pages, now restored, had deteriorated over time and include lacunae, especially near the margins.

Regarding the text, there are frequent typewritten corrections but none by hand, with the exception of page

214. The narrative sequence, which can easily be reconstructed despite a few lacunae which we will discuss later, is the following: pages 231, 162–215, 221–22, and 216–20. However, it is difficult to establish a date for the composition of these pages, because there are no material clues nor clues within the text itself—except for a generic reference to post-conflict events. The only clues can be derived from the order in which the pages were assembled and conserved within the suitcase; for example, page 161, a discarded or misplaced page (found) near a typescript identifiable as "Il Monumento" (see *Opere,* volume 3, and in particular page 1118), a story that was published in the newspaper *Il Mondo* on March 24, 1951. Of course, this proximity does not allow us to date the typescript, in that it may well be accidental and may have occurred at a later date, but it may possibly indicate a *terminus post quem*, if we were to imagine a progressive accumulation of pages on the writer's desk. In general, Version A seems to date from the period after March 1951. Another element, which we will consider later, is the obvious connection between this text and themes and characters in Versions B and C.

The missing sections comprise, for the most part, the beginning and the end of the text. The pages—or page—containing the true *incipit* of the narration have been lost. The top of the first page we do have, typescript page 231, which precedes all others from a narrative perspective, is severely damaged and probably does not contain the beginning of the story. In the present edition, after a lacuna, the beginning of the text seems to suggest a previous event (line 18 of page 231). In the preceding lines, Moravia had written a passage in triplicate, something he often did in the initial phases of composition. The text of lines 1–17 follows:

[. . .] The opportunity arose e<arlier> [. . .] <. . .>o;
when their o<wn> [. . .] completely under<stood>
[. . .] automobile [. . .] [. . .] arose quite a bit earlier
[. . .] their hostility was [. . .] <under>stood. They had
[. . .] and Sergio decided one day [. . .] <auto>mobile
that Maurizio's parents ha<d bou>ght [. . .] <. . .>st
birthday. The opportunity arose quite a bit earlier
than t<hey> [. . .] <wh>en their hostility had not
yet [. . .] completely understood. That year, when
Mau<rizio> [V] <Ser>gio eighteen, also marked the
beginning, for Maurizio, of [. . .] he had a foreign
lover, te<n years> older [. . .] he was moderately infatuated, while she was in love and [. . .].

There is another missing passage between typescript
pages 231 and 162. The passage probably comprises a
single missing page, which in all likelihood contained
the conversation between Emilia and Sergio, the outcome of which is described on page 162.

The story proceeds from there onward without inter-
ruptions for fifty-four typescript pages (162–215), which
constitute the main body of the text that has survived.
After page 215, one or more pages are missing. The two
brief remaining sections (pages 221–22 and 216–20)
have a clear, if not completely identifiable, connection
to the earlier scenes and themes. In the first (pages
221–22), the two characters are still in the park of the
Museo Borghese. This connects the scene to preceding
events; we can hypothesize that there is perhaps only a
single typescript page missing between pages 215 and
221. The final section (pages 216–20), in which Sergio
accompanies the young girl to her new lodgings, clearly
takes place later. What is more difficult to understand,
because of the missing pages, is the scene in which the

two characters shop for a bathing suit—perhaps they were planning to go swimming in the Tevere, given the August heat.

There are a few clear breaks in the text—indicated with empty spaces or typewritten symbols, demarcating sections, however provisional these may be (on pages 164, 188, and 214). Based on these breaks, we can hypothesize regarding the basic structure of the narrative:

    I. (pp. 231, 162–64): Maurizio breaks off relations with Emilia and Sergio.
   II. (pp. 165–70): Sergio in the years leading up to the war
  III. (pp. 170–88): the war years and the fall of Fascism
  IV. (pp. 189–214): the visit to Maurizio's house; the air raid
  V. (pp. 215, 221–22, 216–20): the meeting with Nella

From a narrative standpoint, one can surmise that the first two sections are a kind of prologue, in which Maurizio and Sergio are presented to the reader and the story of their friendship before the war is recounted. The actual story begins in 1943, when Sergio is faced with the choice between taking a political stand and leaving Rome, between Federico's proposal and Maurizio's. It continues with the visit to Maurizio's house and the scene in which Sergio and Maurizio meet Nella.

At the bottom of page 185 we see the only compositional note present on these typescripts: "He goes to Maurizio's villa, decadence, dog and cat, Maurizio's family." This note clearly indicates what is to come in the following pages.

The second typescript consists of eighty-seven unnumbered pages. The archive subsequently numbered the pages, according to the order in which they were found: pages 55–66, 68, 70–74, 76–121, and 123–43, all from Dossier 6 (Incartamento 6). Among the tranches of Moravia's project, the second is the most complete. Most of the corrections are inserted by typewriter, very few by hand (only on pages 62 and 105).

A few visual markings in the text clearly indicate narrative breaks. They consist of either typewritten symbols or empty spaces on pages 62, 84, 90, 108, 118, 131, and 140. The following structure is revealed:

   I. (pp. 55–62): Sergio and Lalla
  II. (pp. 62–84): Sergio and Lalla visit Maurizio's house.
 III. (pp. 84–90): dialogue between Sergio and Lalla
  IV. (pp. 90–108): Sergio and Maurizio's pact regarding Lalla
   V. (pp. 109–18): the party at Moroni's
  VI. (pp. 118–31): the drive to Olevano
 VII. (pp. 131–40): events at Olevano
VIII. (140–43): Sergio and Maurizio's return to Rome

Regarding the dates of composition of this version, we have the following clues:

1) Two of the pages were reused by Moravia and contain, on the back, traces of earlier texts, which can be dated (pages 96 and 115). Typescript page 96 contains a brief narrative note on the back, which, due to

its format, appears to be part of a movie script ("An investor visits a textile factory; the owner of the factory is hoping for an investment. During the visit, the group"). As we will see, we can hypothesize that this note refers to the screenplay for a film by the French director Claude Autant-Lara, but we cannot exclude the possibility that it comes from an updated adaptation of Giovanni Verga's story "La lupa," which Moravia completed in 1953 for the director Alberto Lattuada. According to one critic, this consisted of "a complete revision of the narrative material, containing a new character, invented by Moravia: the owner of the Manifattura Tabacchi" (Agnoletti, 1953).

2) Two lines appear on the reverse of page 115 ("more and more, and everything was useless because the more I spent, the more she said I was stingy and that I hated to spend money, and on and on"). These lines belong to a draft of the "Roman tale" "Sciupone" ("Spendthrift"), which was published in the *Corriere della sera* on April 18, 1953 (see *Opere*, volume 3, page 519). Since Moravia usually completed his stories not long before they were published in the newspaper, this page gives us a *terminus post quem*: the writing on the reverse of the page cannot date from before April 1952. This is perhaps the most certain and significant clue we have regarding the dating of this text.

3) Two letters intermixed with the pages of Version B probably reflect the accumulation of papers on Moravia's desk (pages 75 and 112). Page 75 contains an invitation to an exhibition, written on letterhead from the Centro Nazionale di Studi Umanistici di Roma and dated May 15, 1952. Page 112 is a typewritten

letter dated May 16, 1952, and addressed to "Riccio," probably Attilio Riccio. In the letter Moravia discusses the contract for a screenplay (perhaps the one that appears on page 96).

4) Two pages (67 and 69) belong to Version C but are mixed in with the pages from Version B. This too is an important clue, because the intentional placement of these two pages among the pages of the second draft confirms the chronological precedence of Version B (written in the third person) with respect to Version C (written in the first person). In Version C, Moravia returns to characters and situations from Version B (such as the arrival at Maurizio's villa on page 68 and the description of Maurizio on page 70), but he leaves pages 67 and 69 unfinished, mixed in with the pages of Version B, and decides to write them again. The new pages are placed in Version C (273 and 272*). (To avoid confusion, the pages from Dossier 4 are indicated with an asterisk; the pages without this symbol are all from Dossier 6.)

It appears that the typescript of Version B may date from the period April–May of 1952 and was subsequently used as a draft for Version C.

Version C

The third draft, which we have called C, consists of eighty-two pages, plus twenty-two additional pages abandoned or rewritten at this stage of composition. These are clusters of unordered pages whose narrative continuity can be easily reconstructed: pages 226–29, 230, 238–41, and 242–96 from Dossier 6 and pages 260*–74*, 238*,

237*, 236*, 235*, and 234* from Dossier 4. There are only a few corrections, written in pen on (pages 229, 255, 293, and 273*). Pages 144, 148–60, and 217*–33* were all discarded by the author. There are no page numbers or other notes.

There are very few clues to the dates of composition. The draft includes pages from another typescript (pages 145–47), that of the Roman tale "Il pensatore" ("The Thinker"), which was published in the *Corriere della sera* on May 4, 1962. But it is impossible to pinpoint the moment at which the pages were mixed together. However, since Version C was written after Version B and before Moravia began work on *Il disprezzo* (*Contempt*), as we will discuss, the composition of this version can be dated sometime between May and July 1952.

A few breaks in the text, which we have preserved, indicate breaks in the narration, some of which were probably temporary. The breaks are indicated with blank space or typed symbols and occur on typescript pages 229, 240, 249, 259, and 268*. Page 259 suggests a continuation, after the final line, "I would have liked to s<ay>." Thus, it is possible to theorize the following sequence, in six chapters:

I. (pp. 226–29): the "first important event": Sergio's inscription into the Communist Party
II. (pp. 230, 238–40): the "second important event": the encounter with Nella
III. (pp. 241–49): life with Nella
IV. (pp. 249–59): the encounter with Maurizio
V. (pp. 260–96 and 260*–68*): the party at Maurizio's house
VI. (pp. 268*–74*, 238*, 237*, 236*, 235*, and 234*): Sergio's conversation with Maurizio

Again, this is only a provisional breakdown. If we consider the structure of Moravia's novels from this period, we can imagine that the author intended to include a prologue, distinguishable as such from the start, in which the narrator would illustrate the "two important events" in his life during the period after the end of the war; in other words, Sergio's inscription into the Communist Party and his encounter with Nella. This would be followed by the first real narrative event; in other words, the "first chapter," in which Sergio describes Maurizio's invitation and the party.

The composition of Version C evolved in two phases, as suggested by the change in the name of the female character, from "Lalla" (as in the previous version) to "Nella." Her characterization is profoundly different in each phase. As we will see, we are talking about an important rethinking of the character. This new version introduces, for the first time, the theme of "contempt" which will eventually lead to the abandonment of this project and the starting point of a new novel. For reasons of clarity, we will refer to phases C1 and C2.

The draft of C1 proceeds, without interruption, for about ten pages (226–29, 158–60, and 242–44). Lalla is self-assured, "rough," provocative. But beginning on page 245, she becomes Nella, and is characterized by her timidity and gentleness. In this context, Moravia rewrites the pages describing their first meeting in the offices of the Allied Services, but does not bother to rewrite the pages that precede or follow this scene. He replaces pages 158–60 of C1 with pages 230 and 238–41 of C2. He hastily ties the the new pages together with the previous pages, crossing out (with a pen) the sections of page 229 in which the young woman first appears under the name "Lalla." But he does not bother to do this on following pages. This creates a confusing deformation of the text, caused by a lack of agreement between pages 241 (C2) and 242 (C1). The sequence and the author's intentions are clear, but it seems that a revision parallel to the one on page 229 never took place.

In accordance with our decision to publish the text in its most advanced form, we have adopted phase C2, while including the corresponding pages from C1 in the appendix. In addition, we have made a few indispensible changes in order to connect pages 241 and 242. To begin with, we eliminated the first seven lines of page 242 (which appear in the appendix), just as the author did on page 229. As we have already observed, in this phase of composition, Moravia was not overly concerned with eliminating earlier versions but was careful to distinguish between abandoned versions and more recent ones. Once again we can theorize that the author was simply saving time and was planning to correct the draft in a later revision. Secondly, we changed the name "Lalla" to "Nella" in the three pages from C1 preserved with C2 (242–44). Despite these small edits, there are a few spots in which these pages refer to elements that have been either cut or altered. For example, the beginning of page 243 ("I said earlier that this was a difficult period in my life but in truth it was probably the happiest time I had known") refers to a phrase that the reader will not find in the text but rather in the version that appears in the appendix. The same is true of the reference to the "radio service" (page 243), rather than to a generic office of the Allied Services, which refers back to one of the abandoned pages. Nella's "clumsiness," to which Sergio refers on page 243, is also a leftover from the character of Lalla.

In C2, as we have indicated, the theme of "contempt" is developed for the first time (page 240). It is mentioned only in passing in C1 (page 160). The importance of the appearance of this theme is clear in Moravia's process—this is the point at which the author probably decided to abandon the project at hand, which was centered on the ideological rivalry between two friends, and to instead proceed with a different novel, which would eventually be titled *Il disprezzo* (*Contempt*). Thus, the development of *Il disprezzo* can be said to have begun in July 1952, at the moment the current project was abandoned. We should keep in mind that the feelings of contempt described by the narrator Sergio are quite different from the contempt which provides the subject of the subsequent, eponymous novel. In fact, the original title of the latter novel was *Il fantasma di mezzogiorno* (*A Ghost at Noon*). One significant difference: in the earlier novel, the feeling is experienced by the narrator toward the woman whom he is using as a means to an end, while in the later book, published in 1954, the feeling is experienced by the woman toward her husband.

Among the abandoned pages, a few (219*–220*, included in the appendix) suggest a different narrative direction. Instead of bumping into Maurizio and being invited to a party at his house, Sergio and Nella are invited to "a little gathering at the house of a man called Moroni, a friend, or more specifically a student, of Nella's" (page 219*). As we know, this character and situation already appear in Version B, and it would seem that early on, Moravia intended to continue along those lines. Nella refuses to attend Moroni's "little gathering" because of the poor state of her wardrobe, and Sergio becomes violent. The writer picks up this scene once again in Version C, but in reference to Maurizio's party. One can therefore posit that these three pages were meant to follow the "prologue" (after page 249) and to constitute the first version of the party. The party will later become a gathering organized by Maurizio, and Moroni will become a guest, a small-time cinema producer.

II. EXTERNAL HISTORY

In order to reconstruct the external history of these typescripts, we must first gather all the information that can illuminate Moravia's working process in the period between *Il conformista* (*The Conformist*), which he finished in November 1950 and published in April 1951 (see *Opere*, volume 3, pages 2972–82) and *Il disprezzo* (*Contempt*), which was begun, as we shall see, in July 1952 and published in 1954 (see *Opere*, volume 3, pages 2127–36). We will try to reconstruct, as far as the documents allow, the temporal arc spanning the period from the end of 1950 to the summer of 1952. We must consider the rare references in interviews and letters, even though, as we shall see, they are vague and contradictory.

THE INTERVIEWS

Two interviews are particularly relevant. Moravia was interviewed by Pasquale Festa Campanile on January 8, 1952, for the journal *La Fiera Letteraria* (The book fair) and one year later, on February 8, 1953, for the journal *Il Lavoro Illustrato* (Illustrated work). The first interview allows us some insight into the author's literary and publishing situation during those years. Moravia says:

> I have been suffering from insomnia. I work in
> the morning, and in the afternoon I rest. I've never

been a very assiduous worker. It took me two years
to finish *Il conformista*. I think it will take me some
time to recover from this book. After all, I've written
fifteen books. I'm preparing a volume of 600 pages
for Bompiani, an anthology of stories [. . .] all of the
stories I have written from 1927 onward. I am currently writing a very modern play; I'd rather not say
any more about it, perhaps I'll never finish it. And
besides, I don't even know what the title will be, or
how many acts it will have. On the other hand, I've
been writing a lot of stories for the *Corriere della
sera*. Have you seen them? They are all set in Rome.
I am very attached to these stories; I've written fifty
so far; I'm from Rome, I know it well, and I like
its inhabitants. So I love to write about them in my
own way [. . .] I've been publishing these stories
in the *Corriere*, and toward the end of the year I'm
planning to gather them all into a volume. I think
I will simply call it *Racconti romani*. I've also been
thinking about a very short novel; but this is a project that I am not yet ready to discuss.

It seems that in early 1952 Moravia was mainly thinking about stories. The omnibus volume (*I racconti*) was
in fact published in April 1952. Meanwhile, almost every
month, Moravia published twenty more Roman tales In
the *Corriere*, in addition to the fifty he had already published; they were all collected in a single volume in 1953.
The reference to a project for the theater is more mysterious; it was probably abandoned. Even more mysterious and probably more relevant is the mention of a
"very short novel," which he is still "thinking about." It
seems that at this point early in 1952 Moravia had not
yet begun work on the novel, and that he was still feeling
tired and discouraged in the aftermath of *Il conformista*.

But a year later, in the 1953 interview, a different picture emerges. In the interviewer's words:

> Between 1950 and 1952, for example, [Moravia] wrote a long novel; he was not happy with it and decided to burn it. This novel recounted the story of a group of young Communists and the relationship between their romantic lives and their political ideologies. In other words, he wanted to show the degree to which a political party which does not allow space for individuality can influence the relations of the heart. The novel that Moravia is currently writing is entitled *Fantasma di mezzogiorno*; it too deals with a romantic episode. *Fantasma di mezzogiorno* is now finished, but Moravia is writing it again from the beginning, and he has not yet decided whether he will publish it.

Fantasma di mezzogiorno was the original title of *Il disprezzo*; in fact, the English edition was published under the title *A Ghost at Noon*. But the reference to a "long novel," written between 1950 and 1952 and then incinerated, is a mystery. All we know is its subject ("the story of a group of young Communists and the relationship between their romantic lives and their political ideologies") and the overriding idea ("the degree to which a political party which does not allow space for individuality can influence the relations of the heart").

There are no other explicit references to this project in other interviews, unless we include a mention in the first autobiographical interview given by the author to Enzo Siciliano, published in 1971. The author recalls a sketch for an abandoned novel with a similar plot but dates it to the period after the publication of *Il disprezzo* and before

La ciociara (*Two Women*); in other words, between 1954 and 1956:

Q: So, with *La ciociara* you returned to a Roman subject.

A: Yes. Well, if not a Roman subject, at least a choral theme, like the rest of my Roman writings. I had begun writing a very different novel: I had already written about two hundred pages, but I didn't like them. It was the story of a very rich man who is responsible for the disillusionment of a young Communist because he manipulates him into going to bed with his wife, a very beautiful woman. Some time later I made a story out of it.

The plot sounds similar to the one regarding "a group of young Communists and the relationship between their romantic lives and their political ideologies," or at least it seems to emerge from the same thematic intention. This sketch for a novel, which could be dated to the period 1954–1956, seems to be linked, like the one from the period 1950–1952, to the idea of the romantic life of a young Communist. Among the pages from the suitcase that appear to date from the period of *La ciociara* and *La noia* (*Boredom*), there are none that contain a similar plot featuring a Communist character (see *Opere*, volume 4), nor has a story with a similar subject been identified. This discrepancy could be explained simply by a lack of chronological precision on Moravia's part during the interview, which took place twenty years after the fact. It is possible that in this interview Moravia was in fact referring to the project which he undertook in the period 1951–1952.

But we have no further details with which to support this hypothesis.

Leaving behind the contradictory references in his public declarations, we turn our attention to possible clues in Moravia's private correspondence, especially the correspondence with his editor (see *Opere*, volume 3, pages 2063–2087 and 2126–2149). In this case too there are possible distortions, which may result from the fact that Moravia was attempting to obtain more advantageous conditions and financial assistance, especially during the years after the enormous success of *La romana* (*The Woman of Rome*), when he was seeking financial autonomy.

The failure of *Il conformista*, which the author attributed, not incorrectly, to the hostility of the critics, caused a kind of depression in him, thereby rendering the second half of 1951 unproductive. He writes, in a letter dated July 20: "A great listlessness has come over me after the Italian critics' unjust and stupid reception of my last novel. I have almost no desire to work" (Archivio Bompiani). The first interview with Festa Campanile confirms this state of mind ("I think it will take me some time to recover from this book") as well as his diffidence toward the critics: "Most of the critics are against me; they would be happy if I were to slip on the banana peel of a misguided book."

He seems to have gone back to work around December 1951, after two weeks in Paris, whence he wrote a Christmas letter to his editor: "I feel well again after the exhaustion of the past months, and I've begun to work" (Archivio Bompiani). As we can decipher from fragmentary references over the following months, between January and March 1952 Moravia worked on and off on the "very brief novel" which he later refers to in the January 8, 1952, interview and completed a first version of the book.

But work on the novel was rendered more difficult and later interrupted by financial difficulties, the leitmotif of his correspondence with Valentino Bompiani during these months. It makes sense to take these difficulties into consideration, because they have a real effect, as well as a thematic influence, on the novel. After a first alarm bell sounded in a letter dated January 30 ("I would be very grateful, given that I find myself in a tight spot, if you could speed up the payment of those five hundred dollars"), the author blames the editor for his fiscal problems on February 27:

Dear Bompiani, having declared my income, as you advised me to, I now find myself in a very unpleasant situation which, in part, I had predicted: I must pay so much in taxes that I don't know if I will be able to pull it off. And, even if I am able to do so, I will have to begin writing for money, articles, screenplays, in other words quick projects etc., etc., etc., and no novels. Therefore I will not be able to exercise the profession for which I was born, that of writing novels. I leave it up to you to judge how useful this is to me at this time, when I could, with greater financial tranquility, have produced my best work. So be it. [. . .] I feel that I have many things to say, important things, but unfortunately I am oppressed by material needs. When I think that Armenise, the producer of penicillin, declares a lower income than I do, it makes me laugh.

The complaints return again and again, and Moravia threatens to suspend his literary efforts in order to dedicate himself to screenplays, as in a letter dated March 18: "What will suffer will be my literary output. The taxman must be paid. So for the past two months or so I've been working on a screenplay and have set aside all my beloved manuscripts." The message to the editor is clear: if you want me to write novels, you must offer more support. It is important to note how Moravia distinguishes between the literary work of the novelist and the commercial work of the screenwriter, which will later become an important structural element of *Il disprezzo*, set in the early years of the postwar period.

But despite his work on a screenplay, Moravia did not completely abandon his "beloved manuscripts" (by which he means both the handwritten and the typed scripts). In fact, he completed the first version of a novel, as he writes in a letter dated March 20, 1952, to Bompiani: "I have finished a short *romanzetto* [novella]. But who knows when I will be able to revise it and clean it up. Woe is me, I work to pay the taxman."

Note the wording: "short novella." This does not seem to match the "long novel" that, according to the second interview with Festa Campanile, Moravia completed in 1952, but rather the "very brief novel" mentioned in the first interview. In other words, he is referring not to one of his lengthy novels, such as *La romana* and *Il conformista*, but rather to one of his so-called novellas, such as *La mascherata* (*The Fancy Dress Party*), *Agostino* (*Two Adolescents*), *La disubbidienza* (*Disobedience*), and *L'amore coniugale* (*Conjugal Love*), none of which exceeded 150 typewritten pages and which Moravia would collect in 1953 in a volume titled *Romanzi brevi* (Short novels). (In the same letter, he refers to the English editions of *Agostino* and *La disubbidienza* as *romanzetti*, "novellas.") Note also two other terms—"revise" and "clean up"—which further illuminate Moravia's working methods. A revision refers to a complete rewriting, resulting in a text substantially different from the previous version; cleaning up, on the other hand, refers to small adjustments to the narrative and to the expressive coherence of a definitive text.

It is difficult to ascertain which screenplay in particular was draining time and energy from Moravia's novella. According to the letter dated March 18, he had already been working on it for "the past two months or so." In the March 20 letter he announces his departure for Paris, where he would spend two weeks at Transcontinental Film working on this particular project. On his return from France on May 2, he wrote to Giacomo Antonini, Bompiani's man in Paris: "I spent only three or four days in Paris, and the rest of the time I was in Monfort d'Amaury, working on this accursed film with Autant Lara and a screenwriter [. . .] I've been very involved movie projects lately, while also working on a short novel." (Archivio Vieusseux)

Unfortunately, it has been impossible to establish the title of the "accursed film" by Claude Autant-Lara that Moravia was working on during this period. In the midst of his work for the movies, the literary project was advancing slowly. It would seem that in this letter he is referring to revisions of the "brief *romanzetto*" he had completed in March; in other words, Version B.

In order to fully reconstruct the months between April and July, we must recall two important, connected episodes. First, the publication in April of the volume of collected stories (*I racconti*), which Moravia would have seen on his return from France and which constitutes the first volume of the *Opere complete*, with its blue and black dust jackets. And, perhaps more important, the Church's condemnation of Moravia's entire oeuvre, which, along with André Gide's, was placed in the Index of Forbidden Books maintained by the Congregation of the Holy See, with a decree published in the *Osservatore romano* newspaper on May 27. This ban would be removed only in 1966, after the abolition of the Index during the Second Vatican Council. The ban would cause intense public discussion and a general feeling of solidarity toward the author, especially in cultural circles. This support would be translated into an award, the Premio Strega, for *I racconti* in July of the following year, and Moravia's subsequent liberation from economic worries and the need to work in the film industry. The day after the Strega award ceremony, Moravia left for Sorrento and Capri, where he planned to "finish preparing the novellas for the second volume of the complete works," as he wrote to Bompiani on July 15. It is possible that the project of collecting his four earlier *romanzetti* or "brief novels" (*La mascherata, Agostino, La disubbidienza,* and *L'amore coniugale*) was somehow connected to his work on the mysterious new *romanzetto*, which would have become the fifth work in the collection.

But, as we have seen, it was in July of that year that Moravia began his new novel. In a letter to Bompiani from Anacapri dated September 7, he writes: "This summer I completed a hundred pages of the novel I began writing in July. I've abandoned the other one I was working on, after writing about three hundred pages, at least for now. This new novel looks promising."

It seems likely that this "new novel," begun in July 1952, was *Fantasma di mezzogiorno,* or *Il disprezzo,* which, after several drafts, Moravia would finish in August 1953 and send to the publisher at the beginning of 1954. In this letter, the "abandoned" novel is not referred to as a "very brief novel" (as on January 8), a "brief *romanzetto*" (as on March 20), or a "brief novel" (as on May 2), but rather as a three-hundred-page text, perhaps the "long novel" mentioned to Festa Campanile in February 1953.

III. INTERIM CONCLUSIONS

The contradictory, inconclusive data we have been able to collect does not permit us to completely elucidate the evolution of Moravia's process in the early fifties, or to identify with utter confidence the typescripts in our possession. That said, it is possible to propose the following hypotheses.

THE STORY OF SERGIO AND MAURIZIO

It is likely that the typescript we have called Version B is in fact the "very short novel" referred to by Moravia in his first interview with Festa Campanile as well as in his March 20 letter to Valentino Bompiani, the same book which he referred to as a "brief novel" in his May 2 letter to Giacomo Antonini. More specifically, it appears to be a "revision" of an earlier draft, written between March and May 1952.

Since the two other versions, A and C, can be placed before and after Version B, they can also be considered part of this "brief novel" Moravia was working on. Version A would therefore be a section of the first draft; since the March 20 letter to Bompiani refers to a "finished" text, we can conclude that many pages have been lost. Version C could then be dated to the period between May and July 1952.

It is clear that this is not a finished work. Each version is a revision of the previous one, and there certainly would have been more. At this point it is necessary to shed light on the connections between this "brief novel," written in early 1952, and the "long novel" that seems to have preceded it, as well as the one that followed, *Il disprezzo*.

Regarding the "long novel," we have only a few details of its theme, the effect of political ideology on the amorous relations of young Communists; in addition, we have the information that the draft had reached three hundred pages in July 1952 and that it was subsequently burned, probably sometime between September 1952 and February 1953. The difficulty lies first of all in defining the identity of this unfinished, lost, and burned text. We can exclude the hypothesis that, despite the author's declarations, it might have survived and could be related to one of the novels that came after *Il disprezzo*, such as the project mentioned in the 1971 interview with Siciliano or even *La ciociara*, from 1957, despite that book's long gestation period, which extended back to the forties (see *Opere*, volume 3, pages 2150–67).

Thus, there are only two alternatives: either the "long novel" and the "brief novel" are two separate projects, or they are substantially one and the same. In the first hypothesis, Moravia effectively would have written a long novel of around three hundred pages, already in an advanced state in 1951, and then burned it, perhaps saving one section. It is possible that the story "Luna di miele, sole di fiele" ("Bitter Honeymoon"), which was published in the journal *Paragone* in November 1951 and was subsequently included in the second edition of

Racconti 1927–1951 (1953), bears some relation with this project on the subject of Communism (see *Opere*, volume 3, pages 355–85). The second hypothesis is that the "long novel" and the "brief novel" are actually the same project, and that these contradictory references are the result of different phases, revisions, expansions, or reductions lost to time—or simply of Moravia's imprecision.

At this time, this second hypothesis appears to be the most likely scenario. What is certain is that there is a thematic affinity between the "story of a group of young Communists and the relationship between their romantic lives and their political ideologies" and the plot found in these typescripts at the Fondo Moravia, in which ideology in fact destroys the relationship between two young lovers. The story that emerges from these typescripts breathes life into the ghost of the previously lost novel regarding the lives of young Communists. It would seem likely that Moravia's passing mention in his 1953 interview with Festa Campanile is an indirect reference to the typescripts now at the Fondo Moravia.

THE PREHISTORY OF *IL DISPREZZO* (*CONTEMPT*)

There is one final aspect to consider: the connection between the "brief novel" of 1952 and *Il disprezzo*. The first idea for *Il disprezzo* seems to date from before the composition of the novel on the theme of Communism, as documented by a letter to Valentino Bompiani dated June 1951: "I'm thinking of writing a brief novel that will include a ghost as one of the characters" (Archivio Bompiani). This mysterious note makes sense when one considers the original title of *Il disprezzo*, *Il fantasma di mezzogiorno*, referring to a "ghost" who appears in the epilogue (see *Opere*, volume 3, page 2128). This idea probably emerged from an autobiographical context, Moravia's conjugal crisis, which is worth exploring insofar as it allows us to identify his narrative process. The most explicit reference comes from an interview with Alain Elkann, after the death of his first wife, Elsa Morante:

MORAVIA: Yes, there were days when I wanted to kill her. Not to separate, which would have been a rational solution, but to kill her, because our relationship was so close, so complex, and so thoroughly alive that violence seemed easier than separation.
[. . .] In any case, the idea of killing her soon became a novel, *Il disprezzo*. In my original idea for this novel the protagonist, reacting to his wife's unjust attitude, planned and executed her murder. But this idea of killing her disappeared in the process of writing. The wife dies in an accident. The protagonist of the novel that I actually wrote bears no relation to the one I had imagined.

ELKANN: Did Elsa recognize herself in the book?

MORAVIA: No, and how could she? The only thing the book I never wrote had in common with our experience was the theme of uxoricide. The rest would have been pure invention.

From 1951 onward, the author imagined and perhaps began composing a novel based on the idea of uxoricide; however, he didn't begin seriously working on the book until a year later, in July 1952. Meanwhile, this project intersected and in part absorbed another project on the subject of Communism and the friendship between Sergio and Maurizio. The interaction between these two projects is profound and inevitable, and it is clear that certain narrative elements in *Il disprezzo* had already been developed in the novel about Sergio and Maurizio: the idea of Sergio's writing a screenplay, the love triangle, and even the theme of "contempt." According to the letter dated September 7, 1952, the abandonment of the novel about Communism occurs at the moment that the "new novel" begins to take shape; between July and September the writer has already composed "one hundred pages" and realizes that he is on the right track: "This new novel looks promising." By a few months later, when he is interviewed by Festa Campanile, the new novel has acquired a title: *Il fantasma di mezzogiorno*—which, as we have said, would later become *Il disprezzo*.